THE PICTURE OF DORIAN GRAY

THE PICTURE OF DORIAN GRAY

AN ANNOTATED, UNCENSORED EDITION

OSCAR WILDE

Edited by Nicholas Frankel

THE BELKNAP PRESS OF HARVARD UNIVERSITY PRESS

Cambridge, Massachusetts   London, England   2011

LIBRARY OF CONGRESS CATALOGING-IN-PUBLICATION DATA

Wilde, Oscar, 1854–1900.

The picture of Dorian Gray : an annotated, uncensored edition /
Oscar Wilde ; edited by Nicholas Frankel.

p.   cm.

Includes bibliographical references.

ISBN 978-0-674-05792-0 (alk. paper)

1. Appearance (Philosophy)—Fiction.   2. Conduct of life—Fiction.
3. Portraits—Fiction.   I. Frankel, Nicholas, 1962–   II. Title.

PR5819.A2F73   2011

823'.8—dc22   2010049134

For my children, Max, Theo, and Oliver

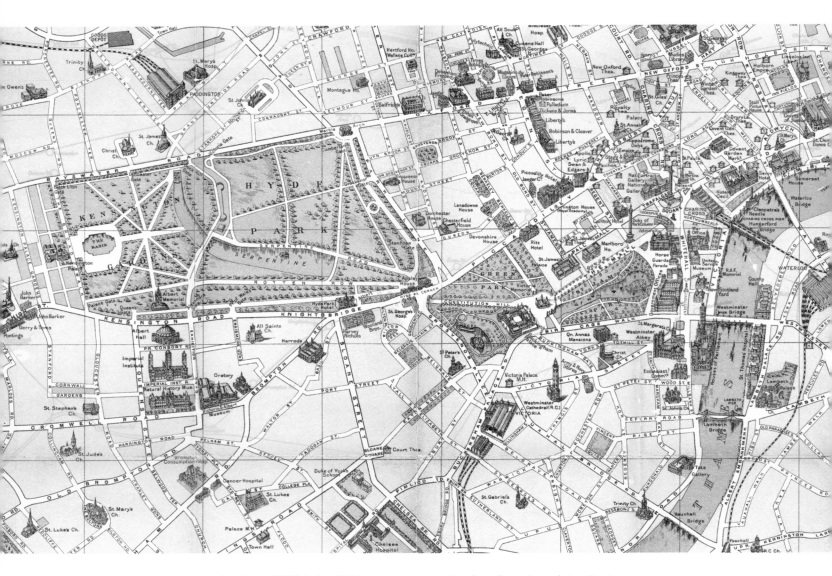

London in Wilde's day: "This grey, monstrous London of ours," proclaims Dorian
Gray, "with its myriads of people, its splendid sinners, and its sordid sins . . .
must have something in store for me."

CONTENTS

GENERAL INTRODUCTION

The remains of Oscar Wilde lie in Père Lachaise Cemetery in Paris. His sleek, modern tomb, designed by the British sculptor Jacob Epstein and commissioned by Wilde's lover and executor, Robert Ross, is one of the most frequently visited and recognizable graves in a cemetery notable for the many famous writers, artists, and musicians buried there (Balzac, Chopin, Proust, Gertrude Stein, Jim Morrison). The surface of Epstein's massive monolith is covered with hundreds of lipstick kisses, some ancient and faded, others new and vibrant. ("The madness of kissing" is what Wilde said Lord Alfred Douglas's "red-roseleaf lips" were made for.) Some observers decry the presence of these marks on Wilde's tomb as a form of defacement or vandalism, rightly pointing out that the lipstick's high fat content does real and lasting damage to the monolith. But to the many men and women, gay and straight, who journey each year to the site, the kisses are a tribute to the famous playwright, novelist, and wit—sentenced in 1895 to two years in prison, with hard labor, after being convicted of "gross indecency"—whom they see as a martyr to Victorian sexual morality.

Five years before his death, Wilde went, almost overnight, from being one of Britain's most colorful and celebrated figures to its most notorious sexual criminal. When he died from cerebral meningitis, in a seedy Parisian hotel room on November 30, 1900, at the age of forty-six, he had been living in exile in France for over three years, broken in spirit and body, bankrupt, and ostracized from respectable

British society. In 1895, at the time of his arrest, he had been Britain's leading playwright and wit, feted in London's West End and intellectual circles, as well as in the country homes and London townhouses of England's ruling class (much of it unaware that Wilde originated from Ireland, since, to use Wilde's own words, "my Irish accent was one of the many things I forgot at Oxford"). Even before his fame as a playwright and novelist, he had been the principal spokesman for the cult of "Aestheticism," or art for art's sake, which had swept much of England and America in the wake of Wilde's stunning arrival on the cultural scene in 1881. His death in 1900, little more than three years after his release from England's Reading prison (the "Reading Gaol" of his celebrated poem "The Ballad of Reading Gaol"), coincided with the end of a decade ("the Yellow Nineties," "the age of Dorian") more closely associated with him than with anyone else, as much for his large personality and life as for his considerable accomplishments as a writer and thinker.

Wilde's final years make for depressing summary. In exile he took the assumed name of "Sebastian Melmoth," invoking the martyrdom of St. Sebastian (a homosexual icon) and the eponymous protagonist of *Melmoth the Wanderer,* a gothic novel by Charles Maturin, Wilde's great-uncle. His wife, Constance, who had visited him just once while he was in jail, in 1896, to break the news of his mother's death, shunned him in his final years before her own premature death in 1898. After his incarceration, Wilde never again saw his two sons. Like their mother, they had adopted the last name of "Holland"; and they were taught by Constance and her relatives "to forget that we had ever borne the name of Wilde and never to mention it to anyone."[1] Four months after his release from prison, Wilde returned briefly to his lover Lord Alfred Douglas, who had barely escaped prosecution himself in 1895. Wilde was convinced that with Douglas he could find the happiness, love, and renewed creativity that he craved, but after a two-month sojourn together in Naples, Douglas abandoned him, leaving Wilde to face his impecunious, uncertain future alone. Harsh prison conditions had taken their toll on Wilde. Isolated and demoralized, he let himself go in the final months of his

Oscar Wilde's tomb, designed by Jacob Epstein in 1909, Père Lachaise
Cemetery, Paris, France. The tomb was unveiled in 1912. Today it stands
covered with lipstick kisses and graffiti, intended as a form of tribute
to Wilde. The high fat content in the lipstick has, unfortunately, done
lasting damage to the monolith. Visitors to Wilde's tomb are urged to
pay homage in a more respectful, less destructive way. Notes of appreciation or flowers—especially sunflowers or lilies—may be left at the
tomb: these are touching and entirely appropriate tributes.

life: "I will never outlive the century," Wilde predicted. "The English people would not stand for it."

Richard Ellmann, Wilde's biographer, estimates that he was bedridden by the end of September 1900. On his deathbed, Wilde, who was unable to speak, assented to be received into the Catholic Church by raising his hand and was administered Last Rites. According to Ellmann, Robert Ross, present at Wilde's deathbed, admitted later that he only "made up his mind to get [Wilde] a priest so there could be formal obsequies and a ceremonial burial." Otherwise, Ross feared, the body might be taken to the morgue and an autopsy performed.[2] "The coffin was cheap, and the hearse was shabby," Ellmann states succinctly (Ellmann, p. 584). According to the writer Ernest La Jeunesse, who was present at Wilde's funeral, only thirteen people followed the coffin to its resting place in Bagneux Cemetery, where Wilde was buried on December 3, his simple grave marked with a single stone on which was inscribed "Job xxix Verbis meis adere nihil audebant et super illos stillebat eloquium meum" ("To my words they durst add nothing, and my speech dropped upon them," from the Book of Job). In 1909 his remains would be moved to Père Lachaise, and three years later the Epstein monument erected over them. Ross's ashes were placed in a compartment in the Père Lachaise tomb after his own death in 1918. The inscription on the tomb is from "The Ballad of Reading Gaol" (which was published under the pseudonym "C.3.3.," Wilde's prison identification, signifying cell block C, landing 3, cell 3):

> And alien tears will fill for him
>   Pity's long-broken urn,
> For his mourners will be outcast men,
>   And outcasts always mourn.

The Picture of Dorian Gray was published simultaneously in England and America in 1890 by the J. B. Lippincott Company of Philadelphia in the July issue of *Lippincott's Monthly Magazine,* five years before the series of sensational trials that would lead to Wilde's in-

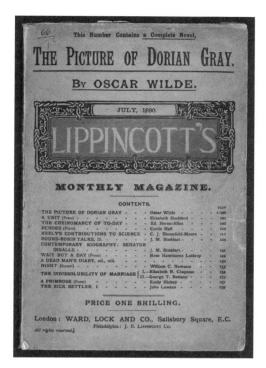

Front cover of British version of the July 1890 issue of *Lippincott's Monthly Magazine. The Picture of Dorian Gray,* published complete in the July issue, occupies its first 100 pages.

carceration. (The British edition of the magazine, copublished with Ward, Lock, and Company, appeared with a table of contents slightly different from that of the American edition.) Wilde soon set about revising and enlarging the novel for a book edition, which was published in 1891 by Ward, Lock, and Company. At the time of the novel's appearance in *Lippincott's Monthly Magazine,* Wilde was already well known to the general public—for his quick wit, theatricality, ostentatious dress, and the many poems, stories, lectures, and journalistic pieces he had written over the previous decade. But *The Picture of Dorian Gray* was the work that made him an iconic figure, in the eyes of both his supporters and his detractors, and that would later play a part in his downfall when it was used as evidence against him in court. The novel altered the way Victorians saw and understood the world they inhabited, particularly with regard to sexuality and masculinity. It heralded the end of a repressive "Victorianism," and, as Ellmann has remarked, after its publication "Victorian literature had a different look" (Ellmann, p. 314).

When the novel appeared in *Lippincott's,* it was immediately controversial. To be sure, appreciative and sensitive reviews appeared in Britain and America, but a significant segment of the British press reacted with outright hostility, condemning the novel as "vulgar," "unclean," "poisonous," "discreditable," and "a sham." In August 1890, Wilde claimed to have received 216 such attacks on his novel since its appearance in *Lippincott's* two months earlier.[3] "Dulness and dirt are the chief features of *Lippincott's* this month," began the reviewer for the *Daily Chronicle:*

The element that is unclean, though undeniably amusing, is furnished by Mr. Oscar Wilde's story of *The Picture of Dorian Gray.* It is a tale spawned from the leprous literature of the

French decadents—a poisonous book, the atmosphere of which is heavy with the mephitic odours of moral and spiritual putrefaction—a gloating study of the mental and physical corruption of a fresh, fair and golden youth, which might be fascinating but for its effeminate frivolity, its studied insincerity, its theatrical cynicism, its tawdry mysticism, its flippant philosophizings. . . . Mr. Wilde says the book has "a moral." The "moral," so far as we can collect it, is that man's chief end is to develop his nature to the fullest by "always searching for new sensations," that when the soul gets sick the way to cure it is to deny the senses nothing.[4]

One of the most pernicious reviews came from the *St. James's Gazette:* "Not being curious in ordure, and not wishing to offend the nostrils of decent persons, we do not propose to analyze *The Picture of Dorian Gray,*" writes the anonymous reviewer. "Whether the Treasury or the Vigilance Society will think it worth while to prosecute Mr. Oscar Wilde or Messrs. Ward, Lock & Co., we do not know," he continues. "The puzzle is that a young man of decent parts, who enjoyed (when he was at Oxford) the opportunity of associating with gentlemen, should put his name (such as it is) to so stupid and vulgar a piece of work."[5] Another contemporary notice, which appeared in the *Scots Observer,* a respectable, even prestigious literary magazine edited by the poet and critic (and Wilde's onetime friend) W. E. Henley, merits fuller quotation:

> Why go grubbing in muck-heaps? The world is fair, and the proportion of healthy-minded men and women to those that are foul, fallen, or unnatural is great. Mr. Oscar Wilde has again been writing stuff that were better unwritten; and while *The Picture of Dorian Gray,* which he contributes to *Lippincott's,* is ingenious, interesting, full of cleverness, plainly the work of a man of letters, it is false art—for its interest is medico-legal; it is false to human nature—for its hero is a devil; it is false to morality—for it is not made sufficiently clear that the writer does not prefer a course of unnatural in-

iquity to a life of cleanliness, health, and sanity. The story
—which deals with matters only fitted for the Criminal In-
vestigation Department or a hearing *in camera* [out of public scrutiny]—is discreditable alike to author and editor. Mr.
Wilde has brains, and art, and style; but if he can write for
none but outlawed noblemen and perverted telegraph boys,
the sooner he takes to tailoring (or some other decent trade)
the better for his own reputation and the public morals.[6]

Today we can easily recognize these references to unhealthiness,
insanity, uncleanliness, and "medico-legal interest" as coded imputa-
tions of homosexuality. It is worth bearing in mind, however, that in
the Victorian era, sexual preference was less clearly seen as an identity; indeed, the word *homosexual* did not enter the English language
until 1892, when it was used adjectivally in a translation of Richard
Krafft-Ebing's book *Psychopathia Sexualis* (it was first used as a noun
in 1912). Wilde and the other men who participated in London's homosexual subculture, many of them leading secret double lives,
would have been viewed by the majority not as homosexuals per se
but as men indulging in "unclean" vices. Even so, homosexual acts
were generally considered repugnant and deviant—and for the first
time, with the passage of the Criminal Law Amendment Act of 1885,
sexual activities of any nature between men were not merely sinful but unlawful. (The criminalization of homosexuality and the example of Wilde's life and work are widely credited with instating homosexuality as a distinct sexual and social identity.) That outraged
British reviews of *The Picture of Dorian Gray* share the same coded
language (unhealthiness, insanity, uncleanliness, and so on), while
making allusions to criminal prosecution, shows very clearly that
many early British readers were cognizant of the ways in which the
novel challenged conventional Victorian notions of masculine sexuality, particularly through its preoccupation with the homoerotic
and emotional relations between the three main male characters
(Dorian, Basil, and Lord Henry) and through its complex interest in
the potentially corruptive nature of interpersonal influence. (Britain's largest bookseller, W. H. Smith & Son, took the unusual step of

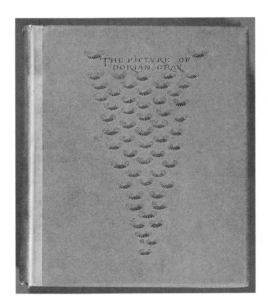

Front cover of the 1891 book edition (large-paper issue) of *The Picture of Dorian Gray,* published by Ward, Lock, and Co., designed by Wilde's friend Charles Ricketts. "Ricketts has just done for me a lovely cover for *Dorian Gray,*" Wilde remarked in October 1890, "grey pastel-paper with a white back and tiny marigolds." Ricketts, whom Wilde called a "subtle and fantastic decorator," went on to design many of Wilde's subsequent books.

pulling the July number of *Lippincott's* from its railway bookstalls as a result of the public outcry.) *The Picture of Dorian Gray* is one of the first novels in the English language to explore the nature of homoerotic and homosocial desire, which is to say it is a subversive novel, even if—or perhaps especially because—it plays a cat-and-mouse game of hiding and revealing the fact that homoerotic desire is the force that animates its still gripping, macabre plot.

Understanding the general atmosphere of hysteria about sexuality that existed in Britain in the years leading up to the publication of *The Picture of Dorian Gray* is important to understanding the hostility that greeted the novel in 1890. The Criminal Law Amendment Act of 1885, under which Wilde was eventually prosecuted, originated in a panic over the corruption of young, innocent girls, following an exposé of London's white slave trade titled "The Maiden Tribute of Modern Babylon," by the journalist W. T. Stead in the *Pall Mall Gazette* (for which Wilde also wrote regularly from 1884 until 1889). Statute 11 of the Act (termed the "Labouchère Amendment" after the radical M. P. Henry Labouchère, who proposed it), criminalizing "gross indecency" between men, was added only at the eleventh hour, shortly before parliamentary debate ended and a vote was taken, but it succeeded in driving homosexual practices further underground and only heightened anxieties about homosexuality in Britain. The key language in the amendment—"gross indecency"—was broad enough to encompass any sexual activities between men, regardless of age or consent, and it was under this statute that Wilde and many other homosexuals were prosecuted in Britain until the Act's repeal in 1956 (under the terms of the Labouchère Amendment, homosexual acts, as well as the procurement or attempted procurement of those acts, were punishable by up to two years' imprisonment with or without hard labor). The vagueness of the language in the Labouchère Amendment invited prosecution, while the criminalization of private acts between consenting adult males encouraged male prostitutes and domestic servants to extort money from patrons and employers (Wilde was himself the victim of several blackmail attempts). The conditions had been created for a series of homosexual scandals that would rock London and increase the level of homophobia in British society.

Prior to Wilde's own downfall, the most notable such scandal to follow in the wake of the Labouchère Amendment was the Cleveland Street Affair of 1889–1890. In late 1889, when Wilde began writing *The Picture of Dorian Gray*, rumors emerged in the press surrounding a number of aristocratic and military men and an address in the Fitzrovia neighborhood in central London. Police investigating a theft from the Central London Post Office had uncovered a ring of male prostitutes or "rent boys" who operated as telegraph messengers by day and as male prostitutes, working out of a male brothel at 19 Cleveland Street, by night (the "perverted telegraph boys" alluded to in the *Scots Observer* review). One of those most tarnished in the unfolding scandal was Lord Arthur Somerset, the Prince of Wales's equerry, who fled to France in October 1889 for fear of prosecution (hence the reference to "outlawed noblemen" in the *Scots Observer* review). Rumor also linked Prince Albert Victor, the eldest son of the Prince of Wales, to the Cleveland Street brothel, though the British press did not dare to mention Prince Albert Victor's name, and no evidence exists to suggest he ever patronized the brothel. But the circulation of the rumor indicates the general level of anxiety about homosexual behavior, now associated in the public mind with aristocratic vices and the corruption of lower-class youth. The scandal even reached the floor of Parliament in the form of heated debate, after allegations were made of a government cover-up to protect the reputations of aristocratic patrons. It was in this heated atmosphere of hysteria and paranoia that *The Picture of Dorian Gray* was greeted by the British press. In the wake of the Cleveland Street Scandal, Wilde's emphasis on Dorian Gray's youthfulness, or susceptibility to the "corruption" of an older aristocratic man (Lord Henry), is one of the features of the novel that most outraged reviewers. The reception of *The Picture of Dorian Gray* in 1890 was a hint of what was yet to come.

It is not surprising that Wilde's novel is a highly "coded" text, given the necessary secrecy and caution that governed England's homosexual community following the passage of the Labouchère Amendment and the Cleveland Street Scandal. The very name *Dorian* is a veiled reference to "Dorian" or "Greek" love—to the Ancient Greek tradition (first openly discussed in Karl Müller's *History and Antiquities of the Doric Race* [1824; English translation 1830]) of an older male "lover" taking a younger man in his charge. Chapter IX of *The Picture of Dorian Gray* especially contains numerous coded allusions to homosexuals and criminal sexual activity throughout history; and such depravity contains a "horrible fascination" for Dorian Gray, we are told, representing to him not evil but rather a "mode through which he might realize his conception of the beautiful." The painting, which is itself a veiled record of Dorian's secret vices and crimes, is similarly cloaked and locked away in an old study so as to be "secure from prying eyes," though Dorian has the key and goes to it repeatedly in order to comprehend the nature and depth of his own depravity. Lord Henry and Dorian rent a small house in Algiers, a vacation place frequented by British homosexuals, though the nature of their relationship is never fully revealed. And there is much other "circumstantial evidence" that points obliquely to the fact that the three principals are engaged in acts of "gross indecency." Above all, Wilde's frequent recourse to terms like *personality, romance of feeling,* and even *friendship* to describe the intense attraction felt by the painter Basil Hallward for Dorian, is a way of encoding its specifically homoerotic nature. Wilde was cross-examined about his use of such terms when the novel was used against him in court.

To be sure, the *Lippincott's* version of the novel—and still more the typescript that Wilde originally submitted to *Lippincott's,* from which some 500 words were excised prior to publication (restored in the present edition)—is more explicit in its sexual references and allusions than the revised 1891 book version, in which Wilde, in response to his critics and at the insistence of his publisher, toned down the novel's homosexual content. In the *Lippincott's* text and the original typescript, for instance, Basil Hallward says to Lord Henry (speaking about Dorian), "I find a strange pleasure in saying things to him I know I shall be sorry for having said. I give myself away. As a rule, he is charming to me, and we walk home together from the club arm in arm." Similarly, Wilde's narrator tells us in the 1890 *Lippincott's* edition and the typescript that "rugged and straightforward as he was," there was something in Hallward's nature "that was purely feminine in its tenderness." Most revealing of all, perhaps, in the present typescript version Hallward says to Dorian: "It is quite true I have worshipped you with far more romance of feeling than a man should ever give to a friend. Somehow I have never loved a woman. . . . From the moment I met you, your personality had the most extraordinary influence over me . . . I adored you madly, extravagantly, absurdly. I was jealous of everyone to whom you spoke. I wanted to have you all to myself. I was only happy when I was with you." This telling confession (altered very slightly by the editor of *Lippincott's* before publication in the magazine) was deleted from the 1891 version, in which the intensity of Hallward's "worship" is at once lessened and transformed into something more innocuous: the painter's quest for a Platonic ideal in art.[7] Wilde made other, similar deletions when preparing the book version of the novel for Ward, Lock, and Company.

In the wake of the Cleveland Street Scandal, Wilde had particular reason to be cautious in his published writings. Like Dorian, he was harboring his own secrets. Since at least 1886, Wilde had been leading a secret double life, designed to conceal his sexual orientation and extramarital affairs from close family members and "respectable" society. In that year he had allowed himself to be seduced by the boyish Robert Ross, with whom he embarked on a two-year love affair, though this did not preclude either man from taking other lovers.[8] The event has traditionally been viewed by Wilde scholars as a critical turning point in Wilde's life. From this time onward, he consciously recognized and acted upon his homosexual predilections and began, in the words of Richard Ellmann, "to think of himself as a criminal, moving guiltily among the innocent" (Ellmann, p. 278). As

Ellmann observes, the event may even be coded into the plot of *Dorian Gray,* since in late 1886, around the time Wilde met Ross, Wilde turned thirty-two, and there is little other explanation for why he felt impelled to change the date on which Dorian Gray commences a life of unprecedented criminality, from "the eve of his own thirty-second birthday," in the 1890 *Lippincott's* version, to "the eve of his thirty-eighth birthday" in the 1891 book version.

Recent scholarship has speculated that Wilde's secret homosexual life dates from an even earlier period than 1886 — that Wilde was not merely conscious of his homosexual desires as early as the mid-1870s, when he was an undergraduate at Oxford, but that he also acted upon them.[9] Certainly it was at Oxford that Wilde met and befriended one of the most notorious sodomites of his day, the artist and connoisseur Lord Ronald Sutherland Gower, eleven years his senior, now generally regarded as an important real-life model for the character of Lord Henry Wotton; and it was shortly after leaving Oxford that Wilde began a two-year cohabitation, in London, with the man who had introduced him to Gower, the onetime society portraitist Frank Miles. (Miles died obscurely in 1891 and is sometimes said to be the real-life figure on whom the painter Basil Hallward is based.) But the need for deception and concealment was undoubtedly heightened by Wilde's marriage to the beautiful Constance Lloyd, with whom Oscar fathered two sons shortly after their wedding in 1884. His marriage to Constance may have been a genuine attempt on Wilde's part to overcome or deny his existing homosexual proclivities. But there can be little question that, especially after his affair with Ross had begun, Wilde was play-acting the roles of dutiful husband and father, and increasingly allowing himself to be drawn into homosexual relationships and modes of behavior that he knew threatened to expose his double life. If he had not known it before he met Ross, certainly Wilde must have felt afterward that, as Lord Henry puts it, "there are certain temperaments that marriage makes more complex" and that "the one charm of marriage is that it makes a life of deception necessary for both parties." According to Constance's brother, Otho, it was not until 1895 and the months leading up to Wilde's arrest that Constance began to suspect her husband's real sexual orientation.

Following the cooling off of his affair with Ross in 1888–1889, and possibly even before this, Wilde entered into a number of other erotic liaisons with men, two of which possess special importance as far as *Dorian Gray* is concerned. From 1889 onward, Wilde began actively courting a young poet named John Gray, twelve years his junior but looking even younger than his years, famed among both men and women of his day for his unearthly good looks: "What a fascinating man," one besotted female admirer remarked upon seeing Gray at the opera; "I never knew that anybody could be so beautiful."[10] There is no evidence to suggest that Wilde's desire for Gray was consummated or even reciprocated before the completion of *Dorian Gray*. And in February 1890, when Wilde's composition of the novel was at its fiercest, Gray converted to Catholicism in a conscious attempt to quash his own "sinfulness." But by Gray's own account, he thereafter "immediately . . . began a course of sin compared with which my previous life was innocence."[11] As with the unspecified crimes of Dorian Gray, we can only speculate on the nature of Gray's "course of sin." But his intimacy with Wilde lasted until late 1892, when, following an intense personal crisis, he renounced Wilde for good in favor of a Catholic religious devotion that would eventually lead him to the priesthood. Gray is often said to constitute a real-life model for Dorian Gray, and at one point he even signed a letter to Wilde, "Yours ever, Dorian." As Ellmann says, for Wilde to call his leading character "Gray" was, as far as the real Gray was concerned, almost certainly a form of courtship (Ellmann, p. 307).

The other crucial erotic relationship into which Wilde entered was the long, complex affair with Lord Alfred Douglas, which would prove to be disastrous for Wilde, as we shall shortly see, though the affair did not start until one year after the publication of *Dorian Gray*. Ironically, it was the novel that was, at least in part, responsible for bringing the two men together: Douglas, who was obsessed with *The Picture of Dorian Gray*, longed to meet its author and, according to Ellmann, read the novel nine times over before the friendship began. Flattered by his young admirer's praise, Wilde carefully inscribed a deluxe copy of the book version to Douglas at their second meeting, in July 1891. At any rate, it was Douglas who initiated Wilde into

London's homosexual subculture of procurers and "rent boys": previously Wilde had sought the company, chiefly, of male poets, attracted as he was to an ideal of masculinity embodied by the beautiful male protagonist of his own poem "Charmides," named after a character in Plato's *Dialogues*. Passionate in his pursuit of "rough trade," Douglas led Wilde down a path of risky, dangerous, and even reckless behavior that would eventually incriminate him. While serving his prison sentence, Wilde famously recalled that he had been "feasting with panthers" and that "the danger was half the excitement."[12]

To identify the continuities between *The Picture of Dorian Gray* and the relationships in Wilde's own life is not to say that the novel must be considered a *roman à clef* or an allegory of Wilde's life. Acknowledging that Dorian and Lord Henry contain elements of John Gray and Lord Ronald Gower does not begin to account for the complexity of these characters or for their vibrancy on the page, and it is a cliché of criticism that novelists draw upon experiences and relationships that are familiar to them personally. Nonetheless, the novel does have numerous autobiographical elements, and Wilde on one occasion remarked that it "contains much of me in it. Basil Hallward is what I think I am: Lord Henry what the world thinks me: Dorian what I would like to be—in other ages, perhaps." Wilde's comment suggests that the novel is a work of art that embodies his own "secret," just as Hallward's portrait of Dorian encodes the painter's illicit love for his younger subject. Wilde's phrase "in other ages" reminds us—like the name *Dorian* itself—that love between men was tolerated and celebrated openly in Ancient Greece but that in Wilde's own day, by contrast, a "harsh, uncomely Puritanism . . . is having . . . its curious revival." Wilde was conscious that the novel reflected the multiple strands of his personality and sexual life. As importantly, he was acutely aware that, like himself, *The Picture of Dorian Gray* stood at odds with an age of heightened intolerance and repression when it came to sexual matters.

That intolerance was, tragically, to be made powerfully manifest in the spring of 1895, when, at the height of his fame, Wilde was to be arrested, convicted, and sentenced to two years' imprisonment with hard labor for the new crime of "gross indecency." The arrest, at least, was partly of his own making. Douglas's father, the Marquess of Queensberry—the "screaming, scarlet Marquess," as Wilde called him, a pugnacious paranoiac whose deep aversion to Wilde and homosexuals was matched only by his passion for the "manly" sports of hunting and boxing (he was the originator of the "Queensberry Rules" in boxing)—had been bridling at his youngest son's involvement with Wilde since its inception. In June 1894, Queensberry appeared unannounced at Wilde's house, accompanied by a prizefighter, and had to be forcibly ejected from the premises; and then on February 14, 1895, on the opening night of *The Importance of Being Earnest,* Wilde had got wind of, and foiled, an attempt by Queensberry to enter the theater and publicly denounce Wilde from the stage. On February 18, 1895, Queensberry left a calling card at Wilde's club, the Albermarle Club, on which he had scrawled (with the word "sodomite" misspelled), "For Oscar Wilde, posing somdomite."[13] Ten days later the club's porter handed the card to Wilde, who felt that Queensberry, having failed to surprise him at his theater, was now invading his club. Because sodomy (the ancient, biblically derived term for "unnatural" sex) was a criminal offense under both the 1885 Criminal Law Amendment Act and the 1861 Offences against the Person Act, Queensberry's scrawl formed the legal basis for libel charges.[14] Encouraged by Douglas, Wilde decided to prosecute Queensberry for criminal libel in an effort to stop Queensberry's virulent harassment. But Wilde had seriously misjudged his opponent; in advance of the libel trial, while Wilde and Douglas vacationed in Monte Carlo, Queensberry and his lawyers were employing private detectives to scour London's homosexual underworld to prove that Wilde was not merely a "posing" but a practicing sodomite. Right up to the commencement of the libel trial, a number of close friends—Frank Harris, George Bernard Shaw, George Alexander—urged Wilde to abandon the prosecution. But Wilde's judgment was seriously impaired by his love for Douglas, who wanted vengeance on his father, as well as by the virulence of Queensberry's persecution, and he foolishly allowed the prosecution to proceed: "My whole life seems ruined by this man," he confessed to Ross on the

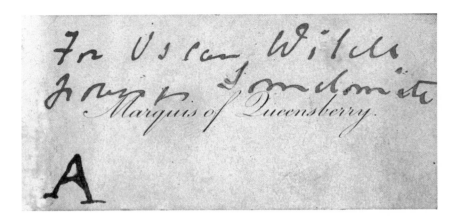

Calling card, left for Wilde at his club by the Marquess of Queensberry, Lord Alfred Douglas's father, on February 18, 1895. On the card Queensberry has scrawled, "For Oscar Wilde, posing somdomite"—evidently in some haste, since "sodomite" is misspelled. This card, which Wilde received ten days later, precipitated the disastrous libel action that Wilde took against Queensberry in April 1895, which in turn led to Wilde's prosecution, conviction, and imprisonment with hard labor for the new crime of "gross indecency."

night Queensberry had left the offensive card. "The tower of ivory is assailed by the foul thing. On the sand is my life spilt."

The libel trial began on April 3, and as it proceeded the evidence against Wilde became overwhelming. Edward Carson, Queensberry's counsel, began defending his client by using passages from the *Lippincott's* text of *Dorian Gray*—Carson was aware that such passages were considerably muted for the 1891 book edition, and in court he referred to the latter as "the purged edition."[15] He also used excerpts from the British press's outraged reactions to *Dorian Gray* to prove that Wilde was "posing as a sodomite," in his writings at least, and that his client's charge was in fact legally justified.[16] Wilde defended himself and his novel vigorously. But a few minutes later, Carson had moved onto surer ground, interrogating Wilde about his relationships with a series of blackmailers, male prostitutes, and the procurer Alfred Taylor, as well as with the bookseller's clerk Edward Shelley. This line of interrogation was especially damaging to Wilde's case and would have implications beyond the libel trial. Wilde and his attorney were unaware that Carson had secured depositions from

Edward Carson Q. C., later 1st Baron Carson, caricatured by "Lib" [Libero Prosperi], from *Vanity Fair,* Nov. 1893. Carson (1854–1935) had been Wilde's contemporary at Trinity College, Dublin, and he represented Lord Alfred Douglas's father, the Marquess of Queensberry, in court during Wilde's disastrous libel action of April 1895. Carson's cross-examination of Wilde during the trial's opening days was extremely damaging to Wilde's case and reputation, and ensured Wilde's criminal prosecution. Later in life, Carson was a leader of the Ulster Unionists and an architect of Irish Partition.

a number of these figures, who were willing to turn witness against Wilde; but before Carson had even mounted his case for the defense, the trial collapsed with Wilde agreeing to his counsel's advice to abandon the proceedings. Wilde evidently hoped that his adversary would be content with a judgment of "not guilty." In the event, he had to listen in court to the judicial ruling that Queensberry's charge was legally justified, or "true in fact," and that it had been "published for the public benefit."

It had become increasingly clear in the course of the libel trial that, as a result of the evidence arrayed in defense of Queensberry, Wilde had opened himself up to criminal prosecution under Statute 11 of the Criminal Law Amendment Act. Moreover, at one point, Wilde's counsel had quoted from a letter, written from Queensberry to his father-in-law, ostensibly about Queensberry's ex-wife's "encouragement" of Lord Alfred Douglas, in which the names of Lord

Rosebery and William Ewart Gladstone—respectively Britain's
prime minister and his predecessor—were mentioned. By reading
from the letter in court, Wilde's counsel had meant to imply that
Queensberry was paranoid and vindictive for suspecting the two
high-ranking politicians of covering up a homosexual affair between
Rosebery and Queensberry's oldest son, Francis Douglas, Viscount
Drumlanrig, who had committed suicide in dubious circumstances
in 1894. But according to Carson's biographer, once Rosebery's and
Gladstone's names were introduced in court, it was inevitable that
Wilde would be tried, in order to avoid the appearance that Rosebery and Gladstone were intervening on Wilde's behalf to protect
themselves.[17] Realizing that the inevitable was coming, Wilde's counsel offered to protract the libel trial by calling further defense witnesses, to give his client (who was not legally obliged to remain in
court) time to flee the country. But Wilde declined, and though some
hours intervened between the end of the collapsed libel trial and the
issuing of an arrest warrant, Wilde was arrested at the Cadogan Hotel at 6:20 P.M. on April 5, 1895, a half-packed suitcase on his bed and
a book with a yellow cover in his hand.[18]

Wilde was tried twice on the criminal charges against him. The
first trial opened at the Old Bailey on April 26, 1895. Two days before
the start of the trial, the entire contents of Wilde's family home were
sold off at public auction, by bailiffs sent in by Queensberry to collect the court costs awarded him. Around this time Wilde's name was
removed from the billboards and programs of the theaters where his
plays *The Importance of Being Earnest* and *An Ideal Husband* were running. The Crown made extensive use of the evidence gathered by
Queensberry's detectives and lawyers, and this time the witnesses
were produced in court. An array of young male prostitutes, hotel
servants, and others were called to offer evidence for the prosecution—some of it quite lurid in its details. "[P]erhaps never in the
nineties was so much unsavory evidence given so much publicity,"
Ellmann writes (Ellmann, p. 462). Charles Gill, the Crown's attorney,
also read aloud to the jury Edward Carson's cross-examination of
Wilde about *Dorian Gray.* The judge, however, took a dim view of the
prosecution's use of literary evidence, and later enjoined the jury not

to base their judgment on the fact that Wilde was the author of *The Picture of Dorian Gray* and not to allow themselves "to be influenced against [Wilde] by the circumstances that he has written a book of which you, in so far as you have read extracts from it, may disapprove."[19] During his cross-examination of Wilde, Gill questioned Wilde about another literary work—Lord Alfred Douglas's poem "Two Loves." He asked Wilde to explain the meaning of the phrase "the love that dare not speak its name" (now of course little more than a clichéd euphemism for homosexuality). Wilde's answer provided what is perhaps the most indelible moment of the two criminal trials:

> "The Love that dare not speak its name" in this century is such a great affection of an elder for a younger man as there was between David and Jonathan, such as Plato made the very basis of his philosophy, and such as you find in the sonnets of Michelangelo and Shakespeare. It is that deep, spiritual affection that is as pure as it is perfect. It dictates and pervades great works of art like those of Shakespeare and Michelangelo. . . . It is in this century misunderstood, so much misunderstood that it may be described as the "Love that dare not speak its name," and on account of it I am placed where I am now. It is beautiful, it is fine, it is the noblest form of affection. There is nothing unnatural about it. It is intellectual, and it repeatedly exists between an elder and a younger man, when the elder man has intellect, and the younger man has all the joy, hope and glamour of life before him. That it should be so, the world does not understand. The world mocks at it and sometimes puts one in the pillory for it.[20]

Wilde's words were met with a spontaneous outburst of applause from the public gallery. When a hung jury was declared, on May 1, matters might have ended there, with Wilde utterly disgraced in the public's eye. Even Edward Carson is said to have appealed to the Crown to let up. But the politics of a highly publicized trial de-

manded the Crown proceed afresh, with Sir Frank Lockwood, the
solicitor-general, leading Wilde's prosecution this time. A verdict of
guilty on all counts was delivered on May 25, four days after the
second criminal trial had begun. The presiding judge, Justice Wills,
called it "the worst case I have ever tried" and imposed a sentence of
two years in prison with hard labor, the maximum sentence allowed
under the law. Addressing Wilde directly, Justice Wills said, "In my
judgment [the sentence] is totally inadequate for a case such as this."
Amid the cries of shame heard in the court, Wilde was reported to
have said, "And I? May I say nothing, my lord?"—but Wills dismissed
Wilde, indicating with a wave of his hand that the warders should
remove him from the courtroom.[21]

That *Dorian Gray* was used as evidence in Wilde's court trials un-
derscores again how incendiary the novel really was and how much
Wilde risked in bringing it before the public. I have already indicated
how, at his publisher's insistence, Wilde toned down much of its homoerotic and sexually explicit material when he revised and enlarged
the novel. Some of his other revisions at this time were also attempts
to deflect criticism—introducing into the 1891 book version more
patently melodramatic and sentimental elements of plot; expanding
Lord Henry's witty repartee so that the novel might be seen as a
work of "silver-fork" fiction, not unlike the novels of Disraeli and
Bulwer-Lytton; incorporating material designed to suggest that Dorian's "sins" consisted at least partly of financial malfeasance and
opium abuse; and bringing the novel to a clearer, more conventional
moral conclusion.[22] The process of purging the novel of its most controversial elements, however, had begun even earlier, before the novel's appearance in *Lippincott's*. When the typescript of the novel, containing over 3,000 words of handwritten emendations by Wilde,
arrived at the Lippincott offices in the spring of 1890, it caused immediate alarm. J. M. Stoddart, the editor of the magazine, had commissioned Wilde to write a fiction of 35,000 words, but he could not
have anticipated the occasionally graphic nature of the novel that finally appeared on his desk. After consulting with a handful of advisors to determine whether—and if so how—the novel might be published, Stoddart decided to proceed cautiously. He now set about

making or overseeing numerous changes to Wilde's typescript, including the excision of some 500 words that he feared would be objectionable—or worse. As the response by the British press and W. H. Smith & Son would soon demonstrate, Stoddart's anxieties were entirely justified, at least from the standpoint of what British readers would tolerate. We can imagine that Stoddart, when he learned of the outcry against the novel in Britain, must have felt he hadn't removed quite enough of the "objectionable passages." For reasons explained in the Textual Introduction that follows, Wilde almost certainly never saw any of the edits to his novel until he opened his personal copy of *Lippincott's Monthly Magazine.* Had he been given the opportunity to review Stoddard's edits, would he have approved them? Such a question cannot be answered with certainty. It is entirely possible that, as a still relatively inexperienced author, he would have been governed by his editor's judgment. On the other hand, Wilde, always the aesthete, might have taken the aesthetic high ground, as he was to do with critics of the novel soon after its publication, and objected to Stoddart's tampering with his "art." In his life and writing, Wilde was playing a dangerous game of hiding and revealing his sexual orientation.

The version of the novel that appears in this book follows Wilde's emended typescript: it represents the novel as Wilde envisioned it in the spring of 1890, before Stoddart began to work his way through the typescript with his pencil and before Wilde's later self-censorship of the novel, when he revised and enlarged it for Ward, Lock, and Company. The result is a more daring and scandalous novel, more explicit in its sexual content, and for that reason less content than either of the two subsequent published versions in adhering to Victorian conventions of representation. The present edition marks the first time Wilde's typescript has been published, more than 120 years after its author submitted it to *Lippincott's* for publication—a fitting, timely embodiment of what Wilde meant when he confessed that Dorian Gray is "what I would like to be—in other ages, perhaps."

When defending *Dorian Gray* against the attacks to which it was subjected in the British press, Wilde repeatedly took the aesthetic high ground in his exchanges with newspaper editors, at least initially, before his resolve was worn down and he felt at last browbeaten into addressing—as openly as he could—charges of the novel's immorality. But early in these exchanges, we see him insisting again and again on the separation of art and ethics ("I am quite incapable of understanding how any work of art can be criticised from a moral standpoint. The sphere of art and the sphere of ethics are absolutely distinct and separate . . .") and asking readers to attend to the artistic merits of his novel.[23] His preface to the 1891 edition and his essay "The Soul of Man under Socialism" also constitute responses to critics of the novel, and in these writings Wilde resorted to the same kind of exalted pronouncements on art that typify his early correspondence with the papers ("They are the elect to whom beautiful things mean only Beauty." "There is no such thing as a moral or immoral book. Books are well written, or badly written. That is all." "The true artist is a man who believes absolutely in himself." "The artist is never morbid. He expresses everything.").[24] On one level of course, Wilde was trying to deflect criticism from the novel's more controversial elements (he knew very well what kind of book he had written); on the other hand, these pronouncements are entirely in concert with the aesthetic principles he had been espousing for years. Art and its proper relationship to life are after all the central preoccupation of Wilde's fictions, plays, essays, and lectures. It is worth keeping in mind, too, that Wilde was a lecturer on art and aesthetics long before his fame as a fiction writer and playwright. An understanding of Wilde's enduring artistic concerns is as important to a larger appreciation of *Dorian Gray* as some knowledge of his biography and the circumstances in which his novel was published.

No reader perhaps can fail to appreciate that *Dorian Gray* is a novel that abounds in commentary on painting and portraiture (Chapter I is an extended conversation between Lord Henry and Basil Hallward about the painter's portrait of Dorian). Wilde was greatly influenced in his writing of the novel by the cult of aesthetic portraiture that then dominated the transatlantic arts scene and that stands at the imaginative center of his novel (the novel takes its title not from its central character but from a *picture* or portrait of him). Artistic portraiture was undergoing a major renaissance in the late

Victorian era: it reached its apogee in the early 1890s in the cele-brated portraits of John Singer Sargent, James McNeill Whistler, and G. F. Watts. These artists were all early members of the Society of Portrait Painters (now the Royal Society of Portrait Painters) estab-lished in 1891. They were less interested in a strictly faithful depic-tion of their subjects than in a more interpretive rendition, and they often exaggerated their sitters' beauty or the lavishness of their dress and surroundings. They were greatly influenced by the poet-painter Dante Gabriel Rossetti, who, in the 1860s and 1870s, strove to cap-ture a transcendent, unearthly ideal in his portraits of his lovers Fanny Cornforth, Alexa Wilding, and Jane Morris. Rossetti's paint-ings—and those of his fellow Pre-Raphaelites—emphasized an aes-thetic of beauty for its own sake, and for that reason Rossetti and the Pre-Raphaelites are often said to be precursors to the Aesthetic movement and an important influence on the thought and writings of Wilde.

The Pre-Raphaelites were also interested in the decorative arts. In 1861, Rossetti and the painter Edward Burne-Jones joined William Morris's design firm, Morris, Marshall, Faulkner & Co. (later Morris & Co.), renowned for its stained glass, furniture, textiles, wallpapers, and jewelry. William Morris, a versatile poet, novelist, designer, and printer, was devoted to handcrafted work and a decorative arts ideal that took its inspiration from the workshop practices of late-medieval Europe. His firm was founded in response to what Morris saw as a growing gap between fine and applied arts and the shoddy machine-made products then making their way into English homes with the expansion of the Industrial Revolution. He also promoted the idea of a completely designed and unified living environment—which explains in part the wide range of Morris's interests in the in-dustrial arts. In his emphasis on such an environment and the need to beautify everyday existence, he was enormously influential on Wilde. "Your work comes from the sheer delight of making beautiful things," Wilde told Morris: "no alien motive ever interests you," so that "in its singleness of aim, as well as in its perfection of result, it is pure art."[25] Wilde's early lectures "Art and the Handicraftsman," "The House Beautiful," and "House Decoration" owe a clear debt to

Morris. Morris's more indirect influence on *Dorian Gray* can be felt in the novelist's careful attention to domestic interiors and furnishings. Wilde often decorates the rooms in his novel according to the principles of the "house beautiful."

In his letter to the *Daily Chronicle* of June 30, 1890, when Wilde called *Dorian Gray* "an essay on decorative art," he was signaling his indebtedness to Morris and Rossetti. He was making a claim, too, about the novel's departure from nineteenth-century realism and the fact that its real power lay in its language:

> Finally, let me say this—the aesthetic movement produced certain colours, subtle in their loveliness and fascinating in their almost mystical tone. They were, and are, our reactions against the crude primaries of a doubtless more respectable but certainly less cultivated age. My story is an essay on decorative art. It reacts against the crude brutality of plain realism. It is poisonous if you like, but you cannot deny that it is also perfect, and perfection is what we artists aim at.[26]

"A lover of words . . . will avail himself of . . . the elementary particles of language . . . realized as colour and light and shade," the critic Walter Pater declared in his essay collection *Appreciations,* a book Wilde enthusiastically reviewed for the *Speaker* in March 1890. "[O]pposing the constant degradation of language by those who use it carelessly," Pater said, "he will not treat coloured glass as if it were clear."[27] Taking his cue from the Pre-Raphaelites and from Pater, Wilde sought to lend color and texture to language by accentuating the rhythms and imagery of his own, often decorative prose. We can see this most clearly perhaps in Chapter IX, the novel's most intractable and difficult chapter, where Wilde largely abandons dialogue and narrative technique in favor of language that approaches prose poetry:

> There was a gem in the brain of the dragon, Philostratus told us, and "by the exhibition of golden letters and a scarlet robe" the monster could be thrown into a magical sleep, and slain.

According to the great alchemist Pierre de Boniface, the Diamond rendered a man invisible, and the Agate of India made him eloquent. The Cornelian appeased anger, and the Hyacinth provoked sleep, and the Amethyst drove away the fumes of wine. The Garnet cast out demons, and the Hydropicus deprived the Moon of her colour. The Selenite waxed and waned with the Moon, and the Meloceus, that discovers thieves, could be affected only by the blood of kids. Leonardus Camillus had seen a white stone taken from the brain of a newly-killed toad, that was a certain antidote against poison. The bezoar, that was found in the heart of the Arabian deer, was a charm that could cure the plague. In the nests of Arabian birds was the Aspilates, that, according to Democritus, kept the wearer from any danger by fire.

Like *Le Secret de Raoul,* the novel that comes to exert such an intoxicating influence over Dorian, Wilde's language in Chapter IX possesses a "curious jewelled style, vivid and obscure at once, full of argot and of archaisms, of technical expressions and of elaborate paraphrases." Foreign and esoteric objects abound in the chapter, and it is a well-documented fact that many of Wilde's descriptions of textiles, jewels, and musical instruments draw heavily from published sources such as William Jones's *History and Mystery of Precious Stones* (1880). Claims that such passages are instances of plagiarism are misplaced, however. Wilde's creative appropriations from nonfiction works are motivated by the imaginative possibilities of the fact—or what Lord Henry would call the "mystery of the visible." Wilde wants to render both the perceptual reality of things and their suggestiveness or mystery. For this reason he uppercases words such as "Diamond," "Cornelian," "Hydropicus," and "Selenite," the unusual capitalization giving them a symbolic value we associate more often with poetry than with prose. Unlike the realist writer, Wilde does not seek to render a familiar world. He seeks to capture the world's strangeness—to *defamiliarize* it, as the Russian formalist critic Victor Shklovsky would say, since "art exists that one may recover the sensation of life: it exists to make one feel things, to make the stone *stony*. The purpose of art is to impart the sensation of things as they are perceived and not as they are known."[28]

Wilde could hardly have escaped the influence of the classicist, historian, and philosopher of art Walter Pater (1839–1894), a fellow in Classics at Brasenose College, Oxford, whose controversial reputation as an aesthete was widely known when Wilde enrolled as an undergraduate at Magdalen College, Oxford, in 1874. Pater was not, as Denis Donoghue observes, an original thinker, but his presence is everywhere felt in the late Victorian era (the Aesthetic movement, Pre-Raphaelitism, Decadence), and he "set modern literature upon its antithetical—[Pater] would say its antinomian—course."[29] Pater's insistence on "experience itself" as an end and the "free play" of the human imagination, his cultivation of intense receptivity to beauty, and his advocacy of a quickened sense of life in the face of mortality—all expressed in highly eroticized language—had great appeal to his devotees (mostly young men), but it put him at odds with both the utilitarian values of the industrial era and contemporary moral reserve. And his embrace of art for art's sake was against the grain of the Victorian belief, articulated by Matthew Arnold and John Ruskin, in art's social and moral function. Shy and reserved by nature, Pater was appointed to his fellowship at Brasenose College in 1864, and for many years he was known only among a small circle at Oxford for his scholasticism and critical views of Christianity. There is little to suggest in his early career that this retiring Casaubon-like scholar would become a countercultural figure and lightning rod.

But in 1873, one year before Wilde's matriculation at Oxford, Pater published *Studies in the History of the Renaissance,* a book that proved immediately offensive to some of its readers and resulted in a controversy that eerily prefigures that surrounding Wilde and *Dorian Gray*. The essays in *Studies* do not form a "history" in the usual sense of the word but rather attempt to define a Renaissance sensibility, locating in some of the greatest paintings, sculptures, and poems of the Italian and French Renaissance, as well as in the career of the eighteenth-century German art historian Johann Joachim Winckelmann, a secret Hellenistic tradition. That tradition, both the book's detractors and admirers understood, embraced both an aestheti-

cism and homoeroticism. (The scandal surrounding Pater intensified when, in the year following the publication of *Studies,* he was
reprimanded by the master of Balliol College for engaging in inap-
propriate correspondence with William Hardinge, an undergraduate student.) It was the "Conclusion" to Pater's *Studies,* adapted from
an earlier review of various poetry by William Morris, that caused
outrage:

> Not the fruit of experience, but experience itself, is the end
> . . . To burn always with this hard, gemlike flame, to maintain
> this ecstasy, is success in life . . . What we have to do is to
> be for ever curiously testing new opinions and courting new
> impressions, never acquiescing in a facile orthodoxy . . . For
> our one chance lies in expanding [this] interval, in getting as
> many pulsations as possible into the given time. Great pas-
> sions may give us this quickened sense of life, ecstasy, sorrow
> of love.[30]

For Pater, always the aesthete, art was best suited to generating such
ecstasy and heightened consciousness. But the highly eroticized language and the emphasis on courting new impressions created an outcry against the book that took him by surprise. Reviewers feared the
book's corrosive moral effect on the young. When the second edition of the book was published in 1877, Pater, chastened, silently
withdrew the "Conclusion," an act of self-censorship that prefigures
Wilde's own revisions to *The Picture of Dorian Gray* (Pater's book was
retitled, with the second edition, *The Renaissance: Studies in Art and
Poetry*). For the third edition, Pater restored the "Conclusion," and
with the fourth he added a short note to his readers that explained
that the "'Conclusion' was omitted in the second edition of this
book, as I conceived it might possibly mislead some young men into
whose hands it might fall." In his novel *Marius the Epicurean* (1885),
Pater put it in slightly different terms: "A book, like a person, has its
fortunes with one; is lucky or unlucky in the precise moment of its
falling in our way, and often by some happy accident counts with us
for something more than its independent value."[31] For Marius, Pat-

er's adolescent Roman hero, that "golden book" is the *Metamorphoses* of Apuleius. But here, more generally, Pater means any book that comes to exert a powerful influence over the lives of its readers— particularly adolescent male readers. He also casts a backward glance at the scandal surrounding his own earlier book and its alleged corrosive influence on youth.

Wilde was one of the young men into whose hands the book "had fallen" soon after its publication. He never ceased referring to *The Renaissance* as "my golden book" (Ellmann, p. 47). And later, writing in *De Profundis,* he called it "that book which has had such a strange influence over my life." He read it for the first time in 1874, during his first term at Oxford, though he was not to meet Pater personally for another three years. According to Richard Ellmann, Wilde knew much of *The Renaissance* by heart, and under Pater's general influence Wilde became, in the words of one of his fellow students, an "extreme aesthete" (Ellmann, p. 84). Wilde would spend much of the next fifteen years reacting to Pater's writings in print and in private. *The Picture of Dorian Gray* can be seen as the climax in a long dialogue between Wilde and Pater. The novel dramatizes Pater's ideas, radicalizes them, and in doing so offers itself as a critique of Pater's aestheticism. Some readers see the novel, which is full of allusions to Pater, as a parody of his ideas. Lord Henry in particular seems intimately familiar with Pater's *Renaissance.* Ellmann suggests that the unnamed book that "revealed much to [Lord Henry] that he had not known before," when he was sixteen, is *The Renaissance:* "Lord Henry is forever quoting, or misquoting, without acknowledgment, from [*The Renaissance*]. . . . He brazenly takes over the best known passages" (Ellmann, p. 317). In Chapter II, for example, when Lord Henry urges Dorian to pursue a life of sensation, he paraphrases from Pater's infamous "Conclusion":

> Live! Live the wonderful life that is in you! Let nothing be lost upon you. Be always searching for new sensations. Be afraid of nothing.
> A new Hedonism! That is what our century wants. You might be its visible symbol. With your personality there is

nothing you could not do. The world belongs to you for a season.

Lord Henry's call for a philosophy of "new Hedonism" also alludes to a chapter in Pater's *Marius the Epicurean* called "The New Cyrenaicism," in which Pater describes his young protagonist's attraction to a life of cultivated sensuousness and his determination to "fill up the measure of that present with vivid sensations, and those intellectual apprehensions which . . . are most like sensations" (*Marius,* p. 96). If "actual moments as they pass" are to "be made to yield their utmost" (*Marius,* p. 97), Pater's narrator says, it will sometimes be necessary to "break beyond the limits of the actual moral order, perhaps not without some pleasurable excitement in so bold a venture" (*Marius,* pp. 99–100). By calling Lord Henry's philosophy the "new Hedonism," Wilde offers an explicit rebuke to Pater, whom he increasingly saw as far too timid in both his life and his work (after Pater's death, Wilde is reported to have said to Max Beerbohm, "Was he ever alive?" [quoted in Ellmann, p. 52]). Ever sensitive to the charge that his ideas about sensation lacked any solid ethical basis, Pater had masked them behind such respectable Classicist terms as *Cyrenaicism* and *Epicureanism.*[32] To the point, Pater took issue with the application of the term *hedonism* to his thought on the grounds that the "reproachful Greek term" is "too large and vague" to be conducive "to any very delicately correct ethical conclusions" (*Marius,* p. 100). Wilde's "new Hedonism" was a slap in the face to his former mentor.

Pater declined to review the *Lippincott's* version of *Dorian Gray* in 1890, fearing that doing so would be too dangerous, and we know he expressed reservations to Wilde about the earlier published version of the novel. In his 1891 review of the novel, which can justly be read as an exercise in damage control, Pater goes out of his way to distance himself from the Paterian mouthpiece Lord Henry Wotton, who has (according to Pater) "too much of a not very really refined world in and about him" and whom Wilde can "hardly have intended . . . to figure the motive and tendency of a true Cyrenaic or Epicurean doctrine of life."[33] Wilde himself viewed Lord Henry as "an excellent corrective of the tedious ideal shadowed forth in the semi-theological novels of our age" and probably classified *Marius* as a semi-theological novel.[34] It was a book that greatly disappointed him. Essentially a revision of Pater's Conclusion, it attempts to show the moral limitations of Cyrenaicism or Epicureanism, and its conclusion brings Marius into contact with a group of Christians: "while [Marius] remains a pagan connoisseur and is not formally converted, he dies in their arms, as if baptized by desire."[35] Wilde later wrote that as a result of his effort to "reconcile the artistic life with the life of religion," Pater had made his central character "little more than a spectator."[36]

No such criticism can fairly be made of *The Picture of Dorian Gray*. Dorian remains a vibrant and dynamic character. And Wilde's novel, at least in the two earlier versions, offers no reconciliations. Wilde seems intent on showing up Pater for his timidity and on pushing the philosophy of "the new Hedonism" to its logical conclusion. When preparing the book edition of 1891, Wilde brought the novel to a moral conclusion that he thought would silence his critics. He did so, in part, by heightening Dorian's monstrosity toward the novel's conclusion, making clearer the suggestion that Dorian's destruction of the portrait was only an attempt to destroy "the evidence" against him, so that he might continue his hedonistic pursuit of sensation and experience with impunity. As a result Dorian is finally a less sympathetic and complex figure than he is in the earlier versions. The earlier Dorian is visited by self-doubts toward the novel's end, though they come too late to be of much use to him. He abandons his plan to seduce the virginal Hetty Merton and to keep her as his mistress, despite the fact that he has taken a house in the city for her; and he is troubled by the thought that "something more" than vanity, curiosity, or hypocrisy had prompted his renunciation of her. But hints of compunction persist despite Wilde's efforts at eradicating them from the ending of the 1891 version, and they are prefigured in Dorian's belated sense of guilt about his cruel treatment of Sybil Vane. "Good resolutions are simply a useless attempt to interfere with scientific laws," Lord Henry tells Dorian. "Their origin is pure vanity." Perhaps. But such vanity makes us human.

Wilde's effort to surpass Pater, then, is complicated, and perhaps even thwarted, by an accompanying and persistent sense of the human and moral price the aesthete must pay for pursuing his life of ecstasy. For this reason Dorian remains a tragic figure in both published versions. The playwright John Osborne, who adapted the novel for the stage in 1973, calls it "a moral entertainment."[37] Richard Ellmann sees the novel as an indictment of aestheticism, intent on "exhibiting its dangers" (Ellmann, p. 315). If one leads a beautiful, shallow life, it will end tragically in an ugly death. A life lived in the untrammeled pursuit of sensation must lead ultimately to anarchy and self-destruction. Ellmann, like Osborne, finds a moral lesson in Wilde's novel that the vast majority of Wilde's own contemporaries found lacking. In a memorable phrase, he calls Dorian "aestheticism's first martyr" (Ellmann, p. 315).

Ellmann is right that *Dorian Gray* is a tragedy but certainly wrong in asserting that the novel is a condemnation of aestheticism. Wilde never ceased to be an aesthete in his writings and pronouncements. His only novel, written in decorative prose that works upon the senses, and full of acknowledgments to its aesthetic precursors, is the fiction of an aesthete, whatever else it is. From an artistic point of view, Wilde felt that emphasizing the human and moral cost of pursuing pleasure to its logical conclusion was the novel's central weakness: "far from wishing to emphasise any moral in my story," he writes, "the real trouble I experienced . . . was that of keeping the extremely obvious moral subordinate to the artistic and dramatic effect. . . . I think the moral too apparent."[38] And according to the artistic tenets that Wilde had articulated for a considerable time by 1890—and that he was to reiterate in the 1891 Preface—Dorian's (and our own) willingness to be judged by the portrait, to see it as the document of his inner corruption, is to misunderstand that "the sphere of art and the sphere of ethics are absolutely distinct." Dorian has, in truth, misconstrued the nature of the portrait from the start, gazing at it as if it were a mirror of his true being or soul. Had he understood the portrait from a more purely "Wildean" perspective, seeing it (like any artwork) not as a truth-telling entity so much as a purely imaginative one, he would never have come to be so haunted or possessed by it, allowing it to dominate his existence at the expense of what makes him human. "Art never expresses anything but itself" and is best understood for its absolute indifference to life, Wilde maintains in "The Decay of Lying."[39] By confusing the relations between life and art—to the degree that he *becomes* the work of art and feels he can act with impunity as a result—Dorian has allowed not merely his humanity to become diminished and shrunken but his "aestheticism" as well.[40] He has morphed, in effect, from an aesthete into a mere decadent. The destruction of art, as of civilized culture more broadly, Wilde writes, begins not when "Life becomes fascinated with [art's] new wonder, and asks to be admitted into the charmed circle" as a result, but when "Life gets the upper hand, and drives Art out into the wilderness."[41]

Dorian is no more an exemplar of Wildean aestheticism than Camus's Mersault is a model of existentialism. Aestheticism, at least initially, promises to fulfill Dorian's human potential, not to thwart it. A life dedicated to sensation and art needs to be lived fully and openly, Wilde suggests; but we should never forget that art "is not meant to instruct, or to influence action in any way."[42] The minute life mistakes its object and tries to *be* sensation or art, to act wholly according to it or to separate itself from those broader elements that define humanity as such, a kind of corruption sets in and both life and art become inescapably spoiled in consequence.

Of course, the freedom to live fully and openly, whether dedicated to sensation, art, or anything else, varies enormously according to time, place, and politics. Dorian living today in London's Mayfair district would not need to live a secret double life. His pursuit of beauty and sensation would not bring him into conflict with a "harsh uncomely Puritanism." As Harold Bloom has suggested, in a different age Wilde himself might have been an "aesthetic superstar" like Andy Warhol or Truman Capote.[43] For all the novel's aesthetic concerns, it is impossible for contemporary readers to see *The Picture of Dorian Gray* apart from Wilde's life and the circumstances in which it was written and brought forth into the world. The novel's potent mixture of high-minded ideas about art and pleasure, on the one hand, and sexual transgressiveness, on the other, suggests at the very least that we need to look at the novel with a kind of double vision. It is a book that admits multiple interpretations. If *Dorian Gray* is a lesson about the consequences of confusing life and art, it is also its embodiment, since the novel would become in the hands of Wilde's contemporaries a way of reading and judging its author's own conduct. Life—cruel, inhospitable, and more powerful than Wilde had ever supposed—would gain the upper hand. Aestheticism's first martyr at the hands of life was not Dorian Gray. It was Oscar Wilde himself.

Notes

1 Vyvyan Holland, *Son of Oscar Wilde* (1954; rpt. Oxford University Press, 1987), p. 76.

2 Richard Ellmann, *Oscar Wilde* (New York: Knopf, 1988), p. 584, hereafter cited in text as Ellmann.

3 *Complete Letters of Oscar Wilde,* ed. Merlin Holland and Rupert Hart-Davis (New York: Holt, 2000), p. 447.

4 Unsigned review of *The Picture of Dorian Gray, Daily Chronicle,* June 30, 1890, rpt. in *Oscar Wilde: The Critical Heritage,* ed. Karl Beckson (London: Routledge & Kegan Paul, 1970), p. 72.

5 Unsigned review of *The Picture of Dorian Gray, St. James's Gazette,* June 20, 1890; rpt. in *Oscar Wilde: The Critical Heritage,* ed. Beckson, pp. 68–69.

6 Unsigned notice of *The Picture of Dorian Gray, Scots Observer,* July 5, 1890; rpt. in *Oscar Wilde: The Critical Heritage,* ed. Beckson, p. 75.

7 See textual note e, Chapter VII, for the publisher's change. See Linda Dowling, *Hellenism and Homosexuality in Victorian Oxford* (Ithaca: Cornell University Press, 1994), pp. 124–127; also Robert Mighall's Introduction to *The Picture of Dorian Gray,* ed. R. Mighall (East Rutherford, NJ: Viking Penguin, 2001), pp. xvii–xviii.

8 Ross, who had "the face of Puck," according to Wilde, remained Wilde's most trusted friend and confidante long after their affair had cooled off. Much later, Ross became Wilde's legal and literary executor. Wilde's "Ballad of Reading Gaol" (1898), written shortly after his release from prison, was originally dedicated to Ross with the words, "When I came out of prison some met me with garments and spices and others with wise counsel. You met me with love." The dedication was removed, at Ross's urging, shortly before publication.

9 See Neil McKenna, *The Secret Life of Oscar Wilde* (New York: Basic Books, 2005).

10 Florence T. Gribbell, quoted in McKenna, *The Secret Life of Oscar Wilde,* p. 116.

11 John Gray, letter to André Raffalovich, February 1899, quoted in McKenna, *The Secret Life of Oscar Wilde,* p. 132; for discussion of Gray's "sin," see also Jerusha

Hull McCormack, *John Gray: Poet, Dandy, Priest* (Hanover, NH: Brandeis University Press/University Press of New England, 1991), pp. 39–52.

12 *Complete Letters,* p. 758.

13 Queensberry's scrawl is hard to decipher and often quoted differently. The club porter, and possibly Wilde too, believed up until Queensberry's arraignment that the latter had written "ponce and sodomite." On testifying to this effect during Queensberry's arraignment on the charge of criminal libel, on March 2, 1895, the porter was interrupted by Queensberry, who interposed that he had written "posing as sodomite."

14 The 1861 Offences against the Person Act proscribed "buggery," and Statute 11 of the Criminal Law Amendment Act of 1885 proscribed "gross indecency." While the sentence under the earlier legislation was harsher (life imprisonment), the burden of proof was higher; and from 1885 onward most "sodomites" were prosecuted under the later Act, which required merely proof of "indecency," not sexual penetration.

15 See Merlin Holland, *The Real Trial of Oscar Wilde* (New York: Perennial, 2004), p. 86. (*The Real Trial* was published in the United Kingdom in 2003 under the title *Irish Peacock and Scarlet Marquess: The Real Trial of Oscar Wilde.*)

16 Queensberry's plea of justification, entered on March 30, specifically accuses Wilde of writing "a certain immoral and obscene work in the form of a narrative entitled *The Picture of Dorian Gray* . . . designed and intended [as well as understood by its readers] . . . to describe the relations, intimacies and passions of certain persons of sodomitical and unnatural habits, tastes, and practices." According to Queensberry's plea, *The Picture of Dorian Gray* was "calculated to subvert morality and to encourage unnatural vice" (Holland, *The Real Trial,* Appendix A, pp. 290–291).

17 Edward Marjoribanks, cited in Ellmann, *Oscar Wilde,* p. 450.

18 French decadent novels were typically bound in yellow paper, and the "poisonous book" given by Lord Henry to Dorian, which comes to exert a powerful influence over him, is a yellow paperback.

19 Mr. Justice Charles, quoted in H. Montgomery Hyde, *The Trials of Oscar Wilde* (1962; rpt. New York: Dover Publications, 1973), pp. 215–226.

20 Quoted in Hyde, *The Trials of Oscar Wilde,* p. 201; also quoted in Ellmann, *Oscar Wilde,* p. 463, and McKenna, *The Secret Life of Oscar Wilde,* p. 391. The legal scholar Leslie J. Moran has questioned whether this speech, as reported in modern biographical accounts, including purportedly factual accounts of Wilde's trials, is a verbatim record or rather an editorial embellishment. See Moran's "Transcripts and Truth: Writing the Trials of Oscar Wilde," in *Oscar Wilde and Modern Culture,* ed. Joseph Bristow (Athens, OH: Ohio University Press, 2008), pp. 243ff.

21 See Hyde, *The Trials of Oscar Wilde,* pp. 272–273.

22 Some of these changes may have been instigated in response to a suggestion from Wilde's publisher, George Lock, that Wilde "depict the misery in
which [Dorian Gray] ends his days," and also give "a little longer" to Lord Henry;
letter to Oscar Wilde, July 7, 1890, printed in "Stuart Mason" [pseud. of Christopher Millard], *Bibliography of Oscar Wilde* (London: T. Werner Laurie, 1914),
p. 105.

23 *Complete Letters,* p. 428.

24 For "They are the elect . . ." and "There is no such thing . . ," see Appendix B
below. "The true artist . . ." and "The artist is never morbid . . ." are quoted from
"The Soul of Man under Socialism," in *Criticism: Historical Criticism, Intentions and
the Soul of Man,* ed. Josephine Guy, vol. 4 of *The Complete Works of Oscar Wilde* (Oxford University Press, 2007), p. 252.

25 *Complete Letters,* p. 476.

26 *Complete Letters,* p. 436.

27 Walter Pater, "Style," in his *Appreciations* (1889; Evanston, IL: Northwestern
University Press, 1987), p. 20. Wilde reviewed Pater's *Appreciations,* singling out
the essay "Style" for special praise, in the *Speaker* in March 1890.

28 Victor Shklovsky, "Art as Technique," in *Russian Formalist Criticism: Four Essays,* trans. and intro. Lee T. Lemon and Marion J. Reis (Lincoln, NE: University
of Nebraska Press, 1965), p. 12.

29 Denis Donoghue, *Walter Pater: Lover of Strange Souls* (New York: Knopf, 1995),
p. 7.

30 Walter Pater, *The Renaissance: Studies in Art and Poetry: The 1893 Text,* ed. Donald Hill (Berkeley: University of California Press, 1980), pp. 188–190. Pater had
first expressed these ideas, in nearly identical language, in 1868 in the course of
reviewing the poetry of William Morris.

31 *Marius the Epicurean: His Sensations and Ideas,* ed. Gerald Monsman (Kansas
City, MO: Vallancourt Books, 2008), p. 62, hereafter cited in text as *Marius.*

32 See especially the accusations of "Hedonism" leveled negatively against *The
Renaissance* in 1873 in reviews by Sidney Colvin, John Morley, and "Z," in *Walter
Pater: The Critical Heritage,* ed. R. M. Seiler (London: Routledge and Kegan Paul,
1980), pp. 53, 68, and 75.

33 Walter Pater, signed review of *The Picture of Dorian Gray,* November 1891, rpt.
in *Oscar Wilde: The Critical Heritage,* p. 84.

34 *Complete Letters,* p. 429.

35 Donoghue, *Walter Pater, Lover of Strange Souls,* p. 192.

36 *Complete Letters,* p. 740.

37 See Osborne, Introduction to *The Picture of Dorian Gray: A Moral Entertain-ment* (London: Samuel French, 1973), p. 5.

38 *Complete Letters,* p. 435.

39 "The Decay of Lying," in *Criticism: Historical Criticism, Intentions and the Soul of Man,* ed. Guy, p. 96.

40 See Mighall, Introduction to *The Picture of Dorian Gray,* pp. xxiii–xxvii, esp. Mighall's comment that the novel is in part "an allegory of interpretation, and an essay in critical conduct" (p. xxvii).

41 "The Decay of Lying," p. 84.

42 *Complete Letters,* p. 478.

43 Harold Bloom, *Genius: A Mosaic of One Hundred Exemplary Creative Minds* (New York: Warner Books, 2002), p. 244.

TEXTUAL INTRODUCTION

This edition of *The Picture of Dorian Gray* is based upon the typescript, with emendations in Wilde's own hand, that the author submitted for publication to the Philadelphia-based *Lippincott's Monthly Magazine* in late March or early April 1890, roughly eleven weeks before the novel was first published in the magazine's July number.[1] This version differs markedly from the one that Lippincott eventually published, as well as from all succeeding published editions: it represents the novel as Wilde envisioned it in the spring of 1890, unaltered and uncensored by its first editor, Lippincott's Joseph Marshall Stoddart, and it gives us a more daring and scandalous version of Wilde's novel than either of the two subsequent published versions.[2] Most modern editions of *Dorian Gray* reprint the expanded version of the novel, published in book form by Ward, Lock, and Company in April 1891, into which Wilde incorporated numerous revisions shortly after the novel's appearance in *Lippincott's*. But Wilde's revisions for the book version were greatly influenced by the hostile reviews in the British press that had greeted the novel the previous year, as well as by his publisher's and his own anxieties about possible obscenity charges. The present edition marks the first time Wilde's typescript has been published, more than 120 years after the author submitted it for publication.

Scholars have long recognized the importance of the earlier *Lippincott's* version of the novel, which had been commissioned by J. M. Stoddart, the magazine's editor. Joseph Bristow, the novel's most recent editor, maintains that the *Lippincott's* version constitutes an entirely separate work from the longer version of 1891, pitched (as it was) toward a different readership and possessing distinct merits from the later version. Elizabeth Lorang has recently argued that *Dorian Gray* owes its profound cultural impact, in Wilde's own day at least, to the fact that it first appeared in magazine form.[3] The best of the many recent editions of Wilde's novel—the Norton Critical Edition, first edited by Donald F. Lawler in 1988 (a second edition was published in 2007, newly edited by Michael Patrick Gillespie, preserving most of Lawler's careful textual work), and Joseph Bristow's 2005 Oxford University Press edition for the multivolume *Complete Works of Oscar Wilde*—reprint the shorter, thirteen-chapter *Lippincott's* version alongside the longer, twenty-chapter book version in recognition of this important difference.

When Wilde's novel appeared in *Lippincott's* in the summer of 1890, it was subjected to a torrent of abuse in the British press, chiefly on account of its latent or not-so-latent homoeroticism. British reviewers were virtually unanimous in condemning Wilde for what one termed "writing stuff that were better unwritten."[4] Two leading magazines, the *St. James's Gazette* and the *Scots Observer,* hinted in their review pages that Wilde should be prosecuted for what he had written. As a consequence, Britain's largest bookseller, W. H. Smith & Son, took the unusual step of pulling the July number of *Lippincott's* from its railway bookstalls. Although some scholars have argued that the twenty-chapter version of 1891 represents the greater artistic achievement, most now accept that when Wilde revised and expanded the novel, many of the changes he made were, in the words of one eminent Wilde scholar, "dictated by expediency and not by artistic considerations."[5] Wilde—already leading a secret double life —had reason to be fearful. Five years later, at the height of his fame, he would be imprisoned for two years' hard labor after being convicted of "gross indecency." During the course of Wilde's disastrous libel suit against Lord Alfred Douglas's father, the Marquess of Queensberry, it was the more salacious thirteen-chapter *Lippincott's* version that was used so damagingly against him in the courtroom. As Queensberry's attorney, Edward Carson, brandished the pages of

Lippincott's Monthly Magazine, he took "great pains" to specify differences between the *Lippincott's* version and the subsequent twenty-chapter version, referring repeatedly to the latter as "the purged edition" because of the greater frankness with which the *Lippincott's* version treated sexual matters.[6]

If Edward Carson had possessed Wilde's typescript, he undoubtedly would have made effective use of it in the courtroom, for it is even more explicit in its sexual allusions and references than the version published in *Lippincott's Monthly Magazine. Lippincott's* had a well-deserved reputation for publishing stories in the so-called Erotic School of American fiction.[7] But even at the relatively liberal magazine, the story immediately raised concerns. Upon receipt of the typescript in Philadelphia, Stoddart consulted with colleagues and a number of close associates to determine whether, and if so in what form, the novel could be published, before himself making or overseeing a number of significant emendations to Wilde's text, including the excision of material he feared was too graphic for the magazine's readership. But not all the changes Stoddart oversaw can be fairly described as censorship. First, not surprisingly, Stoddart or his associates altered Wilde's punctuation, capitalization, and spelling to conform to American usage and the magazine's house style. Second, and more significant, as Stoddart and his associates worked their way through the typescript, they struck nearly 500 words from Wilde's novel. They deleted a number of phrases or sentences, for instance, that make clearer and more vivid the homoerotic nature of the painter Basil Hallward's feelings for Dorian Gray. In Chapter VII, Stoddart or one of his associates struck Hallward's description of his portrait of Dorian as a kind of lovemaking: "There was love in every line, and in every touch there was passion." In the same chapter, he deleted Dorian's concluding reflection on Hallward: there was "something infinitely tragic in a romance that was at once so passionate and sterile." Similarly, Stoddart or one of his associates removed references to Dorian's female lovers, Sybil Vane and Hetty Merton, as his "mistresses." A more detailed consideration of the changes overseen by Stoddart will follow; for the moment it is important to recognize that, insofar as the more substantial of those changes are concerned at least, the process of "purging" had begun even before the novel saw the light of day.

That Stoddart or his associates made alterations to Wilde's text prior to publication has long been evident to the handful of scholars who have scrutinized the prepublication typescript. Wilde's hand is distinct from those of at least two others who emended the typescript upon receipt in Philadelphia (that one of these hands was Stoddart's can be inferred from comparisons with known examples of his handwriting, as Joseph Bristow has argued), and at least two previous scholars have given detailed consideration to the nature of the changes overseen by Stoddart.[8] It is a curious fact in the history of the novel that Wilde's typescript has remained unpublished until now, given the general recognition among Wilde scholars that the *Lippincott's* version was bowdlerized. In the Introduction to his recent edition of the novel for Oxford University Press, for example, Joseph Bristow writes that "Stoddart's emendations make it plain that certain kinds of . . . references to sexual passion were unacceptable to *Lippincott's Magazine,*" and he acknowledges Stoddart's "unwillingness to permit explicit references to Dorian Gray's illicit relations with women."[9] Moreover, in a note to his 1988 Norton Critical Edition (the first modern edition to reprint, in its entirety, the *Lippincott's* text for an English-speaking readership), Donald Lawler describes Stoddart's changes as a "series of bowdlerizations."[10] In the prefatory note to her 1974 Oxford English Novels edition of the book, Isobel Murray writes that "Stoddart far exceeded his brief in making changes for the Lippincott version after Wilde had passed the manuscript"; and in their recent fine study of Wilde's writing practices, *Oscar Wilde's Profession,* Josephine Guy and Ian Small write that "often Stoddart appears to be 'censoring' the text, on occasion striking out Wilde's later thoughts and corrections."[11]

No evidence survives to suggest that before publication Wilde saw, let alone approved, the changes Stoddart and his associates had made. As Guy and Small write, "we can be fairly certain that Stoddart did not consult Wilde about these revisions."[12] Indeed, it would have been highly unusual for Wilde to have been granted such an opportunity, since it was not then customary for American magazine editors to provide British authors with proofs. As N. N. Feltes argues, late-Victorian magazine editors on both sides of the Atlantic typically assumed a privileged position over authors as far as the production of the text itself was concerned; and as John Espey speculates, "the American system of editing gave the publisher far more authority than in England or on the Continent."[13] Even well-established fiction writers were forced to accept what Thomas Hardy called "the necessities of magazine publication": and from the editor's viewpoint, "control of the actual production . . . for a magazine or weekly newspaper did not need to be negotiated; it was a *given*."[14] In the months leading up to the novel's publication, then, Wilde had neither the authority nor the opportunity to challenge the alterations made to his novel by its first editor. There exists little warrant for Joseph Bristow's assertion that "all of the editorial emendations to the typescript have Wilde's authority, since no evidence exists to suggest that Wilde refused to accede to any of the changes."[15] The *Lippincott's* version represents what one relatively liberal-minded editor and his associates thought was permissible in 1890. Highlighting those parts of the novel that were expunged or altered from the version that Wilde actually submitted, as I have done in the Textual Notes to this edition, provides an interesting window onto what was, or was not, acceptable in English-language fiction in the run-up to the novel's earliest publication.

   Some scholars have argued that Wilde's incorporation of many of Stoddart's alterations into the later, enlarged version of the novel amounts to a belated acceptance or endorsement of them. This line of argument, however, overlooks two crucial facts. First, it is almost certain that after Wilde submitted his typescript to *Lippincott's* in late March 1890 he never again had possession of the prepublication materials. The typescript—to which Wilde had added some 3,000 words of new material in his own hand before sending it to Stoddart, and on the top sheet of which Stoddart at some point had lightly inscribed, "This is the original copy of *Dorian Gray*. J. M. Stoddart"— remained in Stoddart's possession until long after Wilde's death: a fact that says a lot about the relations between authors and magazine editors at the time.[16] Stoddart or one of his associates possessed as well the holograph fair-copy manuscript that, earlier in 1890, Wilde had submitted to Miss Dickens's Typewriting Service, in the Strand, as "copy" for the production of the typescript.[17] We know this because the holograph manuscript—which has survived to this day and is now housed at the Morgan Library in New York City—is stamped with the seal of Lippincott's London agent. Furthermore, in a letter to his London agent dated June 2, 1890, just eighteen days before the novel's publication, Stoddart wrote that he expected the arrival of the holograph manuscript "in the next shipment."[18] Perhaps most compellingly, when Stoddart was planning in 1906 to issue a new edition of the novel, he intended to base it on this manuscript, which was then in the possession of Stoddart's friend Ferdinand I. Haber (and which Haber referred to, in his correspondence with Stoddart, as "our manuscript").[19] All scholars agree, moreover, that far from using a prepublication text as a copy-text for the 1891 edition, Wilde relied upon printed sheets or "offprints" from the *Lippincott's* text, which he revised and supplemented by hand, in one or two cases reversing changes that Stoddart or one of his associates had made to the original typescript (see p. 262, n. 3, and 264, n. 8).

But there is a second, more important reason that Wilde's later incorporation of Stoddart's more substantive changes does not suggest that he endorsed them. It has everything to do with the circumstances under which Wilde revised the novel for publication in book form in 1891. The furor surrounding the *Lippincott's* text upon its publication in 1890 meant that, even if Wilde had had recourse to the original wording in his typescript, he was in no position when it came time to revise the novel to restore Stoddart's substantive changes: to do so would have risked precisely the kind of legal and public scrutiny that would prove disastrous in 1895. As already indicated, Britain's largest bookseller, W. H. Smith & Son, removed all copies of the July number of *Lippincott's* from its bookstalls days after its publication. In a letter to Ward, Lock, and Company (the magazine's British distributor as well as, later, the book publisher for *Dorian Gray*), the retailer explained that it felt compelled to do so because the story had "been characterized by the press as a filthy one."[20] More significantly, Ward, Lock, and Company wrote to Wilde on the same day stating that "this is a serious matter to us. If you are in the City during the next day or two, we should be glad if you could give us a call."[21] If Ward, Lock, and Company already had misgivings about the story in its shorter form, it is likely that, in the meeting that followed, the company's officers made painfully clear to Wilde that they would publish his novel only if he muted its most sexually explicit elements.[22] (Ward, Lock, and Company was not the only book publisher to express qualms about Wilde's novel. Macmillan and Company had earlier declined it because it contained offensive material.)

The threat of legal prosecution, hinted at in reviews of the novel, was more real than perhaps modern readers appreciate. In 1890, in the wake of the Cleveland Street Scandal of 1889–1890, segments of the British media, the police, and the political establishment were already inflamed at what they perceived as the government's failure to prosecute "gross indecency" among the wealthy (male homosexuality was seen as an aristocratic vice that corrupted lower-class youths). Lingering resentments about the ways in which the Cleveland Street case was prosecuted would affect Wilde's own prosecution and sentencing in 1895. Though barely five years old in 1890, the National Vigilance Association, founded "for the enforcement and improvement of the laws for the repression of criminal vice and public immorality," had recently succeeded in having Emile Zola's English publisher Henry Vizetelly prosecuted—twice—for obscenity. As a result, Vizetelly spent three months in jail in 1889 and was fined a total of £300, while a number of Zola's most important works remained unpublished in Britain for many years. It is worth recalling as well the fate of such Modernist classics as James Joyce's *Ulysses* and Radcliffe Hall's *Well of Loneliness,* both of which fell foul of American courts in the 1920s and which remained essentially unpublishable in Britain for many years.

Given, then, the public outrage that greeted the novel when it appeared in *Lippincott's,* and given, too, the anxieties of Ward, Lock, and Company, it is entirely understandable that Wilde would not have felt at liberty, as he revised the novel for book publication, to restore controversial material that had already been expunged by Stoddart. Indeed, going one step further than his editor, Wilde now removed additional homosexual allusions that had been left uncensored. He also heightened Dorian's monstrosity in the moments before his fateful, final encounter with the portrait, to bring the story to a more appropriate moral conclusion.[23] In an atmosphere of heightened paranoia, Wilde and his publishers were unwilling to risk prosecution. The potential repercussions were simply too great.

Stoddart received Wilde's typescript in Philadelphia on April 7, 1890, nearly eight months after commissioning it, having been told as early as March 20 that it would be sent to him directly.[24] Stoddart's determination that the story needed substantial editorial intervention seems to have been immediate. "I am not yet able to report thoroughly on the Oscar Wilde story," he wrote to his employer Craige Lippincott in a recently discovered letter, dated April 10, 1890. "I read it and consider it a very powerful story, but it has certain faults which will undoubtedly have to be fixed before we can publish it. Mr. Walsh read it last night and is somewhat of the same opinion, and I now propose to have Miss Annie Wharton read it carefully. You may rest assured that it will not go into the Magazine unless it is proper that it shall, although in its present condition there are a number of things which an innocent woman would make an exception to. But I will go beyond this and make it acceptable to the most fastidious taste."[25]

Over the ensuing twelve days, Stoddart consulted a number of his closest literary associates about the story in an effort to determine the exact form in which it should, or could, be published. Those consulted included J. B. Lippincott—along with Craige Lippincott, a joint-partner in the firm; Anne Wharton, a regular contributor to the magazine and later the author of several books on American colonial life as well as a glowing, perceptive review of *Dorian Gray* that appeared in the September 1890 number of *Lippincott's;* Henry Collins Walsh, a regular book reviewer for the magazine who was also the editor of H. F. Cary's translations of Dante's *Purgatorio* and *Paradiso* and, with his liberal-minded brother William S. Walsh (Stoddart's predecessor as editor of *Lippincott's*), publisher of *American Notes and Queries;* and Melville Philips, another regular book reviewer for *Lip-*

pincott's and sometime literary editor of the *Philadelphia Press.*[26] Arguably this circle included some of the most liberal figures in American publishing. "We have finally concluded to use the Oscar Wilde story," Stoddart wrote to Craige Lippincott on April 22, "after it having been read and carefully considered by Mr. H. C. Walsh, Miss Wharton, Mr. J. B. Lippincott, Mr. Julian Shoemaker and later by Melville Philips, the latter [of] who[m] is practically to edit it by picking out any objectionable passages. The universal feeling is, by all who have read it, in favor of its publication."[27]

Only on this date did Stoddart inform Wilde that the story was acceptable and would be published: "the manuscript of *Dorian Gray* was duly received . . . We will publish it in the July number which appears on June 20th. I beg to express my entire satisfaction with the story as it is in my judgment, and that of the several readers who have gone over it, one of the most powerful works of the time. . . . I expect for it a large sale and a most appreciative reading."[28] Stoddart's letter mentions nothing about the concern with which the story had been met in Philadelphia, by himself and his circle of advisors; nor does it say anything about his plans to "pick out objectionable passages." His caution may have had something to do with the fact that Stoddart, apparently, had failed to draw up a formal contract for the *Lippincott's* story, his agreement with Wilde having been a verbal one.[29] On the same date, Stoddart prepared a memorandum for Wilde's signature, which assigned to Lippincott & Co. "my entire right" in the composition.[30] A few days later, Stoddart announced to another dilatory author that "we can give you a few days more grace" because "we have filled the breach with an Oscar Wilde story which . . . reveals itself to be a remarkable production."[31]

How or whether Melville Philips "picked out objectionable passages" from Wilde's text, as Stoddart had indicated he would, cannot now be ascertained. The typescript bears both deletions and insertions in at least two hands other than Wilde's own; and although some of the editorial insertions can be attributed to Stoddart personally with a high degree of certainty, others (such as the alteration of "Sybil" to "Sibyl," of "curtsey" to "courtesy," and of "leapt" to "leaped") are in a hand that is neither Wilde's nor Stoddart's, so it re-

mains entirely possible that Philips or some other individual besides
Stoddart was responsible for editorial deletions, too.

Readers interested in seeing precisely which parts of Wilde's text
were found objectionable by its first editor and his associates should
consult both the Textual Notes in this volume, where the more substantial of *Lippincott's* alterations are delineated in detail, and the appendix of "accidental" changes at the back, where smaller changes
made by *Lippincott's* editors are laid out. But at this juncture, a fuller
description of the editorial changes overseen by Stoddart—including
those made to Wilde's spelling, capitalization, and punctuation—
is in order. I refer to changes that clearly alter meaning—that is,
changes to entire words, phrases, or larger units of text—as "substantive." "Accidental" changes mean alterations to spelling, punctuation,
and capitalization, which less clearly affect meaning.

The vast majority of the substantive changes introduced by *Lippincott's* center on sexual matters. The deletion in Chapter VII of
passages making more explicit and vivid the homoerotic nature
of Basil Hallward's feelings for Dorian Gray has already been mentioned. The same anxieties about explicit homosexual references
motivate as well a number of alterations in Chapter X, where Basil
laments the corruption of Dorian. Stoddart or one of his associates
cuts, for example, the sentence: "It is quite sufficient to say of a
young man that he goes to stay at Selby Royal, for people to sneer
and titter." In the same chapter, Stoddart alters the salacious question, "Why is it that every young man that you take up seems to
come to grief, to go to the bad at once?" to the more ambiguous question, "Why is your friendship so fateful to young men?" In Chapter
V, Stoddart or one of his associates cuts a sentence that gives an entirely different caste to Dorian's night walking: "A man with curious
eyes had suddenly peered into his face, and then dogged him with
stealthy footsteps, passing and repassing him many times."

Some of the most extensive editorial alterations, however, concern not references to homosexuality but rather passages related to
promiscuous or illicit heterosexuality. I have already alluded to the
elimination of three instances in which Wilde refers to Dorian's fe-

male lovers, Sybil Vane and Hetty Merton, as his "mistresses." By far the longest editorial deletion in this regard is a still shocking passage in Chapter XIII in which Lord Henry speculates on Hetty's "happiness" had she become Dorian's mistress: "Upon the other hand, had she become your mistress, she would have lived in the society of charming and cultured men. You would have educated her, taught her how to dress, how to talk, how to move. You would have made her perfect, and she would have been extremely happy. After a time, no doubt, you would have grown tired of her. She would have made a scene. You would have made a settlement. Then a new career would have begun for her." That Stoddart or his associates deleted a total of nearly 120 words concerning Hetty Merton, including Dorian's confession that "she promised to come with me to town. I had taken a house for her, and arranged everything," suggests that Stoddart was as worried about reactions to the novel's depictions of illicit heterosexual behavior as he was about its seeming endorsement of homosexuality.[32] Anxieties about representations of illicit heterosexual desire also motivated the decision to delete from Chapter XIII Lord Henry's insouciant comment that his estranged wife Victoria had been "desperately in love with [Dorian] at one time," as well as Stoddart's decision to eliminate from Chapter IX Wilde's reference to the death (by suicide?) of those to whom Lady Elizabeth Devereux, Dorian's distant ancestor, "granted her favours." Similarly, Stoddart altered the blunt remark by Lord Henry in Chapter I—"I don't suppose that ten per cent of the lower orders live with their wives"—to the prudishly out-of-character comment, "I don't suppose that ten per cent of the lower orders live correctly."

Stoddart also oversaw the elimination of anything that smacked generally of decadence. There were a number of changes made to Wilde's descriptions in Chapter IX of Dorian's extreme behavior as he pushes to the limit his immersion in a world of sensation and experience. Stoddart or one of his associates altered the phrase "till the people almost drove [Dorian] out in horror and had to be appeased with monstrous bribes" to the less incriminating "until he was driven away," while deleting references to the "strange love that he inspired in women" and to "the sinful creatures who prowl the street at night [and who] cursed him as he passed by, seeing in him a corruption greater than their own." Stoddart was especially concerned with taming descriptions of the yellow novel that is given by Lord Henry Wotton to Dorian and comes to exert such a powerful influence over Dorian's life. To begin with, he eliminated all references to the novel's title and author, *Le Secret de Raoul, par Catulle Sarrazin* [Raoul's Secret, by Catulle Sarrazin], rightly sensing that these fictional names allude to some of the most scandalous works and figures of the French Decadent movement (see Chap. VIII, n. 17). Similarly, Stoddart muted a number of passages concerning the novel's hero, Raoul, who serves as "a kind of prefiguring type of [Dorian]." He expunged, for example, Raoul's imagined reincarnation as Caligula, who "had drank the love-philter of Caesonia, and worn the habit of Venus by night, and by day a false gilded beard." Raoul's specially made tapestries, "on which were pictured the awful and beautiful forms of those whom Vice and Blood and Weariness had made monstrous or mad," came in for harsh treatment. In addition to substituting "Lust" for "Vice," Stoddart deleted Wilde's specific mention of "Manfred, King of Apulia, who dressed always in green, and consorted only with courtezans and buffoons," as well as the narrator's explanation that Filippo, Duke of Milan (depicted on one tapestry), "slew his wife, and painted her lips with a scarlet poison, that her guilty lover might suck swift death from the dead thing that he fondled."

Although previous editors disagree about whether Wilde or Stoddart made the last of these deletions, the pencil line running through the phrase is identical to that with which other words and phrases in the novel were censored, indicating that it was Stoddart or one of his associates who made it (see Textual Note p, Chap. IV). Less certainty, however, surrounds three sentences omitted from the *Lippincott's* text that concern Dorian's discovery of "wonderful stories . . . about jewels." Two of the sentences—"It was a pearl that Julius Caesar had given to Servilia, when he loved her. Their child had been Brutus."—conclude a longer section added to the typescript by Wilde, in his own hand, before it was submitted to *Lippincott's*. These and the sentence that begins the next paragraph in the typescript—"The young priest of the Sun, who while yet a boy had been slain for his sins, liked to walk in jeweled shoes on dust of gold and silver."—were left unaltered by Stoddart and his associates in the typescript (as were Wilde's other references to the effeminate Elagabalus, the "young priest of the Sun"); however, they do not appear in the *Lippincott's* text (or in any later published text). Whether this was due to a typesetting error or because Stoddart or another editor excised them in the proofreading stage cannot now be determined. At any rate, these changes—if they were changes and not typesetting errors—were not alterations that Wilde ever had the opportunity to correct. They are restored here.

Although less dramatic than the edits I have been describing so far, some of the changes Stoddart oversaw to Wilde's punctuation, spelling, and capitalization transform the reading experience and alter meaning no less pervasively. Taken individually, such alterations may appear minor or "accidental," but their cumulative effect, on style and mood, can be profound. For instance, Stoddart or one of his associates inserted numerous dashes into Wilde's dialogue, often where Wilde was content with a comma. The result is speech that appears more disjointed and impulsive. These dashes were inserted not because Wilde's punctuation is in any way deficient but rather because *Lippincott's* wished to make the story's dialogue more sensational. A good example is the re-punctuation of Sybil Vane's whispered remark, in Chapter V, "Take me away, Dorian. Take me away with you," as "Take me away, Dorian—take me away with you." Here the dash changes the tone from wistful to imploring and desperate. With similar results, Stoddart or one of his associates changed Dorian's estimation of Basil Hallward's superiority to Lord Henry, in Chapter VII, from "'You are not stronger. You are too much afraid of life. But you are better,'" to "'You are not stronger,—you are too much afraid of life,—but you are better.'" Stoddart's alteration of Dorian's comment to the frame-maker Ashton, from "I will certainly drop in and look at the frame, though I don't go in much for religious art," to "I will certainly drop in and look at the frame—though I don't go in much for religious art," achieves a similar effect. In nearly all these instances, Stoddart can hardly be faulted as an editor because Wilde himself had punctuated much of his dialogue with dashes in order to make his character's speech and interior thought appear more dramatic. Nonetheless, Stoddart was at best exaggerating Wilde's own preferred punctuation style and at worst distorting it to make *Dorian Gray* more consistent with the reputation of *Lippincott's* for sensational, impulse-driven fiction.

Stoddart or one of his associates made significant alterations to Wilde's spelling, too. The replacement of British spellings of common words such as "colour," "odour," "rumour," "sympathise," and "realise" (but not "theatre"), and so on, with their American equivalents ("color," "odor," "rumor," "sympathize," "realize") is understandable given the primary American readership of the magazine (and in a few instances, it must be admitted, Wilde was inconsistent about British and American spelling). Americanizing British spellings remains a common practice today among American publishers. In one or two instances, Stoddart or one of his associates corrected obvious spelling errors that were made by Wilde or introduced into the typescript by Miss Dickens's Typewriting Service, the agency to whom the production of the typescript had been entrusted in London. Less understandable, however, is the twitchiness of Stoddart or one of his associates about such words as "ribands," "curtsey," "reverie," "spoilt," "leapt," and "syphons" (rendered as "ribbons," "courtesy," "revery," "spoiled," "leaped," and "siphons"), all of which had precedent in American English; while the alteration of "clenched" to the more antiquated "clinched" (p. 145 and p. 170 below) arguably produces an entirely new set of associations.

Three of the spelling changes made by the magazine's officers deserve special comment. First, in altering "sphynxes" to "sphinxes," Stoddart or one of his associates changed the spelling that Wilde preferred at this point in his career (it was not until much later, in a late draft of his poem "The Sphinx," that he adopted the more modern spelling). Second, the alteration of "idyll" to "idyl" must have struck Wilde as arbitrary, because he took the trouble to reverse this change of spelling when he used offprints or unbound sheets of the *Lippincott's* text to prepare the novel for book publication. Finally, the often-noted alteration, by Stoddart or one of his associates, of

Wilde's "Sybil" to "Sibyl," a nod to the name's derivation from the Greek *sibylla,* connoting "prophetess" or "oracle" (see p. 114, n. 16, below), obscures a number of interesting associations. As John Espey has observed, "Sybil" was a common name and spelling in England at this time (Lord Alfred Douglas's mother was born Sybil Montgomery). In "Lord Arthur Savile's Crime," we encounter another of Wilde's fictional Sybils, Sybil Merton, who "was . . . a symbol of all that is good and noble." It must be noted, too, that "Sybil" is the spelling found in *Melmoth the Wanderer,* the 1820 Gothic novel by Wilde's great-uncle Charles Maturin, which served as an inspiration for Wilde's novel and which features a demonic portrait and a bargain for eternal youth.

In an effort to correct spelling or usage, Stoddart or his colleagues sometimes made substitutions that changed meanings and associations of which they were probably unaware. The alteration of "jessamine" to "jasmine," for instance, effaces a spelling that has a long and distinguished tradition in English literature, from Spenser and Milton to Blake to Wilde's own contemporaries and beyond. Not too much should be made of the alteration in Chapter VI of Dorian's memorialization of Sybil (from "a wonderful tragic figure to whom Love had been a great reality" to "a wonderful tragic figure to show Love had been a great reality"), since, absent any editorial markings on the typescript, the change must be attributed to a typesetter's misreading of Wilde's handwriting. However, the typesetter's mistake has been allowed to stand in all editions of *Dorian Gray* before this one, and its reversal is long overdue.[33] Similarly, another typesetter's misreading—"I won't hear it!" rather than "I won't bear it!" (p. 167)—has been reprinted in all previous editions of the novel.

That Stoddart frequently lower-cased words capitalized by Wilde in the typescript ("Club," "King," "Queen," and so on) deserves comment. In a few instances, these changes will strike readers as defensible, and it is certainly true that Wilde was not always consistent in this matter (varying occasionally between "theatre" and "Theatre," or "art" and "Art," for example). But some of the decisions made by Stoddart or his associates seem arbitrary. When revising the typescript, Wilde had changed "genius," "beauty," and "nocturne" to the upper case: Stoddart leaves the first two intact, but reverses "Nocturne" to lower case. This is a debatable case at best. The same cannot be said of the lower-casing of "Hedonism," which, as the annotations to the present edition show, is designed through its upper-casing to contrast with the term "Cyrenaicism" in the writings of Walter Pater (Wilde uppercased the word once again when preparing the book edition). It is true that there is something antiquated, even self-conscious, about Wilde's predilection—common among eighteenth-century writers—to capitalize seemingly common nouns such as "Hospitals," "Bishop," and "Costume Ball." But this was Wilde's preference, and readers interested in what is distinctive about his writing will want to know about it.

In Chapter IX of the typescript, the unusual capitalization of names of various precious stones and ecclesiastical vestments ("Diamond," "Hyacinth," "Hydropicus," "Selenite," "Morse," "Corporals," and "Sudaria") suggests what Wilde in the same chapter calls the "mystic offices" of these things (see p. 201). That is to say, in employing capitalization here, Wilde wishes to transform, at least on the page, common or material objects into spiritual, mystic, or symbolic entities possessed of a power that belies everyday experience. Put another way: the upper case indicates how such objects "quickened [Dorian's] imagination" (p. 201). Except for a small handful of cases where Wilde himself was inconsistent, these, as well as all of his original capitalizations, have been retained in the present edition.

Decisions about such matters as punctuation, spelling, and capitalization are inevitably somewhat subjective, and a number of the changes Stoddart or his associates made in these respects may be defended as improvements.[34] But many of Stoddart's "accidental" changes were arbitrary or driven by commercial considerations, while others had unforeseen and unfortunate consequences, as I have shown. As importantly, Wilde stated categorically to one hostile reviewer that "in prose at any rate, correctness should always be subordinate to artistic effect and musical cadence; and any peculiarities of syntax that occur in *Dorian Gray* are deliberately intended, and are introduced to show the artistic value of the theory in question" (*Complete Letters,* 429–430). For these reasons, this edition presents *Dorian Gray* as Wilde submitted it to *Lippincott's,* stripped of all "accidental" changes that can be attributed with certainty to Stoddart or his associates.

The present restoration of matter excised by Stoddart and colleagues gives us a more scandalous and daring novel than either of its two subsequent published versions. By presenting the typescript Wilde submitted for publication, this edition presents *Dorian Gray,* for the first time, as its author envisioned it in 1890, before commercial, social, and legal pressures motivated a number of changes to Wilde's text, including the excision of graphic homosexual content. Wilde once said that Dorian Gray "contains much of me in it"; that Basil Hallward is "what I think I am" but "Dorian what I would like to be—in other ages, perhaps." Wilde's comment suggests a backward glance to a Greek or "Dorian" Age, but also a forward-looking one to a more permissive time. The appearance of Wilde's novel, in its uncensored form, 120 years after its submission to *Lippincott's,* is reason for celebration.

Notes

1 The novel was first published simultaneously on both sides of the Atlantic on June 20, 1890, in the July number of *Lippincott's.* The typescript on which the present edition is based is now housed at the William Andrews Clark Jr. Memorial Library, at the University of California in Los Angeles.

Wilde was one of the first British authors to embrace the medium of the typewriter as a mechanism for literary production (see Nicholas Frankel, "The Typewritten Self: Media Technology and Identity in Wilde's *De Profundis,*" in Frankel, *Masking the Text: Essays on Literature and Mediation in the 1890s* [High Wycombe: Rivendale Press, 2009]), and there is considerable reason for thinking that the decision to submit the novel in the form of a typescript rests with Wilde alone. "The only thing to do is to be thoroughly modern, and to have it type-written," Wilde said in 1897 about his prison letter *De Profundis;* and the "best edition," he remarked in the four-act version of *The Importance of Being Earnest,* is "one written in collaboration with the typewriting machine." While it is true that none of the short stories and prose criticism that Wilde produced in the period 1885–1890 involved the production of a typescript, Wilde went to considerable lengths, from 1891 onward, to have longer works, such as plays and his poem "The Sphinx," produced in the form of a typescript. In submitting *Dorian Gray* in the form of a typescript, Wilde might possibly have been mindful, too, of the kind of advice that *The Writer: A Monthly Magazine for Literary Workers* gave its readers some months later, that "every editor prefers typewritten manuscripts" (Will P. Hopkins, "What Kind of Manuscripts Do Editors Prefer?" *The Writer: A Monthly Magazine for Literary Workers* [Boston], 4:11 [November 1890], p. 250). *The Picture of Dorian Gray* was commissioned by *Lippincott's* simultaneously with Arthur Conan Doyle's novel *The Sign of Four,* and the fact that Conan Doyle's story was accepted in the form of a holograph manuscript constitutes important evidence that it was Wilde, rather than J. M. Stoddart, the editor of *Lippincott's,* who was responsible for the submission of *Dorian Gray* in the form of a typescript. As importantly, *Dorian Gray* is typewritten on heavy laid paper, not the inexpensive, somewhat shoddy, paper that was typical for Stoddart's business transactions. (Wilde was adamant that "good paper, such as is used for plays," be used for the act of typewriting, not "tissue paper" (*Complete Letters of Oscar Wilde,* ed. Merlin Holland and Rupert Hart-Davis [New York: Holt, 2000], p. 447). This choice of paper was almost certainly Wilde's alone, since Wilde—notoriously extravagant about matters of cost—was consistently alive to how the very materials of writing affected the act of reading.

2 As John Espey writes, "we have in the Clark text [the emended typescript] the original intention of the author at a particular time" or "the full text as Wilde submitted it to Stoddart" ("Resources for Wilde Study at the Clark Library," in *Oscar Wilde; Two Approaches: Papers Read at a Clark Library Seminar, April 17, 1976* [William Andrews Clark Memorial Library, University of California, Los Angeles, 1977], p. 35); and in paraphrasing Espey's argument, Donald Lawler writes that the emended typescript could reasonably be deemed "the only version of the text with unadulterated authorial sanction," given that later texts of the novel incorporate editorial changes that Wilde had little opportunity or authority to reverse ("A Note on the Texts," in Oscar Wilde, *The Picture of Dorian Gray,* ed. Donald L. Lawler, Norton Critical Editions [New York: Norton, 1988], p. xi). While Lawler and Espey are correct in suggesting that later texts of the novel incorporate "adulterations" of one kind or another, the typescript upon which the present text is based by no means represents either Wilde's original intentions or his final intentions for his novel, as this Textual Introduction makes clear. Even if it were possible to recover an author's "original" or "final" intentions, to suggest that such intentions are entirely stable and self-consistent is to misrepresent how literary works often change, in the lifetime of their own authors, as the result of a combination of factors, including readers' reactions, published reviews, editorial control, and the author's own evolving sense of his or her own work. This is especially true of *The Picture of Dorian Gray,* which met fierce resistance from readers—as well as censorship from its first editor—even before it had seen the "published" light of day. Readers interested in texts embodying Wilde's earlier or later intentions for the novel are urged to consult the unpublished holograph manuscript of the novel currently housed in the Morgan Library in New York, as well as Joseph Bristow's excellent edition of the two texts published in Wilde's lifetime (*The Picture of Dorian Gray: The 1890 and 1891 Texts,* ed. Joseph Bristow, Volume 3 of *The Complete Works of Oscar Wilde* [Oxford University Press, 2005]). By contrast, the present edition is designed to clarify how Wilde's own personal intentions for his novel were seriously compromised by the extraordinary circumstances surrounding its early publication. The copytext for the present edition, to be sure, represents an expression of Wilde's intentions for the novel at a crucial moment in its history; but this Textual Introduction and the Textual Notes clarify the social and editorial processes whereby those intentions were "adulterated."

3 Joseph Bristow, Introduction to *The Picture of Dorian Gray: The 1890 and 1891 Texts,* ed. Joseph Bristow, Volume 3 of *The Complete Works of Oscar Wilde,* gen. ed. Ian Small (Oxford University Press, 2005), p. xii; Elizabeth Lorang, "*The Picture of Dorian Gray* in Context: Intertextuality and *Lippincott's Monthly Magazine,*" *Victorian Periodicals Review* 43:1 (Spring 2010), 33. Lorang writes that the articles and stories that appeared alongside Wilde's novel in the July 1890 number of *Lippin-*

cott's Monthly Magazine, far from being incidental elements, are critical for understanding Wilde's novel, since "the individual components of a magazine act as discursive, intertextual counterparts, the ideas in one drawing on, engaging, enriching, and complicating or contradicting ideas in another" (22). Lorang focuses especially on the connections between Wilde's novel and three other articles that appeared in the July 1890 number (two of which appeared only in the British edition): Edward Heron-Allen's "The Cheiromancy of Today"; Coulson Kernehan's unsigned story "A Dead Man's Diary"; and "The Indissolubility of Marriage," by Elizabeth R. Chapman and George Bettany. For details of Lorang's argument, see p. 132, n. 3, and pp. 214–215, n. 10.

4 Unsigned notice of *The Picture of Dorian Gray, Scots Observer,* July 5, 1890; rpt. in *Oscar Wilde: The Critical Heritage,* ed. Karl Beckson (London: Routledge & Kegan Paul, 1970), p. 75.

5 H. Montgomery Hyde, letter to the editor, *Times Literary Supplement,* August 9, 1974. Hyde is here paraphrasing, as well as endorsing, the views of an anonymous *TLS* reviewer who, on reviewing Isobel Murray's Oxford University Press edition of *Dorian Gray* two weeks earlier, had commented that the changes Wilde made to the novel prior to its publication in book form were "inspired by nothing grander than expediency" and amounted to "censorings," not "thematic changes," as Murray claimed ("Not So Fond After All," anon. rev. of *The Picture of Dorian Gray,* ed. I. Murray [Oxford University Press, 1974], in *TLS,* July 26, 1974, p. 3).

6 *The Real Trial of Oscar Wilde,* intro. and commentary by Merlin Holland (New York: Perennial, 2004), pp. 82, 86.

7 See the defense of the Erotic School, published by Stoddart's close associate William S. Walsh in his *Handy Book of Literary Curiosities* (Philadelphia: J. B. Lippincott, 1893), pp. 332–333.

8 Bristow writes that "it is reasonable to infer that Stoddart . . . made most of the editorial changes to the typescript" because "most of the insertions that are not in Wilde's distinctive hand bear a strong resemblance" to known examples of Stoddart's handwriting ("Editorial Introduction" to *The Picture of Dorian Gray: The 1890 and 1891 Texts,* pp. lxi–lxii). While Bristow's inference is true for the most part, the typescript contains at least a few emendations—notably the alteration of "Sybil" to "Sibyl," of "leapt" to "leaped," and of "curtsey" to "courtesy"—in a hand that is neither Wilde's nor Stoddart's. Moreover, Bristow's important comment that "where Wilde tended to cancel passages in squiggly lines with a thicker pen, Stoddart by and large scored through passages with straighter lines and lighter markings" needs qualification, since in places the typescript was censored using squiggly lines in a hand that appears to have been neither Wilde's nor Stoddart's (as Bristow characterizes it here). For more on the nature of the changes overseen by Stoddart, see Espey, "Resources for Study," pp. 26–35; and Bristow, "Editorial Introduction," pp. lxiv–lxvii.

9 Bristow, "Introduction," pp. xxxix–xl.

10 Wilfred Edener's edition of *The Picture of Dorian Gray* (Nuremberg: H. Carl, 1964) had also reprinted the *Lippincott's* text in its entirety. But Edener's edition, with introductory matter and notes in German, was published for a German-speaking readership. For Lawler's characterization see Wilde, *The Picture of Dorian Gray,* ed. Lawler, p. 200, n. 1. Like many of Lawler's textual and critical notes, this note is retained intact in the recent, second edition of Norton's Critical Edition, edited by Michael Patrick Gillespie (New York, 2007), p. 214. In the new Preface that he supplied to the Norton edition, Gillespie notes that "Stoddart did not hesitate to excise portions that he felt would be too graphic for his readers' sensibilities" (p. xii).

11 Isobel Murray, "Note on the Text," in *The Picture of Dorian Gray,* ed. Isobel Murray (Oxford University Press, 1974), p. xxvii; Josephine M. Guy and Ian Small, *Oscar Wilde's Profession* (Oxford University Press, 2000), p. 233.

12 Guy and Small, *Oscar Wilde's Profession,* p. 233.

13 Espey, "Resources for Study," p. 32.

14 N. N. Feltes, *Modes of Production of Victorian Novels* (Chicago: University of Chicago Press, 1986), pp. 64, 63.

15 Bristow, Editorial Introduction, p. lxii.

16 Before being acquired by William Andrews Clark Jr. (in whose library it currently resides) in 1933, the typescript was sold at a 1920 auction of Wilde items previously owned by the Wilde collector John B. Stetson Jr. The sheer number of items listed alongside the typescript as deriving from J. M. Stoddart in the sale catalogue (*The Oscar Wilde Collection of John B. Stetson Jr.* [New York: Anderson Galleries, 1920]) strongly suggests that Stetson—like Stoddart, a Philadelphian—acquired the typescript from Stoddart directly.

17 Donald Lawler speculates that the holograph manuscript is a fair-copy of a now-lost "proto-manuscript." See Lawler, "Oscar Wilde's First Manuscript of *The Picture of Dorian Gray," Studies in Bibliography,* 25 (1972), 125–135; also Lawler, *An Inquiry into Oscar Wilde's Revisions of "The Picture of Dorian Gray"* (New York: Garland, 1988), pp. 145–147.

18 J. M. Stoddart, letter to J. Garmeson, June 2, 1890, J. B. Lippincott Co. Records 1858–1958, Collection 3104, Box 61, Item 2 [foreign letter-book 1889–1894], p. 111, Pennsylvania Historical Society.

19 See the uncatalogued file of print and manuscript materials documenting the efforts of J. M. Stoddart in 1906 to produce a definitive edition of Wilde's works, especially the letter concerning *Dorian Gray* from Ferdinand I. Haber to J. M. Stoddart, dated October 6, 1906, in which Haber reports, "I find several marked

differences between our manuscript and the printed text" (William Andrews Clark Jr. Memorial Library, uncatalogued). I have not yet determined whether Ferdinand I. Haber was related to the Louis I. Haber from whom the Morgan Library's present ownership of the holograph manuscript derives.

20 W. H. Smith and Co, letter to Ward, Lock, and Company, July 10, 1890, quoted by Holland in *The Real Trial of Oscar Wilde,* p. 310., n. 113.

21 Ward, Lock, and Company, letter to Oscar Wilde, July 10, 1890, quoted in Hyde, letter to the editor.

22 See Stoddart's letter to Craige Lippincott, April 29, 1890, in which Stoddart finds it "strange that Ward Lock & Co. do not expect much success with Oscar Wilde's story" (J. B. Lippincott Co. Records 1858–1958, Collection 3104, Box 61, Item 2 [foreign letter-book 1889–1894], Pennsylvania Historical Society); also George Lock's letter to Oscar Wilde, July 7, 1890 (rpt. in "Stuart Mason" [Christopher Millard], *Bibliography of Oscar Wilde* [London: T. W. Laurie, 1914], p. 105), in which Lock suggests changes to the novel's ending and a greater focus on Lord Henry Wotton's character, while commenting approvingly on Wilde's proposal "to add to the story so as to counteract any damage done" by its appearance in *Lippincott's.* Six weeks prior to publication, Ward, Lock, and Company's misgivings were evidently great enough that they reduced their order for the July number: Ward, Lock had ordered 10,000 copies of the January number (J. M. Stoddart, letter to J. Garmeson, October 8, 1889, J. B. Lippincott Co. Records 1858–1958, Collection 3104, Box 61, Item 2 [foreign letter-book 1889–1894], Pennsylvania Historical Society), and in February Stoddart had proposed sending 10,000 copies of the May number, too (J. M. Stoddart, letter to J. Garmeson, February 25, 1890, J. B. Lippincott Co. Records 1858–1958, Collection 3104, Box 61, Item 2 [foreign letter-book 1889–1894], p. 83). On April 22, the date on which he announced his intention to publish *Dorian Gray,* Stoddart wrote to Craige Lippincott, "I should think they could use to advantage 12 or 15,000 copies" of the July number. Two weeks later he was forced to confess to Lippincott, "The order for the July number has just been received; it is for 5000 copies and of course at the full price" (letter to C. Lippincott, May 6).

Circulation figures for the American edition of the July number are harder to come by, but it is certain that in the months preceding the publication of *Dorian Gray,* Stoddart wished to deceive his British distributors about circulation in the United States: "Be careful in conversation with Ward Lock & Co. not to give away our true circulation," Stoddart wrote to Lippincott on April 10, "as I have led everyone to understand that we average a circulation of 100,000 copies. I have not communicated the real facts of the case to Garmeson as it might weaken his appreciation of it. Ward Lock & Co. think we are having a big sale here as we are, and it is better to let them be of the same opinion" (J. M. Stoddart, letter to Craige Lippincott, April 10, 1890). The disintegration of Lippincott's arrangements with Ward, Lock, and Company continued, in the wake of the disastrous publication of *Dorian Gray,* with Ward, Lock's order for just 2,000 copies of the October number. On February 12, 1891, Stoddart lamented that J. B. Lippincott could not "make an additional payment" to Wilde, as he had requested, because "the publication of *Dorian Gray* was, in a comparative sense, a mistake, and instead of being a commercial success it was really in the nature of a failure" (Stoddart, letter to Wilde, February 12, 1891, J. B. Lippincott Co. Records 1858–1958, Collection 3104, Box 61, Item 2 [foreign letter-book 1889–1894], pp. 180–181).

23　In both published versions, when Dorian reflects toward the end of the novel on his "renunciation" of Hetty Merton, Wilde poses an urgent series of questions: "Vanity? Curiosity? Hypocrisy? Had there been nothing more in his renunciation than that?" only to answer them with, "There had been something more. At least he thought so. But who could tell?" This phrasing, as well as suggesting that Dorian is tortured by conscience, implies that Dorian's renunciation of Hetty might have been motivated by altruism, pity, or fellow-feeling. While it is true that Wilde only hints here at the possibility of good in Dorian, the ambiguity seems deliberate, humanizing Dorian and allowing room for moral debate about the deepest well-springs of his nature.

Such subtle hedging of the issue had elicited fierce remonstrance in 1890—for example, that "it is not made sufficiently clear that the writer does not prefer a course of unnatural iniquity to a life of cleanliness, health, and sanity" and that Wilde "does not take the trouble to make his moral logically cohere with his subject matter." In an effort to answer such criticisms, Wilde added the following important rejoinder in 1891:

> No. There had been nothing more. Through vanity he had spared her. In hypocrisy he had worn the mask of goodness. For curiosity's sake he had tried the denial of self. He recognized that now.

The first five sentences of this rejoinder were inserted precisely so as to eradicate the moral ambiguity present in the ending of the first published version and to underscore—as Walter Pater was to iterate upon reviewing the novel in book form—that *Dorian Gray* contained "a very plain moral, pushed home, to the effect that vice and crime make people coarse and ugly."

Wilde made a second revision in 1891 that similarly heightens Dorian's monstrosity and levels the moral ambiguity of the 1890 ending. Dorian determines upon "killing the portrait," Wilde tells us in both published versions, because this "would kill the past, and when that was dead he would be free." Although this motivation seems consistent with Wilde's comment, just previously, that Dorian strikes the portrait to destroy "conscience," since the portrait "brought melancholy across his passions" and "marred" his "joy," Wilde's formulation allows for the possibility, as the scholar Donald F. Lawler puts it, that "Dorian struck against the portrait in revulsion at the monstrous evil he saw in it and that his action was therefore a repudiation of his past life of vice and crime." Such a reading is underscored, in fact, by the lines leading up to this moment, in which

Wilde tells us, with somewhat heavy-handed symbolism, of Dorian's determination to "clean" the murder instrument "till there was no stain left upon it."

But in 1891 Wilde followed these lines with the crucial sentences, "It would kill this monstrous soul-life, and without its hideous warnings, he would be at peace." Again Wilde felt that his 1890 wording had been too ambiguous: the new wording eliminates any suggestion that "freedom" implies salvation, and instead reinforces a straightforward, morally conventional reading whereby Dorian strikes the portrait so as to quiet the "soul-life," with its "hideous reminders" of his criminality.

These changes to the ending confronted head on the criticisms, made publicly in 1890, that *Dorian Gray* was an immoral book. They were dedicated to proving, as Wilde had claimed to the press in 1890, that "it is a story with a moral" and that "Dorian Gray, having led a life of mere sensation and pleasure, tries to kill conscience, and at that moment kills himself" (*Complete Letters,* p. 430). To some degree, they are consistent with the suggestion made by George Lock, publisher of the 1891 book version, that in revising the novel Wilde should "depict the misery in which [Dorian] ends his days" so as to "counteract any damage . . . done" by the novel's appearance in *Lippincott's.* Wilde's changes to the ending were designed, in other words, to increase Dorian's monstrosity and to eradicate any suggestion, inherent in the 1890 version, that Dorian's final act was motivated by moral self-revulsion and by the lingering pangs of a tortured conscience. By eliminating hints of remorse on Dorian's part, Wilde sharpened the reader's dissociation with him, eliminating lingering shreds of sympathy that the reader might still have for Dorian in the moments before he strikes the portrait.

24 In August 1889 Stoddart journeyed to London to make arrangements with Ward, Lock, and Company for distribution of *Lippincott's* in Britain and also to secure British authors for the magazine. As Arthur Conan Doyle relates in his *Memories and Adventures* (1924; rpt. Oxford University Press, 1989), Stoddart commissioned stories from both Wilde and Conan Doyle during a dinner at London's Langham Hotel on August 30, 1889. (Stoddart's contract with Conan Doyle, formalized at Conan Doyle's insistence on the same date as the dinner, specifies "a story consisting of not less than 40,000 words." However, in a letter to Wilde dated October 11, 1889, Stoddart countered Wilde's offer of a story of 30,000 words [*Complete Letters,* p. 413] with, "we want at least 35,000 words as 30,000 words would be entirely too short.") Soon after arriving back in Philadelphia, Stoddart wrote to Wilde that he hoped to place Wilde's story in the January 1890 number and that he was eager to "inaugurate our English venture with it" (J. M. Stoddart, letter to Oscar Wilde, September 18, 1889, J. B. Lippincott Co. Records 1858–1958, Collection 3104, Box 7, Item 5 [letter-book 1889], p. 237, Pennsylvania Historical Society). But *Dorian Gray* was slow in coming, and Wilde evidently spent the last months of 1889 struggling over a story—"The Fisherman and His Soul"—that eventually totaled 15,000 words and that would appear in his 1891 collection *A House of Pomegranates.* In mid-November he was "unable to finish" and "not satisfied" with his efforts to date (*Complete Letters,* p. 414), but in mid-

December he announced, "I have invented a new story . . . and I am quite ready to set to work on it" (*Complete Letters,* p. 416). Possibly Wilde was hard at work drafting *Dorian Gray* soon after this date. But by early February 1890, Stoddart was getting anxious. On February 7, Stoddart wrote to Wilde's friend, the cheiromantist Edward Heron-Allen (whose 1888 novella *The Suicide of Sylvester Gray* dimly influenced Wilde, and whose essay "The Cheiromancy of Today" would appear alongside *The Picture of Dorian Gray* in the July 1890 number of *Lippincott's*): "I have nothing very satisfactory from Oscar Wilde; would it be asking too much of you for you to ask him about his story?" (J. M. Stoddart, letter to E. Heron-Allen, February 7, 1890, J. B. Lippincott Co. Records 1858–1958, Collection 3104, Box 61, Item 2 [foreign letter-book 1889–1894], Pennsylvania Historical Society). That Heron-Allen intervened on Stoddart's behalf shortly after this date can be inferred from a letter dated February 19 in which Wilde informed Heron-Allen that he would "look in on you and discuss the wicked Lippincott if you are at home" (*Complete Letters,* 424). Around this time, Wilde confessed to an unknown correspondent that he was "overwhelmed with work" (*Complete Letters,* 424) and also, to Aglaia Coronio, that "I am so busy I dare not stir out. Publishers are showing that worms will turn, and the editors of magazines are clamorous" (*Complete Letters,* 425). Evidently Heron-Allen's intervention was successful, because on March 25 Stoddart thanked Heron-Allen for "punching OW up to his work, as within the last few days we have received word that he has sent his story in" (J. M. Stoddart, letter to E. Heron-Allen, March 25, 1890, J. B. Lippincott Co. Records 1858–1958, Collection 3104, Box 61, Item 2 [foreign letter-book 1889–1894], Pennsylvania Historical Society). See, too, Stoddart's comment to his London agent, J. Garmeson, on March 25, 1890, "I expect in answer to my telegram of March 20th saying 'Pay Wilde' that we will receive a part of the type written copy by next Monday or Tuesday if sent on the steamer leaving on the 22nd" (J. B. Lippincott Co. Records 1858–1958, Collection 3104, Box 61, Item 2 [foreign letter-book 1889–1894], p. 32, Pennsylvania Historical Society).

25 J. M. Stoddart, letter to Craige Lippincott, April 10, 1890, J. B. Lippincott Co. Records 1858–1958, Collection 3104, Box 61, Item 2 [foreign letter-book 1889–1894], Pennsylvania Historical Society.

26 The contents page to Philips's 1893 collection *The Making of a Newspaper* (New York and London: G. P. Putnam's, 1893) lists him as "Literary Editor of the *Philadelphia Press*" and reveals Philips to have been a leading figure in American journalism at the time. The American edition of the July 1890 number of *Lippincott's,* which differs from the British edition in certain respects (though not in its version of Wilde's novel), lists Philips as copyright-holder. A measure of Stoddart's confidence in Philips is ascertainable from the "Round-Robin Talks" feature printed in the June 1890 number of *Lippincott's,* in which Stoddart self-consciously exposed to his readers the behind-the-scenes processes by which literary manuscripts were collectively adjudicated: "For some months past in various places there have been informal and fraternal meeting of an uncertain

number of congenial spirits," Stoddart declared, their gatherings sometimes prompted by "the advance sheets of a novel" (J. M. Stoddart, "Round-Robin Talks," *Lippincott's Monthly Magazine,* June 1890, pp. 889–907). "Many of the participants are known by their writings to the readers of *Lippincott's.* . . . Why should not that faction of the public that reads the book reviews of Melville Philips know that their author is a smooth-faced, blue-eyed chap, with a profile like Byron?" At the latest meeting of this group, declared Stoddart, which had evidently taken place in April 1890, "we had gathered to discuss the chances for life of a forthcoming novel which it would be manifestly inopportune to mention now."

27 J. M. Stoddart, letter to Craige Lippincott, April 22, 1890, J. B. Lippincott Co. Records 1858–1958, Collection 3104, Box 61, Item 2 [foreign letter-book 1889–1894], Pennsylvania Historical Society.

28 J. M. Stoddart, letter to Oscar Wilde, April 22, 1890, J. B. Lippincott Co. Records 1858–1958, Collection 3104, Box 61, Item 2 [foreign letter-book 1889–1894], Pennsylvania Historical Society. That Stoddart is referring here to receipt of the typescript might seem unclear to modern readers. But by this date, the word *typescript* had not yet come into wide use, and the terms *manuscript* and *typewritten manuscript* were commonly applied to what we would now term *typescript.* See Philo H. Sylvester, "Two Needed New Words," *North American Review,* 148 (1889), p. 647.

29 See Wilde's request to Stoddart, in December 1889, to "let me have half the honorarium in advance—£100" (*Complete Letters,* 416); also his May 1890 comment to a prospective publisher of the book version that "next month there appears in *Lippincott's Magazine* a one-volume novel of mine, 50,000 words in length. After three months the copyright reverts to me" (*Complete Letters,* 425). Stoddart declined Wilde's request for "half the honorarium," writing to Wilde on December 17 that "I greatly regret to be unable to accede to your request for the advancement of the amount. . . . The moment that the manuscript is accepted by our agent in London, the total amount will be paid over to you" (J. M. Stoddart, letter to Oscar Wilde, December 17, 1889, J. B. Lippincott Co. Records 1858–1958, Collection 3104, Box 61, Item 6 [letter-book 1889–1890], p. 279, Pennsylvania Historical Society).

30 The memorandum in which Wilde was to assign and set over his "entire right" in *Dorian Gray* while simultaneously acknowledging that he had "completed and forwarded the manuscript" and "received payment from [Lippincott's] London agent Mr. J. Garmeson" survives today only as an unsigned duplicate, dated simply "London . . . 1890." The original was attached to Stoddart's letter to Craige Lippincott of April 22, in which Stoddart instructed Lippincott (who was visiting London) to "get him to sign the enclosed authorization, which we are going to use for the purpose of securing copyright here." In his letter to Wilde of the same date, Stoddart informed Wilde, "I am going to endeavor to secure the American copyright for [*Dorian Gray*]."

31 J. M. Stoddart, letter to F. C. Baylor, April 25, 1890, J. B. Lippincott Co. Records 1858–1958, Collection 3104, Box 7, Item 6 [letter-book 1890], p. 320, Pennsylvania Historical Society.

32 Stoddart's anxiety in this respect stemmed from the extensive publicity given to the white slave trade by W. T. Stead's exposé "The Maiden Tribute of Modern Babylon," serialized in the *Pall Mall Gazette* in 1885. See pp. 215–216, n. 13 below.

33 In the absence of a text giving his original wording, Wilde used this change as the basis for a further change in the book version, where this phrase is rendered as "a wonderful tragic figure sent on to the world's stage to show the supreme reality of Love" (*The Picture of Dorian Gray: The 1890 and 1891 Texts,* ed. Bristow, p. 257).

34 See Bristow, Editorial Introduction, p. lxv.

THE PICTURE OF DORIAN GRAY

"It is your best work, Basil," wood-engraved illustration by Eugène Dété, from a drawing by Paul Thiriat, frontispiece to *The Picture of Dorian Gray* (Paris: Charles Carrington, 1908 [1910]).

I

THE STUDIO WAS FILLED with the rich odour of roses, and when the light summer wind stirred amidst the trees of the garden there came through the open door the heavy scent of the lilac, or the more delicate perfume of the pink-flowering thorn.[1]

From the corner of the divan of Persian saddle-bags on which he was lying, smoking, as usual, innumerable cigarettes,[2] Lord Henry Wotton[3] could just catch the gleam of the honey-sweet and honey-coloured blossoms of the laburnum, whose tremulous branches seemed hardly able to bear the burden of a beauty so flame-like as theirs;[4] and now and then the fantastic shadows of birds in flight flitted across the long tussore-silk curtains that were stretched in front of the huge window, producing a kind of momentary Japanese effect, and making him think of those pallid jade-faced painters who, in an art that is necessarily immobile, seek to convey the sense of swiftness and motion.[5] The sullen murmur of the bees shouldering their way through the long unmown grass, or circling with monotonous insistence round the black-crocketed spires of the early June hollyhocks,[6] seemed to make the stillness more oppressive, and the dim roar of London was like the bourdon note of a distant organ.[7]

In the centre of the room, clamped to an upright easel, stood the full-length portrait[8] of a young man of extraordinary personal beauty,[9] and in front of it, some little distance away, was sitting the artist himself, Basil Hallward,[10] whose sudden disappearance some years ago caused, at the time, such public excitement, and gave rise to so many strange conjectures.[11]

1 The setting of Hallward's studio adjacent to a garden in full bloom would seem to locate it in one of Victorian London's artists' colonies at St. John's Wood, Hampstead, Chelsea, Kensington, or (the most prestigious address) Holland Park. In Wilde's day, Holland Park was the location for a number of specially commissioned artists' studio-houses, many of them incorporating parts of the garden of old Little Holland House (demolished in 1875), where bohemia had first become respectable (Carolyn Dakers, *The Holland Park Circle: Artists and Victorian Society* [New Haven, CT: Yale University Press, 1999], p. 24). Studio-homes incorporating gardens, such as those built in Holland Park for the artists Marcus Stone, Luke Fildes, Val Prinsep, and Hamo Thorneycroft, were in the forefront of contemporary architecture.

2 Toward the end of the nineteenth century, the cigarette emerged as an important symbol of modernity, its portability and transience compatible with the etiquette of urban culture and the demands of modern life. At the same time, as Robyn L. Schiffman observes, the cigarette belonged to "part of a complex network of fashion accessories that began to carve out a discernible homosexual style and culture" ("Toward a Queer History of Smoking," in *Smoke: A Global History of Smoking*, ed. Sander L. Gilman and Zhou Zun [London: Reaktion Books, 2004], p. 305).

The divan on which Lord Henry sits and smokes may reflect the decor of Wilde's own smoking-room, designed by the explorer Walter Harris. Wilde's youngest son, Vyvyan Holland, recalled, "My father's smoking-room was the most awe-inspiring room in the house. . . . The décor was North African. Divans, ottomans, Moorish hangings, and lanterns filled the room" (*Son of Oscar Wilde* [1954; rpt. Oxford University Press, 1988], p. 44).

3 It is generally accepted by scholars that the witty and urbane Lord Henry Wotton was inspired at least partly by Wilde's friend Lord Ronald Sutherland Gower (1845–1916), who was a sculptor, an art connoisseur, a trustee of the National Portrait Gallery, and the vice president of the Kyrle Society for the Diffusion of Beauty among the People, as well as "a notorious sodomite, with a penchant for 'rough trade'" (Neil McKenna, *Secret Life of Oscar Wilde* [New York: Basic Books, 2005], p. 11). Gower was the subject of an oil portrait by John Everett Millais that Wilde publicly praised for its profile of "a young man with delicate aquiline nose, thoughtful oval face, and artistic abstracted air" ("The Grosvenor Gallery" [1877]).

A number of Wilde's friends, notably Frank Harris and Robert Ross, publicly maintained that Wilde, consciously or not, also put a great deal of himself into Lord Henry. For Wilde's own comment that, while the novel contains "much of me in it . . . Lord Henry Wotton is [merely] what the world thinks me," see *Complete Letters of Oscar Wilde,* ed. Merlin Holland and Rupert Hart-Davis (New York: Holt, 2000), p. 585, hereafter cited as *CL.*

4 *Laburnum x waterer,* or "Goldenchain tree," as it is generally known, explodes in a mass of yellow flowers in spring, cascading in clusters 10–20 inches long. Particularly fine examples of the "laburnum arch," popular with Victorian landscape gardeners, can still be found at Bodnant Gardens, Gwynned, Wales, and at Ness Gardens, in the Wirral.

5 "If you desire to see a Japanese effect, you will not behave like a tourist and go to Tokio. On the contrary, you will stay at home and steep yourself in the work of certain Japanese artists, and then, when you have absorbed the spirit of their style, and caught their imaginative manner of vision, you will go some afternoon

Oil portrait of Lord Ronald Sutherland Gower, painted and gifted to Gower by the artist John Everett Millais, R. A., in 1876; on display at the inaugural exhibition of the Grosvenor Gallery in 1877. Wilde greatly admired this portrait. Gower, an art connoisseur and unapologetic homosexual, came from one of England's wealthiest families and is frequently thought to have been a real-life model for Lord Henry Wotton.

LADY WILDE

Harry Furniss, pen and ink caricature of Wilde's mother, Jane Francesca Elgee, Lady Wilde. Lady Wilde was an important Irish folklorist, poet, and translator. In the 1880s she tried hard to transform her modest Mayfair accommodations into one of London's leading artistic salons. She died, impoverished and heartbroken, in 1896 while Wilde was in jail. Wilde claimed that she appeared to him in his cell on the day she died.

and sit in the Park, or stroll down Piccadilly, and if you cannot see an absolutely Japanese effect there, you will not see it anywhere ("The Decay of Lying," in *Criticism: Historical Criticism, Intentions and the Soul of Man,* ed. Josephine Guy, vol. 4 of *The Complete Works of Oscar Wilde* [Oxford University Press, 2007], p. 98). The "pallid jade-faced painters" Lord Henry is thinking of may include Hokusai and Hokkai—both mentioned by name in "The Decay of Lying"—as well as Hiroshige and Utamaro, whose work was at the forefront of the growing *Japonisme* movement of the late 1880s and early 1890s. Wilde would have been familiar with these artists from important studies of *Japonisme* such as Rutherford Alcock's *Art and Art Industries in Japan* (which he owned), William Anderson's *Pictorial Arts of Japan,* Marcus Huish's *Japan and Its Art,* and the short-lived monthly *Artistic Japan.* It is likely that Wilde attended the exhibition of Hokusai's drawings and prints held at the Fine Art Society in 1890. For *Japonisme* as a movement, see Lionel Lambourne, *Japonisme* (London: Phaidon, 2005).

Wilde's image-laden prose here aspires to "convey the very swiftness of motion" in "an art that is necessarily immobile." By layering phrase upon phrase, Wilde attempts to capture his own "Japanese effect" in language, mimicking the manner in which images are built up in Japanese woodblock printing, gradually and incrementally, through the imposition of one colored mass upon another.

6 This is the first of many bee references in the novel. Marion Thain observes that while "bees have taken part in a discourse central to the aesthetic" since ancient times, when Sophocles and Sappho were known respectively as the "Attic bee" and the "Pierian bee," "bees . . . gained a new and topical currency at the end of the nineteenth century" ("Apian Aestheticism," in *Michael Field and Their World,* ed. Margaret D. Stetz and Cheryl A. Wilson [Rivendale Press, 2007], p. 224). For Thain, "the gently humming bee entering the flower bell is symbolic of the mediation required for the aesthetic voice to be heard by its reader" (p. 231). For other scholars, however, the bee is a signifier for sexual activity, about which Victorians felt obliged to be circumspect. For instance, Nicolette Scourse—who richly describes Victorians' fascination with bee-keeping and apiaries as fashionable adornments to homes of taste, especially following the establishment of the British Bee-Keeper's Association in 1874—demonstrates how Victorians employed elaborate euphemisms and evasions to suppress bees' self-evident role in plants' sexual reproduction (*The Victorians and Their Flowers* [London: Croom Helm, 1983], pp. 9, 39–42, 65). Whereas one Victorian commentator euphemistically describes bees as "venial panders to the flowers" (quoted in Scourse, p. 62), the contemporary botanist Peter Bernhardt quips that "bees are a flower's winged penis" ("The Faithful and Unfaithful Bee," in Bernhardt, *The Rose's Kiss: A Natural History of Flowers* [Chicago: University of Chicago Press, 1999], p. 162).

7 The Oxford English Dictionary (OED) defines *bourdon* as "a bass stop in an organ, usually of 16 ft. tone; a similar stop in a harmonium; also the drone of a bagpipe. Also *attrib.,* as in *bourdon stop.*"

8 Compare Hallward's portrait of Dorian to the one that plays a central role in "The Portrait of Mr. W. H." (one of two stories centering on mysterious portraits that Wilde had written before commencing *Dorian Gray*): "It was a full-length portrait of a young man . . . of quite extraordinary personal beauty, though evidently somewhat effeminate." The picture of Dorian Gray belongs to a class of contemporary full-length portraiture dominated by Whistler, Sargent, and Tissot. About 1884, Wilde commissioned his own full-length portrait by the American artist Harper Pennington, a student of Whistler's. The Pennington portrait, cherished by Wilde, adorned the walls of his Tite Street home until his imprisonment in 1895. Whistler remarks that crispness and sparkle are easily hinted at in tiny pastels, "but a full-length portrait is a very different matter" (*Whistler on Art: Selected Letters and Writings of James McNeill Whistler,* ed. Nigel Thorp [Washington, DC: Smithsonian Institution Press, 2004], p. 152).

9 The presence of an artwork in the center of the room, and the narrator's declaration that it contains a portrait of a young man "of extraordinary personal beauty," make explicit what is already implied by the

gorgeous prose of the previous two paragraphs: that *Dorian Gray* is an "aesthetic" novel, deeply preoccupied with the perception and discrimination of beauty in art, life, and nature. The historical roots of aestheticism are many, reaching back through English Pre-Raphaelitism and Romanticism (especially the poetry of John Keats) to the philosophical writings of Kant and Baumgarten in the eighteenth century. Deriving from the Greek *aisthesis* signifying "perception, or the science of the beautiful" (Walter Hamilton, *The Aesthetic Movement in England,* 3rd ed. [1882; rpt. New York: Garland, 1986], p. vi), the term *aesthetic* originally designated a philosophy or theory of taste. But by 1890, when *Dorian Gray* was written, many British artists, writers, designers, and consumers had become preoccupied with beauty and/or art for their own sakes; a full-fledged "Aesthetic Movement" had sprung up in the English-speaking world, and in the early 1880s Wilde had assumed a position as spokesman for this nascent movement.

For Wilde and for many others of his generation, the golden book of aestheticism was *The Renaissance: Studies in Art and Poetry* (orig. pub. 1873 under the title *Studies in the History of the Renaissance*) by Walter Horatio Pater (1839–1894), fellow and tutor of Brasenose College, with whom Wilde formed a close friendship while at Oxford and whose work casts a long shadow over *Dorian Gray.* In his Preface to *The Renaissance,* Pater writes that the aesthete "regards all the objects with which he has to do, all works of art, and the fairer forms of nature and human life, as powers or forces producing pleasurable sensations, each of a more or less peculiar or unique kind." For Pater, *aestheticism* is an intensely subjective and impressionistic form of criticism, its object being "to distinguish, to analyse, and separate from its adjuncts, the virtue by which a picture, a landscape, a fair personality in life or in a book, produces this special impression of beauty or pleasure, to indicate what the source of that impression is, and under what conditions it is experienced."

10 In "Who Was Basil Hallward?" (*English Language Notes,* 24 [1986], 84–91), Kerry Powell writes that "Wilde's involvement with art and artists—his essays on painting, his lectures on art, his jousting with Whis-

tler—tempts one to imagine that the remarkable portraitist of *Dorian Gray* stands in some relation to the author's own experience" (p. 86). A few different models for Hallward have been suggested by critics. Powell argues compellingly that "the most plausible real-life model for Hallward" was a now-neglected late-Victorian portrait artist named Frank Holl. Powell's argument is based not on any presumed intimacy between Holl and Wilde—there is no evidence that Wilde knew Holl personally, or even that he liked Holl's paintings—but rather on the possibility that Holl's portraits, widely admired in Wilde's day, "present a guilty buried self rather than the 'blameless' and unblemished mask that the sitter wears every day to deceive the world" (p. 88). "[Holl] must, in the course of his painting, have discovered some dreadful secret in those apparently blameless breasts, such 'damnable faces' have his sitters shown," remarks the critic Harry Quilter in a book that Wilde reviewed in 1886 and which Powell quotes at some length. According to Quilter, Holl was also a painter who "threw, to some extent, the cloak of his own personality over all his sitters," thereby lending his portraits another of the features that distinguishes Hallward's work in *The Picture of Dorian Gray.*

11 A direct foreshadowing of Hallward's tragic end and Lord Henry's comment at the novel's conclusion that "people are still discussing poor Basil's disappearance." By mentioning Hallward's "sudden disappearance" barely three paragraphs into his narrative, Wilde generates desire on the part of his readers to know more. Will Hallward commit suicide, be murdered, or simply fake his own disappearance, like Isa Whitney in Arthur Conan Doyle's story "The Man with the Twisted Lip"? Such questions would have pressed themselves on the minds of Wilde's earliest readers, especially Londoners still anxious about the Whitechapel or "Jack the Ripper" Murders of 1888. The gruesome Ripper murders, which were never solved, instigated a massive police hunt. London has been called "The City of Disappearances," and it was not uncommon in Wilde's day for respectable people to go missing in London or for their corpses to materialize months later, washed up on the banks of the River Thames. Arthur Conan Doyle's

James McNeill Whistler, "Harmony in Blue and Gold: The Peacock Room," 1876–1877. Whistler was commissioned by the shipping magnate F. R. Leyland to decorate his dining-room at 49 Prince's Gate, London. Whistler's design is a monument of Victorian Aestheticism or "art for art's sake."

As he looked at the gracious and comely form he had so skilfully mirrored in his art, a smile of pleasure passed across his face, and seemed about to linger there.[12] But he suddenly started up, and, closing his eyes, placed his fingers upon the lids, as though he sought to imprison within his brain some curious dream from which he feared he might awake.

"It is your best work, Basil, the best thing you have ever done," said Lord Henry, languidly. "You must certainly send it next year to the Grosvenor. The Academy is too large and too vulgar. The Grosvenor is the only place."[13]

"I don't think I will send it anywhere," he answered, tossing his head back in that odd way that used to make his friends laugh at him at Oxford. "No: I won't send it anywhere."

Lord Henry elevated his eyebrows, and looked at him in amazement through the thin blue wreaths of smoke that curled up in such fanciful whorls from his heavy opium-tainted cigarette.[14] "Not send it anywhere? my dear fellow, why? Have you any reason? What odd chaps you painters are! You do anything in the world to gain a reputa-

Sign of Four—published in *Lippincott's Monthly Magazine* four months before *Dorian Gray*—turns on one such disappearance.

12 "I am so very pleased with yourself in the picture," remarks Whistler to Louise Kinsella, the subject of an 1896 portrait, "that today I showed the portrait to Sargent . . . and you know I don't show my things—but I couldn't resist it! He was I really believe very much struck—He said it is very beautiful—and I must say I admired it myself quite recklessly for once" (*Whistler on Art,* ed. Thorp, pp. 151–152). Hallward's consciousness of his own artistry, like Whistler's, points to a defining characteristic of portraits generally. "Portraits are not merely recognizable faces and bodies, nor even likenesses in any common sense of the term," remarks Richard Brilliant: what is crucial is "the role of the portrait artist in creating a work shaped by his talent and craft, by the perspicacity of his interpretation, and by the affective relationship between himself and his subject, both as responsive human beings and as 'artist' and 'sitter'" (*Portraiture* [Cambridge, MA: Harvard University Press, 1991], pp. 30–31).

13 "While the yearly exhibition of the Royal Academy may be said to present us with the general characteristics of ordinary English art at its most commonplace level, it is at the Grosvenor Gallery that we are enabled to see the highest development of the modern artistic spirit" (Oscar Wilde, "The Grosvenor Gallery" [1879]). In *Patience, or Bunthorne's Bride* (1881), Gilbert and Sullivan famously caricatured Wilde as a "greenery-yallery-Grosvenor-Gallery-foot-in-the-grave-young-man," thereby ensuring that he remained indelibly associated with the Grosvenor Gallery in British and American minds. In one of several fine recent studies of the Grosvenor Gallery, Christopher Newall notes that "the Grosvenor came to be thought of as an appropriate place to show portraits—preferable in many ways to the Academy" (*The Grosvenor Gallery Exhibitions* [Cambridge University Press, 1995], p. 28).

Wilde's contempt for the Royal Academy, which had rejected early works by Whistler, Millais, and other leading artists of the day, boiled over in "The Rout of the R. A.," his witty review of the satirical work of Harry Furniss. Here, after calling Furniss "a young and ruddy David [come] to slay this lumbering Goliath of middle-class art," Wilde comments that "the Royal Academicians are now in full retreat, and the opinion of the best military and artistic experts is, that they are rapidly retiring in the direction of Bayswater, a desolate tract of country lying to the north of the Park. . . . The final encounter, however, will not take place till the end of this week, when Goliath, who is now occupied in varnishing, the only artistic process with which he is thoroughly familiar, will display his forces in Burlington House, under the patronage of the British public, and under the protection of the British policeman."

14 Lord Henry's opium-tainted cigarette may be similar to the cigarette offered by Ernest to Gilbert in "The Critic as Artist"—an example of the "excellent tobacco" that Ernest tells Gilbert he has obtained "direct from Cairo" (in *Criticism: Historical Criticism, Intentions and the Soul of Man,* ed. Guy, p. 142). Wilde himself loved Egyptian cigarettes, telling Jacques Daurelle that "the English only keep Egypt because it's the country from which we get our best cigarettes" (quoted in Jacques Daurelle, "An English Poet in Paris" [1891], rpt. and trans. in *Oscar Wilde: Interviews and Recollections,* ed. E. H. Mikhail, 2 vols. [London: Macmillan, 1979], 1:169). Wilde publicized the pleasures of cigarette smoking as much by his public appearances as by the numerous references to the practice in his dialogues, fiction, and plays. Henry de Regnier recalled that "Oriental cigarettes with gold tips were ever consuming themselves into smoke in his mouth" ("Recollections of Oscar Wilde" [1901], rpt. and trans. in *Oscar Wilde: Interviews and Recollections,* ed. Mikhail, 1:165), while according to Marcel Schwob, who saw much of Wilde during a visit to Paris in 1891, Wilde "never stopped smoking opium-tainted Egyptian cigarettes" (quoted in Richard Ellmann, *Oscar Wilde* [New York: Knopf, 1988], p. 346). For the connections between Egyptian tobacco and opium-inspired reverie, see Kate Chopin's story "An Egyptian Cigarette."

15 Some art critics maintain that accurate portraiture is a positive impediment to any knowledge of the sitter as subject. "I cannot see the man for his likeness," complains Roger Fry of one of Sargent's portraits (quoted

tion. As soon as you have one, you seem to want to throw it away. It is silly of you, for there is only one thing in the world worse than being talked about, and that is not being talked about. A portrait like this would set you far above all the young men in England, and make the old men quite jealous, if old men are ever capable of any emotion."

"I know you will laugh at me," he replied, "but I really can't exhibit it. I have put too much of myself into it."[15]

Lord Henry stretched his long legs out on the divan and shook with laughter.

"Yes, I knew you would laugh; but it is quite true, all the same."

"Too much of yourself in it! Upon my word, Basil, I didn't know you were so vain; and I really can't see any resemblance between you, with your rugged strong face, and your coal-black hair, and this young Adonis, who looks as if he was made of ivory and rose-leaves.[16] Why, my dear Basil, he is a Narcissus, and you—well, of course you have an intellectual expression, and all that.[17] But Beauty, real Beauty, ends where an intellectual expression begins. Intellect is in itself an exaggeration, and destroys the harmony of any face. The moment one sits down to think, one becomes all nose, or all forehead, or something horrid. Look at the successful men in any of the learned professions. How perfectly hideous they are! Except, of course, in the Church.[18] But then in the Church they don't think. A Bishop keeps on saying at the age of eighty what he was told to say when he was a boy of eighteen, and consequently he always looks absolutely delightful.[19] Your mysterious young friend, whose name you have never told me, but whose picture really fascinates me, never thinks. I feel quite sure of that. He is a brainless, beautiful thing, who should be always here in winter when we have no flowers to look at, and always here in summer when we want something to chill our intelligence. Don't flatter yourself, Basil: you are not in the least like him."

"You don't understand me, Harry. Of course I am not like him. I know that perfectly well. Indeed, I should be sorry to look like him. You shrug your shoulders? I am telling you the truth. There is a fatality about all physical and intellectual distinction, the sort of fatality that seems to dog through history the faltering steps of kings. It is better not to be different from one's fellows. The ugly and the stupid

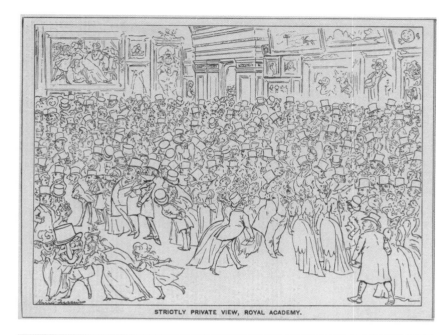

STRICTLY PRIVATE VIEW, ROYAL ACADEMY.

No. 163.—PRIVATE FRITH'S VIEW.—Members of the Salvation Army, led by General Oscar Wilde, joining in a hymn.

Harry Furniss, "Strictly Private View, Royal Academy," and "Our Academy Guide, No. 163—Private Frith's View," satirical engravings that appeared in *Punch* in 1890 and 1883, respectively. Furniss caricatures Frith's painting *A Private View at the Royal Academy, 1881* (see p. 88), even as he sympathizes, in "Private Frith's View," with Frith's own suspicion of the "Aesthetic" cult surrounding Wilde.

in Brilliant, *Portraiture,* p. 26). Modern English portraits are "so like the people they pretend to represent," Wilde writes in "The Decay of Lying," that "a hundred years from now, no one will believe in them. The only portraits in which one believes are portraits where there is very little of the sitter and a great deal of the artist" (p. 99).

16 According to classical legend, Adonis was a beautiful young man. Born of the incestuous love of Myrra for her father, Cinyras, the king of Cyprus, Adonis grew up to become Aphrodite's favorite lover, but he was unlucky and reckless as a hunter: gashed by a boar's tusks, he bled to death. As Aphrodite ran to her dying lover's aid, she sprinkled nectar on the blood-soaked ground and there sprouted up a flower of bloody, red hue, the anemone or *windflower,* whose blossoms are said to be opened by the action of the wind before being blown away shortly after. In his study of the relations between Greco-Roman mythology and the names of plants, Peter Bernhardt writes that "for thousands of years, Greek women worshipped Adonis as the personification of vegetation drying up in the cyclical heat of a Mediterranean summer" (*Gods and Goddesses in the Garden: Greco-Roman Mythology and the Scientific Names of Plants* [Brunswick, NJ: Rutgers University Press, 2008], p. 143).

17 The Narcissus myth preoccupied Wilde and informs the central moment of *Dorian Gray* in which "the sense of his own beauty came on [Dorian] like a revelation." According to classical legend, Narcissus was a beautiful youth of awesome vanity, beloved by suitors of both sexes, all of whom he rejected or ignored. Upon being rejected by Narcissus, one of his lovesick victims uttered a curse dooming him to experience the same intensity of passion for an unattainable object. Thereafter Narcissus came upon a clear, silvery mountain pool, and upon stooping down to drink from its waters, he fell in love with his own reflection. Unable to possess the beautiful boy that he had found in the water, whose image dissipated with the falling of his tears, Narcissus pined away until his body was no more and all that remained was the flower that bears his name. Peter Bernhardt observes that unlike many of the varieties of Narcissus registered today, early species possessed a numbingly sweet odor, re-

flecting the common Greek origin of the words *narcissus* and *narcotic* (*Gods and Goddesses in the Garden*, p. 61).

18 In *The Importance of Being Earnest*, when Canon Chasuble remarks that the Primitive Church was distinctly against matrimony, Miss Prism replies, "you do not seem to realize, dear Doctor, that by persistently remaining single, a man converts himself into a permanent public temptation," and "this very celibacy leads weaker vessels away."

19 "I never intend to grow old," remarks Lord Illingworth in *A Woman of No Importance:* "The soul is born old but grows young." Compare "Those whom the Gods love grow young" (Wilde, "A Few Maxims for the Instruction of the Over-Educated").

20 There has been much speculation about possible real-life models for the title character in Wilde's novel. A number of Wilde's contemporaries believed that Dorian Gray was inspired by the poet John Gray, Wilde's protégé at the time of the novel's composition. The biographer Richard Ellmann says that "to give the hero of his novel the name of 'Gray' was [for Wilde] a form of courtship" (Ellmann, *Oscar Wilde,* p. 307). The only extant letter from John Gray to Wilde—an autograph draft of Gray's poem "Mishka" dating from 1891—is signed "Yours ever, Dorian," and according to the British Library (where this letter is now housed) it was for many years pasted into "copy No. 1" of *The Picture of Dorian Gray.* Gray was for some time eager to embrace the persona of "Dorian" Gray, and up until 1892 he used it to gain entrance into fashionable society. However, when *The Star* publicly reported in its gossip column, in February 1892, that Gray was "said to be the original Dorian of the same name," Gray threatened to sue for libel and the report was immediately recanted. The incident was the beginning of a permanent breach between Wilde and Gray. For discussion of Gray's "Dorian" persona and his possible connection to Wilde's novel, see Jerusha Hull McCormack, *John Gray: Poet, Dandy, Priest* (Hanover, NH: Brandeis University Press/University Press of New England, 1991), pp. 39–102.

But why "Dorian"? The OED defines Dorian as "Of Doris or Doria, a division of ancient Greece," specifically mentioning that in music "Dorian mode" refers

Charles Haslewood Shannon, lithographic portrait of John Gray, 1896. Many of Wilde's contemporaries were convinced that the poet John Gray was the model for Dorian Gray. Gray was for a while happy to indulge such speculations, even signing one letter to Wilde, "Yours ever, Dorian."

have the best of it in this world. They can sit quietly and gape at the play. If they know nothing of victory, they are at least spared the knowledge of defeat. They live as we all should live, undisturbed, indifferent, and without disquiet. They neither bring ruin upon others nor ever receive it from alien hands. Your rank and wealth, Harry; my brains, such as they are, my fame, whatever it may be worth; Dorian Gray's good looks; we will all suffer for what the gods have given us, suffer terribly."

"Dorian Gray? is that his name?" said Lord Henry, walking across the studio towards Basil Hallward.[20]

"Yes; that is his name. I didn't intend to tell it to you."

"But why not?"

"Dorian Gray? Is that his name?" frontispiece by S. A. Moss to *The Picture of Dorian Gray*, vol. 2 of *The Sunflower Edition of the Works of Oscar Wilde* (New York: Lang, 1909).

to "one of the ancient Grecian modes, characterized by simplicity and solemnity; also, the first of the 'authentic' ecclesiastical modes." As an accomplished classicist, Wilde was familiar with this definition of the term, even drawing upon it for his reference to "the noble Dorian music of the Greek" in "The Critic as Artist." However, as John Espey observes, "followers of Walter Pater and John Addington Symonds must have been aware of a second 'coterie' meaning of 'Dorian'—one difficult to document because of its nature. It was a safe enough name to use, a bit dandified and fashionable, and if anyone had challenged it there was [always] the dictionary to turn to with its standard definition of simplicity and severity" (Espey, "Resources for Wilde Studies at the Clark Library," in *Oscar Wilde: Two Approaches; Papers Read at a Clark Library Seminar, April 17, 1976* [Los Angeles: William Andrews Clark Memorial Library, 1977], p. 37). In an essay entitled "The Dantesque and Platonic Ideals of love," the poet and critic John Addington Symonds (1840–1893) uses the terms "Greek love," "masculine love," and "Dorian love" interchangeably. The philologist Karl Müller's *History and Antiquities of the Doric Race*—a book that inspired Symonds—defends the tradition of an older male "lover's" taking a younger man in his charge.

In a poem entitled "In Honorem Doriani Creatorisque Eius" [In Honor of Dorian and His Creator], which was written in Latin, the poet Lionel Johnson —to whom Wilde had given a copy of *The Picture of Dorian Gray*—plays on both the official and the coterie senses of *Dorian:*

Blessed be you, Oscar!
Who deem me worthy of this book
For friendship's sake:
Modulating in the Roman mode
Praises to the Dorian owed,
I give you thanks. . . .

Here are apples of Sodom;
Here the heart of vices;
And sweet sins.
In the heavens and in the depths,
Be to you, who perceive so much,
Glory of all glories. (translated by Ian Fletcher)

21 In *The Importance of Being Earnest,* Jack asks Gwendolen, "But you don't mean to say that you couldn't love me if my name wasn't Ernest? . . . Personally darling, to speak quite candidly, I don't much care about the name of Ernest—I don't think the name suits me at all." "It suits you perfectly," replies Gwendolen: "It is a divine name. It has a music of its own. It produces vibrations. . . . Your Christian name has an irresistible fascination."

22 Wilde had already written one story based upon this idea. The eponymous heroine of "Lady Alroy" (subsequently retitled "The Sphinx without a Secret") rents rooms for three guineas a week and spends time in them merely to surround herself with an air of mystery: "she was a woman with a mania for mystery. She took these rooms for the pleasure of going there with her veil down, and imagining she was a heroine. She had a passion for secrecy, but she was merely a Sphinx without a secret."

23 "You have invented a useful younger brother called Ernest, in order that you may come up to town as often as you like. I have invented an invaluable permanent invalid called Bunbury, in order that I may be able to go down into the country whenever I choose. Bunbury is perfectly invaluable. If it wasn't for Bunbury's extraordinary bad health, for instance, I wouldn't be able to dine with you at Willis's tonight" (*The Importance of Being Earnest*).

24 Prior to the public exposure in 1895 of Wilde's sexual activities with a string of young men, and his subsequent imprisonment for "gross indecency," he kept his sexual preferences secret from his wife, Constance (née Constance Lloyd; 1858–1898). Nearly sixty years after Wilde's imprisonment, his son Vyvyan vividly recalls the moment when his mother found out the truth: "my main recollection is of my mother, in tears, poring over masses of press cuttings, mostly from Continental newspapers. I was, of course, not allowed to see them, though I could not help seeing the name OSCAR WILDE in large headlines" (*Son of Oscar Wilde,* p. 61).

"Oh, I can't explain. When I like people immensely I never tell their names to any one. It seems like surrendering a part of them.[21] You know how I love secrecy. It is the only thing that can make modern life wonderful or mysterious to us.[22] The commonest thing is delightful if one only hides it. When I leave town I never tell my people where I am going. If I did, I would lose all my pleasure. It is a silly habit, I dare say, but somehow it seems to bring a great deal of romance into one's life. I suppose you think me awfully foolish about it?"

"Not at all," answered Lord Henry, laying his hand upon his shoulder;[a] "not at all, my dear Basil. You seem to forget that I am married, and the one charm of marriage is that it makes a life of deception necessary for both parties.[23] I never know where my wife is, and my wife never knows what I am doing. When we meet—we do meet occasionally, when we dine out together, or go down to the Duke's—we tell each other the most absurd stories with the most serious faces. My wife is very good at it—much better in fact than I am. She never gets confused over her dates, and I always do. But when she does find me out, she makes no row at all.[24] I sometimes wish she did, but she merely laughs at me."[b]

"I hate the way you talk about your married life, Harry," said Basil Hallward, shaking his hand off,[c] and strolling towards the door that led into the garden. "I believe that you are really a very good husband, but that you are thoroughly ashamed of your own virtues. You are an extraordinary fellow. You never say a moral thing, and you never do a wrong thing. Your cynicism is simply a pose."[25]

"Being natural is simply a pose, and the most irritating pose I know," cried Lord Henry, laughing; and the two young men went out into the garden together, and for a time they did not speak.

After a long pause Lord Henry pulled out his watch. "I am afraid I must be going, Basil," he murmured, "and before I go I insist on your answering a question I put to you some time ago."

"What is that?" asked Basil Hallward, keeping his eyes fixed on the ground.[26]

"You know quite well."

"I do not, Harry."

Drypoint etching of Edward Carson Q. C., by John George Day, 1914.

"Well, I will tell you what it is."

"Please don't."

"I must. I want you to explain to me why you won't exhibit Dorian Gray's picture. I want the real reason."[27]

"I told you the real reason."

"No, you did not. You said it was because there was too much of yourself in it. Now, that is childish."

"Harry," said Basil Hallward, looking him straight in the face, "every portrait that is painted with feeling is a portrait of the artist, not of the sitter. The sitter is merely the accident, the occasion. It is not he who is revealed by the painter; it is rather the painter who, on the

In *An Ideal Husband,* one of Wilde's characters advances a view somewhat different from Lord Henry's on the subject of marriage and secrecy. "You should have told your wife the whole thing," remarks the dandy Lord Goring to his friend Sir Robert Chiltern. "Secrets from other people's wives are a necessity in modern life. . . . But no man should have a secret from his own wife. She invariably finds it out. Women have a wonderful instinct about things. They can discover everything except the obvious."

25 With its connotations of imposture and insincerity, "posing" was nearly as serious a moral defect in the eyes of earnest heterosexual Victorians as homosexuality. In his reply to Basil Hallward's suggestion that his cynicism is a pose ("Being natural is simply a pose, and the most irritating pose I know"), Lord Henry inverts the terms according to which the charge of *posing* conventionally operated. Helen Swanwick remarked in a memoir that Wilde was a "*Poseur* of genius and perfectly aware that he posed and [was] making an art of the pose" (*I Have Been Young* [London: Gollancz, 1935], p. 67).

26 Wilde the fiction writer possesses a dramatist's eye for body language. Hallward's averted gaze suggests his discomfort in the face of Lord Henry's questioning, though it contrasts sharply with the open, steady ("straight") look he gives Lord Henry moments later when he announces that he has painted "with feeling" and "shown the secret" of his soul.

27 This paragraph all the way through "I take no credit to myself for trying to escape" (on p. 79 below), as well as an extract from pp. 79 to 80 below (see n. 39), was read aloud in court by Queensberry's lawyer, Edward Carson, during Wilde's 1895 unsuccessful libel suit against the Marquess of Queensberry. Carson followed his reading of these extracts with the question, "Now I ask you, Mr. Wilde, do you consider that that description of the feeling of one man towards a youth, just grown up, was a proper or an improper feeling?" (quoted in *The Real Trial of Oscar Wilde,* intro. and commentary by Merlin Holland [New York: Perennial, 2003], p. 85).

28 For Canon H. N. Ellacombe, a writer of sentimental flower books, the daisy is "the special flower of childhood," connoting the innocence and simplicity of "the infant sporting in the sunny field" (quoted in Scourse, *The Victorians and Their Flowers,* p. 52). Ellacombe's connection of the daisy to childlike innocence casts a sinister light over Lord Henry's act of plucking, which in turn comes to prefigure his corruption of the youthful Dorian.

29 A crowded event, in this case a literary and artistic *salon* similar to those hosted in the 1880s by Wilde's mother, Jane Francesca Elgee Lady Wilde. In 1951 Horace Wyndham writes, "That once flourishing London institution, the literary *salon,* has long since disappeared.... Yet fifty and sixty years ago, quite a number of such 'circles'—with young bloods and old bloods, authors and artists, musicians and mummers, and playwrights and poets revolving around them and endeavoring to set the Thames on fire—were in full swing" (Horace Wyndham, *Speranza: A Biography of Lady Wilde* [London: Boardman, 1951], p. 11).

30 Wilde uses the adjective *curious,* and the related noun *curiosity,* dozens of times in *Dorian Gray.* Matthew Arnold notes, in "The Function of Criticism at the Present Time" (1865), that "the word *curiosity,* which in other languages is used in a good sense, to mean, as a high and fine quality of man's nature, just this disinterested love of a free play of the mind on all subjects, for its own sake. . . has in our language no sense of the kind, no sense but a rather bad and disparaging one. But criticism, real criticism, is essentially the exercise of this very quality." But like the word *subtle* (which Wilde also uses numerous times), the word *curious* has been seen as part of Wilde's effort to encode his homosexuality in ways that will escape censure or prosecution in the eyes of the law. Difficult to pin down, the words *curious* and *curiosity* point to an object of knowledge that is "a reflection of the impulse towards knowing it" (Eve Kosofsky Sedgwick, *Epistemology of the Closet,* 2nd ed. [Berkeley and Los Angeles: University of California Press, 2008], p. 174).

coloured canvas, reveals himself. The reason I will not exhibit this picture is that I am afraid that I have shown with it the secret of my own soul."

Lord Harry laughed. "And what is that?" he asked.

"I will tell you," said Hallward, and an expression of perplexity came over his face.

"I am all expectation, Basil," murmured his companion, looking at him.

"Oh, there is really very little to tell, Harry," answered the young painter; "and I am afraid you will hardly understand it. Perhaps you will hardly believe it."

Lord Henry smiled, and, leaning down, plucked a pink-petalled daisy from the grass, and examined it. "I am quite sure I shall understand it," he replied, gazing intently at the little golden white-feathered disk,[28] "and I can believe anything, provided that it is incredible."

The wind shook some blossoms from the trees, and the heavy lilac blooms, with their clustering stars, moved to and fro in the languid air. A grasshopper began to chirrup in the grass, and a long thin dragon-fly floated by on its brown gauze wings. Lord Henry felt as if he could hear Basil Hallward's heart beating, and he wondered what was coming.

"Well, this is incredible," repeated Hallward, rather bitterly,— "incredible to me at times. I don't know what it means. The story is simply this. Two months ago I went to a crush[29] at Lady Brandon's. You know we poor painters have to show ourselves in society from time to time, just to remind the public that we are not savages. With an evening coat and a white tie, as you told me once, anybody, even a stock-broker, can gain a reputation for being civilized. Well, after I had been in the room about ten minutes, talking to huge overdressed dowagers and tedious Academicians, I suddenly became conscious that someone was looking at me. I turned half-way round, and saw Dorian Gray for the first time. When our eyes met, I felt that I was growing pale. A curious instinct of terror came over me.[30] I knew that I had come face to face with some one whose mere personality was so fascinating that, if I allowed it to do so, it would absorb my whole nature, my whole soul, my very art itself.[31] I did not want any external influence in my life. You know yourself, Harry, how independent I am by nature. My father destined me for the army. I insisted on going to Oxford.[32] Then he made me enter my name at the Middle Temple.[33] Before I had eaten half a dozen dinners I gave up the Bar, and announced my intention of becoming a painter.[34] I have always been my own master; had at least always been so till I met Dorian Gray. Then—but I don't know how to explain it to you. Something seemed to tell me that I was on the verge of a terrible crisis in my life. I had a strange feeling that Fate had in store for me exquisite joys and exquisite sorrows. I knew that if I spoke to Dorian I would become absolutely devoted to him, and that I ought not to speak to him.[d] I grew afraid, and turned to quit the room. It was not conscience that made me do so: it was cowardice. I take no credit to myself for trying to escape."

"Conscience and cowardice are really the same things, Basil. Conscience is the trade-name of the firm. That is all."[35]

"I don't believe that, Harry. However, whatever was my motive—and it may have been pride, for I used to be very proud—I certainly struggled to the door. There, of course, I stumbled against Lady Brandon. 'You are not going to run away so soon, Mr. Hallward?' she screamed out. You know her shrill horrid voice?"

"Yes; she is a peacock in everything but beauty,"[36] said Lord Henry, pulling the daisy to bits with his long, nervous fingers.

"I could not get rid of her. She brought me up to Royalties, and people with Stars and Garters,[37] and elderly ladies with gigantic tiaras and hooked noses. She spoke of me as her dearest friend. I had only met her once before, but she took it into her head to lionize me. I believe some picture of mine had made a great success at the time, at least had been chattered about in the penny newspapers, which is the nineteenth-century standard of immortality.[38] Suddenly I found myself face to face with the young man whose personality had so strangely stirred me. We were quite close, almost touching. Our eyes met again. It was mad of me, but I asked Lady Brandon to introduce me to him. Perhaps it was not so mad, after all. It was simply inevitable. We would have spoken to each other without any introduction. I

31 In the course of his unsuccessful libel suit against the Marquess of Queensberry, Wilde was forced by Queensberry's attorney, Edward Carson, to defend his use of the term *personality.* "You mean a beautiful young man?" asked Carson (*The Real Trial,* p. 85). "I would rather say *personality,*" replied Wilde, "I use the word *personality* on account of the peculiar effect on the artist [that] this spectre, this appearance of Dorian Gray, produced" (p. 86). Wilde's interest in the psychology of personal and artistic influence is evident in many of his works, as well as in the notebooks that survive from his days as a student at Oxford. Wilde frequently utilizes the term *personality* when discussing the importance of art to the life or "soul" of man. In "The Critic as Artist" he remarks that *personality* "is an element of revelation" and that just "as art springs from personality, so it is only to personality that it can be revealed" (pp. 165–166).

32 The University of Oxford, the seat of powerful new ideas about culture and masculinity in the late-nineteenth century, has been called "a decisive battle-ground in the Victorian struggle over the sociopolitical order being brought forth by secular materialism and industrial modernity" (Linda Dowling, *Hellenism and Homosexuality in Victorian Oxford* [Ithaca, NY: Cornell University Press, 1994], p. 36). Wilde famously remarks that the moment his father sent him to Oxford was one of the two great turning points of his life (the other was when society sent him to prison); "the young men with me at Oxford," he comments elsewhere, "[were] men of position, taste, and high mental culture" ("The Decorative Arts").

33 Middle Temple is one of the four Inns of Court entitled to call their members to the English bar as barristers. In Elizabethan times, men from outside the legal profession could join as social members, and Middle Temple became a kind of club for the intellectual elite (the first recorded production of Shakespeare's *Twelfth Night* took place there in 1602). But by Wilde's day, Middle Temple was a training ground for barristers. Wilde's brother Willie briefly trained there in 1874, prior to being called to the Irish bar in 1875.

34 Basil Hallward's career has been driven by attachment to culture in the face of his father's insistence upon more active, practical, or "manly" professions. In this respect, Basil embodies an emerging idea of the gentleman, dedicated to civilized or enlightened values, at odds with the crude Toryism on which British imperial strength had earlier been founded. See Regenia Gagnier, "Dandies and Gentlemen," in her *Idylls of the Marketplace: Oscar Wilde and the Victorian Public* (Stanford University Press, 1986), pp. 49–99, and Martin Wiener, *English Culture and the Decline of the Industrial Spirit 1850–1980* (Cambridge University Press, 1981).

35 In *The Duchess of Padua* (1883) Wilde writes, "Conscience is but the name which cowardice / Fleeing from battle scrawls upon its shield"; and in *Hamlet*, Shakespeare's protagonist tells us that "conscience doth make cowards of us all."

36 The peacock—celebrated in Whistler's mural art for the "Peacock Room" (1876–1877) and in Aubrey Beardsley's designs for Wilde's *Salome* (1894)—was a favorite symbol of beauty for the Aesthetes of Wilde's generation. As early as 1851, John Ruskin adduced the example of the peacock as proof that "the most beautiful things in the world are the most useless" (*The Stones of Venice, Vol. 1,* vol. 9 of *The Complete Works of John Ruskin,* ed. E. T. Cook and Alexander Wedderburn [London: George Allen, 1912]). The peacock is the male sex of the species (peafowl), and is usually thought more beautiful than its female counterpart, the peahen, dull brown and lacking the male's long, iridescent tail feathers, which it raises into a spectacular fan-like display during courtship. The peacock is also known for its shrill, raucous cry during mating season. Lady Brandon, then, according to Lord Henry, acts like a cock but looks like a peahen.

37 In *An Ideal Husband,* "the riband and star of the Garter" are worn by Lord Caversham, "an old gentleman of seventy . . . A fine Whig type. Rather like a portrait by Lawrence."

38 One of numerous attacks on the institution of modern journalism to be found in Wilde's works—at-

am sure of that. Dorian told me so afterwards. He, too, felt that we were destined to know each other."[39]

"And how did Lady Brandon describe this wonderful young man? I know she goes in for giving a rapid *précis* of all her guests.[40] I remember her bringing me up to a most truculent and red-faced old gentleman covered all over with orders and ribands, and hissing into my ear, in a tragic whisper which must have been perfectly audible to everybody in the room, something like 'Sir Humpty Dumpty—you know—Afghan Frontier—Russian intrigues: very successful man—wife killed by an elephant—quite inconsolable—wants to marry a beautiful American widow—everybody does nowadays—hates Mr. Gladstone—but very much interested in beetles—ask him what he thinks of Schouvaloff.'[41] I simply fled. I like to find out people for myself. But poor Lady Brandon treats her guests exactly as an auctioneer treats his goods. She either explains them entirely away, or tells one everything about them except what one wants to know. But what did she say about Mr. Dorian Gray?"

"Oh, she murmured, 'Charming boy—poor dear mother and I quite inseparable—engaged to be married to the same man—I mean married on the same day—how very silly of me! Quite forget what he does—afraid he—doesn't do anything—Oh, yes, plays the piano—or is it the violin, dear Mr. Gray?' We could neither of us help laughing, and we became friends at once."

"Laughter is not a bad beginning for a friendship, and it is the best ending for one," said Lord Henry, plucking another daisy.

Hallward buried his face in his hands. "You don't understand what friendship is, Harry," he murmured, "or what enmity is, for that matter. You like every one; that is to say, you are indifferent to every one."

"How horribly unjust of you!" cried Lord Henry, tilting his hat back, and looking up at the little clouds that were drifting across the hollowed turquoise of the summer sky, like ravelled skeins of glossy white silk. "Yes, horribly unjust of you. I make a great difference between people. I choose my friends for their good looks, my acquaintances for their characters, and my enemies for their brains.[42] A man can't be too careful in the choice of his enemies.[43] I have not got one tacks that Wilde only sharpened after the clamor of dissent in the British press that greeted *The Picture of Dorian Gray* upon its publication. See for instance Wilde's comment, in "The Soul of Man under Socialism," that "in old days men had the rack. Now they have the press" (in *Criticism: Historical Criticism, Intentions and the Soul of Man,* ed. Guy, p. 255).

39 Together with an earlier passage (see n. 27 above), the last eight sentences of this paragraph, from "Our eyes met again" to "know each other," were read out in open court by Queensberry's lawyer, Edward Carson, in the course of Wilde's unsuccessful suit for libel.

40 The boorish Lady Brandon finds a real-life antecedent in Wilde's own mother, Lady Wilde, who in the 1880s strove to transform her modest accommodations in Park Street into one of London's leading salons: "If anyone was sitting in a corner unnoticed, Lady Wilde was sure to bring up someone to be introduced. . . . She generally prefaced her introductions with some such remark as 'Mr. A. who has just written a delightful poem,' or 'Mrs. B., who is on the staff of the *Snapdragon,*' or 'Miss. C., whose new novel everybody is talking about'" (Catherine Hamilton, quoted in Wyndham, *Speranza,* p. 172). However, Lady Wilde's garrulousness often got the better of her; and though her weekly receptions sometimes attracted a diverse and interesting crowd, she was "a figure of fun" (*Speranza,* p. 172) to many of her own guests. She dominated proceedings with her "strangely toned voice," and her crowded rooms were filled with people one "had never heard of until Lady Wilde trotted them out" (W. B. Maxwell, quoted in *Speranza,* p. 173).

41 Sir Humpty Dumpty is the embodiment of stuffy English imperialism. "Afghan Frontier" and "Russian intrigues" indicate he was engaged in Britain's unsuccessful military effort of 1878–1880 to wrest control of Afghanistan from Russia. His wife's tragic death, presumably in India ("killed by an elephant"), prefigures the vengeful shooting of an elephant through which George Orwell famously symbolized fatuous attempts by Britain to impose rule violently upon its colonies ("Shooting an Elephant," in *The Orwell Reader* [1961;

rpt. Orlando, FL: Harcourt Brace, 1984], pp. 1–8). He "hates Mr. Gladstone" because William Ewart Gladstone, prime minister of Great Britain from 1868 to 1874 (and again from 1880 to 1885, in 1886, and from 1892 to 1894), embodied Liberal opposition to crass imperial ambition. Sir Humpty has strong views about Count Peter Schouvaloff, the former Russian envoy to London, because Schouvaloff worked tirelessly to preserve amicable relations between Russia and Britain. Finally, Sir Humpty "wants to marry a beautiful American widow" because, according to Wilde, "American women are bright, clever, and wonderfully cosmopolitan. . . . They insist on being paid compliments, and have almost succeeded in making English men eloquent. . . . It is true that they lack repose and that their voices are rather harsh and strident. . . . but after a time one gets to love these pretty whirlwinds in petticoats that sweep so recklessly through society and are so agitating to all duchesses who have daughters." In the "race for coronets," Wilde concluded, the American woman "often carries off the prize. . . . and as there is neither romance nor humility in her love, she makes an excellent wife" (Wilde, "The American Invasion").

42 Wilde's opinion of friendship was vastly different in 1897, after two years of prison life, from the view expressed by Lord Henry here. Just days before leaving Reading Gaol, Wilde writes that "a good friend is a new world. I must be with nice, sweet people" (*CL,* p. 830).

43 After his downfall Wilde came to see the irony of this statement, writing in *De Profundis* that "I little thought that it was by a pariah that I was to be made a pariah myself" (*CL,* p. 758). In suing the Marquess of Queensberry for libel, Wilde had chosen as an "enemy" not only a man with no "brains"—the uncultivated Queensberry had little time for intellectual or artistic pursuits—but someone who was regarded by members of his own family as insane and violent. But Wilde had greatly underestimated the determination of his opponent, who went to the lengths of hiring private detectives to investigate Wilde's participation in the London underworld of homosexual clubs and procurers. On the advice of his lawyers, Wilde dropped the libel charge when Queensberry's attorney Edward Carson

announced in his opening speech for the defense that he intended to call to the witness box several male prostitutes who would testify that they had had sex with Wilde. Immediately following the collapse of Wilde's action against Queensberry, Wilde was arrested, prosecuted, and jailed for the crime of "gross indecency." Adding further injury and humiliation to his situation, he was bankrupted when he was unable to pay the court costs incurred by Queensberry in his defense. *De Profundis* vividly describes the ignominy heaped publicly upon Wilde during his appearances at Bankruptcy Court and also during his transferences between prisons. When Wilde was released on bail, in the short interim between his first criminal trial (in which the jury could not agree) and the second (in which he was found guilty of the counts against him), he found virtually every door in London closed to him. After his prison term ended in 1897, he took the assumed name "Sebastian Melmoth" and retired to the Continent, where genteel English society continued to shun him until his death in 1900.

44 "Now that I think of it, I have never heard any man mention his brother. The subject seems distasteful to most men" (*The Importance of Being Earnest*).

45 "The private lives of men and women should not be told to the public. The public have nothing to do with them at all. In France they manage these things better. There they do not allow the details of the trials that take place in the divorce courts to be published for the amusement or criticism of the public. All that the public are allowed to know is that the divorce has taken place and was granted on petition of one or other or both of the married parties concerned" ("The Soul of Man under Socialism," p. 256).

46 "In London my father always carried a gold-headed malacca cane, about three foot six inches long, as was the fashion among the dandies of the day" (Holland, *Son of Oscar Wilde,* p. 55).

47 "The English are always degrading truths into facts" (Wilde, "A Few Maxims for the Over-Educated").

Lord Alfred Douglas's father, the Marquess of Queensberry—"the screaming, scarlet Marquess," as Wilde called him. Queensberry was widely viewed as unstable and vindictive, even by members of his own family. As Wilde later wrote, "I little thought that it was by a pariah that I was to be made a pariah myself."

who is a fool. They are all men of some intellectual power, and consequently they all appreciate me. Is that very vain of me? I think it is rather vain."

"I should think it was, Harry. But according to your category I must be merely an acquaintance."

"My dear old Basil, you are much more than an acquaintance."

"And much less than a friend. A sort of brother, I suppose?"

"Oh, brothers! I don't care for brothers.[44] My elder brother won't die, and my younger brothers seem never to do anything else."

"Harry!"

"My dear fellow, I am not quite serious. But I can't help detesting my relations. I suppose it comes from the fact that we can't stand other people having the same faults as ourselves. I quite sympathise with the rage of the English Democracy against what they call the vices of the upper classes. They feel that drunkenness, stupidity, and immorality should be their own special property, and that if any one of us makes an ass of himself we are poaching on their preserves.[e] When poor Southwark got into the Divorce Court, their indignation was quite magnificent.[45] And yet I don't suppose that ten per cent of the lower orders live with their own wives."[f]

"I don't agree with a single word that you have said, and, what is more, Harry, I don't believe you do either."

Lord Henry stroked his pointed brown beard, and tapped the toe of his patent-leather boot with a tasselled malacca cane.[46] "How English you are, Basil! If one puts forward an idea to a real Englishman —always a rash thing to do—he never dreams of considering whether the idea is right or wrong.[47] The only thing he considers of any importance is whether one believes it oneself. Now, the value of an idea has nothing whatsoever to do with the sincerity of the man who expresses it.[48] Indeed, the probabilities are that the more insincere the man is, the more purely intellectual will the idea be, as in that case it will not be coloured by either his wants, his desires, or his prejudices. However, I don't propose to discuss politics, sociology, or metaphysics with you. I like persons better than principles. Tell me more about Dorian Gray. How often do you see him?"

"Every day. I couldn't be happy if I didn't see him every day. Of course sometimes it is only for a few minutes. But a few minutes with somebody one worships mean a great deal."[g]

"But you don't really worship him?"

"I do."

"How extraordinary! I thought you would never care for anything but your painting—your art, I should say. Art sounds better, doesn't it?"[49]

"He is all my art to me now. I sometimes think, Harry, that there are only two eras of any importance in the history of the world. The first is the appearance of a new medium for art, and the second is the appearance of a new personality for art also.[50] What the invention of

48 Lord Henry speaks in paradoxes and bon-mots designed to amuse, shock, and provoke, and Dorian will later tell Lord Henry that "you mock at everything." Lord Henry's gift of tongue recalls Wilde's own quick intelligence and ostentatious, mannered displays of speech. Wilde maintained that conversation is an art form and "recreation, not instruction . . . the aim of conversation" ("Aristotle at Afternoon Tea"). Here Lord Henry's reply to Basil Hallward's doubts about his sincerity is a crystallization of Wilde's own ideas about the importance of lying in conversation. Walter Pater comments about *Dorian Gray* that "there is always something of an excellent talker about the writing of Oscar Wilde; and in his hands, as happens so rarely with those who practice it, the form of dialogue is justified by its being really alive" ("A Novel by Mr. Oscar Wilde," signed rev. of *Dorian Gray* [1891], rpt. in *Oscar Wilde: The Critical Heritage,* ed. K. Beckson [London: Routledge & Kegan Paul, 1970], p. 83). *Dorian Gray* would be a very dull book without Lord Henry. When Wilde revised the novel for book publication, he enlarged Lord Henry's character and gave his mouthpiece greater space to dazzle and amuse. Commenting directly on Lord Henry's speech in the book version, Wilde says he played with an "idea, and grew willful; tossed it into the air and transformed it; let it escape and recaptured it, made it iridescent with fancy and winged it with paradox. The praise of folly, as he want on, soared into a philosophy, and Philosophy herself became young" (*The Picture of Dorian Gray: The 1890 and 1891 Texts,* ed. J. Bristow, vol. 3 of *The Complete Works of Oscar Wilde* [Oxford University Press, 2005], p. 204).

49 "Art is the only serious thing in the world" (Wilde, "A Few Maxims").

50 Hallward's comments on the role of art in world history condense ideas that Wilde had entertained seriously since at least his Oxford thesis, "The Rise of Historical Criticism." He would reformulate these ideas on many occasions, most notably in "The Critic as Artist" and "The Soul of Man under Socialism."

51 As the critic Andrew Elfenbein notes, this passage seems indebted to the art-critic and homosexual apologist John Addington Symonds. In *The Renaissance in Italy:* vol. 3, *The Fine Arts* (New York: Henry Holt, 1879), Symonds declares that "the Venetians perfected oil-painting, and set forth the glory of the world as it appeals to the imagination and the senses" (p. 182). "We have before us a favourite of the Roman emperor Hadrian," he says elsewhere of Antinoüs, Hadrian's young male lover (whom Hadrian subsequently transformed into a Roman deity), "a real youth of incomparable beauty, just as nature made him, with all the inscrutableness and undeveloped character, with all the pathos of a most untimely doom" (*Sketches and Studies in Italy* [London: Smith Elder, 1879], p. 50).

52 According to classical legend, Paris, the physically beautiful son of Priam, King of Troy, was destined before birth to be the ruin of his nation. When pregnant with Paris, his mother, Hecuba, dreamed she would give birth to a firebrand. After a soothsayer interpreted her dream to mean that Paris would one day bring calamity on Troy, the infant was abandoned on the exposed slopes of Mt. Ida. But, unknown to his parents, the child survived and was brought up among herdsmen. Later, Paris was called upon by the Gods to judge which of the three goddesses—Hera, Athena, or Aphrodite—was the most beautiful. Paris awarded the prize—a golden apple—to Aphrodite, then sought to claim as his prize the most beautiful woman in the world, Helen, whom he persuaded to abandon her Greek husband, Meneleus, and flee with him to Troy. His actions in alienating Hera and Athena, as well as in turning the Greeks against Troy, precipitated the Trojan wars. The judgment of Paris was a favorite subject in Greek art, Paris nearly always being represented as a beautiful beardless young man, wearing the pointed Phrygian cap, often holding the golden apple in his hand.

53 Antinoüs is reputed to have fallen from Hadrian's barge and drowned in the Nile in the year 130 A.D., though whether by suicide, accident, sacrifice, or foul play is unknown.

oil-painting was to the Venetians, the face of Antinoüs was to late Greek sculpture,[51] and the face of Dorian Gray will some day be to me. It is not merely that I paint from him, draw from him, model from him. Of course I have done all that. He has stood as Paris in dainty armour, and as Adonis with huntsman's cloak and polished boar-spear.[52] Crowned with heavy lotus-blossoms, he has sat on the prow of Adrian's barge, looking into the green, turbid Nile.[53] He has leaned over the still pool of some Greek woodland, and seen in the waters' silent silver the wonder of his own beauty.[54] But he is much more to me than that. I won't tell you that I am dissatisfied with what I have done of him, or that his beauty is such that art cannot express it. There is nothing that art cannot express, and I know that the work I have done, since I met Dorian Gray, is good work, is the best work of my life. But in some curious way—I wonder will you understand me?—his personality has suggested to me an entirely new manner in art, an entirely new mode of style. I see things differently, I think of them differently. I can now recreate life in a way that was hidden from me before. 'A dream of form in days of thought,'[55]—who is it who says that? I forget;—but it is what Dorian Gray has been to me. The merely visible presence of this lad—for he seems to me little more than a lad, though he is really over twenty—his merely visible presence—ah! I wonder can you realise all that that means? Unconsciously he defines for me the lines of a fresh school, a school that is to have in itself all the passion of the romantic spirit, all the perfection of the spirit that is Greek. The harmony of soul and body, —how much that is! We in our madness have separated the two, and have invented a realism that is bestial, an ideality that is void. Harry! Harry! If you only knew what Dorian Gray is to me! You remember that landscape of mine, for which Agnew offered me such a huge price, but which I would not part with?[56] It is one of the best things I have ever done. And why is it so? Because, while I was painting it, Dorian Gray sat beside me."

"Basil, this is quite wonderful! I must see Dorian Gray."

Hallward got up from the seat, and walked up and down the garden. After some time he came back. "You don't understand, Harry," he said. "Dorian Gray is merely to me a motive in art. He is never more present in my work than when no image of him is there. He is simply a suggestion, as I have said, of a new manner. I see him in the curves of certain lines, in the loveliness and the subtleties of certain colours. That is all."

"Then why won't you exhibit his portrait?"

"Because I have put into it all the extraordinary romance[h] of which, of course, I have never dared to speak to him.[57] He knows nothing about it. He will never know anything about it. But the world might guess it; and I will not bare my soul to their shallow, prying eyes. My heart shall never be put under their microscope. There is too much of myself in the thing, Harry, too much of myself!"

"Poets are not so scrupulous as you are. They know how useful passion is for publication. Nowadays a broken heart will run to many editions."[58]

"I hate them for it. An artist should create beautiful things, but should put nothing of his own life into them. We live in an age when men treat art as if it were meant to be a form of autobiography. We have lost the abstract sense of beauty. If I live, I will show the world what it is; and for that reason the world shall never see my portrait of Dorian Gray."

"I think you are wrong, Basil, but I won't argue with you. It is only the intellectually lost who ever argue. Tell me; is Dorian Gray very fond of you?"

Hallward considered for a few moments. "He likes me," he answered, after a pause; "I know he likes me. Of course I flatter him dreadfully. I find a strange pleasure in saying things to him that I know I shall be sorry for having said. I give myself away.[i] As a rule he is charming to me, and we walk home together from the club arm in arm,[j] or sit in the studio and talk of a thousand things. Now and then, however, he is horribly thoughtless, and seems to take a real delight in giving me pain. Then I feel, Harry, that I have given away my whole soul to some one who treats it as if it were a flower to put in his coat, a bit of decoration to charm his vanity, an ornament for a summer's day."

"Days in summer, Basil, are apt to linger. Perhaps you will tire sooner than he will. It is a sad thing to think of, but there is no doubt

54 A confirmation of Lord Henry's earlier remark that Dorian "is a Narcissus." That Dorian has "seen . . . the wonder of his own beauty," even if only in the fantasized shape of Narcissus, prefigures his reaction to the portrait in Chapter II.

55 Austin Dobson, "To a Greek Girl," in his *Proverbs in Porcelain* (1877).

56 Agnew's was—and still is—a leading dealer in contemporary art. In 1890 its premises, in London's Bond Street, were close to the Grosvenor Gallery.

57 On one level, Hallward means by "romance" simply *romanticism* in the sense of "imagination" or "artistry." But Hallward's term *romance* also implies erotic desire, as Wilde's later substitution of the term "curious artistic idolatry" for "extraordinary romance" indicates (one of many acts of self-censorship Wilde undertook as he revised and expanded the novel in 1891 for Ward, Lock, and Company). Hallward's confession in this paragraph, as well as his admission three paragraphs later ("I give myself away"), contradicts his claim, in the previous paragraph, that Dorian "is merely to me a motive in art."

58 An unfortunate foreshadowing of the truth in Wilde's own case. Wilde's heartbroken poem "The Ballad of Reading Gaol," written shortly after the end of his jail sentence, sold more widely than any other of his works during his own lifetime. Seven authorized editions of "The Ballad" (some 7,100 copies) were printed in England alone before Wilde's death.

59 "Education is an admirable thing. But it is well to remember from time to time that nothing that is worth knowing can be taught" (Wilde, "A Few Maxims").

60 "Friendship is far more tragic than love. It lasts longer" (Wilde, "A Few Maxims").

61 Wilde probably refers here to a small match or "vesta" case with a built-in match strike. Such cases were popular with genteel smokers up until the 1930s and were often given as mementos. As a compulsive smoker, Wilde was fascinated by the paraphernalia of smoking.

62 "I summed up all systems in a phrase, and all existence in an epigram" (CL, p. 729).

A "Vesta" case with a built-in match strike, by Archibald Knox (1864–1933), manufactured by William Hair Haseler of Birmingham in 1904. When Lord Henry strikes a light on "a dainty silver case," Wilde is almost certainly referring to a match-case such as this. Knox, active from the late 1890s onward, was Britain's preeminent Art Nouveau designer in silver and pewter.

that Genius lasts longer than Beauty. That accounts for the fact that we all take such pains to overeducate ourselves. In the wild struggle for existence, we want to have something that endures, and so we fill our minds with rubbish and facts, in the silly hope of keeping our place.[59] The thoroughly well informed man—that is the modern ideal. And the mind of the thoroughly well informed man is a dreadful thing. It is like a bric-à-brac shop, all monsters and dust, and everything priced above its proper value. I think you will tire first, all the same. Some day you will look at him,[k] and he will seem to you to be a little out of drawing, or you won't like his tone of colour, or something. You will bitterly reproach him in your own heart, and seriously think that he has behaved very badly to you. The next time he calls, you will be perfectly cold and indifferent. It will be a great pity, for it will alter you. The worst of having a romance[l] is that it leaves one so unromantic."[60]

"Harry, don't talk like that. As long as I live, the personality of Dorian Gray will dominate me. You can't feel what I feel. You change too often."

"Ah, my dear Basil, that is exactly why I can feel it. Those who are faithful know only the pleasures of love; it is the faithless who know love's tragedies." And Lord Henry struck a light on a dainty silver case,[61] and began to smoke a cigarette with a self-conscious and self-satisfied air, as if he had summed up life in a phrase.[62] There was a rustle of chirruping sparrows in the ivy, and the blue cloud-shadows chased themselves across the grass like swallows. How pleasant it was in the garden! And how delightful other people's emotions were! Much more delightful than their ideas, it seemed to him. One's own soul, and the passions of one's friends—those were the fascinating things in life. He thought with pleasure of the tedious luncheon that he had missed by staying so long with Basil Hallward. Had he gone to his aunt's, he would have been sure to meet Lord Goodbody there, and the whole conversation would have been about the housing of the poor, and the necessity for model lodging-houses. It was charming to have escaped all that![63] As he thought of his aunt, an idea seemed to strike him. He turned to Hallward, and said, "My dear fellow, I have just remembered."

"Remembered what, Harry?"

"Where I heard the name of Dorian Gray."

"Where was it?" asked Hallward, with a slight frown.

"Don't look so angry, Basil. It was at my aunt's, Lady Agatha's. She told me she had discovered a wonderful young man, who was going to help her in the East End, and that his name was Dorian Gray.[63] I am bound to state that she never told me he was good-looking. Women have no appreciation of good looks. At least, good women have not. She said that he was very earnest, and had a beautiful nature. I at once pictured to myself a creature with spectacles and lank hair, horridly freckled, and tramping about on huge feet. I wish I had known it was your friend."

"I am very glad you didn't, Harry."

"Why?"

"I don't want you to meet him."

"Mr. Dorian Gray is in the studio, Sir," said the butler, coming into the garden.

"You must introduce me now," cried Lord Henry, laughing.[65]

Basil Hallward turned to the servant, who stood blinking in the sunlight. "Ask Mr. Gray to wait, Parker: I will be in in a few moments." The man bowed, and went up the walk.

Then he looked at Lord Henry. "Dorian Gray is my dearest friend," he said. "He has a simple and a beautiful nature. Your aunt was quite right in what she said of him. Don't spoil him for me. Don't try to influence him. Your influence would be bad. The world is wide, and has many marvellous people in it. Don't take away from me the one person that makes life absolutely lovely to me and that gives to my art whatever wonder or charm it possesses.[m] Mind, Harry, I trust you." He spoke very slowly, and the words seemed wrung out of him almost against his will.

"What nonsense you talk!" said Lord Henry, smiling, and, taking Hallward by the arm, he almost led him into the house.

63 Improving housing for the urban poor of London's East End was a pet topic of late-nineteenth-century British philanthropists, but Wilde held a low opinion of such philanthropic work. In "The Soul of Man under Socialism," he writes that "the majority of people spoil their lives by an unhealthy and exaggerated altruism. . . . They very seriously and very sentimentally set themselves to the task of remedying the evils that they see. But their remedies do not cure the disease: they merely prolong it. Indeed their remedies are part of the disease" (p. 231).

64 In Wilde's day, well-to-do women assumed a central role as social activists in working-class districts such as London's East End. The English historian Jane Lewis writes that "taking a district" was "something that large numbers of young middle-class women felt obliged to do before marriage, and many carried on the work throughout their adult lives" (*Women and Social Action in Victorian and Edwardian England* [Stanford University Press, 1991], p. 10). According to Lewis, such work "remained within the bounds of propriety and middle-class women's sphere" while answering a felt need to serve others that was widely perceived to constitute women's main obligation as active citizens (p. 11). Despite Wilde's professed contempt for such work, he actively solicited a number of articles concerning urban activism among educated and middle-class women while editor of *Woman's World* in the years 1887–1889.

65 Lord Henry is amused at the ironic timing of the butler's announcement, which comes on the heels of Hallward's declaration, "I don't want you to meet him." Victorian social etiquette dictated that Hallward was obligated to introduce Lord Henry to another gentleman present in Hallward's house. The announcement of Dorian Gray's presence punctuates the long, emotionally tense discussion about the subject of Hallward's portrait, which takes up the entirety of the first chapter. Dorian's sudden appearance may amuse the reader as much as it does Lord Henry.

A Private View at the Royal Academy, 1881, oil painting by William Powell Frith,
R. A., first exhibited at the Royal Academy in 1883. Wilde himself is pictured, top-
hatted and gazing upward, toward the right. For Frith, the academy's vulgarity lay
not in the artwork it displayed but in the faddishness of the "aesthetic" crowd and
the cult of publicity that surrounded fine painting.

II

As they entered they saw Dorian Gray. He was seated at the piano, with his back to them, turning over the pages of a volume of Schumann's "Forest Scenes." "You must lend me these, Basil," he cried. "I want to learn them. They are perfectly charming."[1]

"That entirely depends on how you sit to-day, Dorian."

"Oh, I am tired of sitting, and I don't want a life-sized portrait of myself," answered the lad swinging round on the music-stool, in a wilful, petulant manner. When he caught sight of Lord Henry, a faint blush coloured his cheeks for a moment, and he started up. "I beg your pardon, Basil, but I didn't know you had any one with you."

"This is Lord Henry Wotton, Dorian, an old Oxford friend of mine. I have just been telling him what a capital sitter you were, and now you have spoiled everything."

"You have not spoiled my pleasure in meeting you, Mr. Gray," said Lord Henry, stepping forward and shaking him by the hand. "My aunt has often spoken to me about you. You are one of her favourites and, I am afraid, one of her victims also."

"I am in Lady Agatha's black books at present," answered Dorian, with a funny look of penitence. "I promised to go to her club in Whitechapel with her last Tuesday, and I really forgot all about it. We were to have played a duet together,—three duets, I believe.[2] I don't know what she will say to me. I am far too frightened to call."

"Oh, I will make your peace with my aunt. She is quite devoted to you. And I don't think it really matters about your not being there.

1 In "Loving Schumann," the French literary theorist and semiotician Roland Barthes writes that "Schumann is truly the musician of solitary intimacy, of the amorous and imprisoned soul that speaks to itself" (*The Responsibility of Forms,* trans. Richard Howard [Berkeley and Los Angeles: University of California Press, 1991], p. 293). Schumann was one of the most literary nineteenth-century composers: six of the nine pieces constituting his "Forest Scenes," or *Waldszenen* (opus 82), originally had verse fragments attached to them. His music stimulated literary Symbolism in France, leading the poet Camille Mauclair to declare that Schumann "realized everything the Symbolists only dreamed of" (quoted in John Daverio, *Robert Schumann: Herald of a New Poetic Age* [Oxford University Press, 1997], p. 491).

Aesthetic young men frequently show an interest in nineteenth-century piano music in Wilde's writings: *The Importance of Being Earnest* opens with Algernon playing the piano; and in "The Critic as Artist," Gilbert rises from the piano (where he has been playing Chopin), saying, "I feel as if I had been weeping over sins that I had never committed, and mourning over tragedies that are not my own. Music always seems to me to produce that effect. It creates for one a past of which one has been ignorant, and fills one with a sense of sorrows that have been hidden from one's tears. I can fancy a man who led a perfectly commonplace life, hearing by chance some curious piece of music, and suddenly discovering that his soul, without his being conscious of it, had passed through terrible experiences, and known fearful joys, or wild romantic loves, or great renunciations" (pp. 127–128).

2 Lady Agatha is a member of that "very advanced school" of philanthropists who "try to solve the problem of poverty . . . by amusing the poor" (Wilde, "The Soul of Man under Socialism," p. 232; in *A Woman of No Importance,* Wilde calls this trying to solve the problem of "slavery" by "amusing the slaves"). She might well also be a member of the People's Concert Society, established in 1878 by a group of well-intentioned amateurs who, "after a series of experiments in giving good music in the East End of London, founded this Society with the object of increasing the popularity of good music by means of cheap concerts" (*Grove's Dictionary of Music and Musicians,* ed. J. A. Fuller Maitland, 5 vols. [London: Macmillan, 1907], 3:670).

3 Britain had witnessed a rage for pianos, pianists, and piano music since the late eighteenth century. By the late Victorian period, when technological improvements and increased production had made the piano the dominant instrument in British cultural life and Steinway the model *par excellence,* "musicians, professional and amateur, almost fell over each other in their intense desire to explore and exploit the piano's potential for both brilliance and subtlety of expression" (Nicholas Temperley, Foreword to *The Piano in Nineteenth-Century British Culture: Instruments, Performers and Repertoire,* ed. T. Ellsworth and S. Wollenberg, [Ashgate, 2007], p. xv). Women especially relished the possibilities in the instrument: "there is no branch of art which has been so much cultivated by women as pianoforte-playing," remarks Frederick Corder in 1890 ("Women as Pianoforte Players," *Woman's World,* 3, [1890] 141), while Temperley notes the "intensity of feeling which some women, in particular, invested in their piano playing" (xvii).

4 "I like the society of young men," Wilde confessed during the course of his trials (H. Montgomery Hyde, *The Trials of Oscar Wilde* [2nd ed. 1962; rpt. New York:

Lord Alfred Douglas at twenty-one. When Edward Carson defended Douglas's father, the Marquess of Queensberry, against Wilde's charge of libel, he characterized Douglas as a young innocent, corrupted and dominated by Wilde's "vile, abominable passion" for him. But it was Douglas, with his penchant for "rough trade," who introduced Wilde to London's underworld of male prostitutes and homosexual procurers.

The audience probably thought it was a duet. When Aunt Agatha sits down to the piano she makes quite enough noise for two people."[3]

"That is very horrid to her, and not very nice to me," answered Dorian, laughing.

Lord Henry looked at him. Yes, he was certainly wonderfully handsome, with his finely-curved scarlet lips, his frank blue eyes, his crisp gold hair. There was something in his face that made one trust him at once. All the candour of youth was there, as well as all youth's passionate purity.[4] One felt that he had kept himself unspotted from the world. No wonder Basil Hallward worshipped him. He was made to be worshipped.[a]

"You are too charming to go in for philanthropy, Mr. Gray—far too charming." And Lord Henry flung himself down on the divan, and opened his cigarette-case.[5]

Dover Publications, 1973], p. 125): "I am a lover of youth . . . I like to study the young in everything. There is something fascinating in youthfulness" (pp. 202–203). In the wake of the Cleveland Street Scandal of 1889, in which Lord Henry Somerset, the Earl of Euston, and other aristocrats were found to have solicited sexual favors from an organized coterie of telegraph "boys" working at the Central Post Office, it was precisely this emphasis on Dorian Gray's youthfulness, or susceptibility to the "corruption" of an older man, that British reviewers found most objectionable about Wilde's novel. Similarly, it was Wilde's putative exploitation of the youthful Lord Alfred Douglas, and the apparent justice of Queensberry's attempts to protect his son, that Wilde's prosecutors emphasized during the course of his trials. An unsigned review in the *Daily Chronicle* calls *Dorian Gray* "a gloating study of the mental and physical corruption of a fresh, fair and golden youth" (rpt. in *Oscar Wilde: The Critical Heritage,* ed. K. Beckson, p. 72); and in summing up Queensberry's case in the failed libel suit, Edward Carson remarks of Douglas that "the young man was in a dangerous position" (Hyde, *The Trials of Oscar Wilde,* p. 143).

5 "I have a weakness for presenting my acquaintances with cigarette cases," Wilde declared during his first trial for gross indecency (Hyde, *The Trials of Oscar Wilde,* p. 204). Wilde gave silver cigarette cases to numerous young men in 1892 and 1893; when pressed by the prosecution about the expense of this habit, he replied that it was "less extravagant than giving jewelled garters to ladies" (p. 204).

"Dorian Gray," frontispiece to *The Picture of Dorian Gray,* intro. Osbert Burdett, illustr. Henry Keen (London and New York: John Lane / Dodd, Mead & Co., 1925).

Hallward had been busy mixing his colours and getting his brushes ready. He was looking worried, and when he heard Lord Henry's last remark he glanced at him, hesitated for a moment, and then said, "Harry, I want to finish this picture to-day. Would you think it awfully rude of me if I asked you to go away?"

Lifesize oil portrait of W. Graham Robertson, by John Singer Sargent, 1894. Sargent, a close neighbor of Wilde's in Chelsea, was one of the greatest portrait painters of Wilde's day. His portrait of the boyish-looking Robertson captures the essence of the fin-de-siècle dandy or aesthete. Robertson, a painter, illustrator, theater-designer, poet, and collector, was the costume designer for the abortive first production of *Salome,* in May 1892.

Lord Henry smiled, and looked at Dorian Gray. "Am I to go, Mr. Gray?" he asked.

"Oh, please don't, Lord Henry. I see that Basil is in one of his sulky moods; and I can't bear him when he sulks. Besides, I want you to tell me why I should not go in for philanthropy."

"I don't know that I shall tell you that, Mr. Gray. But I certainly will not run away, now that you have asked me to stop. You don't really mind, Basil, do you? You have often told me that you liked your sitters to have someone to chat to."

Hallward bit his lip. "If Dorian wishes it, of course you must stay. Dorian's whims are laws to everybody, except himself."

Lord Henry took up his hat and gloves. "You are very pressing, Basil, but I am afraid I must go. I have promised to meet a man at the Orleans.[6] Good-bye, Mr. Gray. Come and see me some afternoon in Curzon Street.[7] I am nearly always at home at five o'clock. Write to me when you are coming. I should be sorry to miss you."

"Basil," cried Dorian Gray. "If Lord Henry goes I shall go too. You never open your lips while you are painting, and it is horribly dull standing on a platform and trying to look pleasant.[8] Ask him to stay. I insist upon it."

"Stay, Harry, to oblige Dorian, and to oblige me," said Hallward, gazing intently at his picture. "It is quite true, I never talk when I am working and never listen either, and it must be dreadfully tedious for my unfortunate sitters. I beg you to stay."

"But what about my man at the Orleans?"

Hallward laughed. "I don't think there will be any difficulty about that. Sit down again, Harry. And now, Dorian, get up on the platform and don't move about too much, or pay any attention to what Lord Henry says. He has a very bad influence over all his friends, with the exception of myself."

Dorian stepped up on the dais, with the air of a young Greek martyr,[9] and made a little *moue* of discontent to Lord Henry, to whom he had rather taken a fancy. He was so unlike Hallward. They made a delightful contrast. And he had such a beautiful voice. After a few

6 The Orleans, a Mayfair club popular with sports-men, numbered the Marquis of Queensberry among its members. In *De Profundis,* Wilde writes to Douglas that "as for the costs of the trial . . . your father openly said in the Orleans Club that if it had cost him £20,000 he would have considered the money thoroughly well spent" (*CL,* p. 73).

7 In Victorian times, a number of prominent aristo-crats lived on Curzon Street, in the heart of London's expensive Mayfair district, including the writer and former Prime Minister Benjamin Disraeli, Lord Bea-consfield. It features prominently in a number of Wilde's works: Curzon Street is home to Lord Goring in *An Ideal Husband,* to Lady Clementina Beauchamp in "Lord Arthur Savile's Crime," and to Mrs. Erlynne in *Lady Windermere's Fan.* In Thackeray's *Vanity Fair,* Cur-zon Street is the fashionable residence of Becky Sharp and her husband.

8 "In New York, and even in Boston, a good model is so great a rarity that most of the artists are reduced to painting Niagara and millionaires. In Europe, however, it is different. The Italian models are the best. . . . The Italian youth . . . is often quite charming with his large melancholy eyes, his crisp hair, and his slim brown fig-ure. . . . He is always full of pretty compliments, and has been known to have kind words of encouragement for even our greatest artists. As for the English lad of the same age, he never sits at all. Apparently he does not regard the career of the model as a serious profes-sion. In any case he is rarely if ever to be got hold of. English boys too are difficult to find. . . . Occasionally an artist catches a couple of *gamins* in the gutter and asks them to come to his studio. The first time they al-ways appear, but after that they don't keep their ap-pointments. They dislike sitting still, and have a strong and perhaps natural objection to looking pathetic" (Wilde, "London Models").

9 Persecuted by the Romans but venerated as saints in the Catholic Church, the Greek martyrs were early Christian martyrs. In describing Dorian as possessed of "the air of a young Greek martyr," Wilde may have had in mind the martyrdom of St. Pantaleon of Nico-

media, who is depicted in a number of early-Renaissance Venetian paintings bound to an olive tree, both hands over his head nailed to the tree, and "uni-formly represented young, beardless, and of a beautiful countenance" (Anna Jameson, *Sacred and Legendary Art,* 3rd ed. [London: Longman, Brown, Green, 1857], p. 567). But Wilde almost certainly had in mind too Walter Pater's description of the early Christian mar-tyr Hyacinthus, as well as the near-martyrdom of Pat-er's hero Marius, in Pater's novel *Marius the Epicurean.* It is possible, too, that Wilde may have confused the Greek martyr St. Pantaleon with St. Sebastian, a paint-ing of whose martyrdom (by Guido Reni) he had seen and much admired in Genoa in 1877.

A house on Curzon Street, in the exclusive Mayfair district. Lord Henry Wotton lives on Curzon Street, the address of a number of prominent real-life Victori-ans, including British Prime Minister and novelist Benjamin Disraeli.

10 "Progress in thought is the assertion of individual-ism against authority," Wilde writes in his Common-place Book: "those organisms which are entirely sub-ject to external influences do not progress any more than a mind entirely subject to authority" (*Oscar Wilde's Oxford Notebooks,* ed. Philip E. Smith II and Michael S. Helfand [Oxford University Press, 1989], p. 121). In these ideas, Wilde was profoundly influenced by evolu-tionary science, especially as inflected in the sociologi-cal writings of Herbert Spencer and William Clifford.

11 Like many late-Victorians, Wilde was fascinated by the dynamics of interpersonal influence: "Influence is simply a transference of personality, a mode of giving away what is most precious in one's self, and its exer-cise produces a sense, and it may be, a reality of loss. Every disciple takes away something from his master" ("The Portrait of Mr. W. H.").

12 "If you wish to understand others, you must in-tensify your own individualism" ("The Critic as Artist," p. 165). Wilde earlier writes, "Law has its roots in cus-tom" and "custom in the psychological principle of im-itation and dependence on others" (*Oscar Wilde's Oxford Notebooks,* p. 117). By contrast, "individualism, or the at-tempt to affirm one's own essence, is a late product of matured civilization" (p. 117).

13 As Thomas Mann notes in 1947, "around the turn of the century the European intelligentsia was making its first head-on assault upon the hypocritical moral-ity of the middle-class Victorian age" ("Nietzsche's Philosophy in the Light of Recent History," in *Last Essays,* trans. R. Winston et al. [New York: Knopf, 1959], p. 157). Lord Henry's notion that "good" is a form of cowardice compares interestingly with Friedrich Nietzsche's question, "What if the 'good' man repre-sents not merely a retrogression but even a danger, a temptation, a narcotic drug enabling the present to live at the expense of the future? More comfortable, less hazardous, perhaps, but also baser, more petty—so that morality itself would be responsible for man, as a species, failing to reach the peak of magnificence of which he is capable? What if morality should turn out

moments he said to him, "Have you really a very bad influence, Lord Henry? As bad as Basil says?"

"There is no such thing as a good influence, Mr. Gray. All influ-ence is immoral—immoral from the scientific point of view."[10]

"Why?"

"Because to influence a person is to give him one's own soul. He does not think his natural thoughts, or burn with his natural pas-sions. His virtues are not real to him. His sins, if there are such things as sins, are borrowed. He becomes an echo of some one else's music, an actor of a part that has not been written for him.[11] The aim of life is self-development. To realise one's nature perfectly—that is what each of us is here for.[12] People are afraid of themselves, nowadays. They have forgotten the highest of all duties, the duty that one owes to oneself. Of course they are charitable. They feed the hungry, and clothe the beggar. But their own souls starve, and are naked. Cour-age has gone out of our race. Perhaps we never really had it. The ter-ror of society, which is the basis of morals, the terror of God, which is the secret of religion,—these are the two things that govern us.[13] And yet . . ."

"Just turn your head a little more to the right, Dorian, like a good boy," said Hallward, deep in his work, and conscious only that a look had come into the lad's face that he had never seen there be-fore.

"And yet,"[14] continued Lord Henry, in his low, musical voice, and with that graceful wave of the hand that was always so characteristic of him, and that he had even in his Eton days,[15] "I believe that if one man were to live his life out fully and completely, were to give form to every feeling, expression to every thought, reality to every dream —I believe that the world would gain such a fresh impulse of joy that we would forget all the maladies of mediaevalism, and return to the Hellenic ideal to something finer, richer, than the Hellenic ideal, it may be.[16] But the bravest man among us is afraid of himself. The mu-tilation of the savage has its tragic survival in the self-denial that mars our lives. We are punished for our refusals. Every impulse that we strive to strangle broods in the mind, and poisons us. The body to be the danger of dangers?" (*The Genealogy of Morals* [1887], in *The Birth of Tragedy and the Genealogy of Morals,* trans. F. Golffing [Garden City, NY: Doubleday Anchor, 1956], p. 155).

14 During the course of Wilde's unsuccessful libel suit against the Marquess of Queensberry in 1895, Queensberry's lawyer, Edward Carson, read out this and the ensuing five paragraphs in open court. For Carson, these six paragraphs constituted a crucial moment in the "story of a man corrupted by another man and who, by such corruption, is brought to commit . . . sodomitic vice" (*The Real Trial,* p. 261). The defense wished to demonstrate that Queensberry's allegedly libelous remark "posing sodomite" was justified. See *The Real Trial,* pp. 259–261.

15 Eton College, one of England's preeminent private schools for boys, drew its pupils largely from the aristocracy. In "The Portrait of Mr. W. H.," Erskine remarks, "There was . . . a good deal more play than work, but I cannot say I am sorry for that. It is always an advantage not to have received a sound commercial education, but what I learned in the playing fields at Eton has been quite as useful to me as anything I was taught at Cambridge."

16 Ancient Greece or the "Hellenic ideal" represented to many Victorians "the means of rescuing England from the uniformity and stagnation of industrial modernity" as well as a "vehicle for channeling modern progressive thought into the Victorian civic elite" (Dowling, *Hellenism and Homosexuality,* pp. 62, 64). For John Stuart Mill, fifth-century Athens represented a "picture of generous tolerance towards social dissent, and spontaneity of individual taste" (quoted in Dowling, *Hellenism and Homosexuality,* p. 61), while for Matthew Arnold Hellenism was characterized by a "play of thought" and "spontaneity of consciousness" contrasting sharply with "Hebraic" authoritarianism (quoted in *Hellenism and Homosexuality,* p. 78). Walter Pater defines the early Renaissance as the embrace of "that Hellenic ideal in which man is at unity with himself, with his physical nature, with the outward world" (*The Renaissance: Studies in Art and Poetry: The 1893 Text,* ed. Donald

Hill [Berkeley and Los Angeles: University of California Press, 1980], p. 177) and the "return from the overwrought spiritualities of the Middle Age to the earlier, more ancient life of the senses" ("Aesthetic Poetry" [1889]; rpt. in *An Anthology of Pre-Raphaelite Writings,* ed. C. Hares-Stryker [New York: New York University Press, 1997], p. 317). Recent scholarship has suggested that Arnold's and Mill's earlier liberal notion of Hellenism was adapted, in Wilde's writings as well as in the writings of John Addington Symonds and Walter Pater, into a legitimating discourse for homosexuality (see Dowling, *Hellenism and Homosexuality,* esp. pp. 117–154).

17 As Joseph Bristow points out, Lord Henry's remark echoes a "saying" quoted by an Oxford lecturer named Henry Grey in Mrs. Humphrey Ward's novel *Robert Elsmere*: "he would quote to me that saying he was always bringing into lectures—I forget whose it is—*the decisive events of the world take place in the intellect*" (Boston: Houghton and Dutton, 1888, p. 224). Bristow attributes the maxim to the Oxford philosopher T. H. Green, upon whom Mrs. Ward's fictional Henry Grey is modeled. But it is clear from the fact that Grey "quotes" the "saying," as well as from the narrator's dismissive comment, "I forget whose it is," that the remark does not originate with Green himself and must have been in wide circulation at Oxford in the 1880s. Wilde first invokes the saying (in the form given by Mrs. Ward) in his 1889 review "The New President." The saying also bears correspondence to the comment by Walter Pater, Green's close friend, that "the world is but a thought, or series of thoughts . . . it exists, therefore, solely in the mind" (*Imaginary Portraits, with "The Child in the House" and Gaston de Latour,* Intro. Bill Beckley [New York: Allworth, 1997], p. 76).

18 "I said in *Dorian Gray* that the great sins of the world take place in the brain, but it is in the brain that everything takes place. . . . It is in the brain that the poppy is red, that the apple is odorous, that the skylark sings" (*CL,* p. 748).

19 Along with the four paragraphs that follow it and the final two sentences of the previous one, this paragraph, inserted on a separate handwritten sheet, was a late addition to the typescript. This material does much to humanize Dorian by giving expression to his interior life. At the same time, it borrows heavily from Walter Pater's unfinished novel *Gaston de Latour* (serialized 1888–1889): "The gifted poet seemed but to have spoken what was already in Gaston's own mind, what he had longed to say, had been just going to say: so near it came, that it had the charm of a discovery of one's own. Perhaps that was because the poet told one so much about himself, making so free a display of what though personal was very contagious" (Pater, *Gaston de Latour: The Revised Text,* ed. G. Monsman [Greensboro, NC: ELT Press, 1995], p. 29).

sins once, and has done with its sin, for action is a mode of purification. Nothing remains then but the recollection of a pleasure, or the luxury of a regret. The only way to get rid of a temptation is to yield to it. Resist it—and your soul grows sick with longing for the things it has forbidden to itself, with desire for what its monstrous laws have made monstrous and unlawful. It has been said that the great events of the world take place in the brain.[17] It is in the brain, and the brain only, that the great sins of the world take place also.[18] You, Mr. Gray, you yourself, with your rose-red youth and your rose-white boyhood, you have had passions that have made you afraid, thoughts that have filled you with terror, day-dreams and sleeping dreams whose mere memory might stain your cheek with shame . . ."

"Stop!" murmured Dorian Gray, "Stop! You bewilder me. I don't know what to say. There is some answer to you, but I cannot find it. Don't speak. Let me think, or rather let me try not to think."

For nearly ten minutes he stood there motionless, with parted lips, and eyes strangely bright. He was dimly conscious that entirely fresh impulses were at work within him, and they seemed to him to have come really from himself. The few words that Basil's friend had said to him—words spoken by chance, no doubt, and with wilful paradox in them—had yet touched some secret chord, that had never been touched before, but that he felt was now vibrating and throbbing to curious pulses.[19]

Music had stirred him like that. Music had troubled him many times. But music was not articulate. It was not a new world, but rather a new chaos, that it created in us.[20] Words! Mere words! How terrible they were! How clear, and vivid, and cruel! One could not escape from them. And yet what a subtle magic there was in them! They seemed to be able to give a plastic form to formless things, and to have a music of their own as sweet as that of viol or of lute. Mere words! Was there anything so real as words?[21]

Yes: there had been things in his boyhood that he had not understood. He understood them now. Life suddenly became fiery-coloured to him. It seemed to him that he had been walking in fire.

Why had he not known it?

Lord Henry watched him, with his sad smile. He knew the precise psychological moment when to say nothing. He felt intensely interested.[22] He was amazed at the sudden impression that his words had produced, and, remembering a book that he had read when he was sixteen, which had revealed to him much that he had not known before, he wondered whether Dorian Gray was passing through the same experience. He had merely shot an arrow into the air. Had it hit the mark? How fascinating the lad was!

Hallward painted away with that marvellous bold touch of his, that had the true refinement and perfect delicacy that come only from strength. He was unconscious of the silence.

"Basil, I am tired of standing," cried Dorian Gray, suddenly. "I must go out and sit in the garden. The air is stifling here."

"My dear fellow, I am so sorry. When I am painting, I can't think of anything else. But you never sat better. You were perfectly still. And I have caught the effect I wanted, the half-parted lips, and the bright look in the eyes. I don't know what Harry has been saying to you, but he has certainly made you have the most wonderful expression. I suppose he has been paying you compliments. You mustn't believe a word that he says."

"He has certainly not been paying me compliments. Perhaps that is the reason I don't think I believe anything he has told me."

"You know you believe it all," said Lord Henry, looking at him, with his dreamy, heavy-lidded eyes. "I will go out to the garden with you. It is horridly hot in the studio. Basil, let us have something iced to drink, something with strawberries in it."

"Certainly, Harry. Just touch the bell, and when Parker comes I will tell him what you want. I have got to work up this background, so I will join you later on. Don't keep Dorian too long. I have never been in better form for painting than I am to-day. This is going to be my masterpiece. It is my masterpiece as it stands."

Lord Henry went out to the garden, and found Dorian Gray burying his face in the great cool lilac-blossoms, feverishly drinking in their perfume as if it had been wine.[23] He came close to him, and put

20 *Dorian Gray* contains many references to music. While these references often draw on popular late-Victorian attitudes to music, they have been seen by one recent scholar as emblems of Wilde's "perniciously homosexual art": "music—or, more precisely, the idea of music—is intended to suggest more than itself. . . . As an inarticulate medium with the power to stir and trouble while it seems to communicate some indefinite message, music is an ideal emblem for that which could not be named but would be recognized by those who shared in it" (Joe Law, "'The Perniciously Homosexual Art': Music and Homoerotic Desire in *The Picture of Dorian Gray* and Other Fin-de-Siècle Fiction," in *The Idea of Music in Victorian Fiction,* ed. S. Fuller and N. Losseff [Ashgate, 2004], pp. 180–196).

21 "Yes, that was the reason why visible, audible, sensible things glowed so brightly, why there was such luxury in sounds, words, rhythms, of the new light come on the world, of that wonderful freshness. With a masterly appliance of what was near and familiar . . . he found new words for perennially new things, and the novel accent awakened long-slumbering associations. Never before had words, single words, meant so much. What expansion, what liberty of heart, in speech: how associable to music!" (Pater, *Gaston de Latour: The Revised Text,* ed. Monsman, p. 29).

22 Lord Henry brings a combination of intellectual detachment and pleasure to the task of influencing Dorian that is positively Mephistophelian in its connotations. Later, he will refer to Dorian as his "own creation." Lord Henry knows that there are moral consequences to the advice he gives Dorian, but he finds "an exquisite pleasure in playing on the lad's unconscious egotism." There has been much critical speculation about what motivates this combination of pleasure and detachment—about whether it is a sublimated expression of erotic desire, whether it has a purely philosophic or pedagogic basis, or whether it is a sign of Lord Henry's own moral corruption. In filmed adaptations of Wilde's novel, different actors have answered these questions differently. John Gielgud emphasizes Lord Henry's philosophic and erotic motivations in his performance for the BBC in 1976, for instance; by contrast, in his performance for Oliver Parker's 2009 film

adaptation, Colin Firth dramatizes a demonic and Me-phistophelian element.

23 In the language of flowers, purple lilacs symbolize the first emotions of love, while white lilacs represent youthful innocence. The lilacs whose perfume Dorian drinks like wine are purple, we discover later in this chapter.

24 As Wilde makes clear in Chapter III, this idea derives from the pantheistic theology of Giordano Bruno. Interest in the Italian philosopher Giordiano Bruno (1548–1600) peaked in the late 1880s, when a number of books and articles devoted to him appeared and a statue of Bruno was erected by international subscription in Rome. Wilde would have known Walter Pater's essay "Giordano Bruno. Paris: 1586," published in *Fortnightly Review*, n.s. 46 (August 1889), subsequently revised as a chapter titled "The Lower Pantheism" in Pater's posthumously published, unfinished novel *Gaston de Latour.*

25 "The condition of perfection is idleness: the aim of perfection is youth" (Wilde, "Phrases and Philosophies for the Use of the Young").

26 The notion that beauty is a form of genius underwrites many Pre-Raphaelite poems and paintings, notably Dante Gabriel Rossetti's sonnet "Genius in Beauty," where Rossetti writes (reflecting upon a portrait of an unnamed woman), "Beauty like hers is genius" and "the unenvenomed years . . ./Upon this beauty's power shall wreak no wrong" (*Collected Poetry and Prose,* ed. Jerome McGann [New Haven: Yale University Press, 2003], p. 135). Wilde's admiration for Rossetti's poetry is clear from "A Cheap Edition of a Great Man," his review of a poor biography of Rossetti, as well as from "The Critic as Artist."

27 "Only the shallow know themselves" (Wilde, "Phrases and Philosophies").

28 This is an extension, as well as a reversal, of Plato's notion that "it is only when he discerns beauty itself through what makes it visible that a man will be quickened with the true, and not the seeming, virtue" (Plato,

his hand upon his shoulder. "You are quite right to do that," he murmured. "Nothing can cure the soul but the senses, just as nothing can cure the senses but the soul."[24]

The lad started and drew back. He was bare-headed, and the leaves had tossed his rebellious curls, and tangled all their gilded threads. There was a look of fear in his eyes, such as people have when they are suddenly awakened. His finely-chiselled nostrils quivered, and some hidden nerve shook the scarlet of his lips, and left them trembling.

"Yes," continued Lord Henry, "that is one of the great secrets of life—to cure the soul by means of the senses, and the senses by means of the soul. You are a wonderful creature. You know more than you think you know, just as you know less than you want to know."

Dorian Gray frowned and turned his head away. He could not help liking the tall, graceful young man who was standing by him. His romantic olive-coloured face and worn expression interested him. There was something in his low, languid voice that was absolutely fascinating. His cool, white, flower-like hands, even, had a curious charm. They moved, as he spoke, like music, and seemed to have a language of their own. But he felt afraid of him, and ashamed of being afraid. Why had it been left for a stranger to reveal him to himself? He had known Basil Hallward for months, but the friendship between them had never altered him. Suddenly there had come some one across his life who seemed to have disclosed to him life's mystery. And, yet, what was there to be afraid of? He was not a schoolboy, or a girl. It was absurd to be frightened.

"Let us go and sit in the shade," said Lord Henry. "Parker has brought out the drinks, and if you stay any longer in this glare you will be quite spoiled, and Basil will never paint you again. You really must not let yourself become sunburnt. It would be very unbecoming to you."

"What does it matter?" cried Dorian, laughing, as he sat down on the seat at the end of the garden.

"It should matter everything to you, Mr. Gray."

"Why?"

"Because you have now the most marvellous youth, and youth is the one thing worth having."[25]

"I don't feel that, Lord Henry."

"No, you don't feel it now. Someday, when you are old and wrinkled and ugly, when thought has seared your forehead with its lines, and passion branded your lips with its hideous fires, you will feel it, you will feel it terribly. Now, wherever you go, you charm the world. Will it always be so?

"You have a wonderfully beautiful face, Mr. Gray. Don't frown. You have. And Beauty is a form of Genius, is higher indeed than Genius, as it needs no explanation.[26] It is one of the great facts of the world, like sunlight, or spring-time, or the reflection in dark waters of that silver shell we call the moon. It cannot be questioned. It has its Divine right of sovereignty. It makes princes of those who have it. You smile? Ah! when you have lost it you won't smile.

"People say sometimes that Beauty is only superficial. That may be so. But at least it is not so superficial as Thought. To me, Beauty is the wonder of wonders. It is only shallow people who do not judge by appearances.[27] The true mystery of the world is the visible, not the invisible.[28]

"Yes, Mr. Gray, the gods have been good to you. But what the gods give they quickly take away. You have only a few years in which to really live. When your youth goes, your beauty will go with it, and then you will suddenly discover that there are no triumphs left for you, or have to content yourself with those mean triumphs that the memory of your past will make more bitter than defeats. Every month as it wanes brings you nearer to something dreadful. Time is jealous of you, and wars against your lilies and your roses. You will become sallow, and hollow-cheeked, and dull-eyed. You will suffer horribly.

"Realise your youth while you have it. Don't squander the gold of your days, listening to the tedious, trying to improve the hopeless failure, or giving away your life to the ignorant, the common, and the vulgar, which are the aims, the false ideals of our age. Live! Live the wonderful life that is in you! Let nothing be lost upon you. Be always searching for new sensations. Be afraid of nothing.[29]

Symposium, in *Plato: The Collected Dialogues,* ed. E. Hamilton and H. Cairns [Princeton University Press, 1961], p. 563). As Linda Dowling demonstrates, Wilde was an accomplished classicist, his temper formed by the thoroughgoing knowledge of Plato demanded of him by the "Greats" curriculum at Oxford (where he studied from 1874 to 1878). For Plato, the perception of beauty triggers anamnesis, a reminiscence of the "forms" where truth resides. For Lord Henry, however, the perception of beauty ("the visible") remains an end or "mystery" in itself.

29 "What we have to do is to be for ever testing new opinions and courting new impressions. . . . We are all *condamnés,* as Victor Hugo says: we are all under death with a sort of indefinite reprieve . . . we have an interval, and then our place knows us no more. Some spend this interval in listlessness, some in high passions, the wisest, at least among 'the children of this world,' in art and song. For our one chance lies in getting as many pulsations as possible into the given time" (Pater, *The Renaissance,* ed. Hill, pp. 189–190).

Photo of Walter Pater, taken at Oxford around the time he published his controversial book *The Renaissance* (1873). No other writer casts as long a shadow over Wilde's life and work as Pater.

"A new Hedonism![30] That is what our century wants. You might be its visible symbol. With your personality there is nothing you could not do. The world belongs to you for a season.

"The moment I met you I saw that you were quite unconscious of what you really are, what you really might be. There was so much about you that charmed me that I felt I must tell you something about yourself. I thought how tragic it would be if you were wasted. For there is such a little time that your youth will last, such a little time.

"The common hill-flowers wither, but they blossom again. The laburnum will be as golden next June as it is now. In a month there will be purple stars on the clematis, and year after year the green night of its leaves will have its purple stars. But we never get back our youth. The pulse of joy that beats in us at twenty becomes sluggish. Our limbs fail, our senses rot. We degenerate into hideous puppets, haunted by the memory of the passions of which we were too much afraid, and the exquisite temptations that we did not dare to yield to. Youth! Youth! There is absolutely nothing in the world but youth!"

Dorian Gray listened, open-eyed and wondering. The spray of lilac fell from his hand upon the gravel. A furry bee came and buzzed round it for a moment. Then it began to scramble all over the fretted purple of the tiny blossoms. He watched it with that strange interest in trivial things that we try to develop when things of high import make us afraid, or when we are stirred by some new emotion, for which we cannot find expression, or when some thought that terrifies us lays sudden siege to the brain and calls on us to yield.[31] After a time it flew away. He saw it creeping into the stained trumpet of a Tyrian convolvulus. The flower seemed to quiver, and then swayed gently to and fro.

Suddenly Hallward appeared at the door of the studio, and made frantic signs for them to come in. They turned to each other and smiled.

"I am waiting," cried Hallward. "Do come in. The light is quite perfect, and you can bring your drinks."

They rose up, and sauntered down the walk together. Two green-and-white butterflies fluttered past them, and in the pear-tree at the end of the garden a thrush began to sing.

"You are glad you have met me, Mr. Gray," said Lord Henry, looking at him.

"Yes, I am glad now. I wonder shall I always be glad?"

"Always! That is a dreadful word. It makes me shudder when I hear it. Women are so fond of using it. They spoil every romance by trying to make it last for ever. It is a meaningless word, too. The only difference between a caprice, and a life-long passion, is that the caprice lasts a little longer."

As they entered the studio, Dorian Gray put his hand upon Lord Henry's arm. "In that case, let our friendship be a caprice," he murmured, flushing at his own boldness, then stepped upon the platform and resumed his pose.

Lord Henry flung himself into a large wicker arm-chair, and watched him. The sweep and dash of the brush on the canvas made the only sound that broke the stillness, except when Hallward stepped back now and then, to look at his work from a distance. In the silent, slanting beams that streamed through the open door-way, the dust danced and was golden. The heavy scent of the roses seemed to brood over everything.

After about a quarter of an hour, Hallward stopped painting, looked for a long time at Dorian Gray, and then for a long time at the picture, biting the end of one of his huge brushes, and smiling. "It is quite finished," he cried, at last, and stooping down he wrote his name in thin vermilion letters on the left-hand corner of the canvas.

Lord Henry came over and examined the picture. It was certainly a wonderful work of art, and a wonderful likeness as well.

"My dear fellow, I congratulate you most warmly," he said. "Mr. Gray, come and look at yourself."

The lad started, as if awakened from some dream. "Is it really finished?" he murmured, stepping down from the platform.

"Quite finished," said Hallward. "And you have sat splendidly to-day. I am awfully obliged to you."

"That is entirely due to me," broke in Lord Henry. "Isn't it, Mr. Gray?"

Dorian made no answer, but passed listlessly in front of his picture and turned towards it. When he saw it he drew back, and his cheeks flushed for a moment with pleasure. A look of joy came into

30 Lord Henry espouses a much more radical and cartoonish version of the "Aesthetic" philosophy than that articulated by Pater. In his influential Conclusion to *The Renaissance,* Pater urges his readers to cultivate a heightened receptivity to beauty and the splendor of experience: "Not the fruit of experience, but experience itself, is the end. A counted number of pulses only is given to us in a variegated, dramatic life. How may we see in them all that is to be seen by the finest senses? . . . To burn always with this hard, gemlike flame, to maintain the ecstasy, is success in life. In a sense, it might even be said that our failure is to form habits" (*The Renaissance,* ed. Hill, pp. 188–189). When it was published in 1873, Pater's book was widely criticized for promoting hedonism. Pater withdrew the Conclusion from his second edition, but not before it had already done harm to his reputation and academic career. In a note to the third edition of 1888, Pater writes, "This brief 'Conclusion' was omitted in the second edition of this book, as I conceived it might possibly mislead some of those young men into whose hands it might fall" (*The Renaissance,* ed. Hill, p. 186).

In an effort to show that his aesthetic philosophy had been unfairly characterized as amoral, Pater turned to fiction to exemplify and further clarify his ideas. In *Marius the Epicurean,* Pater's narrator specifically cautions against using the word *hedonism* to describe a philosophy of pleasure because "that reproachful Greek term" is too "large and vague" to be conducive "to any very delicately correct ethical conclusions" (*Marius the Epicurean: His Sensations and Ideas,* ed. Gerald Monsman [Kansas City: Vallancourt Books, 2008], p. 100). In trying to "reconcile the artistic life with the life of religion," Wilde writes, Pater made his central character, Marius, "little more than a spectator" (*CL,* p. 740). By labeling Lord Henry's indulgent philosophy a "new Hedonism," Wilde criticizes his intellectual progenitor for his timidity while paying (dubious) homage to him. Pater cannot have been pleased.

31 An idea that finds common expression in Pre-Raphaelite poetry. See, for instance, Dante Gabriel Rossetti's poem "The Woodspurge," in which relief from "perfect grief" is found in the poet's observation of a flowered weed (the "woodspurge"), which has "three cups in one" (*Collected Poetry and Prose,* ed. McGann, p. 177).

32 "The test of a portrait is not whether it attracts attention on the walls of an exhibition, but how far it succeeds, in the house where it is meant to live, in telling its story of sympathy and comprehension through years of silent appeal" (Walter Sickert, rev. of Royal Academy Summer Exhibition, May 15, 1897, rpt. in *Walter Sickert: The Complete Writings on Art*, ed. A. G. Robins [Oxford University Press, 2000], p. 168).

33 Faust, the legendary German astrologer, sells his soul to the Devil in exchange for knowledge and power. Dorian does not realize it, but he has entered a Faustian pact (with Lord Henry—or perhaps with the devilish author of *Dorian Gray*) in expressing his willingness to "give everything" for eternal youth. Irish folklore may play a part, too, in Wilde's creation of unaging youth. According to David Upchurch, the desire to remain forever young has "long been a concern of the Irish folklore tradition. . . . In fact, *Dorian Gray* is an inverted retelling of the *Tír na Nóg* [Land of Youth] theme. Dorian, like Oisín . . . does not age, but the world goes on" (Upchurch, *Wilde's Use of Celtic Elements in "The Picture of Dorian Gray"* [New York: Peter Lang, 1993], p. 24). Critics have long noted the similarities between *Dorian Gray* and the Gothic novel *Melmoth the Wanderer* (1820), by the Irish writer Charles Maturin (Wilde's maternal grand-uncle), in which the eponymous hero buys an extended life and remains youthful as a result of a pact with the Devil. Kerry Powell ("Tom, Dick, and Dorian Gray: Magic-Picture Mania in Late Victorian Fiction," *Philological Quarterly,* 62 [1983], pp. 147–170) detects the influence too of "magic-portrait" fiction from the 1880s—particularly those works in which a Faustian motif features, such as Anton Giulio Barrili's *Devil's Portrait* (1885), Carrick F. Brodie's *Hidden Picture* (1884), and Elizabeth Lysaght's *Veiled Picture* (1889). Whatever the exact combination of influences on Wilde, "the idea of a young man selling his soul in exchange for eternal youth [is] old in the history of literature," as Wilde himself remarks, though it is one "to which I have given a new form" (*CL,* p. 435).

his eyes, as if he had recognized himself for the first time. He stood there motionless, and in wonder, dimly conscious that Hallward was speaking to him, but not catching the meaning of his words. The sense of his own beauty came on him like a revelation.[32] He had never felt it before. Basil Hallward's compliments had seemed to him to be merely the charming exaggerations of friendship. He had listened to them, laughed at them, forgotten them. They had not influenced his nature. Then had come Lord Henry, with his strange panegyric on youth, his terrible warning of its brevity. That had stirred him at the time, and now, as he stood gazing at the shadow of his own loveliness, the full reality of the description flashed across him. Yes: there would be a day when his face would be wrinkled and wizen, his eyes dim and colourless, the grace of his figure broken and deformed. The scarlet would pass away from his lips, and the gold steal from his hair. The life that was to make his soul would mar his body. He would become ignoble, hideous, and uncouth.

As he thought of it, a sharp pang of pain struck like a knife across him, and made each delicate fibre of his nature quiver. His eyes deepened into amethyst, and a mist of tears came across them. He felt as if a hand of ice had been laid upon his heart.

"Don't you like it?" cried Hallward at last, stung a little by the lad's silence, and not understanding what it meant.

"Of course he likes it," said Lord Henry. "Who wouldn't like it? It is one of the greatest things in modern art. I will give you anything you like to ask for it. I must have it."

"It is not my property, Harry."

"Whose property is it?"

"Dorian's, of course."

"He is a very lucky fellow."

"How sad it is!" murmured Dorian Gray, with his eyes still fixed upon his own portrait. "How sad it is! I shall grow old, and horrid, and dreadful. But this picture will remain always young. It will never be older than this particular day of June. . . . If it was only the other way! If it was I who were to be always young, and the picture that were to grow old! For this—for this—I would give everything! Yes: there is nothing in the whole world I would not give!"[33]

"You would hardly care for that arrangement, Basil," cried Lord Henry laughing. "It would be rather hard lines on you."

"I should object very strongly, Harry."

Dorian Gray turned and looked at him. "I believe you would, Basil. You like your art better than your friends. I am no more to you than a green bronze figure. Hardly as much, I dare say."

Hallward stared in amazement. It was so unlike Dorian to speak like that. What had happened? He seemed almost angry. His face was flushed and his cheeks burning.

"Yes," he continued, "I am less to you than your ivory Hermes, or your silver Faun. You will like them always.[34] How long will you like me? Till I have my first wrinkle, I suppose. I know now that when one loses one's good looks, whatever they may be, one loses everything. Your picture has taught me that. Lord Henry is perfectly right. Youth is the only thing worth having. When I find that I am growing old, I will kill myself."[35]

Hallward turned pale, and caught his hand. "Dorian! Dorian!" he cried, "don't talk like that. I have never had such a friend as you, and I shall never have such another. You are not jealous of material things, are you?"

"I am jealous of everything whose beauty does not die. I am jealous of the portrait you have painted of me. Why should it keep what I must lose? Every moment that passes takes something from me, and gives something to it. Oh, if it was only the other way! If the picture could change, and I could be always what I am now! Why did you paint it? It will mock me some day, mock me horribly!" The hot tears welled into his eyes; he tore his hand away, and, flinging himself on the divan, he buried his face in the cushions, as if he was praying.

"This is your doing, Harry," said Hallward, bitterly.

"My doing?"

"Yes, yours, and you know it."

Lord Henry shrugged his shoulders. "It is the real Dorian Gray, that is all," he answered.

"It is not."

"If it is not, what have I to do with it?"

"You should have gone away, when I asked you."

34 Wilde kept a plaster cast of the Hermes of Praxiteles in his Tite Street study, though he told Charles Ricketts that "the plaster did not retain the beauty and transparency of the marble, which is like ivory lit by the sun" (*Oscar Wilde: Recollections by Jean Paul Raymond and Charles Ricketts* [Nonesuch Press, 1932], p. 35).

35 "If I were not afraid that my people might keep it out of the newspapers, I would kill myself tomorrow" (Max Beerbohm to Will Rothenstein, October 22, 1893, in *Max and Will: Max Beerbohm and Will Rothenstein, Their Friendship and Letters, 1893–1945,* ed. Mary M. Lago and Karl Beckson [Cambridge, MA: Harvard University Press, 1975], p. 21). In his discussion of the suicide craze affecting British literature in the early 1890s, John Stokes calls *Dorian Gray* "a novel shot through with self-inflicted deaths" ("'Tired of Life': Letters, Literature and the Suicide Craze," in Stokes, *In the Nineties* [University of Chicago Press, 1989], p. 142).

36 Dorian will later use a knife to kill Basil and then again, in a single self-obliterating stroke, to destroy himself and the portrait. The astute reader will note that it will be murder if Basil *doesn't* destroy the portrait.

The Hermes of Praxiteles, 343 B.C.E. Discovered beneath several meters of earth, it is the only known surviving work of Praxiteles. It depicts Hermes, the messenger of the Gods, holding the infant Dionysos. Wilde owned a plaster caste of the statue. According to Robert Ross, Wilde claimed that he had been present at its unearthing, which took place at Olympia, in Greece, in 1877, shortly after Wilde's visit there in the same year.

"I stayed when you asked me."

"Harry, I can't quarrel with my two best friends at once, but between you both you have made me hate the finest piece of work I have ever done, and I will destroy it. What is it but canvas and colour? I will not let it come across our three lives and mar them."

Dorian Gray lifted his golden head from the pillow, and looked at him with pallid face and tear-stained eyes, as he walked over to the deal painting-table that was set beneath the large curtained window. What was he doing there? His fingers were straying about, among the litter of tin tubes and dry brushes, seeking for something. Yes, it was the long palette-knife, with its thin blade of lithe steel. He had found it at last. He was going to rip up the canvas.

With a stifled sob he leapt from the couch, and, rushing over to Hallward, tore the knife out of his hand, and flung it to the end of the studio. "Don't, Basil, don't!" he cried. "It would be murder!"[36]

"I am glad you appreciate my work at last, Dorian," said Hallward, coldly, when he had recovered from his surprise. "I never thought you would."

"Appreciate it? I am in love with it, Basil. It is part of myself, I feel that."

"Well, as soon as you are dry, you shall be varnished, and framed, and sent home. Then you can do what you like with yourself." And he walked across the room and rang the bell for tea. "You will have tea, of course, Dorian? And so will you, Harry? Tea is the only simple pleasure left to us."

"I don't like simple pleasures," said Lord Henry. "And I don't like scenes, except on the stage. What absurd fellows you are, both of you! I wonder who it was defined man as a rational animal.[37] It was the most premature definition ever given. Man is many things, but he is not rational.[38] I am glad he is not, after all: though I wish you chaps would not squabble over the picture. You had much better let me have it, Basil. This silly boy doesn't really want it, and I do."

"If you let anyone have it but me, Basil, I will never forgive you!" cried Dorian Gray. "And I don't allow people to call me a silly boy."

"You know the picture is yours, Dorian. I gave it to you before it existed."

"And you know you have been a little silly, Mr. Gray, and that you don't really mind being called a boy."[39]

"I should have minded very much this morning, Lord Henry."

"Ah! this morning! You have lived since then."

There came a knock to the door, and the butler entered with the tea-tray, and set it down upon a small Japanese table. There was a rattle of cups and saucers and the hissing of a fluted Georgian urn. Two globe-shaped china dishes were brought in by a page. Dorian Gray went over and poured the tea out.[40] The two men sauntered languidly to the table, and examined what was under the covers.[41]

"Let us go to the theatre to-night," said Lord Henry. "There is sure to be something on, somewhere. I have promised to dine at White's,[42] but it is only with an old friend, so I can send him a wire and say that I am ill, or that I am prevented from coming in consequence of a subsequent engagement. I think that would be a rather nice excuse —it would have the surprise of candour."

"It is such a bore putting on one's dress-clothes," muttered Hallward. "And, when one has them on, they are so horrid."

"Yes," answered Lord Henry, dreamily, "the costume of our day is detestable. It is so sombre, so depressing.[43] Sin is the only colour-element left in modern life."

"You really must not say things like that before Dorian, Harry."

"Before which Dorian? The one who is pouring out tea for us, or the one in the picture?"

"Before either."

"I should like to come to the theatre with you, Lord Henry," said the lad.

"Then you shall come; and you will come too, Basil, won't you?"

"I can't, really. I would sooner not. I have a lot of work to do."

"Well, then, you and I will go alone, Mr. Gray."

"I should like that awfully."

Basil Hallward bit his lip and walked over, cup in hand, to the picture. "I will stay with the real Dorian," he said, sadly.

"Is it the real Dorian?" cried the original of the portrait, running across to him. "Am I really like that?"

"Yes; you are just like that."

37 It was Aristotle (384–322 B.C.E.) in his *Metaphysics* who first offered the definition of man as a rational animal.

38 "One is tempted to define man as a rational animal who always loses his temper when his is called upon to act according to the dictates of reason" ("The Critic as Artist," p. 183).

39 In the 1890s, an older man calling a young man a "boy" was frequently understood as a veiled announcement of homosexual or homosocial desire. The nickname of Wilde's lover Lord Alfred Douglas, "Bosie," originally given to him in childhood (in the form "Boysie"), derives from the word *boy*.

40 There were elaborate rituals to Victorian tea-serving, and the office of pouring out tea—too important to be filled by a servant, according to *Cassell's Book of the Household* (London: Cassells, 1889–1891), 3:95–96 —was usually performed by a woman. "If five o'clock tea is to be made thoroughly enjoyable," etiquette dictated, "the necessaries connected with it must be as pretty and inviting-looking as possible" (*Cassell's Book,* 3:95).

41 "I hate people who are not serious about meals. It is so shallow of them" (*The Importance of Being Earnest*).

42 White's, still the most exclusive of Pall Mall clubs, was in the nineteenth century "*the* club where, in dandy existence, either you must live or have no life" (quoted in Ellen Moers, *The Dandy: Brummell to Beerbohm* [Lincoln: University of Nebraska Press, 1960], p. 42). Beau Brummell had been a member; and in Regency times, Lord Alvanley had famously made a bet of £3,000 with a friend there, while seated in front of the club's famous bow window, as to which of two raindrops would reach the bottom of the windowpane first.

43 "Where there is loveliness of dress, there is no dressing up. And so, were our national attire delightful in colour, and in construction simple and sincere; were dress the expression of the loveliness that it shields . . . then would painting be no longer an artificial reaction against the ugliness of life, but become, as it should be, the natural expression of life's beauty" ("The Relation

of Dress to Art"). Wilde lectured on dress for much of 1884 and 1885 and wrote frequently on the topic. Articles on dress were a conspicuous feature of *Woman's World* during Wilde's tenure as editor (1887–1889).

"How wonderful, Basil!"

"At least you are like it in appearance. But it will never alter," said Hallward. "That is something."

"What a fuss people make about fidelity," murmured Lord Henry. "And after all, it is purely a question for physiology. It has nothing to do with our own will. It is either an unfortunate accident, or an unpleasant result of temperament. Young men want to be faithful and are not; old men want to be faithless, and cannot: that is all one can say."

"Don't go to the theatre to-night, Dorian," said Hallward. "Stop and dine with me."

"I can't really."

"Why?"

"Because I have promised Lord Henry to go with him."

"He won't like you better for keeping your promises. He always breaks his own. I beg you not to go."

Dorian Gray laughed and shook his head.

A hansom cab, designed and patented in 1834 by Joseph Hansom. Like the earlier hackney carriage which it replaced, the hansom cab was a vehicle for hire. It was ubiquitous in London's streets in Wilde's day.

"I entreat you."

The lad hesitated, and looked over at Lord Henry, who was watching them from the tea-table with an amused smile.

"I must go, Basil," he answered.

"Very well," said Hallward; and he walked over and laid his cup down on the tray. "It is rather late, and, as you have to dress, you had better lose no time. Good-bye, Harry. Good-bye, Dorian. Come and see me soon. Come to-morrow."

"Certainly."

"You won't forget?"

"No, of course not."

"And . . . Harry!"

"Yes, Basil?"

"Remember what I asked you, when we were in the garden this morning."

"I have forgotten it."

"I trust you."

"I wish I could trust myself," said Lord Henry, laughing. "Come, Mr. Gray, my hansom⁴⁴ is outside, and I can drop you at your own place. Good-bye, Basil. It has been a most interesting afternoon."

As the door closed behind them, Hallward flung himself down on a sofa, and a look of pain came into his face.

44 A private horse-drawn carriage for hire, akin to a modern taxi. In "The Ballad of an Omnibus" (1889), the poet Amy Levy characterizes hansoms as masculine, luxurious, and unpoetic. In Wilde's story "The Model Millionaire," the impoverished Hughie Erskine gives away a sovereign even though "it means no hansoms for a fortnight."

Aubrey Beardsley, "The Peacock Skirt," line-engraved illustration to Wilde's *Salome, A Tragedy in One Act,* trans. Lord Alfred Douglas (Elkin Mathews and John Lane, 1894). A graphic artist of the first rank, Beardsley refused to consider himself merely an illustrator, insisting that the books he pictured were "embellished" or "embroidered" by his art. The picture corresponds to nothing in *Salome* itself, but it demands to be seen; and in its mastery of line and its sinuous curves, it anticipates Art Nouveau.

III

ONE AFTERNOON, A MONTH LATER, Dorian Gray was reclining in a luxurious arm-chair, in the little library of Lord Henry's house in Curzon Street. It was, in its way, a very charming room with its high panelled wainscoting of olive-stained oak, its cream-coloured frieze and ceiling of raised plaster-work, and its brick-dust felt carpet strewn with long-fringed silk Persian rugs. On a tiny satinwood table stood a statuette by Clodion,[1] and beside it lay a copy of "Les Cent Nouvelles,"[2] bound for Margaret of Valois[3] by Clovis Eve, and powdered with the gilt daisies that the Queen had selected for her device.[4] Some large blue china jars, filled with parrot-tulips, were ranged on the mantel-shelf, and through the small leaded panes of the window streamed the apricot-coloured light of a summer's day in London.[5]

Lord Henry had not come in yet. He was always late on principle, his principle being that punctuality is the thief of time.[6] So the lad was looking rather sulky, as with listless fingers he turned over the pages of an elaborately-illustrated edition of "Manon Lescaut"[7] that he had found in one of the bookcases. The formal monotonous ticking of the Louis Quatorze clock annoyed him. Once or twice he thought of going away.

At last he heard a light step outside, and the door opened. "How late you are, Harry!" he murmured.

"I am afraid it is not Harry, Mr. Gray," said a woman's voice.

1 Claude Michel, called Clodion, the French rococo sculptor of the late eighteenth century, was much in vogue in the 1880s, especially in France. He is known principally for his charming terracotta statuettes and decorative work.

2 *Les Cents Nouvelles Nouvelles* (The Hundred New Tales), one of the most important monuments of Middle French prose, is a miscellany of racy tales dating from the mid-1460s. The tales were initially told by various speakers at the court of Philip the Good, Duke of Burgundy (1396–1467), then subsequently written down, possibly as a gift for the duke, by an anonymous author-compiler.

3 Marguerite of Valois (1553–1615), or "La Reine Margot," wife of Henry of Navarre, daughter of Henri II of France and Catherine de Medici, was one of the most interesting and complex women of the Renaissance, vilified for her promiscuity and praised for her beauty, courage, and intelligence. Her court was known for its cultural and intellectual brilliance. Ste. Beuve describes the "exquisite pages" of her *Memoirs*—one of the first autobiographies ever written by a woman—as "an epoch in our language . . . by reason of which an enduring radiance will cling to her name" (quoted in the Introduction to *Memoirs of Marguerite de Valois, Queen of Navarre,* ed., trans., and intro. Violet Fane [London: Nimmo, 1892], p. 56). In the Introduction to her translation of Marguerite's *Memoirs,* Wilde's friend Violet

Fane writes that while history has judged Marguerite harshly as a woman, wife, and queen, she needs to be regarded altogether differently from a literary standpoint: "by giving the reins to our imagination, we may even picture to ourselves 'La Reine Margot' . . . in her flaxen wig and obsolete sixteenth-century costume, holding out the beautiful hand which she inherited from her mother . . . in welcome to some newly arrived congenial spirit of these latter days" (p. 56).

4   "The bindings which have been traditionally ascribed to Clovis Eve . . . are popularly supposed to have been executed for Marguerite de Valois, the queen of Henri IV. The field of their boards is broken by a series of ovals, in the centre of which are placed various flowers, or sprigs of oak or pomegranate; the hole being surrounded by borders of palm-branches: the central oval of the upper lid is tooled with a shield, charged with three fleurs-de-lys on a bend; that of the lower cover with the legend, Expectata non Elvdet. . . . Tradition has further declared that Marguerite de Valois herself gave the design for these bindings" (Herbert P. Horne, *The Binding of Books* [London: Kegan, Paul, Trench, Trübner, 1894], pp. 123–124).

5   Lord Henry's library is decorated according to the aesthetic principles described by Wilde in his lecture "The House Beautiful," which he delivered on numerous occasions between 1882 and 1885 in North America and Britain. Wilde enjoined his listeners to decorate their houses more beautifully, not by spending large sums of money, but "by the procuring of articles which, however cheaply purchased and unpretending, are beautiful and fitted to impart pleasure." In furnishing the house, the home decorator should select only those beautiful objects that "bear the impress of a distinct personality." In his expression of these ideas, Wilde is a forerunner of modern interior designers.

   Wilde's interest in interior decorating dates back at least to his university days. In his first year at Magdalen College, Oxford, Wilde filled his rooms "with exquisite objects, not only blue china but Tanagra statuettes brought back from Greece, Greek rugs . . . photographs of his favorite paintings, and his famous easel sporting its unfinished painting" (Ellmann, *Oscar Wilde*, p. 87). According to Ellmann, Wilde was famous

Interior of the House Beautiful—An "Aesthetic" Drawing-Room, c. 1882.

He glanced quickly round, and rose to his feet. "I beg your pardon. I thought . . ."

"You thought it was my husband. It is only his wife. You must let me introduce myself. I know you quite well by your photographs.[8] I think my husband has got twenty-seven of them."

"Not twenty-seven, Lady Henry?"

"Well, twenty-six then. And I saw you with him the other night at the Opera." She laughed nervously, as she spoke, and watched him with her vague forget-me-not eyes. She was a curious woman, whose dresses always looked as if they had been designed in a rage and put on in a tempest. She was always in love with somebody, and, as her passion was never returned, she had kept all her illusions. She tried to look picturesque, but only succeeded in being untidy.[9] Her name was Victoria, and she had a perfect mania for going to Church.[10]

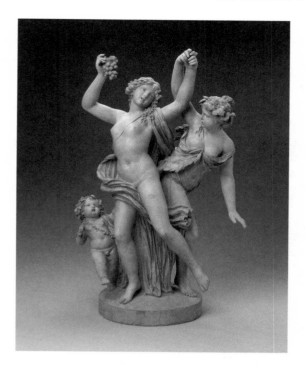

Terracotta statuette, by "Clodion" [Claude Michel, 1738–1814], depicting two dancing bacchantes and a putto, 1800. Clodion was much in vogue in the 1880s.

as early as 1876 for wittily remarking, "I find it harder and harder every day to live up to my blue china" (p. 45). By the time of the publication of *Dorian Gray* no single individual was more associated with the aesthetic interior than Wilde.

6 "Procrastination Is the Thief of Time" (Edward Young, *Night-Thoughts* [1742–1745; London: Printed by C. Whittingham for T. Heptinstall, 1798], Night 1, line 393, p. 13).

7 A French novel written in 1731 by the Abbé Prevost and considered scandalous by many Victorians. It dramatizes the attractions and consequences of a life of untrammeled desire. It was frequently illustrated throughout the eighteenth and nineteenth centuries: the 1885 edition illustrated by Maurice Leloir was considered a monument of illustration in Wilde's day.

8 Wilde was almost as well recognized during his own lifetime as he is today thanks to the many professional photographic portraits he commissioned. During his American lecture tour of 1882, he became especially alive to the importance of photographs in developing his fame and reputation: "I think if some large lithographs of me were got it would help business," he wrote in 1882; "the photograph of me with head looking over my shoulder would be the best" (*CL*, p. 152). For Wilde's fascination with photographic self-portraits, see Daniel Novak, "Sexuality in the Age of Mechanical Reproducibility: Wilde, Photography and Identity," in his *Realism, Photography and Nineteenth Century Fiction* (Cambridge University Press, 2008), pp. 118–145. For the role of photographic portraits in consolidating polite Victorian Society, see B. Hillier, *Victorian Studio Photographs* (Boston: Godine, 1976), pp. 16–19.

9 The biographer Richard Ellmann writes that Wilde imposed his dandyism on his ill-matched wife, Constance, "a half-convinced martyr to his evangel of dress reform" (Ellmann, *Oscar Wilde*, p. 259). Constance's efforts at smart dressing sometimes produced sadly comic results. Ellmann records this diary observation made by Laura Troubridge after the Wildes had come to tea at Troubridge's house in July 1884: "She dressed for the part in limp white muslin with no bustle, saffron coloured silk swathed about her shoulders, a huge cartwheel Gainsborough hat, white and bright yellow stockings and shoes—she looked too hopeless and we thought her shy and dull—he was amusing of course" (Ellmann, *Oscar Wilde*, p. 259).

10 The name associates Lord Henry's wife with Queen Victoria, who once characterized the English higher classes as "frivolous, pleasure-seeking, heartless, selfish, immoral and gambling" (quoted in K. D. Reynolds and H. C. G. Matthew, *Queen Victoria* [Oxford University Press, 2007], p. 66). The term "Victorian" is now a byword for joyless conservatism; and in *A Woman of No Importance,* a woman who is "always going to church" is said to be "not modern, and to be modern is the only thing worth being nowadays." According to one observer, Wilde's wife, Constance, was "entirely devoid of humour and evangelically religious" (Richard Le Gallienne, *The Romantic '90s* [1926; rpt. London: Robin Clark, 1993], p. 144).

Aubrey Beardsley, "The Wagnerites" (1894), line-engraving satirizing the blind devotion to Wagner among the British intelligentsia of the 1890s. Beardsley was himself a devotee of Wagner's music. Many of his drawings, as well as his prose *The Story of Venus and Tannhauser,* were inspired by Wagner's music.

"That was at 'Lohengrin,' Lady Henry, I think?"

"Yes: it was at dear 'Lohengrin.' I like Wagner's music better than any music. It is so loud that one can talk the whole time, without people hearing what one says.[11] That is a great advantage, don't you think so, Mr. Gray?"

The same nervous staccato laugh broke from her thin lips, and her fingers began to play with a long paper-knife.

Dorian smiled, and shook his head. "I am afraid I don't think so, Lady Henry. I never talk during music,—at least during good music. If one hears bad music, it is one's duty to drown it by conversation."

"Ah! that is one of Harry's views, isn't it, Mr. Gray? But you must not think I don't like good music. I adore it, but I am afraid of it. It makes me too romantic. I have simply worshipped pianists,—two at a time, sometimes. I don't know what it is about them. Perhaps it is that they are foreigners. They all are, aren't they? Even those that are born in England become foreigners after a time, don't they? It is so clever of them, and such a compliment to art. Makes it quite cosmopolitan, doesn't it? You have never been to any of my parties, have you, Mr. Gray? You must come. I can't afford orchids, but I spare no expense in foreigners. They make one's rooms look so picturesque. But here is Harry! Harry, I came in to look for you, to ask you something, I forget what it was. And I found Mr. Gray here. We have had such a pleasant chat about music. We have quite the same views. No: I think our views are quite different. But he has been most pleasant. I am so glad I've seen him."

"I am charmed, my love, quite charmed," said Lord Henry, elevating his dark crescent-shaped eyebrows and looking at them both with an amused smile.—"So sorry I am late, Dorian. I went to look after a piece of old brocade in Wardour Street, and had to bargain for hours for it.[12] Nowadays people know the price of everything, and the value of nothing."[13]

"I am afraid I must be going," exclaimed Lady Henry, after an awkward silence, with her silly sudden laugh. "I have promised to drive with the Duchess. Good-bye, Mr. Gray. Good-bye, Harry. You are

11 Wilhelm Richard Wagner's death in 1883 (seven years before the publication of *Dorian Gray*) did nothing to diminish the German composer's international popularity. Love for Wagner's music remained a central feature of the Victorian fin de siècle. British Wagnerism took many forms. In *The Perfect Wagnerite* (1893; rpt. New York: Brentano's, 1907), Bernard Shaw distinguishes merely "enthusiastic admirers" (p. v) of Wagner, or those who attended performances because doing so was fashionable, from "good Wagnerites" (p. 134), zealous fanatics, and "perfect Wagnerites" (p. 1). Like Aubrey Beardsley, whose picture "The Wagnerites" satirizes the blind devotion to Wagner among the British intelligentsia, Shaw was most scornful of those who "are devoted to Wagner merely as a dog is devoted to its master" and who "reverence his superiority without understanding it" (p. v).

12 In Wilde's day, Wardour Street was famous for its curiosity shops. *Dorian Gray* was lambasted by one reviewer upon publication for its "elaborate Wardour Street aestheticism and obtrusively cheap scholarship" (unsigned review, *Daily Chronicle,* June 30, 1890, rpt. in *Oscar Wilde: The Critical Heritage,* ed. Beckson, p. 72).

13 This famous epigram, inserted into the typescript in hand, was reused by Wilde in *Lady Windermere's Fan* and again in *The Importance of Being Earnest.*

14 The preferred perfume of prostitutes since the 1840s, memorialized as follows by Arthur Symons: "Patchouli? Well, why not Patchouli? Is there any 'reason in nature' why we should write exclusively about the natural blush . . . if rouge has any attraction for us? . . . If you prefer your 'new-mown hay' in the hayfield, and I, it may be, in a scent-bottle, why may not my individual caprice be allowed to find expression? (Arthur Symons, "Preface: Being a Word on Behalf of Patchouli," in his *Silhouettes,* 2nd ed. [London: Leonard Smithers, 1896], pp. xiv–xv). See also Max Beerbohm's witty and important essay "A Defence of Cosmetics," *The Yellow Book,* vol. 1, no. 1 (April 1894), pp. 65–82. In the 1891 book edition of *Dorian Gray,* perhaps to mitigate a suggestion of impropriety in the character of Victoria Wotton, Wilde substitutes *frangipani* for *patchouli.*

15 The love of well-to-do men for young actresses is commonplace in both life and fiction in Britain at the fin de siècle. See Frederick Wedmore's "To Nancy" (1896) and Arthur Symons's "Esther Khan" (1905).

16 A variant of the word *sibyl,* from the Greek word *sibylla,* meaning "prophetess." In antiquity, *sibyls* were legendary oracles, such as the Delphic Sibyl who gave prophecies in the sacred precinct of Apollo, at Delphi, on the slopes of Mount Parnassus. "Sybil" was a common name in Wilde's day. Wilde first uses this spelling in *Lord Arthur Savile's Crime* for the character of Sybil Merton, about whom he writes, "Sybil was . . . a symbol of all that is good and noble." Stoddart or one of his associates at Lippincott changed Wilde's spelling from "Sybil" to "Sibyl" in editing *Dorian Gray* for publication. In this edition, Wilde's original spelling is retained.

17 "Owing to their imperfect education, the only works we have had from women were works of genius" (Wilde, as reported in the journals of "Michael Field" [Katherine Bradley and Edith Copper, rpt. in *Oscar Wilde: Interviews and Recollections,* ed. Mikhail], 1:198).

18 "We should . . . deal not merely with what women wear, but with what they think, and what they feel. *The Lady's World* should be made the recognised organ for the expression of women's opinions on all subjects of literature, art, and modern life" (Wilde, to Wemyss Reid, Cassell's business manager, upon assuming the

dining out, I suppose? So am I. Perhaps I shall see you at Lady Thornbury's."

"I dare say, my dear," said Lord Henry, shutting the door behind her, as she flitted out of the room, looking like a bird-of-paradise that had been out in the rain, and leaving a faint odour of patchouli behind her.[14] Then he shook hands with Dorian Gray, lit a cigarette, and flung himself down on the sofa.

"Never marry a woman with straw-coloured hair, Dorian," he said, after a few puffs.

"Why, Harry?"

"Because they are so sentimental."

"But I like sentimental people."

"Never marry at all, Dorian. Men marry because they are tired: women, because they are curious: both are disappointed."

"I don't think I am likely to marry, Harry. I am too much in love. That is one of your aphorisms. I am putting it into practice, as I do everything you say."

"Who are you in love with?" said Lord Henry, looking at him with a curious smile.

"With an actress," said Dorian Gray, blushing.

Lord Henry shrugged his shoulders. "That is a rather commonplace *début,*" he murmured.[15]

"You would not say so if you saw her, Harry."

"Who is she?"

"Her name is Sybil Vane."[16]

"Never heard of her."

"No one has. People will some day, however. She is a genius."

"My dear boy, no woman is a genius; women are a decorative sex.[17] They never have anything to say, but they say it charmingly.[18] They represent the triumph of matter over mind, just as we men represent the triumph of mind over morals. There are only two kinds of women, the plain and the coloured. The plain women are very useful. If you want to gain a reputation for respectability, you have merely to take them down to supper. The other women are very charming. They commit one mistake, however. They paint in order to try and look young. Our grandmothers painted in order to try and talk brilliantly.[a] *Rouge* and *esprit* used to go together.[19] That has all gone out now. As long as a woman can look ten years younger than her own daughter, she is perfectly satisfied. As for conversation, there are only five women in London worth talking to, and two of these can't be admitted into decent society. However, tell me about your genius. How long have you known her?"

"About three weeks. Not so much. About two weeks and two days."

"How did you come across her?"

"I will tell you, Harry; but you mustn't be unsympathetic about it. After all, it never would have happened if I had not met you. You filled me with a wild desire to know everything about life. For days after I met you, something seemed to throb in my veins. As I lounged in the Park,[20] or strolled down Piccadilly, I used to look at every one who passed me, and wonder with a mad curiosity what sort of lives they led.[21] Some of them fascinated me. Others filled me with terror. There was an exquisite poison in the air. I had a passion for sensations.

"One evening about seven o'clock I determined to go out in search of some adventure. I felt that this grey, monstrous London of ours, with its myriads of people, its splendid sinners, and its sordid sins, as you once said, must have something in store for me. I fancied a thousand things. The mere danger gave me a sense of delight. I remembered what you had said to me on that wonderful night when we first dined together, about the search for beauty being the poisonous secret of life. I don't know what I expected, but I went out, and wandered East-ward, soon losing my way in a labyrinth of grimy streets and black grassless squares.[22] About half-past eight I passed by a little third-rate theatre, with great flaring gas-jets and gaudy play-bills. A hideous Jew, in the most amazing waistcoat I ever beheld in my life, was standing at the entrance, smoking a vile cigar. He had greasy ringlets, and an enormous diamond blazed in the centre of a soiled shirt. 'Ave a box, my lord,' he said, when he saw me, and he took off his hat with an act of gorgeous servility. There was something about him, Harry, that amused me. He was such a monster.[23] You will laugh at me, I know, but I really went in and paid a whole guinea for the

editorship of *Woman's World* [then titled *The Lady's World*] in April 1887 [*CL*, p. 297]).

19 "Last century . . . when life was lived by candle-light, and ethics was but etiquette, and even art a question of punctilio, women, we know, gave the best hours of the day to the crafty larding of their faces and the towering of their coiffures" (Max Beerbohm, "A Defence of Cosmetics," p. 66).

20 Either Hyde Park or Green Park, bordered by Piccadilly and the fashionable districts of Mayfair and St. James. In "The Portrait of Mr. W. H.," Cyril Graham occupies rooms in Piccadilly overlooking Green Park. And in "The Critic as Artist," after remarking that "Piccadilly lies at our feet like a long riband of silver," Gilbert (whose house also overlooks Green Park) comments, "A faint purple mist hangs over the Park, and the shadows of the white houses are purple" (p. 206).

21 Piccadilly was (and still is) one of London's preeminent streets, filled with fashionable shops and hotels. In Wilde's day it was also a cruising ground for young male prostitutes, and it was at Piccadilly Circus that "something clutched at [Wilde's] heart like ice" when he saw painted boys on the sidewalk in 1885 while shopping with his wife (Ellmann, *Oscar Wilde*, p. 27). Since the early 1880s, Piccadilly had been associated with Wilde in particular and with homoerotic and effeminate Aestheticism more generally: in *Patience* (1881), W. S. Gilbert had caricatured Wilde as the character Bunthorne, who speaks the following lines:

> Though the Philistines may jostle, you will rank as
>   an apostle in the high aesthetic band,
> If you walk down Piccadilly with a poppy or a lily in
>   your medieval hand.
> And ev'ryone will say,
> As you walk your flow'ry way,
> "If he's content with a vegetable love which would
>   certainly not suit me,
> Why, what a most particularly pure young man this
>   pure young man must be!"

By the early 1890s, Wilde and his circle "increasingly favoured Piccadilly as one of its favourite places to meet and entertain rent boys" (Jason Edwards, *Alfred Gilbert's Aestheticism* [Burlington, VT: Ashgate, 2006], pp. 100–101).

22 "A gentleman never goes east of Temple Bar," Coulson Kernahan reports Wilde as saying (*In Good Company* [London: John Lane, 1917], p. 217).

23 Wilde's "hideous Jew" incorporates a number of anti-semitic stereotypes. It is one of numerous anti-semitic portraits of Jewish men in British fin-de-siècle fiction—other notable examples can be found in Du Maurier's *Trilby* and Stoker's *Dracula*—though anti-semitism has featured in British literature since Chaucer's day. Such portraits reflected a pronounced up-swing in British anti-semitism, among liberals as much as among conservatives, following the exodus of Ashkenazi Jews from Eastern Europe in the 1870s and 1880s. Though the majority of these emigrants settled in the United States, as many as 100,000 arrived in Britain, where they quickly became ghettoized in London's East End (still home to many of Britain's newest immigrants). See Colin Holmes, *Anti-Semitism in British Society, 1876–1939* (London: Edwin Arnold, 1979), pp. 5–6, 13.

24 Though Sybil is later said to have worked at the Royal Theatre, Holborn (Chapter VIII, the *St. James's* account of Sybil's "death by misadventure"), Wilde's "third-rate theatre" is probably modeled on one of seven East End theaters identified by Heidi Holder as thriving in the last decades of the nineteenth century ("The East-End Theater," in *The Cambridge Companion to Victorian and Edwardian Theatre*, ed. Kerry Powell [Cambridge University Press, 2004], pp. 257–258), possibly the Pavilion Theatre in the Whitechapel Road. The Pavilion flourished in the 1880s and early 1890s under the management of the Jewish stage director Isaac Cohen, and was owned from 1872 to 1894 by the Jewish impresario Morris Abrahams. Playgoers entered the Pavilion—nicknamed "the Drury Lane of the East" after one of London's most famous theaters—through "terra cotta arches and Dorian pilasters" before passing into "a classical playground for the masses containing a stately auditorium of stalls, boxes, and a grand circle. Beneath a ceiling covered with cavorting cupids in seats awash in the light of incandescent gas burners, [one] marveled at English melodramas, Yiddish operettas, Christmas pantomimes, Shakespeare, and West End stars. . . . As this circus of acts whirled before

stage-box. To the present day I can't make out why I did so; and yet if I hadn't!—my dear Harry, if I hadn't, I would have missed the greatest romance of my life. I see you are laughing. It is horrid of you!"

"I am not laughing, Dorian; at least I am not laughing at you. But you should not say the greatest romance of your life. You should say the first romance of your life. You will always be loved, and you will always be in love with love. There are exquisite things in store for you. This is merely the beginning."

"Do you think my nature so shallow?" cried Dorian Gray, angrily.

"No: I think your nature so deep."

"How do you mean?"

"My dear boy, people who only love once in their lives are really shallow people. What they call their loyalty, and their fidelity, I call either the lethargy of custom or the lack of imagination. Faithlessness is to the emotional life what consistency is to the intellectual life, simply a confession of failure. But I don't want to interrupt you. Go on with your story."

"Well, I found myself seated in a horrid little private box, with a vulgar drop-scene staring me in the face. I looked out behind the curtain, and surveyed the house. It was a tawdry affair, all Cupids and cornucopias, like a third-rate wedding-cake. The gallery and pit were fairly full, but the two rows of dingy stalls were quite empty, and there was hardly a person in what I suppose they called the dress-circle. Women went about with oranges and ginger-beer, and there was a terrible consumption of nuts going on."24

"It must have been just like the palmy days of the British Drama."

"Just like, I should fancy, and very horrid. I began to wonder what on earth I should do, when I caught sight of the play-bill. What do you think the play was, Harry?"

"I should think 'The Idiot Boy, or Dumb but Innocent.' Our fathers used to like that sort of piece, I believe. The longer I live, Dorian, the more keenly I feel that whatever was good enough for our fathers is not good enough for us. In art, as in politics, *les grand-pères ont toujours tort.*"25

"This play was good enough for us, Harry. It was 'Romeo and Juliet.' I must admit I was rather annoyed at the idea of seeing Shakespeare done in such a wretched hole of a place. Still, I felt interested

Piccadilly, looking east, with Green Park on the right, early 1900s.

them, the audience feasted on and littered away the cakes, apples, oranges, chicken, fish, hot peas, monkey nuts, beer and spirits they brought with them or bought in the hall" (Daniel S. Levy, *Two-Gun Cohen: A Biography* [Macmillan, 2002], p. 25). Such theaters had started life as saloons attached to public houses, but by the late-Victorian period (now licensed as "theaters," as distinct from music halls or saloons, according to the 1843 Theatre Regulation Act) they had developed into well-known thespian centers and attracted audiences rivaling those of the West End stage. Shakespeare's plays were frequently staged there, and many Victorian intellectuals viewed them as bastions of art where prominent actors received a valuable training. Wilde's description of the theater as squalid and low is consistent with mainstream newspaper accounts of East End theaters—accounts Holder calls "more anthropological exercises than reviews" ("The East-End Theatre," 259).

25 "Our grandparents are always wrong."

Piccadilly in 1902. "Few streets in town have so many associations," remarks Charles Dickens, Jr.: Piccadilly is "one of the few streets left in London which are remarkable both from a commercial and from a 'society' point of view" and is "the nearest approach to the Parisian boulevard of which London can boast" (*Dickens's Dictionary of London: An Unconventional Handbook, 1888*).

Photo-portrait of Wilde, by Ward and Downey, c. 1892.

in a sort of way. At any rate, I determined to wait for the first act. There was a dreadful orchestra, presided over by a young Jew who sat at a cracked piano, that nearly drove me away, but at last the drop-scene was drawn up, and the play began. Romeo was a stout elderly gentleman, with corked eyebrows, a husky tragedy voice, and a figure like a beer-barrel. Mercutio was almost as bad. He was played by the low comedian, who had introduced gags of his own, and was on most familiar terms with the pit.[26] They were as grotesque as the scenery, and that looked as if it had come out of a pantomime of fifty years ago. But Juliet! Harry, imagine a girl, hardly seventeen years of age, with a little flower-like face, a small Greek head with plaited coils of dark-brown hair, eyes that were violet wells of passion, lips that were like the petals of a rose.[27] She was the loveliest thing I had ever seen in my life. You said to me once that pathos left you unmoved, but that beauty, mere beauty, could fill your eyes with tears. I tell you, Harry, I could hardly see this girl for the mist of tears that came across me. And her voice—I never heard such a voice. It was very low at first, with deep mellow notes, that seemed to fall singly upon one's ear. Then it became a little louder, and sounded like a flute or a distant hautbois. In the garden-scene it had all the tremulous ecstasy that one hears just before dawn when nightingales are singing. There were moments, later on, when it had the wild passion of violins. You know how a voice can stir one. Your voice and the voice of Sybil Vane are two things that I shall never forget. When I close my eyes, I hear them, and each of them says something different. I don't know which to follow. Why should I not love her? Harry, I do love her. She is everything to me in life. Night after night I go to see her play. One evening she is Rosalind, and the next evening she is Imogen. I have seen her die in the gloom of an Italian Tomb, sucking the poison from her lover's lips. I have watched her wandering through the forest of Arden, disguised as a pretty boy in hose and doublet and dainty cap. She has been mad, and has come into the presence of a guilty King, and given him rue to wear, and bitter herbs to taste of. She has been innocent, and the black hands of jealousy have crushed her reed-like throat. I have seen her in every age and in every costume. Ordinary women never appeal to one's imagination. They are limited to their century. No glamour ever transfigures them. One

26 The "low comedian" was a mainstay of music hall and popular theater repertoire. According to Max Beerbohm, male performers at music halls traditionally made themselves as unsightly as possible in order to "cheer the lower classes by showing them a life uglier and more sordid than their own" ("At the Tivoli," in *Around Theatres* [1924; rpt. New York: Simon & Schuster, 1954], p. 12).

27 Dorian's portrayal of his Sybil bears resemblance to Wilde's own poetic rendering of his future wife, Constance Lloyd, in a letter of January 1884 to his friend Lillie Langtry: "I am going to be married to a beautiful girl . . . with great coils of heavy brown hair which make her flower-like head droop like a blossom, and wonderful ivory hands which draw music from the piano so sweet that the birds stop singing to listen to her" (*CL*, p. 224).

28 "The classic fin-de-siècle performer is a possessed woman who stands for 'instinct,' for an irrational force that threatens to drown out all thought and [to] inhibit constructive ideas. . . . There were times when performing women had to lay claim to a masculine ability to take action without losing their feminine ability to inspire and invoke awe" (John Stokes, "Varieties of Performance at the Turn of the Century," in *The Cambridge Guide to the Fin-de-Siècle,* ed. Gail Marshall [Cambridge University Press, 2007], p. 214).

29 Prior to publishing the novel in *Lippincott's Monthly Magazine,* Wilde's editor J. M. Stoddart eliminated references—here and a few lines later—to Sybil Vane as Dorian's "mistress." He took similar precaution against alarming the sensibilities of his readers in altering passages concerning Dorian's relations with Hettie Merton in the final chapter. The reader should note that Dorian's heated response to Lord Henry's question ("Is Sybil Vane your mistress?") is not quite a denial. His "flushed cheek and burning eyes" may suggest something other than offense. Through sexual scandal he will bring to ruin the lives of many young men and women, including Lord Henry's sister, Lady Gwendolen.

knows their minds as easily as one knows their bonnets. One can always find them. There is no mystery in one of them. They ride in the Park in the morning, and chatter at tea-parties in the afternoon. They have their stereotyped smile, and their fashionable manner. They are quite obvious. But an actress! How different an actress is![28] Why didn't you tell me, Harry, that the only thing worth loving is an actress?"

"Because I have loved so many of them, Dorian."

"Oh, yes, horrid people with dyed hair and painted faces."

"Don't run down dyed hair and painted faces. There is an extraordinary charm in them, sometimes."

"I wish now I had not told you about Sybil Vane."

"You could not have helped telling me, Dorian. All through your life you will tell me every thing you do."

"Yes, Harry, I believe that is true. I cannot help telling you things. You have a curious influence over me. If I ever did a crime, I would come and confide it to you. You would understand me."

"People like you—the wilful sunbeams of life—don't commit crimes, Dorian. But I am much obliged for the compliment, all the same. And now tell me—reach me the matches, like a good boy: thanks—tell me, is Sybil Vane[b] your mistress?"[29]

Dorian Gray leapt to his feet, with flushed cheeks and burning eyes. "How dare you suggest such a thing, Harry? It is horrible. Sybil Vane is sacred!"[c]

"It is only the sacred things that are worth touching, Dorian," said Lord Henry, with a strange touch of pathos in his voice. "But why should you be annoyed? I suppose she will be your mistress[d] some day. When one is in love, one always begins by deceiving oneself, and one always ends by deceiving others. That is what the world calls romance. You know her, at any rate, I suppose?"

"Of course I know her. On the first night I was at the Theatre, the horrid old Jew came round to the box after the performance was over, and offered to bring me behind the scenes and introduce me to her. I was furious with him, and told him that Juliet had been dead for hundreds of years, and that her body was lying in a marble Tomb in Verona.[30] I think, from his blank look of amazement, that he thought I had taken too much champagne, or something."

"I am not surprised."

"I was not surprised either. Then he asked me if I wrote for any of the newspapers. I told him I never even read them. He seemed terribly disappointed at that, and confided to me that all the dramatic critics were in a conspiracy against him,[31] and that they were all to be bought."

"I believe he was quite right there. But, on the other hand, most of them are not at all expensive."

"Well, he seemed to think they were beyond his means. By this time, the lights were being put out in the theatre, and I had to go. He wanted me to try some cigars which he strongly recommended. I declined. The next night, of course, I arrived at the Theatre again. When he saw me he made me a low bow, and assured me that I was a patron of art. He was a most offensive brute, though he had an extraordinary passion for Shakespeare. He told me once with an air of pride that his three bankruptcies were entirely due to the poet, whom he insisted on calling 'The Bard.' He seemed to think it a distinction."

"It was a distinction, my dear Dorian—a great distinction. But when did you first speak to Miss Sybil Vane?"

"The third night. She had been playing Rosalind. I could not help going round. I had thrown her some flowers, and she had looked at me. At least I fancied that she had. The old Jew was persistent. He seemed determined to bring me behind, so I consented. It was curious my not wanting to know her, wasn't it?"

"No; I don't think so."

"My dear Harry, why?"

"I will tell you some other time. Now I want to know about the girl."

"Sybil? Oh, she was so shy, and so gentle. There is something of a child about her. Her eyes opened wide in exquisite wonder when I told her what I thought of her performance, and she seemed quite unconscious of her power. I think we were both rather nervous. The

30 Sybil is a figure of art for Dorian. He loves her precisely for her uncanny ability as an actress to suppress her own personality (to fully inhabit the roles she plays). In a letter to the *Daily Telegraph* in 1892, Wilde defines "the actor's aim" as the conversion of "his own accidental personality into the real and essential personality of the character he is called upon to impersonate" (*CL*, p. 519). In the same letter (entitled "Puppets and Actors" by the *Telegraph*), Wilde praises the many advantages of puppets over modern stage actors, suggesting that the actor is, or should be, a "puppet" of the playwright.

31 Theaters such as the Pavilion, in London's East End, whose audiences reflected the multiethnic and working-class nature of the communities in which they were located, faced considerable class- and race-based prejudice in the mainstream press.

Photo-portrait of Constance Wilde, 1892. Married to Oscar Wilde for eight years when this photo was taken, Constance was to renounce his surname three years later, partly to protect her children, upon his conviction for gross indecency.

old Jew stood grinning at the doorway of the dusty green-room, making elaborate speeches about us both, while we stood looking at each other like children. He would insist on calling me 'My Lord,' so I had to assure Sybil that I was not anything of the kind. She said quite simply to me, 'You look more like a Prince.'"

"Upon my word, Dorian, Miss Sybil knows how to pay compliments."

"You don't understand her, Harry. She regarded me merely as a person in a play. She knows nothing of life. She lives with her mother, a faded tired woman who played Lady Capulet in a sort of magenta dressing-wrapper on the first night, and who looks as if she had seen better days."

"I know that look. It always depresses me."

"The Jew wanted to tell me her history, but I said it did not interest me."

"You were quite right. There is always something infinitely mean about other people's tragedies."

"Sybil is the only thing I care about. What is it to me where she came from? From her little head to her little feet, she is absolutely and entirely divine. I go to see her act every night of my life, and every night she is more marvellous."

"That is the reason, I suppose, that you will never dine with me now. I thought you must have some curious romance on hand. You have; but it is not quite what I expected."

"My dear Harry, we either lunch or sup together every day, and I have been to the Opera with you several times."

"You always come dreadfully late."

"Well, I can't help going to see Sybil play, even if it is only for an act. I get hungry for her presence; and when I think of the wonderful soul that is hidden away in that little ivory body, I am filled with awe."

"You can dine with me to-night, Dorian, can't you?"

He shook his head. "To-night she is Imogen," he answered, "and to-morrow night she will be Juliet."

"When is she Sybil Vane?"

Satirical engraving from *Punch,* June 25, 1881, and sheet music cover for "The Oscar Wilde Galup," arranged by F. H. Snow (New York: R. A. Saalfield, n.d.). In his self-assumed role of spokesman for the Aesthetic Movement, or the "English Renaissance of Art," Wilde was frequently the object of satire in the early 1880s.

32 "This fanciful comedy of unreal romance became to him, as he sat in the audience, the real tragedy of his life. The moods of his own soul seemed to have taken shape and substance, and to be moving before him . . . There are few of us who have not felt something akin to this. We become lovers when we see Romeo and Juliet, and Hamlet makes us students" ("The Portrait of Mr. W. H.").

33 The Bristol appears to be a club of Wilde's own invention; "the Bristol" substituted for "Boodles," the real-life Mayfair club, in the holograph manuscript draft on which the *Lippincott's* typescript was based. (*Picture of Dorian Gray: The 1890 and 1891 Texts,* ed. Bristow, p. 384, n. 23).

"Never."

"I congratulate you."

"How horrid you are! She is all the great heroines of the world in one. She is more than an individual. You laugh, but I tell you she has genius. I love her, and I must make her love me. You, who know all the secrets of life, tell me how to charm Sybil Vane to love me! I want to make Romeo jealous. I want the dead lovers of the world to hear our laughter, and grow sad.[32] I want a breath of our passion to stir their dust into consciousness, to wake their ashes into pain. My God! Harry, how I worship her!" He was walking up and down the room as he spoke. Hectic spots of red burned on his cheeks. He was terribly excited.

Lord Henry watched him with a subtle sense of pleasure. How different he was now from the shy, frightened boy he had met in Basil Hallward's studio! His nature had developed like a flower, had borne blossoms of scarlet flame. Out of its secret hiding-place had crept his Soul, and Desire had come to meet it on the way.

"And what do you propose to do?" said Lord Henry, at last.

"I want you and Basil to come with me some night, and see her act. I have not the slightest fear of the result. You won't be able to refuse to recognise her genius. Then we must get her out of the Jew's hands. She is bound to him for three years—at least for two years and eight months—from the present time. I will have to pay him something, of course. When all that is settled, I will take a West-End Theatre and bring her out properly. She will make the world as mad as she has made me."

"Impossible, my dear boy!"

"Yes, she will. She has not merely art, consummate art-instinct, in her, but she has personality also; and you have often told me that it is personalities, not principles, that move the age."

"Well, what night shall we go?"

"Let me see. To-day is Tuesday. Let us fix to-morrow. She plays Juliet to-morrow."

"All right. The Bristol at eight o'clock; and I will get Basil."[33]

Wilde commissioned this lifesize oil portrait of himself, by Harper Pennington, a student of Whistler's, in or around 1884. The portrait adorned the walls of Wilde's Tite Street home up until the bailiff's sale of Wilde's possessions in April 1895, whereupon it was bought and kept safe for Wilde by his friends Ada and Ernest Leverson. Wilde later called this portrait a "social incubus." One week before his release from Reading prison in 1897 Wilde tried through friends to rent a small room where the portrait could be safely stored and hidden from public view.

When Wilde wrote *The Picture of Dorian Gray,* artistic portraiture was undergoing a renaissance in Britain, and many Victorians understood it as "a sacramental act, involving a mysterious and complex transaction between artist and sitter" (Paul Barlow, "Facing the Past and Present: The National Portrait Gallery and the Search for 'Authentic' Portraiture"). Portraitists of Wilde's day often deviated from strictly truthful or accurate representations of their subjects, either exaggerating their personal beauty and elegance or painting them in settings and clothing that idealized them. The best such portraits bear out Basil Hallward's contention, early in *The Picture of Dorian Gray,* that "every portrait that is painted with feeling is a portrait of the artist, not the sitter." But Wilde's novel may also be said to foreshadow Modernist portraiture: "Freed from the need of describing a particular person, the possibilities [for portraiture] are endless," remarks Mark Rothko in 1943, so much so that "today the artist is no longer constrained by the limitation that all of man's experience is expressed by his outward appearance" ("The Portrait and the Modern Artist").

34 "My frames I have designed as carefully as my pictures—and thus they form as important a part as any of the rest of the work—carrying on the particular harmony throughout" (*Whistler on Art*, p. 48).

35 Dorian dates his birth from the completion of the portrait. The line is ironic in that it is the portrait that is aging, not Dorian.

36 In Chapter I, Hallward confesses to Lord Henry that he has invested in the picture "all the extraordinary romance of which . . . I have never dared to speak." He also tells Lord Henry that Dorian "knows nothing about [my secret]. He will never know anything about it." Here Lord Henry has casually betrayed his friend's confidence. His cutting remark suggests that the repressed artist either won't act, or is incapable of acting, on his desires.

37 "It may be thought that the characteristic which I have occasionally mentioned as proper to aristocracies—their natural inaccessibility, as children of the established fact, to ideas—points to our extending to this class the designation of Philistines; the Philistine being, as is well known, the enemy of the children of light or servant of the idea. Nevertheless . . . if we look into the thing closely, we shall find that the term *Philistine* gives the notion of something particularly stiff-necked and perverse in the resistance to light and its children; and therein it specially suits our middle-class" (Matthew Arnold, "Culture and Anarchy," in *Culture and Anarchy and Other Writings,* ed. Stefan Collini [Cambridge University Press, 1993], p. 104).

38 "A Poet is the most unpoetical of any thing in existence; because he has no identity—he is continually in for—and filling some other body" (*Letters of John Keats,* ed. R. Gittings [Oxford University Press, 1987], p. 157). Wilde's insistence upon the poet's complete dedication to his art—like his insistence upon the actor's surrender of his or her own "accidental personality"—is a variation on Keats's notion of *negative capability,* whereby a "sense of Beauty overcomes every other consideration—or rather obliterates all consideration" as far as the artist is concerned (*Letters of John Keats,* p. 43).

"Not eight, Harry, please. Half-past six. We must be there before the curtain rises. You must see her in the first act, where she meets Romeo."

"Half-past six! What an hour! It will be like having a meat-tea. However, just as you wish. Shall you see Basil between this and then? Or shall I write to him?"

"Dear Basil! I have not laid eyes on him for a week. It is rather horrid of me, as he has sent me my portrait in the most wonderful frame, designed by himself,[34] and, though I am a little jealous of it for being a whole month younger than I am,[35] I must admit that I delight in it. Perhaps you had better write to him. I don't want to see him alone. He says things that annoy me."

Lord Henry smiled. "He gives you good advice, I suppose. People are very fond of giving away what they need most themselves."

"You don't mean to say that Basil has got any passion or any romance in him?"[e]

"I don't know whether he has any passion, but he certainly has romance," said Lord Henry, with an amused look in his eyes. "Has he never let you know that?"[36f]

"Never. I must ask him about it. I am rather surprised to hear it.[g] He is the best of fellows, but he seems to me to be just a bit of a Philistine.[37] Since I have known you, Harry, I have discovered that."

"Basil, my dear boy, puts everything that is charming in him into his work. The consequence is that he has nothing left for life but his prejudices, his principles, and his common sense. The only artists I have ever known who are personally delightful are bad artists. Good artists give everything to their art, and consequently are perfectly uninteresting in themselves. A great poet, a really great poet, is the most unpoetical of all creatures.[38] But inferior poets are absolutely fascinating. The worse their rhymes are, the more picturesque they look. The mere fact of having published a book of second-rate sonnets makes a man quite irresistible.[39] He lives the poetry that he cannot write. The others write the poetry that they dare not realize."

"I wonder is that really so, Harry?" said Dorian Gray, putting some perfume on his handkerchief out of a large gold-topped bottle that stood on the table. "It must be, if you say so. And now I must be off.

39 Wilde may have been thinking here of his own love for the "second-rate" sonneteer and poet Richard Le Gallienne (1866–1947). After receiving a copy of Le Gallienne's *My Ladies' Sonnets and Other Vain and Amatorious Verses,* Wilde diplomatically remarks in a letter of 1887 that it is "full of much that is dainty and delicate in verse" (*CL,* p. 327). After meeting Le Gallienne, however, he confesses, "I think so often of the young poet who came here so wonderfully and so strangely, and whose memory is always with me" (*CL,* p. 367), and again, "Having read the poems, I want to see the poet" (*CL,* p. 395).

Aubrey Beardsley, "The Woman in the Moon," line-engraved illustration to Wilde's *Salome, A Tragedy in One Act,* trans. Lord Alfred Douglas (Elkin Mathews and John Lane, 1894). Beardsley has slyly incorporated into the picture Wilde's own facial features, especially his drooping eyelids, as if to imply that the woman in the moon—if not the entire play—is first and foremost an expression of Wilde himself.

40 Wilde's own drooping eyelids have been frequently remarked upon: they were satirized in Aubrey Beardsley's illustrations to *Salome*. John Cooper Powys says about Wilde's appearance: "the tragic wantonness of that strange countenance, with the heavy eyelids and drooping mouth, means something not easily forgotten" (quoted in *Oscar Wilde: The Critical Heritage*, p. 364). Wilde's emphasis on Lord Henry's eyelids echoes his description of the Devil, in "The Fisherman and His Soul," whose "heavy eyelids drooped over his eyes." See also Chapter X below, where Basil says, "If a wretched man has a vice, it shows itself in . . . the droop of his eyelids."

41 This sentence, like the previous one, is deeply ironic in light of the two-year jail sentence, with hard labor, served by Wilde from 1895 to 1897 as punishment for acts of "gross indecency." In a long letter to his former lover Lord Alfred Douglas written during his incarceration in Reading Gaol, Wilde reflects poignantly and frequently on "the high price one had to pay for knowing you" (*CL*, p. 692).

42 "Let live [sic] the sense of things that are felt, and the understanding of things intelligible, come to the succour of the body with matter and corporeal subject, and let the understanding delight in its own objects, to the end that this composition of the body may be realized, that this machine dissolve not, in which, by means of the spirit, the soul is united to the body" (Giordano Bruno, *The Heroic Enthusiasts, Part One* [15??], tr. L. Williams [London: Redway, 1887], p. 108).

43 Freud does not articulate his principles of psychoanalysis until the Edwardian era. In speculating whether psychology might ever become "so absolute a science that each little spring of life would be revealed to us," Wilde anticipates Freud's great insight that "the concept of the unconscious has long been knocking at the gates of psychology and asking to be let in. Philosophy and literature have often toyed with it, but science could find no use for it. Psychoanalysis has seized upon the concept, has taken it seriously and has given it a fresh content. By its researches it has led to a knowledge of the characteristics of the unconscious mental [life] which have hitherto been unsuspected,

Imogen is waiting for me. Don't forget about to-morrow. Good-bye!"

As he left the room, Lord Henry's heavy eyelids drooped,[40] and he began to think. Certainly few people had ever interested him so much as Dorian Gray, and yet the lad's mad adoration of some one else caused him not the slightest pang of annoyance or jealousy. He was pleased by it. It made him a more interesting study. He had been always enthralled by the methods of Science, but the ordinary subject-matter of Science had seemed to him trivial and of no import. And so he had begun by vivisecting himself, as he had ended by vivisecting others. Human life—that appeared to him the one thing worth investigating. There was nothing else of any value, compared to it. It was true that as one watched life in its curious crucible of pain and pleasure, one could not wear over one's face a mask of glass, or keep the sulphurous fumes from troubling the brain and making the imagination turbid with monstrous fancies and misshapen dreams. There were poisons so subtle that to know their properties one had to sicken of them. There were maladies so strange that one had to pass through them if one sought to understand their nature. And yet what a great reward one received! How wonderful the whole world became to one! To note the curious hard logic of passion, and the emotional coloured life of the intellect: to observe where they met, and where they separated, at what point they became one, and at what point they were at discord—there was a delight in that! What matter what the cost was? One could never pay too high a price for any sensation.[41]

He was conscious—and the thought brought a gleam of pleasure into his brown agate eyes—that it was through certain words of his, musical words said with musical utterance, that Dorian Gray's soul had turned to this white girl and bowed in worship before her. To a large extent, the lad was his own creation. He had made him premature. That was something. Ordinary people waited till life disclosed to them its secrets, but to the few, to the elect, the mysteries of life were revealed before the veil was drawn away. Sometimes this was the effect of Art, and chiefly of the art of literature, which dealt immediately with the passions and the intellect. But now and then a complex personality took the place and assumed the office of art, was indeed, in its way, a real work of art, Life having its elaborate masterpieces, just as poetry has, or sculpture, or painting.

Yes, the lad was premature. He was gathering his harvest, while it was yet spring. The pulse and passion of youth were in him, but he was becoming self-conscious. It was delightful to watch him. With his beautiful face, and his beautiful soul, he was a thing to wonder at. It was no matter how it all ended, or was destined to end. He was like one of those gracious figures in a pageant or a play, whose joys seem to be remote from one, but whose sorrows stir one's sense of beauty, and whose wounds are like red roses.

Soul and body, body and soul—how mysterious they were! There was animalism in the soul, and the body had its moments of spirituality. The senses could refine, and the intellect could degrade. Who could say where the fleshly impulse ceased, or the psychical impulse began? How shallow were the arbitrary definitions of ordinary psychologists! And yet how difficult to decide between the claims of the various schools! Was the soul a shadow seated in the house of sin? Or was the body really in the soul, as Giordano Bruno thought?[42] The separation of spirit from matter was a mystery, and the union of spirit with matter was a mystery also.

He began to wonder whether we should ever make psychology so absolute a science that each little spring of life would be revealed to us.[43] As it was, we always misunderstood ourselves, and rarely understood others. Experience was of no ethical value. It was merely the name we gave to our mistakes. Men had, as a rule, regarded it as a mode of warning, had claimed for it a certain moral efficacy in the formation of character, had praised it as something that taught us what to follow and showed us what to avoid. But there was no motive power in experience. It was as little of an active cause as conscience itself. All that it really demonstrated was that our future would be the same as our past, and that the sin we had done once, and with loathing, we would do many times, and with joy.

It was clear to him that the experimental method was the only method by which one could arrive at any scientific analysis of the passions;[44] and certainly Dorian Gray was a subject made to his hand,

and it has discovered some of the laws which govern it" (Freud, "Some Elementary Lessons in Psycho-analysis," in his *General Psychological Theory: Papers on Metapsychology,* ed. Philip Rieff [New York: Collier Books, 1963], pp. 223–224).

44 Wilde held an abiding interest in the emerging science of psychology and may have felt that *Dorian Gray* had a contribution to make to its future, since psychologists were conflicted about the value of experimental methods at this time: "psychology is passing into a less simple phase. Within a few years what one might call a microscopic psychology has arisen . . . carried on by ex-

Photo-portrait of Richard Le Gallienne, c. 1894. Le Gallienne's poetry was second-rate, but Wilde valued the poet, referring to him as his "always loved friend."

perimental methods, asking of course every moment for introspective data. This method taxes patience to the utmost . . . [and] has brought into the field an array of younger experimental psychologists, bent on studying the *elements* of the mental life" (William James, *Principles of Psychology* [New York: Henry Holt, 1890], p. 9).

45 In the years leading up to his imprisonment, Wilde heavily exploited the telegram as a medium of personal communication; and when the recipient was his friend Ada Leverson, Wilde's telegrams rose to an art form. However, Wilde later accused Alfred Douglas of exploiting such "public" media too recklessly: "you availed yourself of the public telegram and the open postcard," he wrote; "you might have left such modes of annoyance to people like Alfred Wood [blackmailer of Wilde and Douglas] whose sole source of income it is" (*CL,* p. 761). In 1898, eight years after the publication of *Dorian Gray,* Henry James captured the telegram's allure for clandestine courtship and deception in his novella *In the Cage.* An essentially impersonal and electronic medium, the telegram is akin to e-mail and text-messaging, in our own day, in its capacity to reduce human communication to a cipher.

and seemed to promise rich and fruitful results. His sudden mad love for Sybil Vane was a psychological phenomenon of no small interest. There was no doubt that curiosity had much to do with it, curiosity and the desire for new experiences, yet it was not a simple but rather a very complex passion. What there was in it of the purely sensuous instinct of boyhood had been transformed by the workings of the imagination, changed into something that seemed to the boy himself to be remote from sense, and was for that very reason all the more dangerous. It was the passions about whose origin we deceived ourselves that tyrannised most strongly over us. Our weakest motives were those of whose nature we were conscious. It often happened that when we thought we were experimenting on others we were really experimenting on ourselves.

While Lord Henry sat dreaming on these things, a knock came to the door, and his valet entered, and reminded him it was time to dress for dinner. He got up and looked out into the street. The sunset had smitten into scarlet gold the upper windows of the houses opposite. The panes glowed like plates of heated metal. The sky above was like a faded rose. He thought of Dorian Gray's young fiery-coloured life, and wondered how it was all going to end.

When he arrived home, about half-past twelve o'clock, he saw a telegram lying on the hall-table.[45] He opened it and found it was from Dorian. It was to tell him that he was engaged to be married to Sybil Vane.

IV

"I suppose you have heard the news, Basil?" said Lord Henry on the following evening, as Hallward was shown into a little private room at the Bristol where dinner had been laid for three.

"No, Harry," answered Hallward, giving his hat and coat to the bowing waiter. "What is it? Nothing about politics, I hope? They don't interest me. There is hardly a single person in the House of Commons worth painting; though many of them would be the better for a little whitewashing."

"Dorian Gray is engaged to be married," said Lord Henry, watching him as he spoke.

Hallward turned perfectly pale, and a curious look flashed for a moment into his eyes, and then passed away, leaving them dull.[a] "Dorian engaged to be married!" he cried. "Impossible!"

"It is perfectly true."

"To whom?"

"To some little actress or other."

"I can't believe it. Dorian is far too sensible."

"Dorian is far too wise not to do foolish things now and then, my dear Basil."

"Marriage is hardly a thing that one can do now and then, Harry," said Hallward, smiling.

"Except in America.[1] But I didn't say he was married. I said he was engaged to be married. There is a great difference. I have a distinct

1 In *Divorce: An American Tradition* (Oxford University Press, 1991), Glenda Riley writes that "American divorce has a long and venerable history: Puritan settlers first introduced it in the American colonies during the early 1660s. The resulting institution of American divorce was vital, and growing, long before late-twentieth century Americans carried it to its current state" (p. 3). Wilde had toured in America for much of 1882; that he viewed America as a land of more relaxed sexual codes than England is clear from his 1887 essay "The American Man," in which he remarks, "The American man marries early, and the American woman marries often; and they get on extremely well together."

2 Key ingredients, along with gin or whiskey, of the earliest cocktails, such as the Martini and the Manhattan.

3 In *A Woman of No Importance* (1893), Lord Illingworth quips that "the happiness of a married man . . . depends on the people he has not married." And in *The Importance of Being Earnest* (1895), Algernon states that "in married life three is company and two is none." Wilde's own deceptions of his wife, Constance, exemplify these maxims. Two years after their marriage in 1884, Wilde was seduced by his friend Robert Ross. According to the biographer Richard Ellmann, it was Wilde's first homosexual encounter, and Wilde began thereafter to lead a secret double life as a member of London's homosexual subculture. The encounter with Ross had an equally profound impact on Wilde's writing life: "He was now able to make his experience of marriage and countermarriage the center of his career in prose" (Ellmann, *Oscar Wilde*, p. 281).

    Lord Henry's negative views on matrimony may also be seen as part of a more widespread debate about the institution of marriage that was taking place in Britain. It was a debate that gathered force after the appearance of a controversial article by Mona Caird ("Marriage," *Westminster Review*, August 1888) in which Caird declares "the present form of marriage. . . . a vexatious failure." As Elizabeth Lorang notes ("*The Picture of Dorian Gray* in Context: Intertextuality and *Lippincott's Monthly Magazine*," *Victorian Periodicals Review*, 43:1 [Spring 2010]), *Dorian Gray* originally appeared in *Lippincott's Monthly Magazine* alongside a critical dialogue, by Elizabeth Rachel Chapman and George Bettany, entitled "The Indissolubility of Marriage." The piece dramatizes two opposing views of marriage's supposed "indissolubility," both of which "comment discursively on Lord Henry's actions" (Lorang, "*Picture of Dorian Gray* in Context," p. 31).

4 Wilde's secret double life would involve assignations with young men, including not only members of his own class, but also male prostitutes or "renters," a number of whom eventually testified against him in court.

remembrance of being married, but I have no recollection at all of being engaged. I am inclined to think that I never was engaged."

"But think of Dorian's birth, and position, and wealth. It would be absurd for him to marry so much beneath him."

"If you want him to marry this girl, tell him that, Basil. He is sure to do it then. Whenever a man does a thoroughly stupid thing, it is always from the noblest motives."

"I hope the girl is good, Harry. I don't want to see Dorian tied to some vile creature, who might degrade his nature and ruin his intellect."

"Oh, she is more than good, she is beautiful," murmured Lord Henry, sipping a glass of vermouth and orange-bitters.[2] "Dorian says she is beautiful; and he is not often wrong about things of that kind. Your portrait of him has quickened his appreciation of the personal appearance of other people. It has had that excellent effect, amongst others. We are to see her to-night, if that boy doesn't forget his appointment."

"But do you approve of it, Harry?" asked Hallward, walking up and down the room, and biting his lip. "You can't approve of it really. It is some silly infatuation."

"I never approve, or disapprove, of anything now. It is an absurd attitude to take towards life. We are not sent into the world to air our moral prejudices. I never take any notice of what common people say, and I never interfere with what charming people do. If a personality fascinates me, whatever the personality chooses to do is absolutely delightful to me. Dorian Gray falls in love with a beautiful girl who acts Shakespeare, and proposes to marry her. Why not? If he wedded Messalina he would be none the less interesting. You know I am not a champion of marriage.[3] The real drawback to marriage is that it makes one unselfish. And unselfish people are colourless. They lack individuality. Still, there are certain temperaments that marriage makes more complex. They retain their egotism, and add to it many other egos. They are forced to have more than one life.[4] They become more highly organized. Besides, every experience is of value, and whatever one may say against marriage, it is certainly an experience. I hope that Dorian Gray will make this girl his wife, passionately adore her for six months, and then suddenly become fascinated by some one else. He would be a wonderful study."

"You don't mean all that, Harry; you know you don't. If Dorian Gray's life were spoiled, no one would be sorrier than yourself. You are much better than you pretend to be."

Lord Henry laughed. "The reason we all like to think so well of others is that we are all afraid for ourselves. The basis of optimism is sheer terror. We think that we are generous because we credit our neighbour with those virtues that are likely to benefit ourselves. We praise the Banker that we may overdraw our account, and find good qualities in the highwayman in the hope that he may spare our pockets. I mean everything that I have said. I have the greatest contempt for optimism.[5] And as for a spoilt life, no life is spoiled but one whose growth is arrested. If you want to mar a nature, you have merely to reform it. But here is Dorian himself. He will tell you more than I can."

"My dear Harry, my dear Basil, you must both congratulate me!" said the boy, throwing off his evening cape with its satin-lined wings, and shaking each of his friends by the hand in turn. "I have never been so happy. Of course it is sudden. All really delightful things are. And yet it seems to me to be the one thing I have been looking for all my life." He was flushed with excitement and pleasure, and looked extraordinarily handsome.

"I hope you will always be very happy, Dorian," said Hallward, "but I don't quite forgive you for not having let me know of your engagement. You let Harry know."

"And I don't forgive you for being late for dinner," broke in Lord Henry, putting his hand on the lad's shoulder, and smiling as he spoke. "Come, let us sit down and try what the new *chef* here is like, and then you will tell us how it all came about."[6]

"There is really not much to tell," cried Dorian, as they took their seats at the small round table. "What happened was simply this. After I left you yesterday evening, Harry, I had some dinner at that curious little Italian Restaurant in Rupert Street,[7] you introduced me

5 Lord Henry's contempt for optimism reflects the pessimistic philosophy of Arthur Schopenhauer, fashionable with British intellectuals in the 1880s and early 1890s: "To this world, to this scene of tormented and agonised beings, who only continue to exist by devouring each other . . . in which the capacity for feeling pain increases with knowledge, and therefore reaches its highest in man . . . to this world it has been sought to apply the system of optimism, and demonstrate to us that it is the best of all possible worlds. The absurdity is glaring" (Schopenhauer, *The World as Will and Idea,* trans. R. B. Haldane and J. Kemp [1883; 2nd ed. London: Trubner, 1886], vol. 3, p. 392). Wilde was familiar with the general contours of Schopenhauer's thought as early as 1876 (see *CL,* pp. 25–26).

6 "Cookery is an art; are not its principles the subject of South Kensington lectures, and does not the Royal Academy give a banquet once a year?" (Wilde, "Dinners and Dishes").

7 London's Soho district, where Rupert Street is located, is still famous for its Italian restaurants. Wilde favored two Italian restaurants in Rupert Street—Solferino's and the Florence—and often took young men to dine in a private room there (*The Real Trial,* p. 160). When pressed by Queensberry's lawyer, Edward Carson, about why he took Alfred Wood to the Florence, Wilde replied: "I have been for a long time in the habit of supping at the Café Florence—I considered it a pleasant place to sup at—and also . . . in the habit of having cheques cashed by the proprietor" (*Real Trial,* p. 118).

"In her boy's dress," illustration to *The Picture of Dorian Gray,* intro. Osbert Burdett, illustr. Henry Keen (London and New York: John Lane / Dodd, Mead & Co., 1925).

8 "Of all the motives of dramatic curiosity used by our great playwrights, there is none more subtle or fascinating than the ambiguity of the sexes" ("The Portrait of Mr. W. H.").

9 Mold-cast terracotta figurine, dating from the fourth or third century B.C.E., from Tanagra in east-central Greece. Such figurines had been barely noted until the 1860s, but a great quantity were excavated around Tanagra in the 1870s, leading to a flourishing trade in both originals and fakes. Tanagra figurines feature in a number of Wilde's works, notably in "Lord Arthur Savile's Crime," where we are told that Sybil Merton "looked like one of those delicate little figures

to, and went down afterwards to the Theatre. Sybil was playing Rosalind. Of course the scenery was dreadful, and the Orlando absurd. But Sybil! You should have seen her! When she came on in her boy's dress she was perfectly wonderful.[8] She wore a moss-coloured velvet jerkin with cinnamon sleeves, slim brown cross-gartered hose, a dainty little green cap with a hawk's feather caught in a jewel, and a hooded cloak lined with dull red. She had never seemed to me more exquisite. She had all the delicate grace of that Tanagra figurine that you have in your Studio, Basil.[9] Her hair clustered round her face like dark leaves round a pale rose. As for her acting—well, you will see her to-night. She is simply a born artist. I sat in the dingy box absolutely enthralled. I forgot that I was in London and in the nineteenth century. I was away with my love in a forest that no man had ever seen. After the performance was over I went behind, and spoke to her. As we were sitting together, suddenly there came a look into her eyes that I had never seen there before. My lips moved towards hers. We kissed each other. I can't describe to you what I felt at that moment. It seemed to me that all my life had been narrowed to one perfect point of rose-coloured joy. She trembled all over, and shook like a white narcissus. Then she flung herself on her knees and kissed my hands. I feel that I should not tell you all this, but I can't help it. Of course our engagement is a dead secret. She has not even told her own mother. I don't know what my guardians will say! Lord Radley is sure to be furious. I don't care. I shall be of age in less than a year, and then I can do what I like. I have been right, Basil, haven't I, to take my love out of poetry, and to find my wife in Shakespeare's plays? Lips that Shakespeare taught to speak have whispered their secret in my ear.[10] I have had the arms of Rosalind around me, and kissed Juliet on the mouth."

"Yes, Dorian, I suppose you were right," said Hallward, slowly.

"Have you seen her to-day?" asked Lord Henry.

Dorian Gray shook his head. "I left her in the forest of Arden, I shall find her in an orchard in Verona."[11]

Lord Henry sipped his champagne in a meditative manner. "At what particular point did you mention the word marriage, Dorian? and what did she say in answer? Perhaps you forgot all about it."

"My dear Harry, I did not treat it as a business transaction, and I did not make any formal proposal. I told her that I loved her, and she said she was not worthy to be my wife. Not worthy! Why, the whole world is nothing to me compared to her."

"Women are wonderfully practical," murmured Lord Henry,— "much more practical than we are. In situations of that kind we often forget to say anything about marriage, and they always remind us."[12]

Hallward laid his hand upon his arm. "Don't, Harry. You have annoyed Dorian. He is not like other men. He would never bring misery upon any one. His nature is too fine for that."

Lord Henry looked across the table. "Dorian is never annoyed with me," he answered. "I asked the question for the best reason possible, for the only reason, indeed, that excuses one for asking any question, simple curiosity. I have a theory that it is always the women who propose to us, and not we who propose to the women, except, of course, in middle-class life. But then the middle classes are not modern."

men find in the olive-woods near Tanagra." On reviewing Ernst von Wildenbach's *Master of Tanagra* in 1887, Wilde remarked that it is "impossible to reproduce by any process the delicate and exquisite charm of the Tanagra figurines."

10 "Lips that Shakespeare taught to speak" calls to mind the prepubescent boy actors employed by Shakespeare's acting company. Female parts were acted by boys in women's costume, since women were not permitted on the professional stage in Elizabethan England. Wilde's short story "The Portrait of Mr. W. H." concerns an obsessive attempt to demonstrate that "Mr. W. H.," the mysterious dedicatee of Shakespeare's sonnets, was Willie Hughes, an alleged boy actor in Shakespeare's company specializing in playing women. As Rosalind in *As You Like it,* Sybil Vane plays a part originally written for and acted by a boy pretending to be a woman disguised as a man.

11 In 1885 Wilde attended an open-air production of *As You Like It,* mounted by Lady Archie Campbell and E. W. Godwin on the grounds of Coombe House: "we passed into the green pavilion that served as the theatre, the air sweet with odour of the lilac and with the blackbird's song; and when the curtain fell into its trench of flowers, and the play commenced, we saw before us a real forest, and we knew it to be Arden" ("*As You Like It* at Coombe House").

12 "I adore you. But you haven't proposed to me yet. Nothing has been said at all about marriage. The subject has not even been touched upon" (Gwendolen to Jack, in *The Importance of Being Earnest*).

"One afternoon, a month later, Dorian Gray was reclining in a luxurious armchair, in the little library of Lord Henry's house in Mayfair," from *The Picture of Dorian Gray,* illustr. Madjeska (New York: Horace Liveright, 1930).

13 While initially identified with femininity and youth, the cigarette increasingly symbolized the emergence of modernity, rapidly displacing the more "manly" cigar (see Jason Hughes, *Learning to Smoke* [University of Chicago Press, 2003], pp. 89–90). Wilde had an aversion to cigars: upon attempting to light an after-dinner cigar, one unfortunate cigar-smoker was reprimanded by Wilde as follows: "How too terrible of you! But we shall call it a nut-brown cigarette—and you shall smoke it" (*Oscar Wilde: Interviews and Recollections*, 1:224).

14 "There is nothing left for me now but the divine [momentary pleasure] of another cigarette. Cigarettes have at least the charm of leaving one unsatisfied" ("The Critic as Artist," p. 142).

15 A light, four-wheeled, horse-drawn carriage, either invented or made fashionable by the Scottish jurist Henry Brougham, 1st Baron Brougham and Vaux. It had an enclosed cab and sat two, though it sometimes contained an extra pair of foldaway seats in the front corners. An additional passenger could be accommodated on the box seat in front, alongside the driver.

Dorian Gray laughed, and tossed his head. "You are quite incorrigible, Harry; but I don't mind. It is impossible to be angry with you. When you see Sybil Vane you will feel that the man who could wrong her would be a beast without a heart. I cannot understand how anyone can wish to shame what he loves. I love Sybil Vane. I wish to place her on a pedestal of gold, and to see the world worship the woman who is mine. What is marriage? An irrevocable vow. And it is an irrevocable vow that I want to take. Her trust makes me faithful, her belief makes me good. When I am with her, I regret all that you have taught me. I become different from what you have known me to be. I am changed, and the mere touch of Sybil Vane's hand makes me forget you and all your wrong, fascinating, poisonous, delightful theories."

"You will always like me, Dorian," said Lord Henry. "Will you have some coffee, you fellows? Waiter, bring coffee, and *fine-champagne,* and some cigarettes. No: don't mind the cigarettes; I have got some.[b] Basil, I can't allow you to smoke cigars. You must have a cigarette.[13] A cigarette is the perfect type of a perfect pleasure. It is exquisite, and it leaves one unsatisfied.[14] What more can you want? Yes, Dorian, you will always be fond of me. I represent to you all the sins you have never had the courage to commit."

"What nonsense you talk, Harry!" cried Dorian Gray, lighting his cigarette from a fire-breathing silver dragon that the waiter had placed on the table. "Let us go down to the theatre. When you see Sybil you will have a new ideal of life. She will represent something to you that you have never known."

"I have known everything," said Lord Henry, with a sad look in his eyes, "but I am always ready for a new emotion. I am afraid that there is no such thing, for me at any rate. Still, your wonderful girl may thrill me. I love acting. It is so much more real than life. Let us go. Dorian, you will come with me. I am so sorry, Basil, but there is only room for two in the brougham.[15] You must follow us in a hansom."

They got up and put on their coats, sipping their coffee standing. Hallward was silent and preoccupied. There was a gloom over him. He could not bear this marriage, and yet it seemed to him to be better than many other things that might have happened. After a few moments, they all passed down-stairs. He drove off by himself, as had been arranged, and watched the flashing lights of the little brougham in front of him. A strange sense of loss came over him. He felt that Dorian Gray would never again be to him all that he had been in the past. His eyes darkened, and the crowded flaring streets became blurred to him. When the cab drew up at the doors of the Theatre, it seemed to him that he had grown years older.

A brougham. The brougham was designed as a fashionable private vehicle, but second-hand broughams were often refurbished as vehicles for hire.

V

For some reason or other, the house was crowded that night, and the fat Jew Manager who met them at the door was beaming from ear to ear with an oily, tremulous smile. He escorted them to their box with a sort of pompous humility, waving his fat jewelled hands, and talking at the top of his voice. Dorian Gray loathed him more than ever. He felt as if he had come to look for Miranda and had been met by Caliban. Lord Henry, upon the other hand, rather liked him. At least he declared he did, and insisted on shaking him by the hand, and assured him that he was proud to meet a man who had discovered a real genius, and gone bankrupt over Shakespeare. Hallward amused himself with watching the faces in the pit. The heat was terribly oppressive, and the huge sunlight flamed like a monstrous dahlia with petals of fire. The youths in the gallery had taken off their coats and waistcoats and hung them over the side. They talked to each other across the Theatre, and shared their oranges with the tawdry painted girls who sat by them. Some women were laughing in the pit; their voices were horribly shrill and discordant. The sound of the popping of corks came from the bar.

"What a place to find one's divinity in!" said Lord Henry.

"Yes!" answered Dorian Gray. "It was here I found her, and she is divine beyond all living things. When she acts you will forget everything. These common people here, with their coarse faces and brutal gestures, become quite different when she is on the stage.

They sit silently and watch her. They weep and laugh as she wills them to do. She makes them as responsive as a violin. She spiritualises them, and one feels that they are of the same flesh and blood as oneself."

"Oh, I hope not!" murmured Lord Henry, who was scanning the occupants of the gallery through his opera-glass.

"Don't pay any attention to him, Dorian," said Hallward. "I understand what you mean, and I believe in this girl. Any one you love must be marvellous, and any girl that has the effect you describe must be fine and noble. To spiritualise one's age,—that is something worth doing. If this girl can give a soul to those who have lived without one, if she can create the sense of beauty in people whose lives have been sordid and ugly, if she can strip them of their selfishness and lend them tears for sorrows that are not their own, she is worthy of all your adoration, worthy of the adoration of the world. This marriage is quite right. I did not think so at first, but I admit it now. God made Sybil Vane for you. Without her you would have been incomplete."

"Thanks, Basil," answered Dorian Gray, pressing his hand. "I knew that you would understand me. Harry is so cynical, he terrifies me. But here is the Orchestra. It is quite dreadful, but it only lasts for about five minutes. Then the curtain rises, and you will see the girl to whom I am going to give all my life, to whom I have given everything that is good in me."

A quarter of an hour afterwards, amidst an extraordinary turmoil of applause, Sybil Vane stepped on to the stage. Yes, she was certainly lovely to look at, one of the loveliest creatures, Lord Henry thought, that he had ever seen. There was something of the fawn in her shy grace and startled eyes. A faint blush, like the shadow of a rose in a mirror of silver, came to her cheeks as she glanced at the crowded, enthusiastic house. She stepped back a few paces, and her lips seemed to tremble. Basil Hallward leapt to his feet and began to applaud. Dorian Gray sat motionless, gazing on her, like a man in a dream. Lord Henry peered through his opera-glass, murmuring, "Charming, charming!"

Napoleon Sarony photo-portrait of Wilde, 1882. Wilde became increasingly alive to the importance of photographic portraits in developing his fame and reputation during his lecture tour of America in 1882, when the famous series of photo-portraits by Sarony was taken.

1 Wilde's poem "Under the Balcony" was inspired by this most famous of all love scenes (Act II, Scene II, of *Romeo and Juliet*).

2 "The two things the Greeks valued most in actors were grace of gesture and music of voice," Wilde writes in 1886 upon reviewing E. W. Godwin's production of Sophocles' play *Helena in Troas;* "Miss Alma Murray does not possess the physical requisite for our conception of Helen, but the beauty of her movements and the extremely sympathetic quality of her voice gave an indefinable charm to her voice" (*"Helena in Troas"*). A year earlier he had praised Ellen Terry in similar terms, remarking on the "marvelous grace of her movements and gestures" and the impossibility of "escape from the sweet tyranny of her personality" ("*Olivia* at the Lyceum").

The scene was the hall of Capulet's house, and Romeo in his pilgrim's dress had entered with Mercutio and his friends. The band, such as it was, struck up a few bars of music, and the dance began. Through the crowd of ungainly, shabbily-dressed actors, Sybil Vane moved like a creature from a finer world. Her body swayed, as she danced, as a plant sways in the water. The curves of her throat were like the curves of a white lily. Her hands seemed to be made of cool ivory.

Yet she was curiously listless. She showed no sign of joy when her eyes rested on Romeo. The few lines she had to speak,—

> Good pilgrim, you do wrong your hand too much,
> Which mannerly devotion shows in this;
> For Saints have hands that pilgrims' hands do touch,

And palm to palm is holy palmers' kiss,—with the brief dialogue that follows, were spoken in a thoroughly artificial manner. The voice was exquisite, but from the point of view of tone it was absolutely false. It was wrong in colour. It took away all the life from the verse. It made the passion unreal.

Dorian Gray grew pale as he watched her. Neither of his friends dared to say anything to him. She seemed to them to be absolutely incompetent. They were horribly disappointed. Yet they felt that the true test of any Juliet is the balcony scene of the second act.[1] They waited for that. If she failed there, there was nothing in her.

She looked charming as she came out in the moonlight. That could not be denied. But the staginess of her acting was unbearable, and grew worse as she went on. Her gestures became absurdly artificial. She over-emphasised everything that she had to say.[2] The beautiful passage,—

> Thou knowest the mask of night is on my face,
> Else would a maiden blush bepaint my cheek
> For that which thou hast heard me speak to-night,—

was declaimed with the painful precision of a school-girl who has
been taught to recite by some second-rate Professor of Elocution.
When she leaned over the balcony and came to those wonderful
lines,—

> Although I joy in Thee,
> I have no joy of this contract to-night:
> It is too rash, too unadvised, too sudden;
> Too like the lightning, which doth cease to be
> Ere one can say, "It lightens." Sweet, good-night!
> This bud of love by summer's ripening breath
> May prove a beauteous flower when next we meet,—

The actress Ellen Terry (1847–1928), photographed at the
age of sixteen, by Julia Margaret Cameron. Wilde befriended
Terry and many other leading actresses in the late 1870s and
early 1880s.

3 According to Charles Ricketts, the story of the actress who loses her talent when she falls in love was conceived apart from *Dorian Gray* and only later incorporated into the novel (*Oscar Wilde: Recollections,* p. 15). Wilde entertained listeners with earlier versions of the story on multiple occasions: one version is reprinted in Holland, *Son of Oscar Wilde,* Appendix C; another version is given in *Table Talk: Oscar Wilde,* ed. T. Wright (London: Cassell, 2000), pp. 26–31. Both versions end with the actress recovering her dramatic genius while simultaneously falling back out of love.

4 London's gentlemen's clubs developed from eighteenth-century coffeehouses, generally in the area around St. James and Pall Mall. They provided a means of establishing gentlemanly status and making useful connections, but they were also a way for unmarried gentlemen to enter the legitimate social sphere. The number of clubs grew dramatically in the decade before *Dorian Gray.* During this period, they opened their doors to middle-class and professional men and became important testing-grounds for new styles of Victorian masculinity. Wilde was a member of one of the few London clubs (the Albermarle Club) that welcomed women as well as men. The Albermarle fell into decline, however, after featuring prominently in Wilde's scandal. It eventually closed its doors in 1941.

she spoke the words as if they conveyed no meaning to her. It was not nervousness. Indeed, so far from being nervous, she seemed absolutely self-contained. It was simply bad art. She was a complete failure.

Even the common uneducated audience of the pit and gallery lost their interest in the play. They got restless, and began to talk loudly and to whistle. The Jew Manager, who was standing at the back of the dress-circle, stamped and swore with rage. The only person unmoved was the girl herself.

When the second act was over there came a storm of hisses, and Lord Henry got up from his chair and put on his coat. "She is quite beautiful, Dorian," he said, "but she can't act. Let us go."

"I am going to see the play through," answered the lad in a hard, bitter voice. "I am awfully sorry that I have made you waste an evening, Harry. I apologise to both of you."

"My dear Dorian, I should think Miss Vane was ill," interrupted Hallward. "We will come some other night."

"I wish she was ill," he rejoined. "But she seems to me to be simply callous and cold. She has entirely altered. Last night she was a great artist. To-night she is merely a commonplace, mediocre actress."[3]

"Don't talk like that about any one you love, Dorian. Love is a more wonderful thing than art."

"They are both simply forms of imitation," murmured Lord Henry. "But do let us go. Dorian, you must not stay here any longer. It is not good for one's morals to see bad acting. Besides, I don't suppose you will want your wife to act. So what does it matter if she plays Juliet like a wooden doll? She is very lovely, and if she knows as little about life as she does about acting, she will be a delightful experience. There are only two kinds of people who are really fascinating, —people who know absolutely everything, and people who know absolutely nothing. Good Heavens, my dear boy, don't look so tragic! The secret of remaining young is never to have an emotion that is unbecoming. Come to the Club with Basil and myself.[4] We will smoke cigarettes and drink to the beauty of Sybil Vane. She is beautiful. What more can you want?"

"Please go away, Harry," cried the lad. "I really want to be alone. Basil, you don't mind my asking you to go? Ah! can't you see that my heart is breaking?" The hot tears came to his eyes. His lips trembled, and, rushing to the back of the box, he leaned up against the wall, hiding his face in his hands.

"Let us go, Basil," said Lord Henry, with a strange tenderness in his voice; and the two young men passed out together.

A few moments afterwards the footlights flared up, and the curtain rose on the third act. Dorian Gray went back to his seat. He looked pale, and proud, and indifferent. The play dragged on, and seemed interminable. Half of the audience went out, tramping in heavy boots, and laughing. The whole thing was a *fiasco*. The last act was played to almost empty benches.

As soon as it was over, Dorian Gray rushed behind the scenes into the green-room. The girl was standing alone there, with a look of triumph on her face. Her eyes were lit with an exquisite fire. There was a radiance about her. Her parted lips were smiling over some secret of their own.

When he entered, she looked at him, and an expression of infinite joy came over her. "How badly I acted to-night, Dorian!" she cried.

"Horribly!" he answered, gazing at her in amazement, "horribly! It was dreadful. Are you ill? You have no idea what it was. You have no idea what I suffered."

The girl smiled. "Dorian," she answered, lingering over his name with long-drawn music in her voice, as though it were sweeter than honey to the red petals of her lips, "Dorian, you should have understood. But you understand now, don't you?"

"Understand what?" he asked, angrily.

"Why I was so bad to-night. Why I shall always be bad. Why I shall never act well again."

He shrugged his shoulders. "You are ill, I suppose. When you are ill you shouldn't act. You make yourself ridiculous. My friends were bored. I was bored."

She seemed not to listen to him. She was transfigured with joy. An ecstasy of happiness dominated her.

5 "I am half sick of shadows" is the cry of Tennyson's Lady in his ballad "The Lady of Shalott." Embowered on a lonely isle, she weaves her magic web of the scenes (witnessed through a mirror) that pass below her on the road to Camelot. A nameless curse will be placed on her if she looks directly on Camelot. When she sees the comely Lancelot in her mirror, she abandons her loom, the mirror cracks, and she descends from her tower. Hoping to find love, the artist discovers only death.

6 Turning from the ideal of art to life is the source of "bad art," for "when Art surrenders her imaginative medium, she surrenders everything" (Wilde, "The Decay of Lying," p. 85). In supposing life to offer a higher reality than art—in suddenly finding the theater's "painted scenes" to be all "shadows" and "hollowness"— Sybil misconceives the very essence of drama, as Wilde articulates it, holding it up to the standards of verisimilitude or truthfulness by which no art should, properly speaking, be judged. "Art finds her own perfection within, and not outside of, herself," declares Wilde in "The Decay of Lying": "she is not to be judged by any external standard of resemblance. She is a veil, rather than a mirror" (pp. 89–90). For Wilde "the self-conscious aim of Life is to find expression"; and "Art offers it certain beautiful forms" through which it may "realize" that aim (p. 102). Thus, in Wilde's memorable formulation, "Life imitates Art far more than Art imitates Life" (p. 102).

"Dorian, Dorian," she cried, "before I knew you, acting was the one reality of my life. It was only in the theatre that I lived. I thought that it was all true. I was Rosalind one night, and Portia the other. The joy of Beatrice was my joy, and the sorrows of Cordelia were mine also. I believed in everything. The common people who acted with me seemed to me to be godlike. The painted scenes were my world. I knew nothing but shadows, and I thought them real. You came,—oh, my beautiful love!—and you freed my soul from prison. You taught me what reality really is. To-night, for the first time in my life, I saw through the hollowness, the sham, the silliness, of the empty pageant in which I had always played. To-night, for the first time, I became conscious that the Romeo was hideous, and old, and painted, that the moonlight in the orchard was false, that the scenery was vulgar, and that the words I had to speak were unreal, were not my words, not what I wanted to say. You had brought me something higher, something of which all art is but a reflection. You have made me understand what love really is. My love! my love! I am sick of shadows.[5] You are more to me than all art can ever be.[6] What have I to do with the puppets of a play? When I came on to-night, I could not understand how it was that everything had gone from me. Suddenly it dawned on my soul what it all meant. The knowledge was exquisite to me. I heard them hissing, and I smiled. What should they know of love? Take me away, Dorian. Take me away with you, where we can be quite alone. I hate the stage. I might mimic a passion that I do not feel, but I cannot mimic one that burns me like fire. Oh, Dorian, Dorian, you understand now what it all means? Even if I could do it, it would be profanation for me to play at being in love. You have made me see that."

He flung himself down on the sofa, and turned away his face. "You have killed my love," he muttered.

She looked at him in wonder, and laughed. He made no answer. She came across to him, and stroked his hair with her little fingers. She knelt down and pressed his hands to her lips. He drew them away, and a shudder ran through him.

Then he leapt up, and went to the door. "Yes," he cried, "you have killed my love. You used to stir my imagination. Now you don't even stir my curiosity.[7] You simply produce no effect. I loved you because you were wonderful, because you had genius and intellect, because you realised the dreams of great poets, and gave shape and substance to the shadows of art. You have thrown it all away. You are shallow and stupid. My God! how mad I was to love you! What a fool I have been! You are nothing to me now. I will never see you again. I will never think of you. I will never mention your name. You don't know what you were to me, once. Why, once. . . . oh, I can't bear to think of it! I wish I had never laid eyes upon you! You have spoiled the romance of my life. How little you can know of love, if you say it mars your art! What are you without your art? Nothing. I would have made you famous, splendid, magnificent. The world would have worshipped you, and you would have belonged to me. What are you now? A third-rate actress with a pretty face."

The girl grew white, and trembled. She clenched her hands together, and her voice seemed to catch in her throat. "You are not serious, Dorian?" she murmured. "You are acting."

"Acting! I leave that to you. You do it so well," he answered, bitterly.

She rose from her knees, and, with a piteous expression of pain in her face, came across the room to him. She put her hand upon his arm, and looked into his eyes. He thrust her back. "Don't touch me!" he cried.

A low moan broke from her, and she flung herself at his feet, and lay there like a trampled flower. "Dorian, Dorian, don't leave me." she whispered. "I am so sorry I didn't act well. I was thinking of you all the time. But I will try,—indeed I will try. It came so suddenly across me, my love for you. I think I should never have known it if you had not kissed me, if we had not kissed each other. Kiss me again, my love. Don't go away from me. I couldn't bear it. Can't you forgive me for to-night? I will work so hard, and try to improve. Don't be cruel to me because I love you better than anything in the world. After all, it is only once that I have not pleased you. But you are quite right, Dorian. I should have shown myself more of an artist. It was foolish of me; and yet I couldn't help it. Oh, don't leave me, don't leave me." A fit of passionate sobbing choked her. She crouched on

7 Compare with Wilde's harsh words in 1897 about his now-estranged wife, Constance: "Women are so petty, and Constance has no imagination. . . . I wish to goodness she would leave me alone" (*CL*, p. 955).

8 This graphic sentence was deleted by Stoddart or one of his associates at Lippincott. Its restoration certainly puts Dorian's night walking in a different light.

9 This surreal distortion of the London cityscape, foreshadowed in much of Wilde's poetry of the 1870s and 1880s, contains many echoes from Wilde's story "Lord Arthur Savile's Crime": following a palm-reader's prediction that he will commit murder, Lord Arthur Savile wanders haphazardly through London streets at

"She crouched on the floor like a wounded thing, and Dorian Gray, with his beautiful eyes, looked down at her," from *The Picture of Dorian Gray*, illustr. Madjeska (New York: Horace Liveright, 1930).

the floor like a wounded thing, and Dorian Gray, with his beautiful eyes, looked down at her, and his chiselled lips curled in exquisite disdain. There is always something ridiculous about the passions of people whom one has ceased to love. Sybil Vane seemed to him to be absurdly melodramatic. Her tears and sobs annoyed him.

"I am going," he said at last, in his calm, clear voice. "I don't wish to be unkind, but I can't see you again. You have disappointed me."

She wept silently, and made no answer, but crept nearer to him. Her little hands stretched blindly out, and appeared to be seeking for him. He turned on his heel, and left the room. In a few moments he was out of the Theatre.

Where he went to, he hardly knew. He remembered wandering through dimly-lit streets with gaunt black-shadowed archways and evil-looking houses. Women with hoarse voices and harsh laughter had called after him. Drunkards had reeled by cursing, and chattering to themselves like monstrous apes. A man with curious eyes had suddenly peered into his face, and then dogged him with stealthy footsteps, passing and repassing him many times.[8a] He had seen grotesque children huddled upon door-steps, and had heard shrieks and oaths from gloomy courts.[9]

When the dawn was just breaking he found himself at Covent Garden. Huge carts filled with nodding lilies rumbled slowly down the polished empty street.[10] The air was heavy with the perfume of the flowers, and their beauty seemed to bring him an anodyne for his pain. He followed into the Market, and watched the men unloading their waggons. A white-smocked carter offered him some cherries. He thanked him, wondered why he refused to accept any money for them, and began to eat them listlessly. They had been plucked at midnight, and the coldness of the moon had entered into them.[11] A long line of boys carrying crates of striped tulips, and of yellow and red roses, defiled in front of him, threading their way through the huge jade-green piles of vegetables. Under the portico, with its grey sun-bleached pillars, loitered a troop of draggled bare-headed girls, waiting for the auction to be over. After some time he hailed a hansom and drove home. The sky was pure opal now, and the roofs of the houses glistened like silver against it.

'HOW UTTER.'

Wilde caricatured as an "Apostle of the Lily" in a satirical engraving from 1878.

night, tortured by guilt, imagining that "he could detect the stain of blood already upon" his hands.

10 Wilde had been associated with the lily ever since the late 1870s: "he would drop into Covent Garden flower market, buy me a single gorgeous amaryllis (all his slender purse would allow), and stroll down Piccadilly carefully carrying the solitary flower. The scribblers construed this act of homage as a pose, and thus I innocently conferred on him the title 'Apostle of the Lily'" (Lily Langtry, "The Oscar I Knew" [1925], rpt. in *Oscar Wilde: Interviews and Recollections,* ed. Mikhail, 2:261).

11 In Christina Rossetti's poem "Goblin Market" (1862; rpt. in *The Complete Poems,* ed. R. W. Crump [London: Penguin, 2001], pp. 5–19), a young maiden is offered enticing fruits from an "unknown orchard" (line 135) by "wicked, quaint, fruit-merchant men" (line 553). Upon succumbing to the temptation, we are told, she "sucked their fruit globes fair or red" and "knew not was it night or day/As she turned home alone" (lines 134–140). The proffering of cherries is a significant revision of "Lord Arthur Savile's Crime," where we are told merely that "the white-smocked carters, with their pleasant sunburnt faces and coarse curly hair, strode sturdily on, cracking their whips, and calling out now and then to each other."

12 This is the first suggestion of what Wilde later calls "the horrible sympathy" between Dorian and his portrait. This sentence recalls Wilde's earlier story "Lady Alroy" (now usually reprinted under its later title "The Sphinx without a Secret"), in which the protagonist carefully examines a photographic portrait contained in a silver-clasped morocco case: "it seemed to me the face of someone who had a secret, but whether that secret was good or evil I could not say. Its beauty was a beauty moulded out of many mysteries—the beauty, in fact, which is psychological, not plastic—and the faint smile that played across the lips was far too subtle to be really sweet."

A fruit auction at Covent Garden, London's main fruit, vegetable, and flower market. The market, housed in a neo-Classical building designed by Charles Fowler, closed in 1973, and Covent Garden is now a major shopping and tourist mecca. For much of the eighteenth and nineteenth centuries, the Covent Garden area was a notorious red-light district.

As he was passing through the library towards the door of his bedroom, his eye fell upon the portrait Basil Hallward had painted of him. He started back in surprise, and then went over to it and examined it. In the dim arrested light that struggled through the cream-coloured silk blinds, the face seemed to him to be a little changed. The expression looked different. One would have said that there was a touch of cruelty in the mouth.[12] It was certainly curious.

He turned round, and, walking to the window, drew the blinds up. The bright dawn flooded the room, and swept the fantastic shadows into dusky corners, where they lay shuddering. But the strange expression that he had noticed in the face of the portrait seemed to linger there, to be more intensified even. The quivering, ardent sunlight showed him the lines of cruelty round the mouth as clearly as if

Flower selling at Covent Garden.

he had been looking into a mirror after he had done some dreadful thing.

He winced, and, taking up from the table an oval glass framed in ivory Cupids, that Lord Henry had given him, he glanced hurriedly into it. No line like that warped his red lips. What did it mean?

He rubbed his eyes, and came close to the picture, and examined it again. There were no signs of any change when he looked into the actual painting, and yet there was no doubt that the whole expression had altered. It was not a mere fancy of his own. The thing was horribly apparent.[13]

He threw himself into a chair, and began to think. Suddenly there flashed across his mind what he had said in Basil Hallward's studio the day the picture had been finished. Yes, he remembered it per-

13 Supernatural pictures had featured in English-language fiction ever since Horace Walpole's novel *The Castle of Otranto* (1764). But the 1880s witnessed a flood of stories and novels in which magic portraits loomed large. Wilde drew from no one of these stories exclusively but rather incorporated into *The Picture of Dorian Gray* "a veritable lexicon of motifs associated with magic-portrait fiction" (Kerry Powell, "Tom, Dick, and Dorian Gray: Magic-Picture Mania in Late Victorian Fiction," *Philological Quarterly,* 62 [1983], p. 152). Wilde's novel can thus be viewed as culminating a literary tradition that includes not only such well-known works as Nathaniel Hawthorne's "Prophetic Pictures" (1837), Edgar Allen Poe's "Oval Portrait" (originally published in 1842 under the title "Life in Death"), and Nikolai Gogol's "The Portrait" (1835; trans. 1847) but also such lesser-known works as W. H. Pollock's *Picture's Secret* (1883), Elizabeth Lysaught's *Veiled Portrait* (1889), S. Weir Mitchell's *Portrait and the Ghost* (1887), and E. J. Goodman's *His Other Self* (1889). Wilde was almost certainly strongly influenced by *Melmoth the Wanderer* (1820), written by his maternal grand-uncle Charles Maturin, in which a hidden, closeted portrait of the evil Melmoth (who has bargained with the Devil for extended life and an unchanging appearance) contains eyes that move. Balzac's *Peau de Chagrin* (1831; trans. as *The Wild Ass's Skin*) no doubt also deeply affected Wilde. In the novel a picture of Christ exerts a sinister influence and a magic ass's skin becomes an objective, visual register of its owner's dissipation. Raphael, the skin's owner, acquires the skin because he has been promised that it will grant its owner's every wish. After plunging into a life of dissipation and extravagance, however, he discovers that the skin magically shrinks, until, in the end, his life ceases along with it.

fectly. He had uttered a mad wish that he himself might remain young, and the portrait grow old; that his own beauty might be untarnished, and the face on the canvas bear the burden of his passions and his sins; that the painted image might be seared with the lines of suffering and thought, and that he might keep all the delicate bloom and loveliness of his then just conscious boyhood. Surely his prayer had not been answered? Such things were impossible. It seemed monstrous even to think of them. And, yet, there was the picture before him, with the touch of cruelty in the mouth.

Cruelty! Had he been cruel? It was the girl's fault, not his. He had dreamed of her as a great artist, had given his love to her because he had thought her great. Then she had disappointed him. She had been shallow and unworthy. And, yet, a feeling of infinite regret came over him, as he thought of her lying at his feet sobbing like a little child. He remembered with what callousness he had watched her. Why had he been made like that? Why had such a soul been given to him? But he had suffered also. During the three terrible hours that the play had lasted, he had lived centuries of pain, æon upon æon of torture. His life was well worth hers. She had marred him for a moment, if he had wounded her for an age. Besides, women were better suited to bear sorrow than men. They lived on their emotions. They only thought of their emotions. When they took lovers, it was merely to have some one with whom they could have scenes. Lord Henry had told him that, and Lord Henry knew what women were. Why should he trouble about Sybil Vane? She was nothing to him now.

But the picture? What was he to say of that? It held the secret of his life, and told his story. It had taught him to love his own beauty. Would it teach him to loathe his own soul? Would he ever look at it again?

No; it was merely an illusion wrought on the troubled senses. The horrible night that he had passed had left phantoms behind it. Suddenly there had fallen upon his brain that tiny scarlet speck that makes men mad. The picture had not changed. It was folly to think so.

Yet it was watching him, with its beautiful marred face, and its cruel smile. Its bright hair gleamed in the early sunlight. Its blue eyes met his own. A sense of infinite pity, not for himself, but for the painted image of himself, came over him. It had altered already, and would alter more. Its gold would wither into grey. Its red and white roses would die. For every sin that he committed, a stain would fleck and wreck its fairness.[b]

But he would not sin. The picture, changed or unchanged, would be to him the visible emblem of conscience. He would resist temptation. He would not see Lord Henry any more, would not, at any rate, listen to those subtle poisonous theories that in Basil Hallward's garden had first stirred within him the passion for impossible things. He would go back to Sybil Vane, make her amends, marry her, try to love her again. Yes, it was his duty to do so.[14] She must have suffered more than he had. Poor child! He had been selfish and cruel to her. The fascination that she had exercised over him would return. They would be happy together. His life with her would be beautiful and pure.

He got up from his chair, and drew a large screen right in front of the portrait, shuddering as he glanced at it. "How horrible!" he murmured to himself, and he walked across to the window and opened it. When he stepped out on the grass, he drew a deep breath. The fresh morning air seemed to drive away all his sombre passions. He thought only of Sybil Vane. A faint echo of his love came back to him. He repeated her name over and over again. The birds that were singing in the dew-drenched garden seemed to be telling the flowers about her.[15]

14 Duty was a paramount virtue for many Victorians. Wilde's writings are peppered with criticism of it: "duty is what one expects from others, it is not what one does oneself," remarks Lord Illingworth in *A Woman of No Importance.* Wilde's story "Lord Arthur Savile's Crime" is subversively subtitled "A Study in Duty." And in "The Soul of Socialism," Wilde praises Individualism partly because "it does not come to man with any sickly cant about duty, which merely means doing what other people want because they want it" (p. 263).

15 Compare this garden with the "large lovely garden with soft green grass" in Wilde's Christian fable "The Selfish Giant," where "beautiful flowers like stars" stand over the grass and birds sing sweetly. In "The Selfish Giant," the beautiful garden turns desolate and wintry following the giant's act of monumental selfishness.

VI

It was long past noon when he awoke. His valet had crept several times into the room on tiptoe to see if he was stirring, and had wondered what made his young master sleep so late. Finally his bell sounded, and Victor came in softly with a cup of tea, and a pile of letters, on a small tray of old Sèvres china, and drew back the olive-satin curtains, with their shimmering blue lining, that hung in front of the three tall windows.

"Monsieur has well slept this morning," he said, smiling.

"What o'clock is it, Victor?" asked Dorian Gray, sleepily.

"One hour and a quarter, Monsieur."

How late it was! He sat up, and, having sipped some tea, turned over his letters. One of them was from Lord Henry, and had been brought by hand that morning. He hesitated for a moment, and then put it aside. The others he opened listlessly. They contained the usual collection of cards, invitations to dinner, tickets for private views, programmes of Charity Concerts and the like, that are showered on fashionable young men every morning during the season. There was a rather heavy bill, for a chased silver Louis-Quinze toilet-set, that he had not yet had the courage to send on to his guardians, who were extremely old-fashioned people and did not realise that we live in an age when only unnecessary things are absolutely necessary to us; and there were several very courteously worded communications from Jermyn Street money-lenders offering to advance any sum of money at a moment's notice, and at the most reasonable rates of interest.[1]

1 Jermyn Street, in London's St. James district, was and still is associated with gentlemen tailors. As Joseph Bristow observes, in Wilde's day many of these tailors were effectively moneylenders too, since they preferred extending credit, often at exorbitant rates of interest, to suing their customers for unpaid bills.

After about ten minutes he got up, and, throwing on an elaborate dressing-gown, passed into the onyx-paved bath-room. The cool water refreshed him after his long sleep. He seemed to have forgotten all that he had gone through. A dim sense of having taken part in some strange tragedy came to him once or twice, but there was the unreality of a dream about it.

As soon as he was dressed, he went into the library and sat down to a light French breakfast, that had been laid out for him on a small round table close to an open window. It was an exquisite day. The warm air seemed laden with spices. A bee flew in, and buzzed round the blue-dragon bowl, filled with sulphur-yellow roses, that stood in front of him. He felt perfectly happy.

Suddenly his eye fell on the screen that he had placed in front of the portrait, and he started.

"Too cold for Monsieur?" asked his valet, putting an omelette on the table. "I shut the window?"

Dorian shook his head. "I am not cold," he murmured.

Was it all true? Had the portrait really changed? Or had it been simply his own imagination that had made him see a look of evil where there had been a look of joy? Surely a painted canvas could not alter? The thing was absurd. It would serve as a tale to tell Basil some day. It would make him smile.

And, yet, how vivid was his recollection of the whole thing! First in the dim twilight, and then in the bright dawn, he had seen the touch of cruelty in the warped lips. He almost dreaded his valet leaving the room. He knew that when he was alone he would have to examine the portrait. He was afraid of certainty. When the coffee and cigarettes had been brought and the man turned to go, he felt a mad desire to tell him to remain. As the door closed behind him he called him back. The man stood waiting for his orders. Dorian looked at him for a moment. "I am not at home to anyone, Victor," he said with a sigh. The man bowed and retired.

He rose from the table, lit a cigarette, and flung himself down on a luxuriously-cushioned couch that stood facing the screen. The screen was an old one of gilt Spanish leather, stamped and wrought with a rather florid Louis-Quatorze pattern.[2] He scanned it curi-

2 Together with the Louis Quatorze clock mentioned in Chapter III and the Louis Quinze toilet set mentioned earlier in the present chapter, this screen identifies Dorian as a rococo revivalist and a disciple of the Goncourt brothers, who "translated their anger and resentment toward the nineteenth century into the creation of an alternative world," where they "found compensatory association with the dead generations of the Old Regime" (Debora L. Silverman, *Art Nouveau in Fin de Siècle France* [Berkeley: University of California Press, 1989], p. 19).

3 The road to hell is paved with good intentions. Wilde's deliberate and repeated use of the subjunctive mood (could, would) suggests Dorian's unwillingness to change and make reparations. He merely longs to be something he is not. This moment compares interestingly with a later one in Chapter IX when Dorian wakens to "a world in which the past [has] little or no place, or survive[s], at any rate, in no conscious form of obligation or regret." See, too, Lord Henry's remark, later in this chapter, that "good resolutions are simply a useless attempt to interfere with scientific laws. Their origin is pure vanity. Their result is absolutely *nil*."

ously, wondering if it had ever before concealed the secret of a man's life.

Should he move it aside, after all? Why not let it stay there? What was the use of knowing? If the thing was true, it was terrible. If it was not true, why trouble about it? But what if, by some fate or deadlier chance, other eyes than his spied behind, and saw the horrible change? What should he do if Basil Hallward came and asked to look at his own picture? He would be sure to do that. No; the thing had to be examined, and at once. Anything would be better than this dreadful state of doubt.

He got up, and locked both doors. At least he would be alone when he looked upon the mask of his shame. Then he drew the screen aside, and saw himself face to face. It was perfectly true. The portrait had altered.

As he often remembered afterwards, and always with no small wonder, he found himself at first gazing at the portrait with a feeling of almost scientific interest. That such a change should have taken place was incredible to him. And yet it was a fact. Was there some subtle affinity between the chemical atoms, that shaped themselves into form and colour on the canvas, and the soul that was within him? Could it be that what that soul thought, they realised? that what it dreamed, they made true? Or was there some other, more terrible reason? He shuddered, and felt afraid, and, going back to the couch, lay there, gazing at the picture in sickened horror.

One thing, however, he felt that it had done for him. It had made him conscious how unjust, how cruel, he had been to Sybil Vane. It was not too late to make reparation for that. She could still be his wife. His unreal and selfish love would yield to some higher influence, would be transformed into some nobler passion, and the portrait that Basil Hallward had painted of him would be a guide to him through life, would be to him what holiness was to some, and conscience to others, and the fear of God to us all.[3] There were opiates for remorse, drugs that could lull the moral sense to sleep. But here was a visible symbol of the degradation of sin. Here was an ever-present sign of the ruin men brought upon their souls.

Three o'clock struck, and four, and half-past four, but he did not stir. He was trying to gather up the scarlet threads of life, and to weave them into a pattern; to find his way through the sanguine labyrinth of passion through which he was wandering. He did not know what to do, or what to think. Finally, he went over to the table and wrote a passionate letter to the girl he had loved, imploring her forgiveness, and accusing himself of madness. He covered page after page with wild words of sorrow, and wilder words of pain. There is a luxury in self-reproach. When we blame ourselves we feel that no one else has a right to blame us.[4] It is the confession, not the priest, that gives us absolution. When Dorian Gray had finished the letter, he felt that he had been forgiven.

Suddenly there came a knock to the door, and he heard Lord Henry's voice outside. "My dear Dorian, I must see you. Let me in at once. I can't bear your shutting yourself up like this."

He made no answer at first, but remained quite still. The knocking still continued, and grew louder. Yes, it was better to let Lord Henry in, and to explain to him the new life he was going to lead, to quarrel with him if it became necessary to quarrel, to part if parting was inevitable. He jumped up, drew the screen hastily across the picture, and unlocked the door.

"I am so sorry for it all, my dear boy," said Lord Henry, coming in. "But you must not think about it too much."

"Do you mean about Sybil Vane?" asked Dorian.

"Yes, of course," answered Lord Henry, sinking into a chair, and slowly pulling his gloves off. "It is dreadful, from one point of view, but it was not your fault. Tell me, did you go behind and see her after the play was over?"

"Yes."

"I felt sure you had. Did you make a scene with her?"

"I was brutal, Harry, perfectly brutal. But it is all right now. I am not sorry for anything that has happened. It has taught me to know myself better."

"Ah, Dorian, I am so glad you take it in that way. I was afraid I would find you plunged in remorse, and tearing your nice hair."

4 Wilde's narrator switches to the first-person plural here, possibly a sign of Wilde's own identification with Dorian. For other important switches to the first person, see Chapter IX, notes 14 and 41.

5 A sad example of life imitating art. Wilde did not make his debut with a scandal—but he didn't exactly reserve scandal for old age, either. At the age of forty, he went from being the most celebrated writer of his day to Britain's most notorious sexual criminal.

6 Adelina Patti (1841–1919) was one of the most highly regarded opera singers of the nineteenth century. In the years just prior to *Dorian Gray*'s publication, she was at the height of her success. George Bernard Shaw felt that she spoiled the effects of her vocal artistry with a "coquetry of the footlights" (*London Music in 1888–1889, as Heard by Corno di Bassetto* [George Bernard Shaw] [London: Constable, 1937], p. 54).

7 In London's theaters and opera houses, different sections of the auditorium were rigidly stratified by class; the "smart" people were mainly to be found in private boxes or the dress circle.

"I have got through all that," said Dorian, shaking his head, and smiling. "I am perfectly happy now. I know what conscience is, to begin with. It is not what you told me it was. It is the divinest thing in us. Don't sneer at it, Harry, any more, at least not before me. I want to be good. I can't bear the idea of my soul being hideous."

"A very charming artistic basis for ethics, Dorian! I congratulate you on it. But how are you going to begin?"

"By marrying Sybil Vane."

"Marrying Sybil Vane!" cried Lord Henry, standing up, and looking at him in perplexed amazement. "But, my dear Dorian . . ."

"Yes, Harry, I know what you are going to say. Something dreadful about marriage. Don't say it. Don't ever say things of that kind to me again. Two days ago I asked Sybil to marry me. I am not going to break my word to her. She is to be my wife."

"Your wife! Dorian! . . . Didn't you get my letter? I wrote to you this morning, and sent the note down, by my own man."

"Your letter? Oh yes, I remember. I have not read it yet, Harry. I was afraid there might be something in it that I wouldn't like."

Lord Henry walked across the room, and, sitting down by Dorian Gray, took both his hands in his, and held them tightly. "Dorian," he said, "my letter—don't be frightened—was to tell you that Sybil Vane is dead."

A cry of pain rose from the lad's lips, and he leapt to his feet, tearing his hands away from Lord Henry's grasp. "Dead! Sybil dead! It is not true. It is a horrible lie."

"It is quite true, Dorian," said Lord Henry, gravely. "It is in all the morning papers. I wrote down to you to ask you not to see any one till I came. There will have to be an inquest, of course, and you must not be mixed up in it. Things like that make a man fashionable in Paris. But in London people are so prejudiced. Here, one should never make one's *début* with a scandal.[5] One should reserve that to give an interest to one's old age. I don't suppose they know your name at the Theatre. If they don't, it is all right. Did anyone see you going round to her room? That is an important point."

Dorian did not answer for a few moments. He was dazed with horror. Finally he murmured, in a stifled voice, "Harry, did you say an inquest? What did you mean by that? Did Sybil . . . Oh, Harry, I can't bear it. But be quick. Tell me everything at once."

"I have no doubt it was not an accident, Dorian, though it must be put in that way to the public. As she was leaving the Theatre with her mother, about half-past twelve or so, she said she had forgotten something upstairs. They waited some time for her, but she did not come down again. They ultimately found her lying dead on the floor of her dressing-room. She had swallowed something by mistake, some dreadful thing they use at theatres. I don't know what it was, but it had either prussic acid or white lead in it. I should fancy it was prussic acid, as she seems to have died instantaneously. It is very tragic, of course, but you must not get yourself mixed up in it. I see by the *Standard* that she was seventeen. I should have thought she was almost younger than that. She looked such a child, and seemed to know so little about acting. Dorian, you mustn't let this thing get on your nerves. You must come and dine with me, and afterwards we will look in at the Opera. It is a Patti night, and everybody will be there.[6] You can come to my sister's box. She has got some smart women with her."[7]

"So I have murdered Sybil Vane," said Dorian Gray, half to himself, "murdered her as certainly as if I had cut her little throat with a knife.[8] And the roses are not less lovely for all that. The birds sing just as happily in my garden. And to-night I am to dine with you, and then go on to the Opera, and sup somewhere, I suppose, afterwards. How extraordinarily dramatic life is! If I had read all this in a book, Harry, I think I would have wept over it. Somehow, now that it has happened actually, and to me, it seems far too wonderful for tears. Here is the first passionate love-letter I have ever written in my life. Strange, that my first passionate love-letter should have been ad-dressed to a dead girl. Can they feel, I wonder, those white silent people we call the dead? Sybil! Can she feel, or know, or listen? Oh, Harry, how I loved her once! It seems years ago to me now. She was everything to me. Then came that dreadful night—was it really only last night?—when she played so badly, and my heart almost broke. She explained it all to me. It was terribly pathetic. But I was not moved a bit. I thought her shallow. Then something happened that

8 This line would have resonated powerfully with Wilde's earliest readers, especially Londoners. The no-torious Whitechapel murders of 1888, committed by an individual never positively identified but commonly known as "Jack the Ripper," all featured female vic-tims from London's East End whose throats had been slashed.

"Dead! Sybil, dead! It is not true," illustration by S. A. Moss to *The Picture of Dorian Gray,* vol. 2 of *The Sun-flower Edition of the Works of Oscar Wilde* (New York: Lang, 1909).

9 As Talia Schaffer observes, this line of dialogue may be indebted to a line in Ouida's novel *Guilderoy*—quoted approvingly by Wilde in an unsigned review—about "admirably virtuous women who are more likely to turn men away from the paths of virtue than the wickedest of sirens" (quoted in Schaffer, "The Origins of the Aesthetic Novel: Ouida, Wilde and the Popular Romance," in *Wilde Writings: Contextual Conditions,* ed. Joseph Bristow [University of Toronto Press, 2003], p. 223). Of his estranged wife's fruitless attempts to reform him, Wilde once remarked, "How can she really imagine that she can influence or control my life? She might just as well try to influence and control my art" (*CL,* p. 955).

10 Lord Henry says he would have cared less about the "social mistake" (Dorian's marrying below his class) than about the misery the marriage would have brought. He cares far more about the "social mistake" in the 1891 book version, however, in which Wilde rewrites this sentence as follows: "I say nothing about the social mistake, which would have been abject, which, of course, I would not have allowed, but I assure you that in any case the whole thing would have been an absolute failure." In any event, Lord Henry's calculus and cynicism are shocking in both versions.

made me afraid. I can't tell you what it was, but it was awful. I said I would go back to her. I felt I had done wrong. And now she is dead. My God! my God! Harry, what shall I do? You don't know the danger I am in, and there is nothing to keep me straight. She would have done that for me. She had no right to kill herself. It was selfish of her."

"My dear Dorian, the only way a woman can ever reform a man is by boring him so completely that he loses all possible interest in life.[9] If you had married this girl you would have been wretched. Of course you would have treated her kindly. One can always be kind to people about whom one cares nothing. But she would have soon found out that you were absolutely indifferent to her. And when a woman finds that out about her husband, she either becomes dreadfully dowdy, or wears very smart bonnets that some other woman's husband has to pay for. I say nothing about the social mistake, but I assure you that in any case the whole thing would have been an absolute failure."[10]

"I suppose it would," muttered the lad, walking up and down the room, and looking horribly pale. "But I thought it was my duty. It is not my fault that this terrible tragedy has prevented my doing what was right. I remember your saying once, that there is a fatality about good resolutions. That they are always made too late. Mine certainly were."

"Good resolutions are simply a useless attempt to interfere with scientific laws. Their origin is pure vanity. Their result is absolutely *nil.* They give us, now and then, some of those luxurious sterile emotions that have a certain charm for us. That is all that can be said for them."

"Harry," cried Dorian Gray, coming over and sitting down beside him, "why is it that I cannot feel this tragedy as much as I want to? I don't think I am heartless. Do you?"

"You have done too many foolish things in your life to be entitled to give yourself that name, Dorian," answered Lord Henry, with his sweet, melancholy smile.

The lad frowned. "I don't like that explanation, Harry," he rejoined, "but I am glad you don't think I am heartless. I am nothing of the kind. I know I am not. And yet I must admit that this thing that has happened does not affect me as it should. It seems to me to be simply like a wonderful ending to a wonderful play. It has all the terrible beauty of a great tragedy, a tragedy in which I took part, but by which I have not been wounded."

"It is an interesting question," said Lord Henry, who found an exquisite pleasure in playing on the lad's unconscious egotism, "an extremely interesting question. I fancy that the explanation is this. It often happens that the real tragedies of life occur in such an inartistic manner that they hurt us by their crude violence, their absolute incoherence, their absurd want of meaning, their entire lack of style.[11] They affect us, just as vulgarity affects us. They give us an impression of sheer brute force, and we revolt against that. Sometimes, however, a tragedy that has artistic elements of beauty crosses our lives. If these elements of beauty are real, the whole thing simply appeals to our sense of dramatic effect.[12] Suddenly we find that we are no longer the actors, but the spectators of the play. Or rather we are both. We watch ourselves, and the mere wonder of the spectacle enthralls us. In the present case, what is it that has really happened? Some one has killed herself for love of you. I wish I had ever had such an experience. It would have made me in love with love for the rest of my life. The people who have adored me—there have not been very many, but there have been some—have always insisted on living on, long after I had ceased to care for them, or they to care for me. They have become stout and tedious, and, when I meet them, they go in at once for reminiscences. That awful memory of woman! What a fearful thing it is! And what an utter intellectual stagnation it reveals! One should absorb the colour of life, but one should never remember its details. Details are always vulgar.

"Of course, now and then things linger. I once wore nothing but violets all through one season, as mourning for a romance that would not die. Ultimately, however, it did die. I forget what killed it. I think it was her proposing to sacrifice the whole world for me. That is always a dreadful moment. It fills one with the terror of eternity. Well, would you believe it? A week ago, at Lady Hampshire's, I found myself seated at dinner next the lady in question, and she insisted on going over the whole thing again, and digging up the past, and raking

11 "The only beautiful things are the things that do not concern us" ("The Decay of Lying," p. 102).

12 "It is exactly because Hecuba is nothing to us that her sorrows are such an admirable motive for a tragedy" ("The Decay of Lying," p. 82).

The diva Adelina Patti, dressed for the lead role in Verdi's *Aida,* which she performed at the Royal Opera House, in London's Covent Garden, in June 1876.

13 "Who, indeed, in these degenerate days, would hesitate between an ode and an omelette, a sonnet and a salami?" (Wilde, "Dinners and Dishes").

up the future. I had buried my romance in a bed of poppies. She dragged it out again, and assured me that I had spoilt her life. I am bound to state that she ate an enormous dinner, so I did not feel any anxiety.[13] But what a lack of taste she showed! The one charm of the past is that it is the past. But women never know when the curtain has fallen. They always want a sixth act, and as soon as the interest of the play is entirely over they propose to continue it. If they were allowed to have their way, every comedy would have a tragic ending, and every tragedy would culminate in a farce. They are charmingly artificial, but they have no sense of art. You are more fortunate than I am. I assure you, Dorian, that not one of the women I have known would have done for me what Sybil Vane did for you. Ordinary women always console themselves. Some of them do it by going in for sentimental colours. Never trust a woman who wears mauve, whatever her age may be, or a woman over thirty-five who is fond of pink ribands. It always means that they have a history. Others find a great consolation in suddenly discovering the good qualities of their husbands. They flaunt their conjugal felicity in one's face, as if it was the most fascinating of sins. Religion consoles some. Its mysteries have all the charm of a flirtation, a woman once told me; and I can quite understand it. Besides, nothing makes one so vain as being told that one is a sinner. There is really no end to the consolations that women find in modern life. Indeed, I have not mentioned the most important one of all."

"What is that, Harry?" said Dorian Gray listlessly.

"Oh, the obvious one. Taking some one else's admirer when one loses one's own. In good society that always whitewashes a woman. But really, Dorian, how different Sybil Vane must have been from all the women one meets! There is something to me quite beautiful about her death. I am glad I am living in a century when such wonders happen. They make one believe in the reality of the things that shallow, fashionable people play with, such as romance, passion, and love."

"I was terribly cruel to her. You forget that."

"I believe that women appreciate cruelty more than anything else. They have wonderfully primitive instincts. We have emancipated

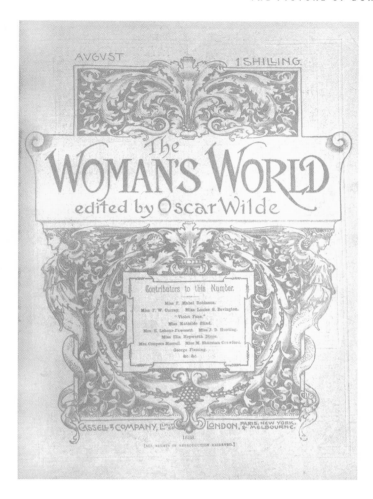

Front wrapper to *The Woman's World,* almost certainly designed at Wilde's instigation, by Lewis F. Day, 1888. Wilde edited the magazine from 1887 to 1889. When Wilde took over editorship of the magazine, he changed its name from *The Lady's World* to *The Woman's World.*

14 John Stuart Mill would have concurred with Lord Henry's view: "The rule of men over women differs from . . . others in not being a rule of force: it is accepted voluntarily; women make no complaint, and are consenting parties to it. . . . All causes, social and natural, combine to make it unlikely that women should be collectively rebellious to the power of men . . . All men, except the most brutish, desire to have, in the woman most nearly connected with them, not a forced slave but a willing one, not a slave merely but a favourite" (J. S. Mill, *The Subjection of Women* [1869; rpt. Peterborough, Ontario: Broadview Press, 2000], pp. 20–22). Despite his low opinion of marriage and wives, Wilde was a keen advocate for the empowerment and education of women. When he took over the editorship of *Lady's World* in 1887, he retitled it *Woman's World* and transformed it from "a magazine for fashion and society" (as its original subtitle declared) into an intellectual venue for educated women and a forum for debate about the legitimacy of women's representation in mainstream British society. For the first two issues of the new magazine he commissioned articles titled "The Position of Woman" and "The Fallacy of the Superiority of Man." In *A Woman of No Importance* (1893), Wilde writes that "the world was made for men and not for women" and that "the growing influence of women is the one reassuring thing in our political life."

them, but they remain slaves looking for their masters, all the same. They love being dominated.[14] I am sure you were splendid. I have never seen you angry, but I can fancy how delightful you looked. And, after all, you said something to me the day before yesterday that seemed to me at the time to be merely fanciful, but that I see now was absolutely true, and it explains everything."

15 "As for Life, she is the solvent that breaks up Art, the enemy that lays waste to her house" ("The Decay of Lying," p. 83).

"What was that, Harry?"

"You said to me that Sybil Vane represented to you all the heroines of romance. That she was Desdemona one night, and Ophelia the other. That if she died as Juliet, she came to life as Imogen."

"She will never come to life again now," murmured the lad, burying his face in his hands.

"No, she will never come to life. She has played her last part. But you must think of that lonely death in the tawdry dressing-room simply as a strange lurid fragment from some Jacobean tragedy, as a wonderful scene from Webster, or Ford, or Cyril Tourneur. The girl never really lived, and so she has never really died. To you at least she was always a dream, a phantom that flitted through Shakespeare's plays, and left them lovelier for its presence, a reed through which Shakespeare's music sounded richer and more full of joy. The moment she touched actual life, she marred it, and it marred her, and so she passed away.[15] Mourn for Ophelia, if you like. Put ashes on your head because Cordelia was strangled. Cry out against Heaven because the daughter of Brabantio died. But don't waste your tears over Sybil Vane. She was less real than they are."

There was a silence. The evening darkened in the room. Noiselessly, and with silver feet, the shadows crept in from the garden. The colours faded wearily out of things.

After some time Dorian Gray looked up. "You have explained me to myself, Harry," he murmured, with something of a sigh of relief. "I felt all that you have said, but somehow I was afraid of it, and I could not express it to myself. How well you know me! But we will not talk again of what has happened. It has been a marvellous experience. That is all. I wonder if life has still in store for me anything as marvellous."

"Life has everything in store for you, Dorian. There is nothing that you, with your extraordinary good looks, will not be able to do."

"But suppose, Harry, I became haggard, and grey, and wrinkled? What then?"

"Ah, then," said Lord Henry rising to go: "Then, my dear Dorian, you would have to fight for your victories. As it is, they are brought to you. No, you must keep your good looks. We live in an age that reads too much to be wise, and that thinks too much to be beautiful. We cannot spare you. And now you had better dress, and drive down to the club. We are rather late, as it is."

"I think I shall join you at the Opera, Harry. I feel too tired to eat anything. What is the number of your sister's box?"

"Twenty-seven, I believe. It is on the grand tier. You will see her name on the door. But I am sorry you won't come and dine."

"I don't feel up to it," said Dorian wearily. "But I am awfully obliged to you for all that you have said to me. You are certainly my best friend. No one has ever understood me as you have."

"We are only at the beginning of our friendship, Dorian," answered Lord Henry, shaking him by the hand. "Good-bye. I shall see you before nine-thirty, I hope. Remember, Patti is singing."

As he closed the door behind him, Dorian Gray touched the bell, and in a few minutes Victor appeared with the lamps and drew the blinds down. He waited impatiently for him to go. The man seemed to take an interminable time about everything.

As soon as he had left, he rushed to the screen, and drew it back. No; there was no further change in the picture. It had received the news of Sybil Vane's death before he had known of it himself. It was conscious of the events of life as they occurred. The vicious cruelty that marred the fine lines of the mouth had, no doubt, appeared at the very moment that the girl had drunk the poison, whatever it was. Or was it indifferent to results? Did it merely take cognizance of what passed within the soul? He wondered and hoped that some day he would see the change taking place before his very eyes, shuddering as he hoped it.

Poor Sybil! What a romance it had all been! She had often mimicked death on the stage, and at last Death himself had touched her, and brought her with him. How had she played that dreadful scene? Had she cursed him, as she died? No; she had died for love of him, and love would always be a sacrament to him now. She had atoned for everything, by the sacrifice she had made of her life. He would not think any more of what she had made him go through, that horrible night at the theatre. When he thought of her, it would be as a wonderful tragic figure to whom Love had been a great reality.[a] A won-

"Dorian Gray," by "Basil Hallward," published as the frontispiece to *The Picture of Dorian Gray* (New York: Charterhouse Press, 1904).

16 "The figure of Narcissus wandered down from classic to modern times, from legend into literature, and thence into popular phrase, long before it entered into sexual psychology," says Havelock Ellis ("The Conception of Narcissism," in his *Studies in the Psychology of Sex* [New York: Random House, 1942], p. 347). Nonetheless, "there really was present in the Greek mind the idea of Narcissus as embodying an attitude of mind which would now be termed autoerotic," and the figure of Narcissus "was clearly predestined to be the emblem of the absorbed self-love of youths and maidens who had not yet reached the stage of falling in love with another person of the opposite sex" ("The Conception of Narcissism," p. 348). Wilde was instrumental in transforming Narcissus into an icon of masculine beauty and homoerotic desire. For the importance of Narcissus to Wilde, as well as to modern concepts of queer camp, see Gregory W. Bredbeck, "Narcissus in the Wilde," in *The Politics and Poetics of Camp,* ed. Moe Meyer [London: Routledge, 1994], pp. 51–74).

17 Wilde was a firm believer in the power of spiritualists and mediums to reanimate dead things.

18 Telepathy, thought transference, and the psychic animation of inorganic matter were in Wilde's day legitimate subjects of scientific research, formalized in the creation, in 1882, of the Society for Psychical Research. Among the society's early members were many prominent intellectuals and public figures, including the physicist Sir William Fletcher Barrett and Arthur Balfour, prime minster of Great Britain from 1902 to 1905 and an advocate for the creation of Palestine.

derful tragic figure? Tears came to his eyes as he remembered her child-like look, and winsome fanciful ways, and shy tremulous grace. He wiped them away hastily, and looked again at the picture.

He felt that the time had really come for making his choice. Or had his choice already been made? Yes, life had decided that for him—life, and his own infinite curiosity about life. Eternal youth, infinite passion, pleasures subtle and secret, wild joys and wilder sins—he was to have all these things. The portrait was to bear the burden of his shame: that was all.

A feeling of pain came over him as he thought of the desecration that was in store for the fair face on the canvas. Once, in boyish mockery of Narcissus, he had kissed, or feigned to kiss, those painted lips that now smiled so cruelly at him.[16] Morning after morning he had sat before the portrait wondering at its beauty, almost enamoured of it, as it seemed to him at times. Was it to alter now with every mood to which he yielded? Was it to become a hideous and loathsome thing, to be hidden away in a locked room, to be shut out from the sunlight that had so often touched to brighter gold the waving wonder of the hair? The pity of it! the pity of it!

For a moment he thought of praying that the horrible sympathy that existed between him and the picture might cease. It had changed in answer to a prayer. Perhaps in answer to a prayer it might remain unchanged. And, yet, who, that knew anything about Life, would surrender the chance of remaining always young, however fantastic that chance might be, or with what fateful consequences it might be fraught? Besides, was it really under his control? Had it indeed been prayer that had produced the substitution? Might there not be some curious scientific reason for it all? If thought could exercise its influence upon a living organism, might not thought exercise an influence upon dead and inorganic things?[17] Nay, without thought or conscious desire, might not things external to ourselves vibrate in unison with our moods and passions, atom calling to atom, in secret love or strange affinity?[18] But the reason was of no importance. He would never again tempt by a prayer any terrible power. If the picture was to alter, it was to alter. That was all. Why inquire too closely into it?

For there would be a real pleasure in watching it. He would be able to follow his mind into its secret places. This portrait would be to him the most magical of mirrors. As it had revealed to him his own body, so it would reveal to him his own soul. And when winter came upon it, he would still be standing where spring trembles on the verge of summer. When the blood crept from its face, and left behind a pallid mask of chalk with leaden eyes, he would keep the glamour of boyhood. Not one blossom of his loveliness would ever fade. Not one pulse of his life would ever weaken. Like the Gods of the Greeks he would be strong, and fleet, and joyous. What did it matter what happened to the coloured image on the canvas? He would be safe. That was everything.

He drew the screen back into its former place in front of the picture, smiling as he did so, and passed into his bedroom, where his valet was already waiting for him. An hour later he was at the Opera, and Lord Henry was leaning over his chair.

1 Hallward feared that Dorian might take his own life once he knew of Sibyl's suicide. His refusal to believe that Dorian had gone to the opera on the evening following Sybil's suicide speaks to his goodness and decency, and stands in sharp contrast to Lord Henry's invitation.

2 In 1837, Samuel Morse, an American inventor, developed the prototype for the first commercially viable telegraph. "What hath God wrought" was the first message sent by electric telegraph, from the Capitol building to the railway depot in Baltimore on May 23, 1844. With subsequent improvements to Morse's apparatus, the telegraph system spread quickly across America and Europe in the second half of the nineteenth century. Basil's reprimand, today, might find equivalent expression in the question, "Why didn't you text me as soon as you heard?"

3 Euston Road was in Wilde's day a main artery housing three of London's principal main-line railway stations. Some blocks contained "a few thoroughly bad places, insanitary and dilapidated, and occupied by a very low class," while others contained a "fair number of the labouring-class," "no extreme poverty," a "fair number of decent artisans and clerks . . . and a few well to do people" (*Life and Labour of the People of London*, ed. William Booth [London: Macmillan, 1892], Appendix, p. 10).

As he was sitting at breakfast next morning, Basil Hallward was shown into the room.

"I am so glad I have found you Dorian," he said gravely. "I called last night, and they told me you were at the Opera. Of course I knew that was impossible. But I wish you had left word where you had really gone to. I passed a dreadful evening, half afraid that one tragedy might be followed by another.[1] I think you might have telegraphed for me when you heard of it first.[2] I read of it quite by chance in a late edition of the *Globe,* that I picked up at the club. I came here at once and was miserable at not finding you. I can't tell you how heartbroken I am about the whole thing. I know what you must suffer. But where were you? Did you go down and see the girl's mother? For a moment I thought of following you there. They gave the address in the paper. Somewhere in the Euston Road, isn't it?[3] But I was afraid of intruding upon a sorrow that I could not lighten. Poor woman! What a state she must be in! And her only child too! What did she say about it all?"

"My dear Basil, how do I know?" murmured Dorian, sipping some pale-yellow wine from a delicate gold-beaded bubble of Venetian glass, and looking dreadfully bored. "I was at the Opera. You should have come on there. I met Lady Gwendolen, Harry's sister, for the first time. We were in her box. She is perfectly charming; and Patti sang divinely. Don't talk about horrid subjects. If one doesn't talk about a thing, it has never happened. It is simply expression, as Harry says, that gives reality to things. Tell me about yourself and what you are painting."

"You went to the Opera?" said Hallward, speaking very slowly, and with a strained touch of pain in his voice. "You went to the Opera while Sybil Vane was lying dead in some sordid lodging? You can talk to me of other women being charming, and of Patti singing divinely, before the girl you loved has even the quiet of a grave to sleep in? Why, man, there are horrors in store for that little white body of hers!"

"Stop, Basil, I won't bear it!"ᵃ cried Dorian, leaping to his feet. "You must not tell me about things. What is done is done. What is past is past."

"You call yesterday the past?"

"What has the actual lapse of time got to do with it? It is only shallow people who require years to get rid of an emotion. A man who is master of himself can end a sorrow as easily as he can invent a pleasure.[4] I don't want to be at the mercy of my emotions. I want to use them, to enjoy them, and to dominate them."

"Dorian, this is horrible! Something has changed you completely. You look exactly the same wonderful boy who used to come down to my studio, day after day, to sit for his picture. But you were simple, natural, and affectionate then. You were the most unspoiled creature in the whole world. Now, I don't know what has come over you. You talk as if you had no heart, no pity in you. It is all Harry's influence. I see that."

The lad flushed up, and, going to the window, looked out on the green flickering garden for a few moments. "I owe a great deal to Harry, Basil," he said at last, "more than I owe to you. You only taught me to be vain."

"Well, I am punished for that, Dorian, or shall be some day."

"I don't know what you mean, Basil," he exclaimed, turning round. "I don't know what you want. What do you want?"

"I want the Dorian Gray I used to know."

"Basil," said the lad, going over to him, and putting his hand on his shoulder, "you have come too late. Yesterday when I heard that Sybil Vane had killed herself. . . ."

4 Experience would provide a different lesson for Wilde personally. After his conviction for "gross indecency," he was sentenced to two years' hard labor and spent time in Pentonville and Wandsworth prisons in London before being transferred to Reading prison. The conditions Wilde met in prison were as harsh as his treatment. In *De Profundis,* Wilde laments, "For [prisoners like himself] there is only one season, the season of Sorrow," and "Sorrow . . . and all that it teaches one, is my new world" (*CL,* p. 720 and p. 736). Compare Dorian's notion of self-mastery with the view expressed in W. E. Henley's "Invictus":

I thank whatever gods may be
For my unconquerable soul.

In the fell clutch of circumstance
I have not winced nor cried aloud.
. . . the menace of the years
Finds, and shall find, me unafraid.

It matters not how strait the gate,
How charged with punishments the scroll,
I am the master of my fate:
I am the captain of my soul.

5 "[T]he chief thing that makes life a failure from [an] artistic point of view is . . . the fact that one can never repeat exactly the same emotion" ("The Critic as Artist," p. 167).

6 "L'art est ce qui console le mieux de vivre" ("art is the best consolation for living"), Théophile Gautier, Preface to *Albertus* (1833), rpt. in *Ouevres de Théophile Gautier: Poésies* (Paris, 1890), p. 7. This is the first of three mentions in *Dorian Gray* of the late-Romantic French poet and man of letters Théophile Gautier (1811–1872). Gautier is widely credited with having invented the slogan "art for art's sake" *(l'art pour l'art),* a rallying cry for the artists and writers associated with the Aesthetic movement. Wilde's Preface to the expanded book version of *Dorian Gray* draws heavily from Gautier's 1835 Preface to *Mademoiselle du Maupin.* See also Peter Whyte, "Oscar Wilde et Théophile Gautier: le cas du *Portrait Du Dorian Gray," Bulletin de la Société Théophile Gautier,* 21 (1999), 279–294.

7 A misspelling of "Marlow," the Thames-side town in Buckinghamshire about thirty miles west of London, altered to "Marlow" in the 1891 book edition. R. Mighall notes, "This may of course be merely a typo, missed by Wilde and his editor. . . . However the reference to the two men being 'down at Marlowe together' does seem somewhat gratuitous in this context, and may be a sly homoerotic reference" to the "homosexual poet and playwright Christopher Marlowe" (*Picture of Dorian Gray,* ed. R. Mighall [London: Penguin, 2003] p. 242).

"Killed herself! Good heavens! Is there no doubt about that?" cried Hallward, looking up at him with an expression of horror.

"My dear Basil! Surely you don't think it was a vulgar accident? Of course she killed herself It is one of the great romantic tragedies of the age. As a rule, people who act lead the most commonplace lives. They are good husbands, or faithful wives, or something tedious. You know what I mean—middle-class virtue and all that kind of thing. How different Sybil was! She lived her finest tragedy. She was always a heroine. The last night she played—the night you saw her—she acted badly because she had known the reality of love. When she knew its unreality, she died, as Juliet might have died. She passed again into the sphere of art. There is something of the martyr about her. Her death has all the pathetic uselessness of martyrdom, all its wasted beauty. But, as I was saying, you must not think I have not suffered. If you had come in yesterday at a particular moment, about half-past five, perhaps, or a quarter to six, you would have found me in tears. Even Harry, who was here, who brought me the news, in fact, had no idea what I was going through. I suffered immensely, then it passed away. I cannot repeat an emotion.[5] No one can, except sentimentalists. And you are awfully unjust, Basil. You come down here to console me. That is charming of you. You find me consoled, and you are furious. How like a sympathetic person! You remind me of a story Harry told me about a certain philanthropist who spent twenty years of his life in trying to get some grievance redressed, or some unjust law altered,—I forget exactly what it was. Finally he succeeded, and nothing could exceed his disappointment. He had absolutely nothing to do, almost died of *ennui,* and became a confirmed misanthrope. And besides, my dear old Basil, if you really want to console me, teach me rather to forget what has happened, or to see it from a proper artistic point of view. Was it not Gautier who used to write about *la consolation des arts?*[6] I remember picking up a little vellum-covered book in your studio one day and chancing on that delightful phrase. Well, I am not like that young man you told me of when we were down at Marlowe together,[7] the young man who used to say that yellow satin could console one for all the miseries of life. I love beautiful things that one can touch and handle. Old brocades, green bronzes, lacquer-work, carved ivories, exquisite surroundings, luxury, pomp,—there is much to be got from all these. But the artistic temperament that they create, or at any rate reveal, is still more to me. To become the spectator of one's own life, as Harry says, is to escape the suffering of life.[8] I know you are surprised at my talking to you like this. You have not realised how I have developed. I was a school-boy when you knew me. I am a man now. I have new passions, new thoughts, new ideas. I am different, but you must not like me less. I am changed, but you must always be my friend. Of course I am very fond of Harry. But I know that you are better than he is. You are not stronger. You are too much afraid of life. But you are better. And how happy we used to be together! Don't leave me, Basil, and don't quarrel with me. I am what I am. There is nothing more to be said."

Hallward felt strangely moved. Rugged and straightforward as he was, there was something in his nature that was purely feminine in its tenderness.[b] The lad was infinitely dear to him, and his personality had been the great turning-point in his art. He could not bear the idea of reproaching him any more. After all, his indifference was probably merely a mood that would pass away. There was so much in him that was good, so much in him that was noble.

"Well, Dorian," he said, at length, with a sad smile, "I won't speak to you again about this horrible thing, after to-day. I only trust your name won't be mentioned in connection with it. The inquest is to take place this afternoon. Have they summoned you?"

Dorian shook his head, and a look of annoyance passed over his face at the mention of the word "inquest." There was something so crude and vulgar about everything of the kind. "They don't know my name," he answered.

"But surely she did?"

"Only my Christian name, and that I am quite sure she never mentioned to anyone. She told me once that they were all rather curious to learn who I was, and that she invariably told them my name was Prince Charming. It was pretty of her. You must do me a drawing of her, Basil. I should like to have something more of her than the memory of a few kisses and some broken pathetic words."

8 "If we lived long enough to see the results of our actions, it may be that those who call themselves good would be sickened with a full remorse, and those whom the world calls evil stirred by a noble joy . . . Sin is an essential element of progress" ("The Critic as Artist," p. 147).

Engraved portrait of Théophile Gautier by L. Wolff, after a photo by Nadar, c. 1856. Gautier, a pioneer of aestheticism, is widely credited with having invented the slogan "art for art's sake." His writings deeply influenced *Dorian Gray* as well as Wilde's ideas about art generally.

"I will try and do something, Dorian, if it would please you. But you must come and sit to me yourself again. I can't get on without you."

"I will never sit to you again, Basil. It is impossible!" he exclaimed, starting back.

Hallward stared at him, "My dear boy, what nonsense!" he cried. "Do you mean to say you don't like what I did of you? Where is it? Why have you pulled the screen in front of it? Let me look at it. It is the best thing I have ever painted. Do take that screen away, Dorian. It is simply horrid of your servant hiding my work like that. I felt the room looked different as I came in."

"My servant has nothing to do with it, Basil. You don't imagine I let him arrange my room for me? He settles my flowers for me sometimes, that is all. No; I did it myself. The light was too strong on the portrait."

"Too strong! Impossible, my dear fellow! It is an admirable place for it. Let me see it." And Hallward walked towards the corner of the room.

A cry of terror broke from Dorian Gray's lips, and he rushed between Hallward and the screen. "Basil," he said, looking very pale, "you must not look at it. I don't wish you to."

"Not look at my own work! you are not serious. Why shouldn't I look at it?" exclaimed Hallward, laughing.

"If you try to look at it, Basil, on my word of honour I will never speak to you again as long as I live. I am quite serious. I don't offer any explanation, and you are not to ask for any. But, remember, if you touch this screen, everything is over between us."

Hallward was thunderstruck. He looked at Dorian Gray in absolute amazement. He had never seen him like this before. The lad was absolutely pallid with rage. His hands were clenched, and the pupils of his eyes were like disks of blue fire. He was trembling all over.

"Dorian!"

"Don't speak!"

"But what is the matter? Of course I won't look at it if you don't want me to," he said rather coldly, turning on his heel, and going over towards the window. "But, really, it seems rather absurd that I shouldn't see my own work, especially as I am going to exhibit it in Paris, in the autumn. I shall probably have to give it another coat of varnish before that, so I must see it some day, and why not to-day?"

"To exhibit it! You want to exhibit it?" exclaimed Dorian Gray, a strange sense of terror creeping over him. Was the world going to be shown his secret? Were people to gape at the mystery of his life? That was impossible. Something, he did not know what, had to be done at once.

"Yes, I don't suppose you will object to that. Georges Petit is going to collect all my best pictures for a special exhibition in the Rue de Sêze,[9] which will open the first week in October. The portrait will only be away a month. I should think you could easily spare it for that time. In fact you are sure to be out of town. And if you hide it always behind a screen, you can't care much about it."

Dorian Gray passed his hand over his forehead. There were beads of perspiration there. He felt that he was on the brink of a horrible danger. "You told me a month ago that you would never exhibit it," he said. "Why have you changed your mind? You people who go in for being consistent have just as many moods as others. The only difference is that your moods are rather meaningless. You can't have forgotten that you assured me most solemnly that nothing in the world would induce you to send it to any exhibition. You told Harry exactly the same thing." He stopped suddenly, and a gleam of light came into his eyes. He remembered that Lord Henry had said to him once, half seriously and half in jest, "If you want to have an interesting quarter of an hour, get Basil to tell you why he won't exhibit your picture. He told me why he wouldn't, and it was a revelation to me." Yes; perhaps Basil, too, had his secret. He would ask him and try.[10]

"Basil," he said, coming over quite close, and looking him straight in the face, "we have each of us a secret. Let me know yours, and I will tell you mine. What was your reason for refusing to exhibit my picture?"

Hallward shuddered in spite of himself. "Dorian, if I told you, you might like me less than you do, and you would certainly laugh at me.

9 Georges Petit's fashionable gallery, at 8 Rue de Sêze in Paris, was a preeminent exhibition space for contemporary French Impressionist painting and sculpture at this time.

10 In the course of Wilde's disastrous libel suit, Queensberry's attorney, Edward Carson, used *Dorian Gray* against Wilde to prove that his client's claim—that Wilde was "posing as a sodomite"—was justified. It was the shorter, more salacious Lippincott version of the novel that Carson adduced as evidence. Carson read aloud in court the ensuing five and a half paragraphs through "I resolved never to allow the picture to be exhibited." He prefaced his reading with the comment, "I believe this was left out of the purged edition afterwards," and followed it by asking, "Do you mean to say that that passage describes a natural feeling of one man towards another?" (*The Real Trial*, pp. 86–89). If Carson had had access to the typescript version of the novel submitted to Lippincott, he undoubtedly would have used it instead, for it is even more explicit and graphic than the published Lippincott version in its homosexual references.

I could not bear your doing either of those two things. If you wish me never to look at your picture again, I am content. I have always you to look at. If you wish the best work I have ever done to be hidden from the world, I am satisfied. Your friendship is dearer to me than any fame or reputation."

"No, Basil, you must tell me," murmured Dorian Gray. "I think I have a right to know." His feeling of terror had passed away. Curiosity had taken its place. He was determined to find out Basil Hallward's mystery.

"Let us sit down, Dorian," said Hallward, looking pale and pained. "Let us sit down. I will sit in the shadow, and you shall sit in the sunlight. Our lives are like that. Just answer me one question. Have you noticed in the picture something that you did not like? Something that probably at first did not strike you, but that revealed itself to you suddenly?"

"Basil!" cried the lad, clutching the arms of his chair with trembling hands, and gazing at him with wild, startled eyes.

"I see you did. Don't speak. Wait till you hear what I have to say. It is quite true that I have worshipped you with far more romance of feeling than a man should ever give to a friend.[c] Somehow, I had never loved a woman. I suppose I never had time. Perhaps, as Harry says, a really *'grande passion'* is the privilege of those who have nothing to do, and that is the use of the idle classes in a country.[d] Well, from the moment I met you, your personality had the most extraordinary influence over me. I quite admit that I adored you madly, extravagantly, absurdly.[e] I was jealous of every one to whom you spoke. I wanted to have you all to myself. I was only happy when I was with you. When I was away from you, you were still present in my art. It was all wrong and foolish. It is all wrong and foolish still.[f] Of course I never let you know anything about this. It would have been impossible. You would not have understood it; I did not understand it myself. One day I determined to paint a wonderful portrait of you. It was to have been my masterpiece. It is my masterpiece. But, as I worked at it, every flake and film of colour seemed to me to reveal my secret. There was love in every line, and in every touch there was passion.[g] I grew afraid that the world would know of my idolatry. I felt, Dorian, that I had told too much. Then it was that I resolved never to allow the picture to be exhibited. You were a little annoyed; but then you did not realize all that it meant to me. Harry, to whom I talked about it, laughed at me. But I did not mind that. When the picture was finished, and I sat alone with it, I felt that I was right. Well, after a few days, the portrait left my studio, and as soon as I had got rid of the intolerable fascination of its presence, it seemed to me that I had been foolish in imagining that I had said anything in it, more than that you were extremely good-looking and that I could paint. Even now I cannot help feeling that it is a mistake to think that the passion one feels in creation is ever really shown in the work one creates. Art is more abstract than we fancy. Form and colour tell us of form and colour, that is all. It often seems to me that art conceals the artist far more completely than it ever reveals him. And so when I got this offer from Paris I determined to make your portrait the principal thing in my exhibition. It never occurred to me that you would refuse. I see now that you were right. The picture must not be shown. You must not be angry with me, Dorian, for what I have told you. As I said to Harry, once, you are made to be worshipped."

Dorian Gray drew a long breath. The colour came back to his cheeks, and a smile played about his lips. The peril was over. He was safe for the time. Yet he could not help feeling infinite pity for the young man who had just made this strange confession to him. He wondered if he would ever be so dominated by the personality of a friend. Lord Harry had the charm of being very dangerous. But that was all. He was too clever and too cynical to be really fond of. Would there ever be someone who would fill him with a strange idolatry? Was that one of the things that life had in store?

"It is extraordinary to me, Dorian," said Hallward, "that you should have seen this in the picture. Did you really see it?"

"Of course I did."

"Well, you don't mind my looking at it now?"

Dorian shook his head. "You must not ask me that, Basil. I could not possibly let you stand in front of that picture."

"You will some day, surely?"

Napoleon Sarony, photo-portrait of Wilde. In 1882 Wilde journeyed to New York at his own expense to be photographed by Napoleon Sarony, whose famous subjects included Lilly Langtry and Sarah Bernhardt. One of Sarony's portraits of Wilde, widely reproduced without Sarony's permission, became the subject of a landmark U.S. Supreme Court case, in 1884, in which the court upheld the extension of copyright protection to photographs.

"Never."

"Well, perhaps you are right. And now, good-bye Dorian. You have been the one person in my life of whom I have been really fond. I don't suppose I shall often see you again. You don't know what it cost me to tell you all that I have told you."

"My dear Basil," cried Dorian, "what have you told me? Simply that you felt that you liked me too much. That is not even a compliment."

"It was not intended as a compliment. It was a confession."

"A very disappointing one."

"Why, what did you expect, Dorian? You didn't see anything else in the picture, did you? There was nothing else to see?"

"No: there was nothing else to see. Why do you ask? But you mustn't talk about not meeting me again, or anything of that kind. You and I are friends, Basil, and we must always remain so."

"You have got Harry," said Hallward sadly.

"Oh, Harry!" cried the lad with a ripple of laughter. "Harry spends his days in saying what is incredible, and his evenings in doing what is improbable. Just the sort of life I would like to lead. But still I don't think I would go to Harry if I was in trouble. I would sooner go to you, Basil."

"But you won't sit to me again?"

"Impossible!"

"You spoil my life as an artist by refusing, Dorian. No man comes across two ideal things. Few come across one."

"I can't explain it to you, Basil, but I must never sit to you again. I will come and have tea with you. That will be just as pleasant."

"Pleasanter for you, I am afraid," murmured Hallward, regretfully. "And now, good-bye. I am sorry you won't let me look at the picture once again. But that can't be helped. I quite understand what you feel about it."

As he left the room Dorian Gray smiled to himself. Poor Basil, how little he knew of the true reason! And how strange it was that instead of having been forced to reveal his own secret, he had succeeded, almost by chance, in wresting a secret from his friend. How much that strange confession explained to him! Basil's absurd fits of jealousy, his wild devotion, his extravagant panegyrics, his curious reticences,—he understood them all now, and he felt sorry. There was something tragic in a friendship so coloured by romance, something infinitely tragic in a romance that was at once so passionate and so sterile.[11h]

He sighed and touched the bell. The portrait must be hidden away at all costs. He could not run such a risk of discovery again. It had been mad of him to have the thing remain, even for an hour, in a room to which any of his friends had access.

11 Nothing would have declared more loudly to Victorian readers that Hallward harbored homosexual feelings than the *sterility* of his "romance" ("sterile" was widely understood as a coded expression for "homosexual"). Understandably cautious, the editor of *Lippincott's*, J. M. Stoddart, deleted the entire sentence before publication.

Pencil sketch of Vernon Lee, by John Singer Sargent, 1889. Vernon Lee was the pen-name of the writer Violet Paget (1856–1935), a lifelong friend of Sargent's. Wilde drew upon her book *Euphorion* (1883) for some of his anecdotes about Renaissance debauchery.

VIII

1 The "distinction" of the "Ideal Butler," Wilde wrote in the stage directions to *An Ideal Husband,* "is his impassivity.... The Sphinx is not so incommunicable. He is a mask with a manner. Of his intellectual or emotional life, history knows nothing. He represents the dominance of form."

2 Victorians fetishized miniature portraits of the dead. But like all portraits, such miniatures represent idealized subjects, not actual persons. In *Lady Windermere's Fan,* Lady Windermere "kisses every night" the miniature portrait of her mother ("a young innocent-looking girl"), whom she believes died when she was herself just a baby. In fact, the mother, still living, eloped scandalously with a lover, deserting her husband and child. Now, under the guise "Mrs. Erlynne," she blackmails Lady Windermere's husband in exchange for her silence about her true identity.

WHEN HIS SERVANT ENTERED, he looked at him steadfastly, and wondered if he had thought of peering behind the screen. The man was quite impassive, and waited for his orders. Dorian lit a cigarette, and walked over to the glass, and glanced into it. He could see the reflection of Victor's face perfectly. It was like a placid mask of servility.[1] There was nothing to be afraid of, there. Yet he thought it best to be on his guard.

Speaking very slowly, he told him to tell the housekeeper that he wanted to see her, and then to go to the frame-maker's and ask him to send two of his men round at once. It seemed to him that as the man left the room he peered in the direction of the screen. Or was that only his fancy?

After a few moments, Mrs. Leaf, a dear old lady in a black silk dress, with a photograph of the late Mr. Leaf framed in a large gold brooch at her neck,[2] and old-fashioned thread mittens on her wrinkled hands, bustled into the room.

"Well, Master Dorian," she said, "what can I do for you? I beg your pardon, Sir,"—here came a curtsey,—"I shouldn't call you Master Dorian any more. But, Lord bless you, Sir, I have known you since you were a baby, and many's the trick you've played on poor old Leaf. Not that you were not always a good boy, Sir, but boys will be boys, Master Dorian, and jam is a temptation to the young, isn't it, Sir?"

He laughed. "You must always call me Master Dorian, Leaf. I will be very angry with you if you don't. And I assure you I am quite as fond of jam now as I used to be. Only when I am asked out to tea I am never offered any. I want you to give me the key of the room at the top of the house."

"The old school-room, Master Dorian? Why, it's full of dust. I must get it arranged and put straight before you go into it. It's not fit for you to see, Master Dorian. It is not, indeed."

"I don't want it put straight, Leaf. I only want the key."

"Well, Master Dorian, you'll be covered with cobwebs if you goes into it. Why, it hasn't been opened for nearly five years. Not since his Lordship died."

He winced at the mention of his dead uncle's name. He had hateful memories of him. "That does not matter, Leaf," he replied. "All I want is the key."

"And here is the key, Master Dorian," said the old lady, after going over the contents of her bunch with tremulously uncertain hands. "Here is the key. I'll have it off the ring in a moment. But you don't think of living up there, Master Dorian, and you so comfortable here?"

"No, Leaf, I don't. I merely want to see the place, and perhaps store something in it. That is all. Thank you, Leaf. I hope your rheumatism is better; and mind you send me up jam for breakfast."

Mrs. Leaf shook her head. "Them foreigners doesn't understand jam, Master Dorian. They calls it 'compot.' But I'll bring it to you myself some morning, if you lets me."

"That will be very kind of you, Leaf," he answered, looking at the key; and, having made him an elaborate curtsey, the old lady left the room, her face wreathed in smiles. She had a strong objection to the French valet. It was a poor thing, she felt, for anyone to be born a foreigner.

As the door closed, Dorian put the key in his pocket, and looked round the room. His eye fell on a large purple satin coverlid heavily embroidered with gold, a splendid piece of late seventeenth-century Venetian work that his uncle had found in a convent near Bologna.[3] Yes, that would serve to wrap the dreadful thing in. It had perhaps served often as a pall for the dead. Now it was to hide something that had a corruption of its own, worse than the corruption of death it-

3 "Agents for the English nobility and men of fashion desirous of forming collections ransacked Italy in the 17th century, and the days of the grand tour extracted a further toll in the 18th. . . . No embroideries of any country are more worth the serious attention of all students. The Italians have a real genius for embroidery, showing great skill and care in adapting design, workmanship and material to the particular end each article has to serve" (*A Book of Old Embroidery,* ed. G. Holme [London: The Studio, 1921], p. 120). The ecclesiastic origins of the satin coverlet (later termed a "purple pall") confer a sacramental dimension on Dorian's decision to wrap the portrait with it. This foreshadows Ashton's offer, a few moments later, of a Florentine frame suitable for "a religious picture."

4 Johann Joachim Winckelmann (1717–1768), a German scholar, was a pioneering Hellenist. Michelangelo, Montaigne, Winckelmann, and Shakespeare were either homosexual or bisexual. The sentence anticipates a moment in the first of Wilde's criminal trials when Charles Gill, the prosecutor in the case, questioned Wilde about the meaning of the line "the love that dare not speak its name" in Alfred Lord Douglas's poem "Two Loves." Wilde replied as follows: "'The love that dare not speak its name' in this century is such a great affection of an elder for a younger man as there was between Jonathan and David, such as Plato made the very basis of his philosophy, and such as you find in the sonnets of Michelangelo and Shakespeare. It dictates and pervades great works of art like those of Shakespeare and Michelangelo . . . It is in this century misunderstood, so much misunderstood that it may be described as 'The love that dare not speak its name'" (quoted in Hyde, *The Trials of Oscar Wilde,* p. 201).

self, something that would breed horrors and yet would never die. What the worm was to the corpse, his sins would be to the painted image on the canvas. They would mar its beauty, and eat away its grace. They would defile it, and make it shameful. And yet the thing would still live on. It would be always alive.

He shuddered, and for a moment he regretted that he had not told Basil the true reason why he had wished to hide the picture away. Basil would have helped him to resist Lord Henry's influence, and the still more poisonous influences that came from his own temperament. The love that he bore him, for it was really love, had something noble and intellectual in it. It was not that mere physical admiration of beauty that is born of the senses, and that dies when the senses tire. It was such love as Michael Angelo had known, and Montaigne, and Winckelmann, and Shakespeare himself.[4] Yes, Basil could have saved him. But it was too late now. The past could always be annihilated. Regret, denial, or forgetfulness could do that. But the future was inevitable. There were passions in him that would find their terrible outlet, dreams that would make the shadow of their evil real.

He took up from the couch the great purple-and-gold texture that covered it, and, holding it in his hands, passed behind the screen. Was the face on the canvas viler than before? It seemed to him that it was unchanged; and yet his loathing of it was intensified. Gold hair, blue eyes, and rose-red lips—they all were there. It was simply the expression that had altered. That was horrible in its cruelty. Compared to what he saw in it of censure or rebuke, how shallow Basil's reproaches about Sybil Vane had been! How shallow, and of what little account! His own soul was looking out at him from the canvas and calling him to judgment. A look of pain came across him, and he flung the rich pall over the picture. As he did so, a knock came to the door. He passed out as his servant entered.

"The persons are here, monsieur."

He felt that the man must be got rid of at once. He must not be allowed to know where the picture was being taken to. There was something sly about him, and he had thoughtful, treacherous eyes. Sitting down at the writing-table, he scribbled a note to Lord Henry,

THE PICTURE OF DORIAN GRAY

asking him to send him round something to read, and reminding him that they were to meet at eight-fifteen that evening.

"Wait for an answer," he said, handing it to him, "and show the men in here."

In two or three minutes there was another knock and Mr. Ashton himself, the celebrated frame-maker of South Audley Street, came in with a somewhat rough-looking young assistant.[5] Mr. Ashton was a florid, red-whiskered little man, whose admiration for art was considerably tempered by the inveterate impecuniosity of most of the artists who dealt with him. As a rule, he never left his shop. He waited for people to come to him. But he always made an exception in favour of Dorian Gray. There was something about Dorian that charmed everybody. It was a pleasure even to see him.

"What can I do for you, Mr. Gray?" he said, rubbing his fat freckled hands. "I thought I would do myself the honour of coming round in person. I have just got a beauty of a frame, sir. Picked it up at a sale. Old Florentine.[6] Came from Fonthill, I believe.[7] Admirably suited for a religious picture, Mr. Gray."

"I am so sorry you have given yourself the trouble of coming round, Mr. Ashton. I will certainly drop in and look at the frame, though I don't go in much for religious art; but to-day I only want a picture carried to the top of the house for me. It is rather heavy, so I thought I would ask you to lend me a couple of your men."

"No trouble at all, Mr. Gray. I am delighted to be of any service to you. Which is the work of art, Sir?"

"This," replied Dorian, moving the screen back. "Can you move it, covering and all, just as it is? I don't want it to get scratched going up-stairs."

"There will be no difficulty, Sir," said the genial frame-maker, beginning, with the aid of his assistant, to unhook the picture from the long brass chains by which it was suspended. "And now, where shall we carry it to, Mr. Gray?"

"I will show you the way, Mr. Ashton, if you will kindly follow me. Or perhaps you had better go in front. I am afraid it is right at the top of the house. We will go up by the front staircase, as it is wider."

5 Coulson Kernahan records Wilde saying the following, before altering "Ashton" to "Hubbard" for the book edition: "Ashton is a gentleman's name . . . and I've given it—God forgive me—to a tradesman! It must be changed to Hubbard. Hubbard positively smells of the tradesman" (*In Good Company,* p. 213).

6 Henry Heydenryk describes the Florentine frame to Gentile da Fabiano's *Adoration of the Magi* (1423) as follows: "Typically Florentine are the arches and tall, triangular pinnacles with medallions containing busts. Here, as in many Florentine altarpieces . . . a flamelike leaf motif is used along the arches and upper parts, and like the scalloping along the inner edge of the arch, this motif is also common in Florentine sculpture and architecture" (*The Art and History of Frames* [1963; New York: Lyons and Burford, 1993], p. 16).

7 Fonthill Abbey, a country house built in 1796–1807 in Wiltshire for William Beckford, the notoriously dissolute and reclusive author of *Vathek,* was at the forefront of the Gothic Revival in architecture. No expense was spared in its construction, and the interior, reflecting the passionate Gothic tastes of its owner, was said to be as splendid as the exterior: "the pictures were an aid to Gothic scholarship," comments one biographer, such that "Fonthill must have been a Mecca for gothicisers" (Boyd Alexander, *England's Wealthiest Son: A Study of William Beckford* [London: Centaur, 1962], p. 169). But scant attention was paid to principles of solid construction, and in 1807 the building's central tower collapsed. It drifted into a state of permanent disrepair even before Beckford's sale of his estate in 1822.

8 Large wooden dowry chest, dating from the early Renaissance. For much of the fifteenth century, when alliances between Florentine families were especially important, *cassone* were decorated by preeminent artists such as Botticelli, Uccello, and Donatello. Shortly before *Dorian Gray* was written, Wilde published in *Woman's World* E. F. Dickinson's essay "About Wedding Chests," in which fifteenth-century *cassone* are richly described and illustrated.

9 The schoolroom is eerily unchanged since Dorian's last lesson. We have all experienced the odd sensation of encountering a former self when we come across some trinket or memento of our childhood. The act of hiding the corrupted portrait from "prying eyes" in a space associated with "the stainless purity of [Dorian's] boyish life" begs for psychoanalytic explanation. The critic Ellie Ragland-Sullivan speculates that the attic is "a kind of metaphor for the Lacanian unconscious. Full of remnants and traces of Dorian's childhood, it is not easily accessible. Not only is it physically distant within the house, it is also dusky, dusty, and eerie just as the Lacanian unconscious, with its archaic accounts of the past, is opaque. Only occasionally does it surface into view—into the light—and just as quickly it shuts back on itself" ("The Phenomenon of Aging in *The Picture of Dorian Gray*: A Lacanian View," in *Memory and Desire: Aging—Literature—Psychoanalysis,* ed. K. M. Woodward and M. M. Schwartz [Bloomington: Indiana University Press, 1986], pp. 120–121).

He held the door open for them, and they passed out into the hall, and began the ascent. The elaborate character of the frame had made the picture extremely bulky, and now and then, in spite of the obsequious protests of Mr. Ashton, who had a true tradesman's dislike of seeing a gentleman doing anything useful, Dorian put his hand to it so as to help them.

"Something of a load to carry, sir," gasped the little man, when they reached the top landing. And he wiped his shiny forehead.

"A terrible load to carry," murmured Dorian, as he unlocked the door that opened into the room that was to keep for him the curious secret of his life and hide his soul from the eyes of men.

He had not entered the place for more than four years,—not indeed since he had used it, first as a playroom when he was a child and then as a study when he grew somewhat older. It was a large, well-proportioned room, which had been specially built by the last Lord Sherard for the use of the little nephew whom, being himself childless, and perhaps for other reasons, he had always hated and desired to keep at a distance. It did not appear to Dorian to have much changed. There was the huge Italian cassone,[8] with its fantastically-painted panels and its tarnished gilt mouldings, in which he had so often hidden himself as a boy. There was the satinwood bookcase filled with his dog-eared schoolbooks. On the wall behind it was hanging the same ragged Flemish tapestry where a faded King and Queen were playing chess in a garden, while a company of hawkers rode by, carrying hooded birds on their gauntleted wrists. How well he recalled it all! Every moment of his lonely childhood came back to him, as he looked round. He remembered the stainless purity of his boyish life, and it seemed horrible to him that it was here that the fatal portrait was to be hidden away.[9] How little he had thought, in those dead days, of all that was in store for him!

But there was no other place in the house so secure from prying eyes as this. He had the key, and no one else could enter it. Beneath its purple pall, the face painted on the canvas could grow bestial, sodden, and unclean. What did it matter? No one could see it. He himself would not see it. Why should he watch the hideous corruption of his soul? He kept his youth,—that was enough. And, besides, might not his nature grow finer, after all? There was no reason that the future should be so full of shame. Some love might come across his life, and purify him, and shield him from those sins that seemed to be already stirring in spirit and in flesh, those curious unpictured sins whose very mystery lent them their subtlety and their charm. Perhaps, some day, the cruel look would have passed away from the scarlet sensitive mouth, and he might show to the world Basil Hallward's masterpiece.

No; that was impossible. The thing upon the canvas was growing old, hour by hour, and week by week. Even if it escaped the hideousness of sin, the hideousness of age was in store for it. The cheeks would become hollow or flaccid. Yellow crow's-feet would creep round the fading eyes and make them horrible. The hair would lose its brightness, the mouth would gape or droop, would be foolish or gross, as the mouths of old men are. There would be the wrinkled throat, the cold blue-veined hands, the twisted body, that he remembered in the uncle who had been so stern to him in his boyhood. The picture had to be concealed. There was no help for it.

"Bring it in, Mr. Ashton, please," he said wearily, turning round. "I am sorry I kept you so long. I was thinking of something else."

"Always glad to have a rest, Mr. Gray," answered the frame-maker, who was still gasping for breath. "Where shall we put it, sir?"

"Oh, anywhere, Here, this will do. I don't want to have it hung up. Just lean it against the wall. Thanks."

"Might one look at the work of art, sir?"

Dorian started. "It would not interest you, Mr. Ashton," he said, keeping his eye on the man. He felt ready to leap upon him and fling him to the ground if he dared to lift the gorgeous hanging that concealed the secret of his life. "I won't trouble you any more now. I am much obliged for your kindness in coming round."

"Not at all, not at all, Mr. Gray. Ever ready to do anything for you, sir," and Mr. Ashton tramped down-stairs, followed by the assistant, who glanced back at Dorian with a look of shy wonder in his rough, uncomely face. He had never seen any one so marvellous.[10]

When the sound of their footsteps had died away, Dorian locked the door, and put the key in his pocket. He felt safe now. No one

10 Wilde accentuated the hint of homoeroticism in the glance of the frame-maker's assistant by adding to the typescript, in handwriting, "He had never seen any one so marvellous."

11 *Nacre* is "mother-of-pearl." Just prior to being released from Reading Gaol in 1897, Wilde wrote to a friend, saying, "I want two or three sets of plain mother-of-pearl (by the way I want to make 'nacred' an English word) studs—nacred studs" (*CL,* p. 809).

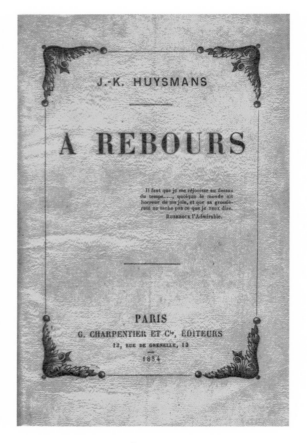

Joris-Karl Huysmans, *À Rebours* (Paris: Charpentier, 1884). French *décadent* fiction was synonymous with the yellow paper wrappers in which it was often bound. It was partly through Wilde—he was purportedly carrying a yellow book at the time of his arrest in 1895—that the color yellow became associated, in English and American minds, with decadence and the 1890s more broadly.

would ever look on the horrible thing. No eye but his would ever see his shame.

On reaching the library he found that it was just after five o'clock, and that the tea had been already brought up. On a little table of dark perfumed wood thickly incrusted with nacre,[11] a present from his guardian's wife, Lady Radley, who had spent the preceding winter in Cairo, was lying a note from Lord Henry, and beside it was a book bound in yellow paper, the cover slightly torn and the edges soiled.[12] A copy of the third edition of the *St. James's Gazette* had been placed on the tea-tray.[13] It was evident that Victor had returned. He wondered if he had met the men in the hall as they were leaving the house and had wormed out of them what they had been doing. He would be sure to miss the picture, had no doubt missed it already, while he had been laying the tea-things. The screen had not been replaced, and the blank space on the wall was visible. Perhaps some night he might find him creeping upstairs and trying to force the door of the room. It was a horrible thing to have a spy in one's house. He had heard of rich men who had been blackmailed all their lives by some servant who had read a letter, or overheard a conversation, or picked up a card with an address, or found beneath a pillow a withered flower or a bit of crumpled lace.

He sighed, and, having poured himself out some tea, opened Lord Henry's note. It was simply to say that he sent him round the evening paper, and a book that might interest him, and that he would be at the Club at eight-fifteen. He opened the *St. James's* languidly, and looked through it. A red pencil-mark on the fifth page caught his eye. He read the following paragraph:

INQUEST ON AN ACTRESS

An inquest was held this morning at the Bell Tavern, Hoxton Road, by Mr. Danby, the District Coroner, on the body of Sybil Vane, a young actress recently engaged at the Royal Theatre, Holborn.[14] A verdict of death by misadventure was returned. Considerable sympathy was expressed for the Mother of the deceased, who was greatly affected during the

OSCAR WILDE.

Copyright 1882, by N. Sarony.

37 UNION SQR., N. Y.

Napoleon Sarony, photo-portrait of Wilde seated with a book (1882).

12 The book's color and the material in which it is bound are significant details. Popular English sensation novels had been bound in yellow paper since the 1840s, and in the 1880s, fiction by French *Décadent* writers often came bound in yellow paper, too, giving rise in Britain to the association of the color yellow with decadence. When in 1894 Wilde's publisher John Lane called his new English-language quarterly *The Yellow Book,* he sought to profit from this association in the popular imagination. He was so successful in his gambit that the entire decade—including Oscar Wilde and his works—are often subsumed under the term "the yellow nineties." It was reported in some newspapers that when Oscar Wilde was arrested at the Cadogan Hotel, he walked out carrying a book with a yellow cover under his arm.

13 The *St. James's Gazette,* a penny review edited by Sidney Low and published three times daily, represented the more intellectual and literary side of Tory journalism. As a *review* rather than a mere chronicle of news, it was conspicuous for its literary character and for the number of distinguished literary men who wrote for it, though it appealed to and influenced a comparatively small circle of cultivated readers. Its politics were reactionary, and in June 1890 it published a scurrilous review of *Dorian Gray,* causing Wilde to say that its editor had "employed Caliban as his art-critic" (*CL,* p. 439). Wilde attempted to defend himself and his novel in a series of letters to the paper that were published alongside abusive editorial notes; the *St. James's Gazette* sustained its attack on Wilde for nearly a full week. Wilde would later characterize the *St. James's Gazette* as occupying "the gutter of English journalism" (*CL,* p. 533) and as one of the "ordinary newspapers" whose "criticisms . . . are of no interest whatsoever, except in so far as they display in its crudest form the extraordinary Boeotianism of a country that has produced some Athenians" (*CL,* p. 522). When Wilde was imprisoned for two years with hard labor, in 1895, the *St. James's Gazette* praised the verdict (Ellmann, *Oscar Wilde,* p. 479).

14 The Theatre Royal at 42 High Holborn (renamed the Royal Holborn Theatre in 1870) burned down in 1880.

15 Compare this denial with Dorian's earlier utterance, "So I have murdered Sybil Vane . . . murdered her
as certainly as if I had cut her little throat with a knife"
(p. 157 above).

16 This paragraph through the first paragraph of
Chapter IX was read out (in their first published ver-
sion) in open court by Queensberry's attorney, Edward
Carson, in 1895. Carson interrogated Wilde at length

William Rothenstein, lithographic portrait of Joris-
Karl Huysmans, 1895. Huysmans's novel *À Rebours*
(Against Nature) greatly influenced Wilde in writing
Dorian Gray. Unimpressed by the great *décadent,* Rothenstein described Huysmans as "a small, shrunken,
nervous man, with a parchment skin—looking rather
like a *fonctionnaire* . . . with his bourgeois collar and tie,
and provincial clothes."

giving of her own evidence, and that of Dr. Birrell, who had
made the post-mortem examination of the deceased.

He frowned slightly, and, tearing the paper in two, went across the
room and flung the pieces into a gilt basket. How ugly it all was! And
how horribly real ugliness made things! He felt a little annoyed with
Lord Henry for having sent him the account. And it was certainly
stupid of him to have marked it with red pencil. Victor might have
read it. The man knew more than enough English for that.

Perhaps he had read it, and had begun to suspect something. And
yet what did it matter? What had Dorian Gray to do with Sybil Vane's
death? There was nothing to fear. Dorian Gray had not killed her.[15]

His eye fell on the yellow book that Lord Henry had sent him.[16]
What was it, he wondered. He went towards the little pearl-coloured
octagonal stand, that had always looked to him like the work of some
strange Egyptian bees who wrought in silver, and took the volume
up. *"Le Secret de Raoul, par Catulle Sarrazin."*[17] What a curious title![a]
He flung himself into an armchair, and began to turn over the leaves.
After a few minutes, he became absorbed. It was the strangest book
he had ever read. It seemed to him that in exquisite raiment, and to
the delicate sound of flutes, the sins of the world were passing in
dumb-show before him. Things that he had dimly dreamed of were
suddenly made real to him. Things of which he had never dreamed
were gradually revealed.

It was a novel without a plot, and with only one character, being,
indeed, simply a psychological study of a certain young Parisian, who
spent his life trying to realise in the nineteenth century all the passions and modes of thought that belonged to every century except
his own, and to sum up, as it were, in himself the various moods
through which the world-spirit had ever passed, loving for their mere
artificiality those renunciations that men have unwisely called virtue, as much as those natural rebellions that wise men still call sin.[18]
The style in which it was written was that curious jewelled style, vivid
and obscure at once, full of argot and of archaisms, of technical expressions and of elaborate paraphrases, that characterises the work
of some of the finest artists of the French school of *Décadents*.[19] There

about them, attempting to demonstrate that the "novel without a plot" was an allusion to Joris-Karl Huysmans's book *À Rebours* (Against the Grain) (1884), a seminal work of French *Décadent* literature. *À Rebours* revolves around the inner life of its reclusive antihero, Jean Des Esseintes, an aesthete and homosexual. Wilde testified that, while he had no "particular novel in . . . mind at the time," a "suggestion" for it came from Huysmans's *À Rebours* (*The Real Trial,* p. 94). Carson pressed Wilde as to whether *À Rebours* (and by implication, *Dorian Gray*) was "a sodomitical book." The presiding judge later ruled that this line of questioning was inadmissible.

17 *Le Secret de Raoul* and its author, Catulle Sarrazin, are made-up names. *Catulle Sarrazin* is a composite of the first and last names of two contemporary French writers—Catulle Mendès and Gabriel Sarrazin—both of whom Wilde knew personally. *Le Secret de Raoul* perhaps alludes to Rachilde's novel *Monsieur Venus* (1884), in which Rachilde's cross-dressing female protagonist, Raoule de Vénérande, takes the effeminate Jacques Silvert as a "mistress." Mendès and Rachilde were at the forefront of the French *Décadent* school—their works transgress accepted notions of gender and sexual propriety. Sarrazin was an anglophile French man of letters, whose work on English writers Wilde admired, and with whom Wilde was friendly at least as early as 1885 (*CL,* p. 273). J. M. Stoddart or one of his associates struck the words "'*Le Secret de Raoul, par Catulle Sarrazin.*' What a curious title!" from the typescript of the novel submitted to Lippincott.

18 The passage of time has not put an end to speculation about the identity of this "novel without a plot." Much ink has been spilled over the question by literary scholars. While most of them agree that *À Rebours* was a key inspiration, the question of influence is complicated by Wilde's well-known love for the works of Walter Pater, as well as by his (less well known) admiration for Ouida's fiction: Wilde's references to *The Renaissance* as "the book which has exerted such a strange influence over my life" (*CL,* p. 735) and "my golden book" (Ellmann, *Oscar Wilde,* p. 47) have led some to speculate that *The Renaissance* was a model. Isobel Murray notes too the possible influence of Pater's novels

Marius the Epicurean and *Gaston de Latour* (*The Picture of Dorian Gray,* ed. Isobel Murray [Oxford University Press, 1974], p. 244); and Talia Schaffer sees the influence of Ouida's novels *Princess Napraxene* and *Othmar* ("The Origins of the Aesthetic Novel," p. 224). In 1894, Wilde writes that "the book that poisoned, or made perfect, Dorian Gray does not exist; it is a fancy of mine merely" (*CL,* p. 585).

19 The *Décadents* were a school of French writers active in the 1870s and 1880s, including Huysmans, Rimbaud, Verlaine, Mendès, Villiers de L'Isle Adam, and Rachilde. They indulged in a highly refined, artificial style, seeing art as autonomous and opposed to nature as well as to bourgeois values, and therefore stressed in their work and lives the bizarre and the transgressive. The Decadents also showed a fascination with decay and annihilation. In 1893 the poet and critic Arthur Symons writes, "The most representative literature of the day—the writing which appeals to, which has done so much to form the younger generation . . . is perhaps [best] characterized by the word *Decadence.* . . . It has all the qualities that mark the end of great periods; the qualities that we find in the Greek, the Latin, decadence: an intense self-consciousness, a restless curiosity in research, an over-subtilizing refinement upon refinement, a spiritual and moral perversity. If what we call the *classic* is indeed the supreme art . . . then this representative literature of today, interesting, beautiful, novel as it is, is really a new and beautiful and interesting disease" ("The Decadent Movement in Literature" [1893], rpt. in *Aesthetes and Decadents of the 1890s,* ed. Karl Beckson [Chicago: Academy Chicago, 1982], pp. 135–136).

In the years following the publication of *Dorian Gray,* the term "decadent" was increasingly used to describe English-language writers, including Wilde and Symons, whose work was now seen as part of a larger European "Decadent Movement." In his book *Degeneration* (1895; originally published in German in 1892), the Hungarian medic and journalist Max Nordau wrote a scathing, highly influential critique in which he portrayed the Decadents and Wilde, as well as many other contemporary European intellectuals including Ibsen and Nietzsche, as examples of *degenerate* writers.

20 An idea reiterated at the end of the next chapter, when Wilde declares that "Dorian Gray had been poisoned by a book," and again in Chapter XIII, when Dorian tells Lord Henry, "[Y]ou poisoned me with a book once." Wilde, too, believed that he had been poisoned by a book (Robert Harborough Sherard, *The Life of Oscar Wilde* [New York: Brentano's, 1911], p. 59); and upon publication in *Lippincott's* in 1890, *Dorian Gray* itself was called "a poisonous book, the atmosphere of which is heavy with the mephitic odours of moral and spiritual putrefaction" (unsigned review in *Daily Chronicle,* rpt. in *Oscar Wilde: The Critical Heritage,* ed. Beckson, p. 72).

21 The novel acts upon Dorian in such a way that its effects are more easily described than its content. One is tempted to say that it is the kind of novel that can only be experienced.

were in it metaphors as monstrous as orchids, and as evil in colour. The life of the senses was described in the terms of mystical philosophy. One hardly knew at times whether one was reading the spiritual ecstasies of some mediæval saint or the morbid confessions of a modern sinner. It was a poisonous book.[20] The heavy odour of incense seemed to cling about its pages and to trouble the brain. The mere cadence of the sentences, the subtle monotony of their music, so full as it was of complex refrains and movements elaborately repeated, produced in the mind of the lad, as he passed from chapter to chapter, a form of reverie, a malady of dreaming, that made him unconscious of the falling day and the creeping shadows.[21]

Cloudless, and pierced by one solitary star, a copper-green sky gleamed through the windows. He read on by its wan light till he could read no more. Then, after his valet had reminded him several times of the lateness of the hour, he got up, and, going into the next room, placed the book on the little Florentine table that always stood at his bedside, and began to dress for dinner. It was almost nine o'clock before he reached the Club, where he found Lord Henry sitting alone, in the morning-room, looking very bored.

"I am so sorry, Harry," he cried, "but really it is entirely your fault. That book you sent me so fascinated me that I forgot what the time was."

"I thought you would like it," replied his host, rising from his chair.

"I didn't say I liked it, Harry. I said it fascinated me. There is a great difference."

"Ah, if you have discovered that, you have discovered a great deal," murmured Lord Henry, with his curious smile. "Come, let us go in to dinner. It is dreadfully late, and I am afraid the champagne will be too much iced."

IX

FOR YEARS, Dorian Gray could not free himself from the memory of this book.[1] Or perhaps it would be more accurate to say that he never sought to free himself from it. He procured from Paris no less than five large-paper copies[2] of the first edition, and had them bound in different colours, so that they might suit his various moods and the changing fancies of a nature over which he seemed, at times, to have almost entirely lost control. Raoul,[a] the wonderful young Parisian, in whom the romantic temperament and the scientific temperament were so strangely blended, became to him a kind of prefiguring type of himself. And, indeed, the whole book seemed to him to contain the story of his own life, written before he had lived it.

In one point he was more fortunate than Catulle Sarrazin's fantastic hero.[b] He never knew, never indeed had any cause to know, that somewhat grotesque dread of mirrors, and polished metal surfaces, and still water, which came upon Raoul[c] so early in his life, and was occasioned by the sudden decay of a beauty that had once, apparently, been so remarkable. It was with an almost cruel joy—and perhaps in nearly every joy, as certainly in every pleasure, cruelty has its place—that he used to read the latter part of the book, with its really tragic, if somewhat over-emphasised, account of the sorrow and despair of one who had himself lost what in others, and in the world, he had most valued.

He, at any rate, had no cause to fear that. The boyish beauty that had so fascinated Basil Hallward, and many others besides him,

1 This is the most difficult, intractable, and densely referential chapter in the novel. Not surprisingly it has given directors fits in their numerous efforts to bring the novel to life on the stage, in film, and on television. Here Wilde largely abandons witty dialogue and dramatic interpersonal exchanges in favor of descriptions of Dorian's interests in religion, mysticism, music, perfumes, jewels, ancient tapestries, and the study of his own ancestors, as he enacts Lord Henry's philosophy of a "new Hedonism." Wilde's object is to capture the texture of Dorian's experiences and the almost scientific spirit in which they are pursued—and thus to capture also the "various moods and changing fancies" of Dorian's own shifting, experimental nature. Wilde's language here is highly ornate, frequently poetic, and it possesses all the characteristics ascribed by Arthur Symons to writings of the Decadent Movement. Like *Le Secret de Raoul,* the chapter possesses a "curious jewelled style, vivid and obscure at once, full of argot and of archaisms, of technical expressions and of elaborate paraphrases" (Chap. 8, p. 184).

2 Altered to "nine large-paper copies" in 1891. Dorian has hired a professional bookbinder to strip and rebind the novel. This private edition, bound in different colors to reflect Dorian's "various moods and changing fancies," has become a reflection of Dorian himself. Like a Bible or religious almanac, it is a physical object that has become fused in its owner's mind with the aura of something sacred. What is being enshrined is Dorian himself.

3 Dorian's youthful, innocent appearance allows him to act with impunity. The influences of the Faust legend and Maturin's *Melmoth the Wanderer* on Wilde's story of unaging youth have already been mentioned. But the story may also owe something to Plato's myth of the Ring of Gyges, which Wilde—an accomplished classicist—would have known well. In the *Republic*, Plato uses the myth as a thought-experiment to ask whether an individual would be moral if he didn't have to fear the consequences of his actions. According to the myth, Gyges, a shepherd, witnesses an earthquake that rents the ground, opening a chasm where he tends his flock. Amazed, he enters the chasm and discovers a corpse wearing a gold ring on its hand. He takes the ring and soon discovers it has the power to make its wearer invisible. He then seduces the wife of the king, murders him with her aid, and takes possession of his kingdom. The myth is related by Plato's character Glaucon to demonstrate his contention that "those who practice justice do so unwillingly and from want of power to commit injustice" and that "every man, when he supposes himself to have the power to do wrong, does wrong" (*The Republic,* II 359b and 360c, in *Plato: The Collected Dialogues*).

4 London's East End and Docklands, mythologized in the novels of Israel Zangwill and Arthur Morrison, were an endless source of fascination to British fiction writers in the 1890s. In Arthur Conan Doyle's story "The Man with The Twisted Lip," Kate Whitney's addict-husband can be found in the "Bar of Gold," an opium den, in Upper Swandam-Lane, sleeping off the effects of opium "among the dregs of the docks" (*The Adventures of Sherlock Holmes,* ed. Richard Lancelyn Green [Oxford University Press, 1994], p. 124). In George Du Maurier's *Trilby,* the painter Little Billee finds pleasure in "study[ing] London life at its lowest end—the eastest end of all. Whitechapel, The Minories, The Docks, Ratcliffe Highway, Rotherhithe, soon got to know him well, and he found much to interest him and much to like among their denizens" (*Trilby* [1894], intro. by Elaine Showalter, notes by Denis Denisoff [Oxford University Press, 1998], pp. 157–158).

seemed never to leave him. Even those who had heard the most evil things against him (and from time to time strange rumours about his mode of life crept through London and became the chatter of the Clubs) could not believe anything to his dishonour when they saw him.[3] He had always the look of one who had kept himself unspotted from the world. Men who talked grossly became silent when Dorian Gray entered the room. There was something in the purity of his face that rebuked them. His mere presence seemed to recall to them the innocence that they had tarnished. They wondered how one so charming and graceful as he was could have escaped the stain of an age that was at once sordid and sensuous.

He himself, on returning home from one of those mysterious and prolonged absences that gave rise to such strange conjecture among those who were his friends, or thought that they were so, would creep upstairs to the locked room, open the door with the key that never left him, and stand, with a mirror, in front of the portrait that Basil Hallward had painted of him, looking now at the evil and aging face on the canvas, and now at the fair young face that laughed back at him from the polished glass. The very sharpness of the contrast used to quicken his sense of pleasure. He grew more and more enamoured of his own beauty, more and more interested in the corruption of his own soul. He would examine with minute care, and often with a monstrous and terrible delight, the hideous lines that seared the wrinkling forehead or crawled around the heavy sensual mouth, wondering sometimes which were the more horrible, the signs of sin or the signs of age. He would place his white hands beside the coarse bloated hands of the picture, and smile. He mocked the misshapen body and the failing limbs.

There were moments, indeed, at night, when, lying sleepless in his own delicately-scented chamber, or in the sordid room of the little ill-famed tavern near the Docks,[4] which, under an assumed name, and in disguise, it was his habit to frequent, he would think of the ruin he had brought upon his soul, with a pity that was all the more poignant because it was purely selfish. But moments such as these were rare. That curiosity about life that, many years before, Lord Henry had first stirred in him, as they sat together in the garden

Photo-portrait of Wilde by Hills and Saunders, taken in Oxford, 1876. Dandies abound in Wilde's plays and fictions, but Wilde's greatest dandified invention was himself.

5 To his contemporaries, Dorian appears the embodiment of the gentlemanly ideal, an ideal predicated in part on education at England's elite institutions: "The young men with me at Oxford," Wilde remarks, "[were] men of position, taste, and high mental culture" ("The Decorative Arts").

6 This quotation, which does not derive from Dante directly, echoes Walter Pater's description of Marius the Epicurean as one "of the number of those who, in the words of a poet who came long after, must be 'made perfect by the love of visible beauty'" (*Marius the Epicurean,* p. 25). The notion that beauty possesses a spiritualizing dimension, popular among the Aesthetes of Wilde's generation, was given currency in Britain in the writings of Walter Pater and Dante Gabriel Rossetti, but its ultimate source is the Dialogues of Plato. According to Plato, the perception of beauty induces *eros,* or the passion that drives the soul upward in its spiritual journey, which culminates in a purely intellectual understanding of beauty, goodness, justice, and wisdom (which are inseparable). In "The Critic as Artist," Wilde writes: "The true critic will, indeed, always be sincere in his devotion to the principle of beauty, but he will seek for beauty in every age and in each school, and will never suffer himself to be limited to any settled custom or thought, or stereotyped mode of looking at things" (p. 189).

7 An adaptation of Gautier's comment *je suis un homme pour qui le monde visible existe* ("I am a man for whom the visible world exists"), uttered by Gautier on May 1, 1857 (quoted in *Selections from Edmond and Jules de Goncourt,* ed. Arnold G. Cameron [New York: American Book Co., 1898], p. 147). Wilde quotes the remark again verbatim, this time with reference to himself, in *De Profundis:* "I have always been one of those *pour qui le monde visible existe*" (*CL,* p. 777).

8 "A Dandy is a Clothes-wearing Man, a Man whose trade, office, and existence consists in the wearing of Clothes," writes Thomas Carlyle in *Sartor Resartus* (1833–1834; rpt. in *A Carlyle Reader,* ed. G. B. Tennyson [Cambridge University Press, 1984], p. 313). But dandyism goes beyond an intense concern for sartorial excellence: "Dandyism does not . . . consist, as many

of their friend, seemed to increase with gratification. The more he knew, the more he desired to know. He had mad hungers that grew more ravenous as he fed them.

Yet he was not really reckless, at any rate in his relations to society. Once or twice every month during the winter, and on each Wednesday evening while the season lasted, he would throw open to the world his beautiful house and have the most celebrated musicians of the day to charm his guests with the wonders of their art. His little dinners, in the settling of which Lord Henry always assisted him, were noted as much for the careful selection and placing of those invited, as for the exquisite taste shown in the decoration of the table, with its subtle symphonic arrangements of exotic flowers, and embroidered cloths, and antique plate of gold and silver. Indeed, there were many, especially among the very young men, who saw, or fancied that they saw, in Dorian Gray the true realisation of a type of which they had often dreamed in Eton or Oxford days, a type that was to combine something of the real culture of the scholar with all the grace and distinction and perfect manner of a citizen of the world.[5] To them he seemed to belong to those whom Dante describes as having sought to "make themselves perfect by the worship of beauty."[6] Like Gautier, he was one for whom "the visible world existed."[7]

And, certainly, to him life itself was the first, the greatest, of the arts, and for it all the other arts seemed to be but a preparation. Fashion, by which what is really fantastic becomes for a moment universal, and Dandyism, which, in its own way, is an attempt to assert the absolute modernity of beauty, had, of course, their fascination for him.[8] His mode of dressing, and the particular styles that he affected from time to time, had their marked influence on the young exquisites of the Mayfair balls and Pall Mall Club windows, who copied him in everything that he did, and tried to reproduce the accidental charm of his graceful, though to him only half-serious, fopperies.

For, while he was but too ready to accept the position that was almost immediately offered to him on his coming of age, and found, indeed, a subtle pleasure in the thought that he might really become to the London of his own day what to imperial Neronian Rome the

Oil portrait of Robert Ross, by William Rothenstein, 1896. Wilde wrote that Ross, who was perhaps his first male sexual partner, had "the face of Puck." Ross remained the most steadfast and trusted of Wilde's friends long after their two-year affair ended. After Wilde's death, Ross dedicated much of the rest of his life to restoring Wilde's reputation, removing Wilde's estate from bankruptcy and providing financially for Wilde's orphaned sons. Ross's ashes rest alongside Wilde's remains in the Père Lachaise tomb.

thoughtless people seem to believe, in an immoderate taste for the toilet and material elegance. . . . It is first and foremost the burning need to create for oneself a personal originality, bounded only by the limits of the proprieties. It is a kind of cult of the self," Baudelaire says ("The Painter of Modern Life," in *"The Painter of Modern Life" and Other Essays,* trans. and ed. Jonathan Mayne, 2nd ed. [London: Phaidon, 1995], p. 27). This cult of the self should not be mistaken merely for egotism, the *poète maudit* elaborates, for the dandy is the "supreme incarnation of the idea of beauty transported into the sphere of material life, the dictator of form and ruler of manners. His clothes, his adornments, his arms, his calumet bear witness to an inventive faculty which has long since deserted us" ("Further Notes on Edgar Poe," in *"The Painter of Modern Life" and Other Essays,* p. 99).

Wilde was fascinated with fashion and dandyism. Dandies abound in his prose writings and society comedies. Wilde's dandies are modern men, and they are often drawn in sharp juxtaposition to more traditional, less extravagant models of masculine self-fashioning. At the beginning of Act 3 of *An Ideal Husband,* for instance, after we have just witnessed a profound crisis in the marriage of the conventional Sir Robert Chiltern, the stage direction concerning the dandified bachelor Lord Goring reads: "Enter Lord Goring in evening dress with a buttonhole. He is wearing a silk hat and Inverness cape. White gloved, he carries a Louis Seize cane. His are all the delicate fopperies of Fashion. One sees that he stands in immediate relation to modern life, makes it indeed, and so masters it. He is the first well-dressed philosopher in the history of thought." But Wilde's greatest dandified invention was himself. From an early age, and with impressive fastidiousness, he transformed himself into a work of art through careful attention to matters of dress, appearance, and behavioral form. Anecdotes, prints, and photographs record the immense care Wilde took with his appearance—his hair, his clothing, and his buttonhole (in which a green carnation featured on at least two public occasions).

9 Gaius Petronius Arbiter (c. 27–66), a Roman court-ier and advisor of Nero, is the author of the *Satyricon,* a satirical, hedonistic novel documenting the decadence of Imperial Rome. Petronius is referred to by the Roman historian Tacitus as the *elegantiae arbiter,* or "judge of elegance," at Nero's court.

10 The ensuing paragraphs are as indebted to the evolutionary writings of Herbert Spencer and W. K. Clifford as they are to Walter Pater's ideas about sensory experience. The notebooks that Wilde kept while a student at Oxford University, edited and published in 1989, demonstrate that Wilde was profoundly affected by Spencer's and Clifford's attempts to marry evolutionary science and biology with concepts of civilization, culture, and ethics.

11 This "harsh, uncomely puritanism" manifested itself in the late-Victorian era in the form of repressive laws and codes: the formation of the National Vigilance Association (1885), the passage of the Criminal Law Amendment Act (1885), the banning of Emile Zola's novels following their denouncement in the House of Commons as "pernicious literature" (1888), and the imprisonment of Zola's English translator (1889). As Judith Walkowitz observes, "the 1880s witnessed the proliferation of clubs and armies to train the young in sexual repression. . . . complemented by repressive public measures against unrespectable sexual activity" (*Prostitution and Victorian Society* [Cambridge University Press, 1980], p. 246).

In his writings, Wilde frequently inveighs against a resurgent "puritanism": in "The Critic as Artist," he writes that although "the sphere of Art and the sphere of Ethics are absolutely distinct and separate . . ." they are "too often confused in England now" (p. 189). Writing to the *St. James's Gazette* in response to attacks on *Dorian Gray,* Wilde complains, "Puritanism is never so offensive and destructive as when it deals with art matters. It is there that its influence is radically wrong. It is this Puritanism, to which your critic has given expression, that is always marring the artistic instinct of the English" (*CL,* p. 432). In a passage deleted in manuscript from *A Woman of No Importance,* Lord Illingworth goes further: "the real enemy of modern life, of everything that makes life lovely and joyous and coloured for us, is Puritanism, and the Puritan spirit."

author of the "Satyricon" had once been, yet in his inmost heart he desired to be something more than a mere *arbiter elegantiarum,* to be consulted on the wearing of a jewel, or the knotting of a neck-tie, or the conduct of a cane.[9] He sought to elaborate some new scheme of life that would have its reasoned philosophy and its ordered principles and find in the spiritualizing of the senses its highest realisation.

The worship of the senses has often, and with much justice, been decried, men feeling a natural instinct of terror about passions and sensations that seem stronger than ourselves, and that we are conscious of sharing with the less highly organized forms of existence.[10] But it appeared to Dorian Gray that the true nature of the senses had never been understood, and that they had remained savage and animal merely because the world had sought to starve them into submission or to kill them by pain, instead of aiming at making them elements of a new spirituality, of which a fine instinct for beauty was to be the dominant characteristic. As he looked back upon Man moving through History, he was haunted by a feeling of loss. So much had been surrendered! And to such little purpose! There had been mad wilful rejections, monstrous forms of self-torture and self-denial, whose origin was fear, and whose result was a degradation infinitely more terrible than that fancied degradation from which, in their ignorance, they had sought to escape, Nature in her wonderful irony driving the anchorite out to herd with the wild animals of the desert, and giving to the hermit the beasts of the field as his companions.

Yes, there was to be, as Lord Henry had prophesied, a new Hedonism that was to recreate life, and to save it from that harsh, uncomely puritanism that is having, in our own day, its curious revival.[11] It was to have its service of the intellect, certainly; yet it was never to accept any theory or system that would involve the sacrifice of any mode of passionate experience. Its aim, indeed, was to be experience itself, and not the fruits of experience, sweet or bitter as they might be.[12] Of the asceticism that deadens the senses, as of the vulgar profligacy that dulls them, it was to know nothing. But it was to teach man to concentrate himself upon the moments of a life that is itself but a moment.[13]

There are few of us who have not sometimes wakened before dawn,[14] either after one of those dreamless nights that make one almost enamoured of death, or one of those nights of horror and misshapen joy, when through the chambers of the brain sweep phantoms, more terrible than reality itself and instinct[15] with that vivid life that lurks in all grotesques and that lends to Gothic art its enduring vitality, this art being, one might fancy, especially the art of those whose minds have been troubled with the malady of reverie.[16] Gradually white fingers creep through the curtains, and they appear to tremble. Black fantastic shadows crawl into the corners of the room, and crouch there. Outside, there is the stirring of birds among the leaves, or the sound of men going forth to their work, or the sigh and sob of the wind coming down from the hills, and wandering round the silent house, as though it feared to wake the sleepers. Veil after veil of thin dusky gauze is lifted, and by degrees the forms and colours of things are restored to them, and we watch the dawn remaking the world in its antique pattern. The wan mirrors get back their mimic life. The flameless tapers stand where we have left them, and beside them lies the half-read book that we had been studying, or the wired flower that we had worn at the ball, or the letter that we had been afraid to read, or that we had read too often. Nothing seems to us changed. Out of the unreal shadows of the night comes back the real life that we had known. We have to resume it where we had left off, and there steals over us a terrible sense of the necessity for the continuance of energy in the same wearisome round of stereotyped habits, or a wild longing, it may be, that our eyelids might open some morning upon a world that had been re-fashioned anew for our pleasure in the darkness, a world in which things would have fresh shapes and colours, and be changed, or have other secrets, a world in which the past would have little or no place, or survive, at any rate, in no conscious form of obligation or regret, the remembrance even of joy having its bitterness, and the memories of pleasure their pain.[17]

It was the creation of such worlds as these that seemed to Dorian Gray to be the true object, or amongst the true objects of life, and in his search for sensations that would be at once new and delightful, and possess that element of strangeness that is so essential to ro-

12 "Not the fruit of experience, but experience itself, is the end. . . . With this sense of the awful splendour of our experience and of its awful brevity, gathering all we are into one desperate effort to see and touch, we shall hardly have time to make theories about the things we see and touch. What we have to do is to be for ever testing new opinions and courting new impressions, never acquiescing in a facile orthodoxy . . . The theory or idea or system which requires of us the sacrifice of any part of this experience . . . has no real claim upon us" (Pater, *The Renaissance,* ed. Hill, pp. 188–189).

13 Another of Wilde's debts to Pater's *Renaissance.* After commenting that "to regard all things and principles of things as inconstant . . . has more and more become the tendency of modern thought," Pater writes, "This at least of flame-like our life has, that it is but the concurrence, renewed from moment to moment, of forces parting sooner or later on their ways" (pp. 186–187).

14 Note throughout this paragraph the use of the personal pronoun ("we," "us"), suggesting the narrator's—and by extension the reader's—close association with Dorian at this point in the novel.

15 Like Shelley and Carlyle before him, Wilde uses the word *instinct* in the adjectival and Latinate sense, meaning "replete," "imbued," or "charged" with.

16 An idea popularized by John Ruskin. Commenting on the essentially *grotesque* qualities of Gothic art, Ruskin observes that "To delight in fantastic and ludicrous, as well as sublime, images is a universal instinct of the Gothic imagination" (*The Stones of Venice*).

17 "How natural the determination to rely exclusively upon the phenomena of the senses, which certainly never deceive us about themselves, about which alone we can never deceive ourselves. So the merely abstract skeptical apprehension that the little point of the present moment alone really is . . . became practical with Marius, as the resolution, as far as possible, to exclude regret and desire, and yield himself to . . . the present with an absolutely disengaged mind" (Pater, *Marius the Epicurean,* p. 93).

18 "What we call a state of feeling, or emotion, is a transitory outburst from a permanent condition approaching to indifference" (Alexander Bain, *Mental and Moral Science: A Compendium of Psychology and Ethics* [London: Longmans, Green & Co., 1868], p. 224).

19 The opening sentences of this paragraph describe Wilde's own interests in Catholicism. It is not surprising that the aesthetic dimensions of Catholic ritual strongly appealed to Wilde's imagination. Brought up in an Irish Protestant household, Wilde considered converting to Catholicism while at Oxford, even journeying to Rome in 1877 for this purpose. After further dalliances with Catholicism late in his life, he is reputed to have given his consent to being received into the Roman Catholic Church upon his deathbed, at which point he was anointed and given the Last Sacrament by a Roman Catholic priest.

20 German nationalist movement that harnessed Darwin's scientific evolutionism to racially inflected political ideas about the purity of the German *volk*. *Darwinismus* (Darwinism) originated in a speech by Ernst Haeckel to the Association of German Scientists in 1863; it "preached the racial inheritance of acquired characteristics" and favored "a state based on aristocratic Junker leadership of a peasant people" (Mary C. King, "Digging for Darwin: Bitter Wisdom in *The Picture of Dorian Gray* and 'The Critic as Artist,'" *Irish Studies Review*, 12:3 [2004], 318).

21 This paragraph is modeled on Huysmans's *À Rebours,* in which the hero, Des Esseintes, briefly devotes himself to the study of rare scents and perfumes in the belief that perfumery is a "language" possessing a "diction as varied, as subtle, as literature itself" (translated as *Against the Grain* [1923; rpt. New York: Dover Publications, 1969], p. 107). For Huysmans, "the sense of smell was qualified to experience pleasures equal to those pertaining to the eye and the ear" (p. 106), and perfumery is an art distinguished by the "precision with which it can artificially imitate" the aromas of real or natural flowers (p. 106). By combining alcoholates and essences, the perfumier "extracts from the model its inmost individuality while adding that something

mance, he would often adopt certain modes of thought that he knew to be really alien to his nature, abandon himself to their subtle influences, and then, having, as it were, caught their colour and satisfied his intellectual curiosity, leave them with that curious indifference that is not incompatible with a real ardour of temperament, and that indeed, according to certain modern psychologists, is often a condition of it.[18]

It was rumoured of him once that he was about to join the Roman Catholic Communion; and certainly the Roman ritual had always a great attraction for him. The daily sacrifice, more awful really than all the sacrifices of the antique world, stirred him as much by its superb rejection of the evidence of the senses as by the primitive simplicity of its elements, and the eternal pathos of the human tragedy that it sought to symbolise.[19] He loved to kneel down on the cold marble pavement, and with the priest, in his stiff flowered cope, slowly and with white hands moving aside the veil of the tabernacle, and raising aloft the jewelled lantern-shaped monstrance with that pallid wafer that at times, one would feign think, is indeed the "panis celestis," the bread of Angels, or, robed in the garments of the Passion of Christ, breaking the Host into the Chalice, and smiting his breast for his sins. The fuming censers, that the grave boys, in their lace and scarlet, tossed into the air like great gilt flowers, had their subtle fascination for him. As he passed out, he used to look with wonder at the black confessionals, and long to sit in the dim shadow of one of them and listen to men and women whispering through the tarnished grating the true story of their lives.

But he never fell into the error of arresting his intellectual development by any formal acceptance of creed or system, or of mistaking, for a house in which to live, an inn that is but suitable for the sojourn of a night, or for a few hours of a night in which there are no stars and the moon is in travail. Mysticism, with its marvellous power of making common things strange to us, and the subtle antinomianism that always seems to accompany it, moved him for a season; and for a season he inclined to the materialistic doctrines of the Darwinismus movement in Germany,[20] and found a curious pleasure in tracing the thoughts and passions of men to some ivory cell in the brain, or some scarlet nerve in the body,[d] delighting in the conception of the absolute dependence of the spirit on certain physical conditions, morbid or healthy, normal or diseased. Yet, as has been said of him before, no theory of life seemed to him to be of any importance compared with life itself. He felt keenly conscious of how barren all intellectual speculation is when separated from action and experiment. He knew that the senses, no less than the soul, have their mysteries to reveal.

And so he would now study perfumes, and the secrets of their manufacture, distilling heavily-scented oils, and burning odorous gums from the East.[21] He saw that there was no mood of the mind that had not its counterpart in the sensuous life, and set himself to discover their true relations, wondering what there was in frankincense that made one mystical, and in ambergris that stirred one's passions, and in violets that woke the memory of dead romances, and in musk that troubled the brain, and in champak that stained the imagination; and seeking often to elaborate a real psychology of perfumes, and to estimate the several influences of sweet-smelling roots, and scented pollen-laden flowers, of aromatic balms, and of dark and fragrant woods, of spikenard that sickens, of hovenia that makes men mad, and of aloes that are said to be able to expel melancholy from the soul.

At another time he devoted himself entirely to music, and in a long latticed room, with a vermilion-and-gold ceiling and walls of olive-green lacquer, he used to give curious concerts in which mad gypsies tore wild music from little zithers, or grave yellow-shawled Tunisians plucked at the strained strings of monstrous lutes, while grinning negroes beat monotonously upon copper drums, or turbaned Indians, crouching upon scarlet mats, blew through long pipes of reed or brass, and charmed, or feigned to charm, great hooded snakes and horrible horned adders.[22] The harsh intervals and shrill discords of barbaric music stirred him at times when Schubert's grace, and Chopin's beautiful sorrows, and the mighty harmonies of Beethoven himself, fell unheeded on his ear. He collected together from all parts of the world the strangest instruments that could be found, either in the tombs of dead nations or among the few sav-

... that rare touch which makes it a work of art. In one word, in perfumery the artist completes and consummates the original odour, which he cuts, so to speak, and mounts as a jeweller improves and brings out the water of a precious stone" (p. 107). In his capacity as editor of *Woman's World,* Wilde had in 1889 published an essay on "Scents and Scent Bottles," by Anne Hathaway [pseud.].

22 While this passage may seem racist or orientalist to modern readers, Wilde here follows Huysmans in using "the radically foreign (non-Western) as the occasion for showing that the discriminating observer can desire and regulate his body differently from the vulgar, inartistic bourgeois" (Julia Kent, "Oscar Wilde's 'False Notes': *Dorian Gray* and English Realism," *Romanticism & Victorianism on the Net,* 48 [November 2007]). It is also one of many passages in the novel in which Wilde associates Dorian with strange music in order to suggest unconscious, even illicit, desire.

23 Wilde's descriptions of strange-sounding, exotic instruments in this paragraph are adapted from a single chapter ("The American Indians") in Carl Engel, *Musical Instruments,* 2nd ed. [London, 1874], an "Art Handbook" designed to accompany the collections of the South Kensington Museum (now the Victoria and Albert Museum). Although indebted to Engel on a purely factual basis, Wilde's adaptation is transformational, for he renders Engel's material in a prose of subtle poetic power and rhythm. As Arthur Symons remarks about another of Wilde's works, "Wilde . . . can be admirable even when his eloquence reminds us of the eloquent writing of others. He is conscious of the charm of graceful echoes, and is always original in his quotations" (rev. of Wilde's *Intentions* [1891], rpt. in *Oscar Wilde: The Critical Heritage,* p. 96).

24 The German medieval legend of Venus and Tannhäuser dramatizes the conflict between sacred and profane love. After discovering Venus's abode (the "Venusberg") and devoting a full year to the worship of Venus, the knight Tannhäuser journeys to Rome seeking absolution for his sins. The pope tells him that absolution would be as impossible as it would be for the papal staff to sprout in bloom, whereupon Tannhäuser returns dejectedly to the Venusberg. Three days after his departure, the pope's staff does indeed sprout blossoms, and the pope sends messengers to retrieve Tannhäuser, but no trace of him is found and he remains unabsolved. The story had been popular with British aesthetes before the first performances in Britain of Wagner's opera *Tannhäuser* in 1876. But Wagner's opera popularized the story on a massive scale and, along with others of Wagner's works, became the object of cultlike devotion among different elements of the British intelligentsia in the 1890s.

25 Anne de Joyeuse (1561–1587), a man not a woman, was a court favorite or minion of the homosexual Henri III of France (1551–1589). Before elevating him to the peerage (first as Duke of Joyeuse in 1581, then as Admiral of France in 1582), Henri arranged for Anne's marriage to the younger sister of the queen. At the wedding, king and bridegroom were adorned alike with "broderies, perles et pierreries [embroideries, pearls,

age tribes that have survived contact with Western civilizations, and loved to touch and try them.[23] He had the mysterious *juruparis* of the Rio Negro Indians, that women are not allowed to look at, and that even youths may not see till they have been subjected to fasting and scourging, and the earthen jars of the Peruvians that have the shrill cries of birds, and flutes of human bones such as Alfonso de Ovalle heard in Chili, and the sonorous green stones that are found near Cuzco and give forth a note of singular sweetness. He had painted gourds filled with pebbles that rattled when they were shaken; the long *clarin* of the Mexicans, into which the performer does not blow, but through which he inhales the air; the harsh *turé* of the Amazon tribes, that is sounded by the sentinels who sit all day long in trees, and that can be heard, it is said, at a distance of three leagues; the *teponaztli,* that has two vibrating tongues of wood, and is beaten with sticks that are smeared with an elastic gum obtained from the milky juice of plants; the *yotl*-bells of the Aztecs, that are hung in clusters like grapes; and a huge cylindrical drum, covered with the skins of great serpents, like the one that Bernal Diaz saw when he went with Cortes into the Mexican temple, and of whose doleful sound he has left us so vivid a description. The fantastic character of these instruments fascinated him, and he felt a curious delight in the thought that Art, like Nature, has her monsters, things of bestial shape and with hideous voices. Yet, after some time, he wearied of them, and would sit in his box at the Opera, either alone, or with Lord Henry, listening in rapt pleasure to "Tannhäuser," and seeing in that great work of art a presentation of the Tragedy of his own soul.[24]

On another occasion he took up the study of jewels, and appeared at a Costume Ball as Anne de Joyeuse, Admiral of France, in a dress covered with five hundred and sixty pearls.[25] He would often spend a whole day settling and resetting in their cases the various stones that he had collected, such as the olive-green chrysoberyl that turns red by lamplight, the cymophane with its wire-like line of silver, the pistachio-coloured peridot, rose-pink and wine-yellow topazes, carbuncles of fiery scarlet with tremulous four-rayed stars, flame-red cinnamon-stones, orange and violet spinels, and amethysts with their alternate layers of ruby and sapphire.[26] He loved the red gold of the sunstone, and the moonstone's pearly whiteness, and the broken rainbow of the milky opal. He procured from Amsterdam three emeralds of extraordinary size and richness of colour, and had a turquoise *de la vieille roche* that was the envy of all the connoisseurs.

He discovered wonderful stories, also, about jewels.[27] In Alphonso's "Clericalis Disciplina" a serpent was mentioned with eyes of real jacinth, and in the romantic history of Alexander he was said to have found snakes in the vale of Jordan "with collars of real emeralds growing on their backs." There was a gem in the brain of the dragon, Philostratus told us, and "by the exhibition of golden letters and a scarlet robe" the monster could be thrown into a magical sleep, and slain. According to the great alchemist Pierre de Boniface, the Diamond rendered a man invisible, and the Agate of India made him eloquent. The Cornelian appeased anger, and the Hyacinth provoked sleep, and the Amethyst drove away the fumes of wine. The Garnet cast out demons, and the Hydropicus deprived the Moon of her colour. The Selenite waxed and waned with the Moon, and the Meloceus, that discovers thieves, could be affected only by the blood of kids. Leonardus Camillus had seen a white stone taken from the brain of a newly-killed toad, that was a certain antidote against poison. The bezoar, that was found in the heart of the Arabian deer, was a charm that could cure the plague. In the nests of Arabian birds was the Aspilates, that, according to Democritus, kept the wearer from any danger by fire.

The King of Ceilan rode through his city with a large ruby in his hand, as the ceremony of his coronation. The gates of the Palace of John the Priest were "made of sardius, with the horn of the horned snake inwrought, so that no man might bring poison within." Over the gable were "two golden apples, in which were two carbuncles," so that the gold might shine by day, and the carbuncles by night. In Lodge's strange romance "A Margarite of America" it was stated that in the chamber of Margarite were seen "all the chaste ladies of the world, inchased out of silver, looking through fair mirrours of chrysolites, carbuncles, sapphires, and greene emeraults." Marco Polo had

and precious stones]" (J. Quicherat, *Histoire du Costume en France* [1875], quoted in *The Picture of Dorian Gray*, ed. Murray, p. 245). As Joseph Bristow observes, in "The Young King" Wilde's young monarch cries with pleasure when he sees "the delicate raiment and rich jewels that had been prepared for him" while simultaneously delighting in "the wonderful palace—*Joyeuse*, as they called it—of which he now found himself lord."

26 All the descriptions of rare and exotic stones in this paragraph are adapted from A. H. Church, *Precious Stones* (London, 1883), a handbook to the Townsend collection of precious stones in the South Kensington Museum (now the Victoria and Albert Museum). Wilde renders this source material in a prose of subtle power, transforming it drastically in the process.

27 The "wonderful stories about jewels" contained in this paragraph and the two following it were inserted into the typescript by Wilde on three handwritten sheets. They represent the largest single alteration Wilde made to the typescript prior to sending it off for publication. These anecdotes are closely adapted—often word for word—from William Jones, *History and Mystery of Precious Stones* (London: Richard Bentley, 1880). With one exception, all the phrases quoted by Wilde had been previously quoted by Jones; similarly, with the same exception, all names and sources cited by Wilde had previously been cited by Jones, though here their esoteric qualities are decidedly more pronounced. The exception is Wilde's reference to the jeweled gifts that Edward II gave to Piers Gaveston, his male lover—a homoerotic reference which, as Joseph Bristow notes, has no precedent in Jones's work.

28 As Joseph Bristow observes, in Wilde's source (Jones, *History and Mystery*) the young priest of the Sun is identified as Elagabalus, a figure whom late in life Wilde consistently identified with male beauty and homosexual desire.

29 All of Wilde's references in this paragraph and the next derive from Ernest Lefébure, *Embroidery and Lace,* trans. Alan S. Cole (London: H. Grevel & Co., 1888). Wilde had reviewed Lefébure's book enthusiastically in *Woman's World* in November 1888 ("A Fascinating Book"). Much of the present paragraph is adapted, often word for word, from Wilde's review.

"As Anne De Joyeuse," illustration to *The Picture of Dorian Gray,* intro. Osbert Burdett, illustr. Henry Keen (London and New York: John Lane / Dodd, Mead & Co., 1925).

watched the inhabitants of Zipangu place a rose-coloured pearl in the mouth of the dead. A sea-monster had been enamoured of the pearl that the diver brought to King Perozes, and had slain the thief, and mourned for seven moons over his loss. When the Huns lured the king into the great pit, he flung it away,—Procopius tells the story—nor was it ever found again, though the Emperor Anastasius offered five hundred weight of gold pieces for it. The King of Malabar had shown a Venetian a rosary of one hundred and four pearls, one for every god that he worshipped. It was a pearl that Julius Caesar had given to Servilia, when he loved her. Their child had been Brutus.[e]

The young priest of the Sun, who while yet a boy had been slain for his sins, used to walk in jewelled shoes on dust of gold and silver.[28] When the Duke de Valentinois, son of Alexander VI., visited Louis XII. of France, his horse was loaded with gold leaves, according to Brantôme, and his cap had double rows of rubies that threw out a great light. Charles of England had ridden in stirrups hung with three hundred and twenty-one diamonds. Richard II. had a coat, valued at 30.000 marks, which was covered with balas rubies. Hall described Henry VIII., on his way to the Tower previous to his coronation, as wearing "a jacket of raised gold, the placard embroidered with diamonds and other rich stones, and a great bauderike about his neck of large balasses." The favourites of James I. wore ear-rings of emeralds set in gold filigrane. Edward II. gave to Piers Gaveston a suit of red-gold armour studded with jacinths, and a collar of gold roses set with turquoise-stones, and a skull-cap *parsemé* with pearls. Henry II. wore jewelled gloves reaching to the elbow, and had a hawk-glove set with twelve rubies and fifty-two great pearls. The ducal hat of Charles the Rash, the last Duke of Burgundy of his race, was studded with sapphires and hung with pear-shaped pearls.[f] How exquisite life had once been! How gorgeous in its pomp and decoration! Even to read of the luxury of the dead was wonderful.

Then he turned his attention to embroideries, and to the tapestries that performed the office of frescos in the chill rooms of the Northern nations of Europe.[29] As he investigated the subject,—and he always had an extraordinary faculty of becoming absolutely ab-

sorbed for the moment in whatever he took up,—he was almost sad-
dened by the reflection of the ruin that time brought on beautiful and wonderful things. He, at any rate, had escaped that. Summer
followed summer, and the yellow jonquils bloomed and died many
times, and nights of horror repeated the story of their shame, but he
was unchanged. No winter marred his face or stained his flowerlike
bloom. How different it was with material things! Where had they
gone to? Where was the great crocus-coloured robe, on which the
Gods fought against the Giants, that had been worked for Athena?
Where the huge velarium that Nero had stretched across the Colos-
seum at Rome, on which was represented the starry sky, and Apollo
driving a chariot drawn by white gilt-reined steeds? He longed to see
the curious table-napkins wrought for Elagabalus, on which were
displayed all the dainties and viands that could be wanted for a feast;
the mortuary cloth of King Chilperic, with its three hundred golden
bees; the fantastic robes that excited the indignation of the Bishop
of Pontus, and were figured with "lions, panthers, bears, dogs, for-
ests, rocks, hunters,—all, in fact, that a painter can copy from nature;" and the coat that Charles of Orleans once wore, on the sleeves
of which were embroidered the verses of a song beginning "Madame,
je suis tout joyeux," the musical accompaniment of the words being wrought in gold thread, and each note, a square shape in those
days, formed with four pearls. He read of the room that was prepared at the palace at Rheims for the use of Queen Joan of Burgundy,
and was decorated with "thirteen hundred and twenty-one parrots,
made in broidery, and blazoned with the King's arms, and five hundred and sixty-one butterflies, whose wings were similarly orna-
mented with the arms of the Queen, the whole worked in gold."
Catherine de Médicis had a mourning-bed made for her of black
velvet powdered with crescents and suns. Its curtains were of damask, with leafy wreaths and garlands, figured upon a gold and silver ground, and fringed along the edges with broideries of pearls,
and it stood in a room hung with rows of the Queen's devices in cut
black velvet upon cloth of silver. Louis XIV. had gold-embroidered
caryatides fifteen feet high in his apartment. The state bed of
Sobieski, King of Poland, was made of Smyrna gold brocade em-

30 This paragraph—inserted into the typescript of *Dorian Gray* on two separate, handwritten sheets—represents one of Wilde's most substantial handwritten alterations of the typescript. Wilde's descriptions of ecclesiastical vestments are loosely based on an essay that he had edited for *Woman's World* in 1889 ("Notes on a Few Specimens of Ancient Ecclesiastical Embroidery," by Ellen T. Masters). Isobel Murray identifies a second source in Daniel Rock, *Textile Fabrics* (London: Chapman and Hall, 1870), a South Kensington Museum Art Handbook that Wilde had likely consulted when he visited the museum. An ecclesiologist and Roman Catholic priest, Rock assumed his readers would be familiar with the terms *cope, chasuble, chalice-veil,* and *dalmatic*—all repeated by Wilde without definition. All four terms denote vestments still worn during the Catholic Liturgy. Recognizing that *orphrey, corporal,* and *diaper* were beyond the comprehension of most readers, Rock provided definitions. *Orphrey* he defines as an old English word meaning embroidery "wrought in solid gold wire or golden thread" (p. 79), *corporal* as "a handkerchief in which the Eucharist had formerly been held" (p. 107), and *diaper* as "a one-coloured yet patterned silk" (p. 32). *Morse* and *sudaria* are not terms used by Rock. A *morse* is a "clasp or fastening of a cope, frequently made of gold or silver, and set with precious stones" (OED). A *sudarium* is a "napkin or cloth for wiping the face; a handkerchief; *spec.* the cloth with which, according to legend, St. Veronica wiped the face of Christ on the way to Calvary, and on which his features were impressed; hence, any similar cloth venerated as a relic; a portrait of Christ on a cloth" (OED).

broidered in turquoises with verses from the Koran. Its supports were of silver gilt, beautifully chased, and profusely set with enamelled and jewelled medallions. It had been taken from the Turkish camp before Vienna, and the standard of Mahomet had stood under it.

And so, for a whole year, he sought to accumulate the most exquisite specimens that he could find of textile and embroidered work, getting the dainty Delhi muslins, finely wrought, with gold thread palmates, and stitched over with iridescent beetles' wings; the Agra gauzes, that from their transparency are known in the East as "woven air," and "running water," and "evening dew;" strange figured cloths from Java; elaborate yellow Chinese hangings; books bound in tawny satins, or fair blue silks, and wrought with *fleurs de lys,* birds, and images; veils of *lacis* worked in Hungary point; Sicilian brocades, and stiff Spanish velvets; Georgian work with its gilt coins, and Japanese *Foukousas* with their green-toned golds and their marvellously-plumaged birds.

He had a special passion, also, for Ecclesiastical vestments, as indeed he had for every thing connected with the service of the Church.[30] In the long cedar chests that lined the West Gallery of his house he had stored away many rare and beautiful specimens of what is really the raiment of the Bride of Christ, who must wear purple and jewels and fine linen that she may hide the pallid macerated body that is worn by the suffering that she seeks for, and wounded by self-inflicted pain. He had a gorgeous cope of crimson silk and gold-thread damask, figured with a repeating pattern of golden pomegranates set in six-petalled formal blossoms, beyond which on either side was the pine-apple device wrought in seed-pearls. The orphreys were divided into panels representing scenes from the life of the Virgin, and the Coronation of the Virgin was figured in coloured silks upon the Hood. This was Italian work of the fifteenth century. Another cope was of green velvet, embroidered with heart-shaped groups of acanthus-leaves, from which spread long-stemmed white blossoms, the details of which were picked out with silver thread and coloured crystals. The Morse bore a seraph's head in gold-thread raised work. The orphreys were woven in a diaper of red and gold silk, and were starred with medallions of many saints and martyrs, among whom was St. Sebastian. He had Chasubles, also, of amber-coloured silk, and blue silk and gold brocade, and yellow silk damask and cloth of gold, figured with representations of the Passion and Crucifixion of Christ, and embroidered with lions and peacocks and other emblems; dalmatics of white satin and pink silk damask, decorated with tulips and dolphins and fleurs de lys; Altar Frontals of crimson velvet and blue linen; and many Corporals, Chalice-veils, and Sudaria. In the mystic offices to which these things were put there was something that quickened his imagination.

For these things, and everything that he collected in his lovely house, were to be to him means of forgetfulness, modes by which he could escape, for a season, from the fear that seemed to him at times to be almost too great to be borne. Upon the walls of the lonely locked room where he had spent so much of his boyhood, he had hung with his own hands the terrible portrait whose changing features showed him the real degradation of his life, and had draped the purple-and-gold pall in front of it as a curtain. For weeks he would not go there, would forget the hideous painted thing, and get back his light heart, his wonderful joyousness, his passionate pleasure in mere existence. Then, suddenly, one night[g] he would creep out of the house, go down to dreadful places near Blue Gate Fields,[31] and stay there, day after day, till the people almost drove him out in horror, and had to be appeased by monstrous bribes.[h] On his return he would sit in front of the picture, sometimes loathing it and himself, but filled, at other times, with that pride of rebellion that is half the fascination of sin, and smiling, with secret pleasure, at the misshapen shadow that had to bear the burden that should have been his own.

After a few years he could not endure to be long out of England, and gave up the villa that he had shared at Trouville with Lord Henry, as well as the little white walled-in house at Algiers where he had more than once spent his winter.[32] He hated to be separated from the picture that was such a part of his life, and he was also afraid that during his absence some one might gain access to the room, in spite

31 The "favourite haunt of degraded Lascars, Malays, and Chinamen, who may, in some of the dens, be seen smoking opium" (Henry B. Wheatley, *London Past and Present*, 3 vols. [London: John Murray, 1891], 1:212).

32 Trouville, a fashionable French seaside resort on the Normandy coast, had been popular with aesthetes since Whistler and Courbet had painted there in the 1860s. Algiers, capital city of Algeria, on the North African coast, is famous for the glistening whiteness of its buildings. For many decades prior to the Algerian War of Independence (1954–1962), it was also a popular destination for Western sex tourists, particularly homosexual tourists. In January 1895, Wilde spent two weeks there in the company of Lord Alfred Douglas, writing to Robert Ross that "[t]here is a great deal of beauty here. The Kabyle boys are quite lovely" and that "Bosie and I have taken to haschish [sic]: it is quite exquisite: three puffs of smoke and then peace and love . . . The beggars here have profiles, so the problem of poverty is easily solved" (*CL,* p. 629). What Lord Henry and Dorian were doing in Trouville, and why they were sharing a villa, Wilde leaves to his readers to conjecture.

33 Dorian's town and country abodes reflect two distinct parts of his character, one social and public, the other private or secret. As Jack remarks in *The Importance of Being Earnest,* "When one is in town one amuses oneself. When one is in the country, one amuses other people."

34 Both definitions of "blackball" given in OED are relevant here: "1. To exclude (a person) from a club or other society by adverse votes. . . . 2. To exclude from society; to ostracize, taboo." Wilde was himself effectively blackballed from a West End club in 1888 (though technically, his candidacy for the Savile Club was not voted down but simply postponed indefinitely). Wilde likened his presence within the club's walls to "a poor lion who has rashly intruded into a den of Daniels" (*CL,* p. 362).

35 The Carlton Club, altered to the fictive "Churchill" in 1891, was (and still is) a politically conservative London club. Dorian's treatment in the Carlton's smoking-room, at the hands of the Duke of Berwick and his friend, replicates Wilde's own treatment, when visiting the Hogarth Club as a guest of Robert Ross: "as we entered the room, an old member of the Club, ostentatiously staring at Wilde, rose from his chair and made for the door. One or two other members also got up. Everyone felt uncomfortable" (William Rothenstein, *Men and Memories: Recollections, 1872–1938,* ed. Mary Lago [Columbia, MO: University of Missouri Press, 1978], p. 82).

36 Usually written in the upper-case, Wilde means "society" in the restricted sense of *polite* society or *high* society—what he calls farther down this page "civilized society at least," namely, the wealthy, fashionable, and prominent. The action of Wilde's play *Lady Windermere's Fan* centers on Mrs. Erlynne's desire to "get back into society" in precisely this sense. In *A Woman of No Importance,* Lady Caroline Pontefract remarks that "in my young days . . . one never met anyone in society who worked for their living."

of the elaborate bolts and bars that he had caused to be placed upon the door.

He was quite conscious that this would tell them nothing. It was true that the portrait still preserved, under all the foulness and ugliness of the face, its marked likeness to himself, but what could they learn from that? He would laugh at any one who tried to taunt him. He had not painted it. What was it to him how vile and full of shame it looked? Even if he told them, would they believe it?

Yet he was afraid. Sometimes when he was down at his great house in Nottinghamshire, entertaining the fashionable young men of his own rank who were his chief companions, and astounding the county by the wanton luxury and gorgeous splendour of his mode of life, he would suddenly leave his guests and rush back to town to see that the door had not been tampered with and that the picture was still there.[33] What if it should be stolen? The mere thought made him cold with horror. Surely the world would know his secret then. Perhaps the world already suspected it.

For while he fascinated many, there were not a few who distrusted him. He was blackballed at a West End Club of which his birth and social position fully entitled him to become a member,[34] and on one occasion when he was brought by a friend into the smoking-room of the Carlton, the Duke of Berwick and another gentleman got up in a marked manner and went out.[35] Curious stories became current about him after he had passed his twenty-fifth year. It was said that he had been seen brawling with foreign sailors in a low den in the distant parts of Whitechapel, and that he consorted with thieves and coiners and knew the mysteries of their trade. His extraordinary absences became notorious, and, when he used to reappear again in society,[36] men, who were jealous of the strange love that he inspired in women,[i] would whisper to each other in corners, or pass him with a sneer, or look at him with cold searching eyes, as if they were determined to discover his secret.

Of such insolences and attempted slights he, of course, took no notice, and in the opinion of most people his frank debonair manner, his charming boyish smile, and the infinite grace of that wonderful youth that seemed never to leave him, were in themselves a sufficient answer to the calumnies, for so they called them, that were circulated about him. It was remarked, however, that those who had been most intimate with him appeared, after a time, to shun him. Of all his friends, or so-called friends, Lord Henry Wotton was the only one who remained loyal to him.ʲ Women who had wildly adored him, and for his sake had braved all social censure and set convention at defiance, were seen to grow pallid with shame or horror if Dorian Gray entered the room. It was said that even the sinful creatures who prowl the streets at night had cursed him as he passed by, seeing in him a corruption greater than their own, and knowing but too well the horror of his real life.ᵏ

Yet these whispered scandals only lent him, in the eyes of many, his strange and dangerous charm. His great wealth was a certain element of security. Society, civilized society at least, is never very ready to believe anything to the detriment of those who are both rich and charming. It feels instinctively that manners are of more importance than morals,[37] and the highest respectability is of less value in its opinion than the possession of a good *chef*. And after all, it is a very poor consolation to be told that the man who has given one a bad dinner, or poor wine, is irreproachable in his private life.[38] Even the cardinal virtues cannot atone for cold *entrées,* as Lord Henry remarked once,[39] in a discussion on the subject; and there is possibly a good deal to be said for his view. For the canons of good society are, or should be, the same as the canons of art.[40] Form is absolutely essential to it. It should have the dignity of a ceremony, as well as its unreality, and should combine the insincere character of a romantic play with the wit and beauty that make such plays charming. Is insincerity such a terrible thing? I think not.[41] It is merely a method by which we can multiply our personalities.

Such, at any rate, was Dorian Gray's opinion. He used to wonder at the shallow psychology of those who conceive the Ego in man as a thing simple, permanent, reliable, and of one essence.[42] To him, man was a being with myriad lives and myriad sensations, a complex multiform creature that bore within itself strange legacies of thought and passion, and whose very flesh was tainted with the monstrous maladies of the dead.[43] He loved to stroll through the gaunt cold

37 An epigram repeated in *Lady Windermere's Fan.*

38 "After a good dinner, one can forgive anybody, even one's own relations" (*A Woman of No Importance*).

39 "The real difficulty . . . we all have to face in life is not so much the science of cookery as the stupidity of cooks. . . . For the British cook is a foolish woman, who should be turned, for her iniquities, into a pillar of that salt which she never knows how to use" (Wilde, "Dinners and Dishes").

40 "One should either be a work of art, or wear a work of art" (Wilde, "Phrases and Philosophies").

41 Here is another instance where Wilde drops the persona of the objective narrator and inserts himself into the text. Readers can decide for themselves whether the opening phrase of the ensuing paragraph ("Such, at any rate, was Dorian Gray's opinion") sufficiently mitigates this interruption.

42 An idea derived from the Oxford Hegelian William Wallace: "The difficulty of passing from the world of being to the world of thoughts . . . from Ego to non-Ego, is a difficulty which men have made for themselves in their theories. They reasoned on the ground that the individual mind was a fixed and absolute center" (quoted in *Oscar Wilde's Oxford Notebooks,* ed. Smith and Helfand, p. 19).

43 According to Phillip E. Smith II and Michael S. Helfand, Wilde here rejects ego psychology in favor of the idea, advanced in the writings of Herbert Spencer and William Clifford, that "the human psyche is a collective inheritance of acquired characteristics" (*Oscar Wilde's Oxford Notebooks,* ed. Smith and Helfand, p. 101). As Wilde had written in his commonplace book, while a student at Oxford, "This preservation of *self* is not the individual self but what Clifford calls the 'Tribal self' . . . it is the Tribal self whi[ch] is the mainspring of action, and canon of right and wrong" (pp. 129–130).

44 The picture gallery in Dorian's country house marks him as an aristocrat: country houses, the "seat" of the aristocratic family, typically possessed a picture gallery in which portraits of the present generation's forebears were preserved and ancient lineages could be traced. As he strolls through the picture gallery, Dorian sees aspects of himself in every portrait he studies. These resemblances, however, are not primarily physical. There is the strong suggestion that Dorian's moral character is "racial" or genetically determined, that his "blood" is not his own. Dorian, at any rate, seems convinced of his degenerate lineage: "Has some strange poisonous germ crept from body to body till it had reached his own?" Or, has the toxin in his bloodstream been introduced by some other agent—by "the poisonous book"? In *À Rebours,* Huysmans's antihero, Des Esseintes, traces in the portraits of his own forebears "the vitiation of an exhausted race, the excess of lymph in the blood" (trans. as *Against the Grain,* p. 1).

45 Wilde's source here is Thomas Tyler, *Shakespeare's Sonnets* (London: D. Nutt, 1890). Tyler had quoted (p. 71) the phrase "a man caressed by King James for his handsome face, which kept him not long company" from Francis Osborne, *Historical Memoirs on Elizabeth and King James* (1658), though Wilde has subtly altered Tyler's quotation.

46 Giovanna I (born 1326) ruled Naples for thirty-seven years after the death in 1345 of her first husband, Andreas of Hungary, whom she had married in 1342 after a nine-year betrothal. She is reputed to have arranged Andreas's murder out of love for her cousin Luigi of Taranto. The story is immortalized in the dramas of Walter Savage Landor. In F. Marion Crawford's *With the Immortals* (London: Macmillan, 1888), a fictionalized Heinrich Heine asks whether Giovanna's love for Luigi was "a romantic passion" (p. 81).

47 An invented historical figure. In combining the name of Elizabeth I (1533–1603) with that of the 2nd Earl of Essex, Robert Devereux (1567–1601), Wilde may be alluding to the intimacy between them, as Bristow suggests.

48 These elements of dress, all redolent of luxury and eroticized femininity, feature prominently in a number

picture-gallery of his country-house and look at the various portraits of those whose blood flowed in his veins.[44] Here was Philip Herbert, described by Francis Osborne, in his "Memoires on the Reigns of Queen Elizabeth and King James," as one who was "caressed by the court for his handsome face, which kept him not long company."[45] Was it young Herbert's life that he sometimes led? Had some strange poisonous germ crept from body to body till it had reached his own? Was it some dim sense of that ruined grace that had made him so suddenly, and almost without cause, give utterance, in Basil Hallward's studio, to that mad prayer that had so changed his life? Here, in gold-embroidered red doublet, jewelled surcoat, and gilt-edged ruff and wristbands, stood Sir Anthony Sherard, with his silver-and-black armour piled at his feet. What had this man's legacy been? Had the lover of Giovanna of Naples bequeathed him some inheritance of sin and shame?[46] Were his own actions merely the dreams that the dead man had not dared to realise? Here, from the fading canvas, smiled Lady Elizabeth Devereux[47] in her gauze hood, pearl stomacher, and pink slashed sleeves.[48] A flower was in her right hand, and her left clasped an enamelled collar of white and damask roses. On a table by her side lay a mandolin and an apple. There were large green rosettes upon her little pointed shoes.[49] He knew her life, and the strange stories that were told about the death of those to whom she granted her favours.[1] Had he something of her temperament in him? Those oval heavy-lidded eyes seemed to look curiously at him. What of George Willoughby, with his powdered hair and fantastic patches?[50] How evil he looked! The face was saturnine and swarthy, and the sensual lips seemed to be twisted with disdain. Delicate lace ruffles fell over the lean yellow hands that were so overladen with rings. He had been a macaroni of the eighteenth century, and the friend, in his youth, of Lord Ferrars.[51] What of the second Lord Sherard, the companion of the Prince Regent in his wildest days, and one of the witnesses at the secret marriage with Mrs. Fitzherbert?[52] How proud and handsome he was, with his chestnut curls and insolent pose! What passions had he bequeathed? The world had looked upon him as infamous. He had led the orgies at Carlton House. The star of the Garter glittered upon his breast.[53] Beside him hung the of portraits of Elizabeth I. In the Tudor courts, "dress . . . was strongly informed by an appreciation of its symbolic expressiveness"—an appreciation "redoubled in the manner of its representation in portraiture"—with the result that Tudor portraits "intimately detail the textures of the sitter's brocades, velvets, lace, and jewels" and "obtain a rich surface patterning at the expense of a sense of depth" (Lara Perry, *History's Beauties: Women and the National Portrait Gallery, 1856–1900* [Ashgate, 2006], p. 46). Elizabeth I often used such portraits of herself as pawns in "an intricate game of matrimonial alliances with suitors from all over Europe"—a game whose success depended a great deal upon her appearance and the illusion of eternal youth" (Janet Arnold, *Queen Elizabeth's Wardrobe Unlock'd* [Leeds: Maney, 1988], pp. 2–3). In Alciato's *Book of Emblems,* lasciviousness is pictured as a richly attired woman.

49 In English Renaissance portraits, character is often represented allegorically through the deployment of emblems: "riddling emblematics became all the rage in late-Elizabethan England and to read these portrait icons correctly requires a mind well versed in late Renaissance allegory" (Roy Strong, *The English Icon: Elizabethan and Jacobean Portraiture* [New Haven: Yale University Press, 1969], p. 30). The fading portrait of Lady Elizabeth Devereux in Dorian's picture gallery is no exception. Here, the mandolin represents artifice, the apple sexual knowledge. Some of the emblems are of Wilde's own invention. The rose is traditionally a symbol of chaste female beauty, but Wilde invites us to see it as an emblem for the sexual favors that ultimately proved fatal to Lady Elizabeth's lovers. Similarly, the large green rosettes on Lady Elizabeth's shoes are a Wildean emblem of ostentatious artifice, like the dyed green carnations that Wilde sometimes wore in his buttonhole.

50 A *patch* is "a small piece of black silk cut into a decorative shape and worn on the face, either for adornment or to conceal a blemish, esp. in the 17th and 18th centuries" (OED). Wilde's characterization of George Willoughby as a depraved Restoration dandy bears little relation to the actual George Willoughby, 17th Lord of Parham, who died childless in 1779 at the age of thirty-seven.

51 A *macaroni* is an eighteenth-century precursor of the Regency dandy. Named for the pasta dish that rich young Englishmen brought back from their Grand Tours in Europe, the term was applied in the 1770s to a young man who exceeded the perceived standards of good taste through his adoption of elite Continental dress and manners. Widely perceived as effeminate and inauthentic, particularly in his excessive attention to his wig or hairpiece, the macaroni "represented an apotheosis of aristocratic values that seemed to fly in the face of calls to sober, masculine virtue" (A. Rauser, "Hair, Authenticity, and the Self-Made Macaroni," *Eighteenth Century Studies,* 38:1 [2004], p. 102). Laurence Shirley (1720–1760), the 4th Earl Ferrers (not *Ferrars*), was the last British aristocrat to be condemned and executed as a felon. A notoriously dissolute figure, he shot his own steward for refusing to break a family trust, whereupon he was publicly hanged with a silken cord.

52 Wilde's startling characterization of "the second Lord Sherard" bears little correspondence to the Lord Sherard who actually existed in Regency times (as 5th Earl of Harborough after 1807), and scholars agree that the name derives from Wilde's friend—and later, biographer—Robert Harborough Sherard (1861–1943). According to Donald Lawler, Robert Harborough Sherard objected to this characterization because he had a living relative by the name of Lord Sherard. In deference to Sherard's wishes, Wilde substituted "Lord Beckenham" for "Lord Sherard" in the 1891 book version, though he retained the reference to "Sir Anthony Sherard" earlier in this paragraph.

    In 1811 the Prince of Wales became prince regent, the *de facto* ruler of Britain, owing to the insanity of his father, George III (he finally ascended to the throne in 1820 as George IV). The nine years of his Regency, in which he resided at Carlton House, are famous for the profligate, luxurious style that he licensed and personally exemplified. In 1785 he had incurred his father's displeasure by secretly contracting marriage to the Roman Catholic widow Maria Anne Herbert (1756–1837). George III never granted his assent, and since the marriage contravened both the 1701 Act of Settlement (which declared those who married Roman Catholics ineligible to succeed to the throne) and also the 1772 Royal Marriages Act (under which the Prince of Wales could not marry without the consent of the king), the marriage was declared legally void.

53 The Order of the Garter, limited to just twenty-four members, or "companions," in addition to the British sovereign and the Prince of Wales, is the oldest and highest order of British Chivalry. Its enameled insignia, the Garter Star, depicting the heraldic shield of St. George's Cross encircled by a garter, is worn pinned to the left side of the chest.

54 The first of five references to the lives of some of Rome's most decadent rulers. The first four adapt anecdotes from Suetonius's *Lives of the Caesars,* which Wilde had studied as an undergraduate. Julius Caesar Augustus Tiberius (b. 42 B.C.E.) ruled as emperor of Rome from A.D. 14–A.D. 37, though in A.D. 26 he abruptly retired to Capri, where he set aside a suite of rooms in which to pursue "the vices he had so long struggled to conceal" (Suetonius, *Lives of the Caesars,* trans. C. Edwards [Oxford University Press, 2000], p. 118). According to Suetonius, the bedrooms—each decked out with lewd paintings and sculptures—were adjacent to a "library . . . equipped with the works of Elephantis, so that an illustration of the required position would always be available if anyone needed guidance" (p. 119). Elephantis was a Greek woman poet whose works (now lost) apparently described numerous modes of sexual coition.

When the *St. James's Gazette* attacked Wilde's "cheap research" and erudition on reviewing *Dorian Gray* in June 1890, Wilde replied, "I cannot imagine how a casual reference to Suetonius and Petronius Arbiter can be construed into evidence of a desire to impress an unoffending and ill-educated public by an assumption of superior knowledge. I should fancy that the most ordinary of scholars is perfectly acquainted with the *Lives of the Caesars* and the *Satyricon.* The *Lives of the Caesars,* at any rate, forms part of the curriculum at Oxford for those who take the Honour School of *Literae Humaniores;* and as for the *Satyricon,* it is popular even among passmen, though I suppose they are obliged to read it in translations" (*CL,* p. 430).

portrait of his wife, a pallid, thin-lipped woman in black. Her blood, also, stirred within him. How curious it all seemed!

Yet one had ancestors in literature, as well as in one's own race, nearer perhaps in type and temperament, many of them, and certainly with an influence of which one was more absolutely conscious. There were times when it seemed to Dorian Gray that the whole of history was merely the record of his own life, not as he had lived it in act and circumstance, but as his imagination had created it for him, as it had been in his brain and in his passions. He felt that he had known them all, those strange terrible figures that had passed across the stage of the world, and made sin so marvellous, and evil so full of wonder. It seemed to him that in some mysterious way their lives had been his own.

Raoul, the hero of the dangerous novel that had so influenced his life,[m] had himself had this curious fancy. In the fourth chapter of the book he tells us how,[n] crowned with laurel, lest lightning might strike him, he had sat, as Tiberius, in a garden at Capri, reading the shameful books of Elephantis, while dwarfs and peacocks strutted round him and the flute-player mocked the swinger of the censer;[54] and, as Caligula, had drank the love-philter of Caesonia, and worn the habit of Venus by night, and by day a false gilded beard, and caroused with the green-shirted jockeys in their stables,[o] and supped in an ivory manger with a jewel-frontleted horse; and, as Domitian, had wandered through a corridor lined with marble mirrors, looking round with haggard eyes for the reflection of the dagger that was to end his days, and sick with that ennui, that *tædium vitæ,* that comes on those to whom life denies nothing; and had peered through a clear emerald at the red shambles of the Circus, and then, in a litter of pearl and purple drawn by silver-shod mules, been carried through the Street of Pomegranates to a House of Gold, and heard men cry on Nero Caesar as he passed by; and, as Elagabalus, had painted his face with colours, and plied the distaff among the women, and brought the Moon from Carthage, and given her in mystic marriage to the Sun.[55]

Over and over again Dorian used to read this fantastic chapter, and the chapter immediately following, in which Raoul describes the curious tapestries that he had had woven for him from Gustave Moreau's designs,[56] and on which were pictured the awful and beau-

Gustave Moreau, *Sappho,* watercolor, c. 1884. Moreau's watercolor depicts the poet Sappho, who purportedly killed herself by jumping off the Leucadian cliffs for love of Phaon, a ferryman. Moreau returned to this subject many times. The watercolor was once owned by the poet John Gray, often called a real-life model for Dorian Gray.

Dorian's delight in imaginative reconstructions of depraved Roman lives corresponds to a passage in Chapter 3 of Huysmans's *À Rebours,* where Des Esseintes delights in the debaucheries depicted in Petronius's *Satyricon.*

55 These anecdotes about Marcus Aurelius Antoninus, the emperor of Rome (A.D. 218–222) who called himself Elagabalus (meaning "formed god" or "plastic god"), derive from Edward Gibbon, *The Decline and Fall of the Roman Empire* (1776), ed. J. B. Bury, 7 vols. (New York: Macmillan, 1914). After stating that Elagabalus's "eyebrows were tinged with black, and his cheeks painted with an artificial red and white" (1:157), Gibbon describes how, on Elagabalus's instructions, an image of the moon was "transported with solemn pomp from Carthage to Rome," where Elagabalus had erected a temple to the sun (1:159). He also tells us that "the master of the Roman world affected to copy the dress and manners of the female sex, [and] preferred the distaff to the sceptre" (1:160).

56 Gustave Moreau (1826–1898) was a French painter beloved by French Decadent writers. He painted intensely personal interpretations, at once visionary and perverse, of ancient myths and legends, and according to Joris Karl Huysmans—who devoted many pages of *À Rebours* to describing how Moreau's paintings "ravished" Des Esseintes (trans. as *Against the Grain,* p. 50) —"there breathed from his pictures, so despairing and so erudite, a strange magic, a sorcery that moved you to the bottom of your soul . . . disconcerted by this art that crossed the last frontiers of painting, borrowing from literature its most subtle suggestions, from the art of the enameller its most marvellous effects of brilliancy, from the art of the lapidary and the engraver its most exquisite delicacies of touch" (p. 57). According to one modern critic, Moreau "might well be credited as a pioneer in the opening of hazy, disquieting vistas that could begin to plumb the depths of that subconscious fantasy life so prominent in the art and thought of the twentieth century" (Robert Rosenblum, *Paintings in the Musée D'Orsay* [New York: Steward, Tabori and Chang, 1989], p. 78).

57 Manfred, king of Apulia and Sicily (c. 1232–1266), whom Dante encounters in Canto 3 of *Purgatorio*. In *Dante's Divine Comedy: Notes on the Translation* (London: Longman, Brown, etc., 1855), C. B. Cayley says that Manfred was "steeped in all manner of debauchery . . . fond of seeing about him jongleurs, buffoons . . . and fair mistresses: he dressed always in green and . . . in his mode of living was an epicure" (p. 137).

58 Wilde's source here is Vernon Lee's *Euphorion: Being Studies of the Antique and the Medieval in the Renaissance,* 2nd ed. rev. (London: Fisher Unwin, 1885). In describing how "[t]he crimes of Italy furnished the subjects for nearly half of the tragedies written in the reigns of Elizabeth and of James I," Lee states that "numberless ghastly incidents [were] picked up, perhaps, from old chronicles and travellers' tales . . . like the corpse painted up with poison that the guilty lover might suck death in kissing its revived beauties, tacked on by Massinger to his play of the jealousy of some mythical Duke of Milan, himself a compromise between Maximilian Sforza . . . and Filippo Maria Visconti murdering his guiltless wife Beatrice di Tenda" (p. 71).

59 Wilde's source for these and other details of Renaissance debauchery is John Addington Symonds, *The Renaissance in Italy: The Age of the Despots,* the sixth and final volume of one of the most distinguished works of Renaissance scholarship of Wilde's day. Like Walter Pater before him, Symonds (1840–1893) used scholarship on the Renaissance to explore taboo subjects. Wilde was a great admirer of Symonds's work. He favorably reviewed Symonds's *Sketches and Studies of Italy,* in 1879, as well as *The Renaissance in Italy* when the final volume appeared in 1886—and he sent Symonds a copy of *Dorian Gray* shortly after its publication in *Lippincott's*. At the end of "Pen Pencil and Poison" (1889), Wilde compliments Symonds along with Vernon Lee and A. Mary F. Robinson for "the fine spirit of disinterested curiosity" with which they had written "so many charming studies of the great criminals of the Italian Renaissance" (in *Criticism: Historical Criticism, Intentions and the Soul of Man,* ed. Guy, p. 121). Pietro Barbi (1417–1471) became Pope Paul II in 1464, but what Barbi's "terrible sin" was (the phrase is Wilde's own) is un-

tiful forms of those whom Lust and Blood and Weariness had made monstrous or mad. Here was Manfred, King of Apulia, who dressed always in green, and consorted only with courtezans and buffoons;[57] Filippo, Duke of Milan, who slew his wife, and painted her lips with a scarlet poison, that her guilty lover might suck swift death from the dead thing that he fondled;[58] Pietro Barbi, the Venetian, known as Paul the Second, who sought in his vanity to assume the title of Formosus, and whose tiara, valued at 200,000 florins, was bought at the price of a terrible sin;[59] Gian Maria Visconti, who used hounds to chase living men, and whose murdered body was covered with roses by a harlot who had loved him;[60] the Borgia on his white horse, with Incest and Fratricide riding beside him, and his mantle stained with the blood of Perotto;[61p] Pietro Riario, the young Cardinal Archbishop of Florence, child and minion of Sixtus IV., whose beauty was equalled only by his debauchery, and who received Leonora of Aragon in a pavilion of white and crimson silk, filled with nymphs and centaurs, and gilded a boy that he might serve her at the feast as Ganymede or Hylas;[62] Ezzelin, whose melancholy could be cured only by the spectacle of death, and who had a passion for red blood, as other men have for red wine, the son of the Fiend, as was reported, and one who had cheated his father at dice, when gambling with him for his own soul;[63] Giambattista Cibo, who in mockery took the name of Innocent, and into whose torpid veins the blood of three lads was infused by a Jewish Doctor; Sigismondo Malatesta, the lover of Isotta, and the lord of Rimini, whose effigy was burned at Rome as the enemy of God and man, who strangled Polyssena with a napkin, and gave poison to Ginevra d'Este in a cup of emerald, and in honour of a shameful passion built a pagan church for Christian worship;[64] Charles VI., who had so wildly adored his brother's wife that a leper had warned him of the insanity that was coming on him, and who could only be soothed by Saracen cards, painted with the images of Love and Death and Madness;[65] and, in his trimmed jerkin and jewelled cap, and acanthus-like curls, Grifonetto Baglioni, who slew Astorre with his bride, and Simonetto with his page, and whose comeliness was such that, as he lay dying in the yellow piazza of Perugia, those who had hated him could choose not but weep, and Atalanta, who had cursed him, blessed him.[66]

clear from Wilde's source. Symonds writes that "his court was luxurious and in private he was addicted to sensual lust. This would not, however, have brought his name into bad odour in Rome" (194). Joseph Bristow speculates that Barbi's "terrible sin" was his violent, merciless persecution of Platonist scholars.

60 Symonds, *Renaissance in Italy: The Age of the Despots* (1886; new ed. London: Smith Elder, 1898), p. 118.

61 Symonds, *Renaissance in Italy*, pp. 333–334. Symonds refers to Roderick Borgia (1431–1503), who would become Pope Alexander VI, as "The Borgia." Symonds reports that Borgia, approaching the Lateran, "rode in triumph . . . upon a snow-white horse" (p. 319). Roderick was reputed to have been the lover of his own daughter, Lucrezia Borgia; and Symonds says his "priestly mantle" was stained with blood when his minion Perotto was cruelly murdered in his arms (p. 334). Wilde alludes also to Roderick's son, Cesare Borgia (1475–1507), who (among other sins) performed the stabbing and arranged the murder of his brother the Duke of Gandia (p. 333) while also being the lover of his sister Lucrezia.

62 Symonds, *Renaissance in Italy*, pp. 305–306. That Riario's gilded boy "might serve . . . as Ganymede or Hylas" is a detail of Wilde's invention. In Greek mythology, Ganymede was a Trojan prince, the most handsome among mortals, abducted by Zeus in the form of an eagle to serve as cupbearer to the gods and as Zeus's beloved: in poetry, he symbolizes the ideally beautiful young man and homosexual desire. Hylas was similarly an exceptionally handsome youth, beloved by Heracles and taken by him to serve alongside Jason on the ship Argo (as an "Argonaut"), on the expedition to Colchis in search of the Golden Fleece. During the voyage, Hylas was purportedly carried away by nymphs enamoured of his beauty, never to be found again, whereupon Heracles grieved disconsolately and abandoned the expedition.

63 The crimes of the despot Ezzelino da Romano (1192–1259), who ruled much of northern Italy in the mid-thirteenth century, were made legendary by poets after his death, and he lurks as a monstrous presence in the works of Byron and Dante. Symonds describes Ezzelino's lust for blood or "Haematomania" (*Renaissance in Italy*, pp. 83–84); Vernon Lee attempts to redeem Ezzelino from the myths surrounding him when she writes of "such popular legends as gave to Ezzelin the Fiend for a father, and Death and Sin for adversaries at dice" (*Euphorion*, p. 105). In the first of two letters to the *Daily Chronicle* about the cruelty of the prison system, written shortly after his release from Reading prison in 1897, Wilde cites Ezzelino (printed as "Eccelino" by the *Daily Chronicle*) as one of that "race of men . . . to whom the deliberate infliction of pain [gives] a real madness of pleasure" (*CL*, p. 848). But men of the "stamp of Eccelino," Wilde goes on to say, "are merely abnormal types of perverted individualism" (*CL*, p. 848).

64 Details taken from Symonds, *Renaissance in Italy: The Age of the Despots*, p. 135, and from Symonds, *Sketches in Italy and Greece*, 2nd ed. (London: Smith Elder, 1879), pp. 218–222. Polissena and Ginevra D'Este were wives of Sigismondo Malatesta. Details of their murders are taken from A. Mary F. Robinson, "The Malatestas of Rimini," in *The End of the Middle Ages* (London: T. Fisher Unwin, 1889), pp. 273–299, though the "cup of emerald" is of Wilde's invention.

65 These details about Charles VI, who ruled France from 1380 to 1422, are taken from A. Mary F. Robinson, *The End of the Middle Ages*, pp. 127–136.

66 Details taken from Symonds, *Sketches in Italy and Greece*, pp. 74–80.

67 Here and in the preceding paragraph Wilde takes issue with one of his principal sources. In her *Euphorion* (to which Wilde was indebted for anecdotes about Ezzelino da Romano and Filippo Maria Visconti) Vernon Lee sets out to redeem Italian Renaissance despots from the myths surrounding them, arguing that Renaissance criminality was exaggerated and that "the sin of the Renaissance, which the art of Italy could neither pourtray nor perceive, appeared on the stage decked in superb and awful garb by the tragic imagination of Elizabethan England" (p. 108). Whereas Lee recounts well-known anecdotes about Ezzelin and Visconti with skepticism, Wilde recasts them as if they were historical fact.

There was a horrible fascination in them all. He saw them at night, and they troubled his imagination in the day. The Renaissance knew of strange manners of poisoning, poisoning by a helmet and a lighted torch, by an embroidered glove and a jewelled fan, by a gilded pomander and by an amber chain.[67] Dorian Gray had been poisoned by a book. There were moments when he looked on evil simply as a mode through which he could realize his conception of the beautiful.

Photo-portrait of John Addington Symonds, 1886. Symonds was a pioneering apologist for homosexuality as well as one of the greatest Victorian scholars of the Renaissance. Wilde admired Symonds's work greatly but not uncritically.

X

IT WAS ON THE SEVENTH OF NOVEMBER, the eve of his own thirty-second birthday, as he often remembered afterwards.[1]

He was walking home about eleven o'clock from Lord Henry's, where he had been dining, and was wrapped in heavy furs, as the night was cold and foggy. At the corner of Grosvenor Square and South Audley Street a man passed him in the mist, walking very fast, and with the collar of his grey ulster turned up.[2] He had a bag in his hand. He recognised him. It was Basil Hallward. A strange sense of fear, for which he could not account, came over him. He made no sign of recognition, and went on slowly, in the direction of his own house.

But Hallward had seen him. Dorian heard him first stopping, and then hurrying after him. In a few moments his hand was on his arm.

"Dorian! What an extraordinary piece of luck! I have been waiting for you ever since nine o'clock in your library. Finally I took pity on your tired servant, and told him to go to bed, as he let me out. I am off to Paris by the midnight train, and I wanted particularly to see you before I left. I thought it was you, or rather your fur coat, as you passed me. But I wasn't quite sure. Didn't you recognise me?"

"In this fog, my dear Basil? Why, I can't even recognise Grosvenor Square.[3] I believe my house is somewhere about here, but I don't feel at all certain about it. I am sorry you are going away, as I have not seen you for ages. But I suppose you will be back soon?"

1 Altered to "9th of November, the eve of his own thirty-eighth birthday" for the 1891 book edition. Ellmann sees this change as Wilde's effort to efface the parallel between Dorian's criminality and his own initiation into active homosexuality at the age of thirty-two: "Altering Dorian's age would be gratuitous if Wilde had not begun to feel that the first reference was too close to actuality" (Ellmann, *Oscar Wilde*, p. 277).

2 An ulster is a long, heavy, loose-fitting overcoat with a cape and sleeves. Now iconic thanks to its associations with Conan Doyle's Sherlock Holmes, it was popular with travelers and more functional than fashionable in Wilde's day.

3 Grosvenor Square, in London's expensive Mayfair district, is also the home of Sir Robert Chiltern in *An Ideal Husband*.

4 Along with Charing Cross Station, Victoria Station was then one of two London rail terminals serving the south coast ports, whence passengers took boats to the Continent.

5 A light traveling bag developed in the 1880s and named after Prime Minister W. E. Gladstone.

Victoria Station, terminus of the London, Brighton, and South Coast Railway, early 1900s.

"No: I am going to be out of England for six months. I intend to take a studio in Paris, and shut myself up, till I have finished a great picture I have in my head. However, it wasn't about myself I wanted to talk. Here we are at your door. Let me come in for a moment. I have something to say to you."

"I shall be charmed. But won't you miss your train?" said Dorian Gray languidly, as he passed up the steps and opened the door with his latchkey.

The lamplight struggled out through the fog, and Hallward looked at his watch. "I have heaps of time," he answered. "The train doesn't go till 12.15, and it is only just eleven. In fact, I was on my way to the club to look for you, when I met you. You see, I shan't have any delay about luggage, as I have sent on my heavy things. All I have with me is in this bag, and I can easily get to Victoria in twenty minutes."[4]

Dorian looked at him and smiled. "What a way for a fashionable painter to travel! A Gladstone bag,[5] and an ulster! Come in, or the fog will get into the house. And mind you don't talk about anything

Grosvenor Square, in London's aristocratic Mayfair district, in the 1850s.

6 French term meaning "Anglomania."

7 See on p. 178 Dorian's earlier estimation of his "sly" French valet Victor and his determination to dismiss him. In acknowledging that "one often imagines things that are quite absurd," Dorian may now be saying that he was mistaken about the valet: that his dread of Victor was nothing more than the projection of a guilty conscience. But Dorian's remark—and his apparent dismissal of the valet—also suggests the depth of his suspicions. Nothing could have convinced him that Victor's devoted servitude was anything more than fraudulent.

serious. Nothing is serious nowadays. At least nothing should be."

Hallward shook his head, as he entered, and followed Dorian into the library. There was a bright wood fire blazing in the large open hearth. The lamps were lit, and an open Dutch silver spirit-case stood, with some syphons of soda-water and large cut-glass tumblers, on a little table.

"You see your servant made me quite at home, Dorian. He gave me everything I wanted, including your best cigarettes. He is a most hospitable creature. I like him much better than the Frenchman you used to have. What has become of the Frenchman, by the bye?"

Dorian shrugged his shoulders. "I believe he married Lady Ashton's maid, and has established her in Paris as an English dressmaker. *Anglomanie*[6] is very fashionable over there now, I hear. It seems silly of the French, doesn't it? But do you know, he was not at all a bad servant. I never liked him, but I had nothing to complain about. One often imagines things that are quite absurd.[7] He was really very devoted to me, and seemed quite sorry when he went away. Have an-

An ulster. This men's overcoat, with its unmistakable cape and sleeves, popular in the 1890s, is now iconic thanks to its associations with Conan Doyle's Sherlock Holmes.

A "Gladstone bag," a small portmanteau bag, named after Britain's four-time prime minister, William Ewart Gladstone.

8 Popular Victorian drink, composed of *hock* (white Rhine wine, from the German *Hochheimer Wein*) and seltzer water, a naturally carbonated mineral water originally from the Prussian spa of Selters. When Wilde was arrested at the Cadogan Hotel in room 118, he was drinking hock and seltzer in an effort to calm his nerves.

9 The first half of this paragraph, through the sentence, "What gentleman would associate with him?" was read out, in its Lippincott version, in open court by Queensberry's lawyer, Edward Carson. Carson followed up by asking Wilde, "Do you think that, taken in its natural meaning, would suggest that what they were talking about was a charge of sodomy?" (*The Real Trial*, p. 102).

10 Hallward expresses views that were commonplace in Wilde's day. Victorian interest in physiognomy (the interpretation of physical, especially facial, features), phrenology (the study of the shape of the skull), and cheiromancy (palm reading) demonstrates how widespread the belief was that inner character reveals itself in physical traits. That sin must write itself across a man's face is indeed the novel's central conceit. This would not have struck Victorian readers as a fantastic notion. Only the magic portrait would have placed the novel into the realm of the impossible.

other brandy-and-soda? Or would you like hock-and-seltzer?[8] I always take hock-and-seltzer myself. There is sure to be some in the next room."

"Thanks, I won't have anything more," said Hallward, taking his cap and coat off, and throwing them on the bag that he had placed in the corner. "And now, my dear fellow, I want to speak to you seriously. Don't frown like that. You make it so much more difficult for me."

"What is it all about?" cried Dorian, in his petulant way, flinging himself down on the sofa. "I hope it is not about myself. I am tired of myself to-night. I should like to be somebody else."

"It is about yourself," answered Hallward, in his grave, deep voice, "and I must say it to you. I shall only keep you half an hour."

Dorian sighed, and lit a cigarette. "Half an hour!" he murmured.

"It is not much to ask of you, Dorian, and it is entirely for your own sake that I am speaking. I think it right that you should know that the most dreadful things are being said about you in London, things that I could hardly repeat to you."[a]

"I don't wish to know anything about them. I love scandals about other people, but scandals about myself don't interest me. They have not got the charm of novelty."

"They must interest you, Dorian.[9] Every gentleman is interested in his good name. You don't want people to talk of you as something vile and degraded. Of course you have your position, and your wealth, and all that kind of thing. But position and wealth are not everything. Mind you, I don't believe these rumours at all. At least, I can't believe them when I see you. Sin is a thing that writes itself across a man's face. It cannot be concealed. People talk of secret vices. There are no such things as secret vices. If a wretched man has a vice, it shows itself in the lines of his mouth, the droop of his eyelids, the moulding of his hands even.[10] Somebody—I won't mention his name, but you know him—came to me last year to have his portrait done. I had never seen him before, and had never heard anything about him at the time, though I have heard a good deal since. He offered an extravagant price. I refused him. There was something in the shape of his fingers that I hated. I know now that I was quite right in what I fancied about him. His life is dreadful. But you, Dorian, with your

pure, bright, innocent face, and your marvellous untroubled youth—
I can't believe anything against you. And yet I see you very seldom,
and you never come down to the studio now, and when I am away
from you, and I hear all these hideous things that people are whispering about you, I don't know what to say. Why is it, Dorian, that a
man like the Duke of Berwick leaves the room of a club when you
enter it?[11] Why is it that so many gentlemen in London will neither
go to your house nor invite you to theirs? You used to be a friend of
Lord Cawdor. I met him at dinner last week. Your name happened
to come up in conversation, in connection with the miniatures you
have lent to the exhibition at the Dudley.[12] Cawdor curled his lip, and
said that you might have the most artistic tastes, but that you were
a man whom no pure-minded girl should be allowed to know, and
whom no chaste woman should sit in the same room with.[13] I reminded him that I was a friend of yours, and asked him what he
meant. He told me. He told me right out before everybody. It was
horrible! Why is it that every young man that you take up seems to
come to grief, to go to the bad at once?[b] There was that wretched boy
in the Guards who committed suicide. You were his great friend.
There was Sir Henry Ashton, who had to leave England, with a tarnished name.[14] You and he were inseparable. What about Adrian Singleton, and his dreadful end? What about Lord Kent's only son, and
his career? I met his father yesterday in St. James Street. He seemed
broken with shame and sorrow. What about the young Duke of
Perth? What sort of life has he got now? What gentleman would associate with him? Dorian, Dorian, your reputation is infamous. I
know you and Harry are great friends. I say nothing about that now,
but surely you need not have made his sister's name a by-word. When
you met Lady Gwendolen, not a breath of scandal had ever touched
her. Is there a single decent woman in London now who would drive
with her in the Park?[15] Why, even her children are not allowed to live
with her. Then there are other stories, stories that you have been
seen creeping at dawn out of dreadful houses and slinking in disguise
into the foulest dens in London. Are they true? Can they be true?
When I first heard them, I laughed. I hear them now, and they make
me shudder. What about your country-house, and the life that is led

Wilde had a particular interest in cheiromancy.
Elizabeth Lorang observes that "throughout *Dorian
Gray*, descriptions of hands are a common component
of the narrator's overall descriptions of individuals.
Similarly, the narrator emphasizes characters' hands at
many of the most significant moments in the text"
(Elizabeth Lorang, "*The Picture of Dorian Gray* in Con-
text: Intertextuality and *Lippincotts Monthly Magazine*,"
Victorian Periodicals Review, 43:1 [Spring 2010], p. 26).
In the same (July 1890) issue of *Lippincott's Monthly
Magazine* in which *Dorian Gray* debuted was an article by Wilde's friend the cheiromantist Edward Heron-
Allen entitled "The Cheiromancy of Today." As Lorang
notes, the appearance of Heron-Allen's article alongside Wilde's novel, in both British and American editions of *Lippincott's*, "allows one to read the hands of
the characters in the novel and, indeed . . . encourages
one to do so" (p. 26). Note in Chapter XII Dorian's fascination with Gautier's poem about the monstrous
embalmed hand of the murderer Lacenaire.

11 For Wilde's contemporary readers the "Duke of
Berwick" signified aristocratic masculinity at its most
upright and traditional, much as the "Duke of Wellington" did for Tennyson's readers in his "Ode on the
Death of the Duke of Wellington" (1852). The Berwick
title was created in 1687 for James FitzJames, the ille-
gitimate son of King James II.

12 Art gallery within London's Egyptian Hall, named
after Lord Dudley, who had lent many of the pictures
on exhibit. Annual exhibitions of cabinet paintings or
"miniatures," watercolors, and drawings in black and
white were held there in Wilde's day.

13 Cawdor's reported concern about Dorian's effect
on chaste and pure-minded females reminds us that
modern homophobia began in fears for the chastity
of young women. Section 11 of the 1885 Criminal Law
Amendment Act, which criminalized homosexuality
by mandating imprisonment for "gross indecency" between men, was added at the last minute by the M. P.
Henry Labouchère as an amendment—the so-called
Labouchère Amendment—to a bill essentially concerned with the protection of women and girls. The

Act was motivated, initially at least, by a series of inflammatory articles on female prostitution in London, particularly focused on the entrapment and enslavement of young girls, published in the *Pall Mall Gazette* in 1885 under the heading, "The Maiden Tribute of Modern Babylon." Wilde was himself prosecuted and imprisoned under section 11 of the Act, which was not repealed until 1956.

14 This sentence would have resonated with Wilde's early readers. In late 1889, when Wilde began writing *Dorian Gray*, scandalous rumors surrounded a number of aristocratic and military men suspected of involvement in the unfolding Cleveland Street Scandal. The previous summer, police investigating a theft from the Central London Post Office had uncovered a nest of male prostitutes or "rent boys" who operated as telegraph boys by day and as male prostitutes, working out of a male brothel on London's Cleveland Street, by night. By the fall of 1889, it had become clear to the press and the police that a number of male aristocrats had solicited sexual favors from these "boys." One of those most tarnished in the unfolding scandal was Lord Arthur Somerset, the Prince of Wales's equerry, who fled to France in October 1889 for fear of prosecution. Wilde was urged by many friends to do the same following the collapse of his libel trial against the Marquis of Queensberry in April 1895. He stayed to face the music.

15 To be seen on horseback or in a carriage in London's Hyde Park was an important society ritual in the nineteenth century: "The part of the Park near the statue of Achilles, between it and 'The Row,' is, during the London season . . . the very maze and centre of fashion. Here . . . the pride and beauty of England may be seen upon their own stage, and on a fine day in 'the season' no other spot in the world can outrival in rich display and chaste grandeur the scene" (Edward Walford, *Old and New London: Volume 4, Westminster and the Western Suburbs* [1878; new ed. London: Cassell, 1891], p. 397). In *An Ideal Husband*, Lord Goring is forced to miss an appointment to ride in Hyde Park with Mabel Chiltern, whereupon she tells him that "people who don't keep their appointments in the Park are horrid."

there? It is quite sufficient to say of a young man that he goes to stay at Selby Royal, for people to sneer and titter.[c] Dorian, you don't know what is said about you. I won't tell you that I don't want to preach to you. I remember Harry saying once that every man who turned himself into an amateur curate for the moment always said that, and then broke his word. I do want to preach to you. I want you to lead such a life as will make the world respect you. I want you to have a clean name and a fair record. I want you to get rid of the dreadful people you associate with. Don't shrug your shoulders like that. Don't be so indifferent. You have a wonderful influence. Let it be for good, not for evil. They say that you corrupt everyone whom you become intimate with, and that it is quite sufficient for you to enter a house, for shame of some kind to follow after you. I don't know whether it is so or not. How should I know? But it is said of you. I am told things that it seems impossible to doubt. Lord Gloucester was one of my greatest friends at Oxford. He showed me a letter that his wife had written to him when she was dying alone in her villa at Mentone.[16] It was the most the most terrible confession I ever read. He said that he suspected you.[d] I told him that it was absurd, that I knew you thoroughly, and that you were incapable of anything of the kind. Know you? I wonder do I know you? Before I could answer that, I should have to see your soul."

"To see my soul!" muttered Dorian Gray, starting up from the sofa and turning almost white from fear.

"Yes," answered Hallward, gravely, and with infinite sorrow in his voice, "to see your soul. But only God can do that."

A bitter laugh of mockery broke from the lips of the younger man. "You shall see it yourself, to-night!" he cried, seizing a lamp from the table. "Come: it is your own handiwork. Why shouldn't you look at it? You can tell the world all about it afterwards, if you choose. Nobody would believe you. If they did believe you, they'd like me all the better for it. I know the age better than you do, though you will prate about it so tediously. Come, I tell you. You have chattered enough about corruption. Now you shall look on it face to face."

There was the madness of pride in every word he uttered. He stamped his foot upon the ground in his boyish insolent manner. He

Carriages driving in Hyde Park, c. 1896. "The part of the Park near the statue of Achilles, between it and 'The Row,' is, during the London season . . . the very maze and centre of fashion. . . . No other spot in the world can outrival in rich display and chaste grandeur the scene" (Edward Walford, *Old and New London: Volume 4, Westminster and the Western Suburbs* [1878; new ed. London: Cassell, 1891], p. 397).

16 Fashionable resort on the French Riviera, popular with English aristocrats in Wilde's day.

17 Dorian's divorce from his soul echoes that of the love-lorn fisherman in Wilde's story "The Fisherman and His Soul," in which the fisherman's soul possesses a separate, physical, and visible existence. Although the priest in the story reassures the fisherman that "the soul is the noblest part of man, and was given to us by God that we should nobly use it," the fisherman, who must shed his soul to attain the mermaid he loves, replies, "[W]hat doth my soul profit me if it stand between me and the thing that I love?" After several failed attempts at separating himself from his soul, the fisherman eventually succeeds, whereupon his soul "rose up and stood before him, and looked at him, and it was even as himself."

felt a terrible joy at the thought that some one else was to share his secret, and that the man who had painted the portrait that was the origin of all his shame was to be burdened for the rest of his life with the hideous memory of what he had done.

"Yes," he continued, coming closer to him, and looking steadfastly into his stern eyes, "I will show you my soul. You shall see the thing that you fancy only God can see."[17]

Hallward started back. "This is blasphemy, Dorian!" he cried. "You must not say things like that. They are horrible, and they don't mean anything."

"You think so?" He laughed again.

"I know so. As for what I said to you to-night, I said it for your good. You know I have been always devoted to you."[e]

"Don't touch me. Finish what you have to say."

18 In *The Importance of Being Earnest,* Cecily confesses, "I keep a diary in order to enter the wonderful secrets of my life. If I didn't write them down, I should probably forget all about them." Gwendolen, in the same play, says, "I never travel without my diary. One should always have something sensational to read in the train."

"'Come upstairs, Basil,' he said quietly," illustration by S. A. Moss to *The Picture of Dorian Gray,* vol. 2 of *The Sunflower Edition of the Works of Oscar Wilde* (New York: Lang, 1909).

A twisted flash of pain shot across Hallward's face. He paused for a moment, and a wild feeling of pity came over him. After all, what right had he to pry into the life of Dorian Gray? If he had done a tithe of what was rumoured about him, how much he must have suffered! Then he straightened himself up, and walked over to the fireplace, and stood there, looking at the burning logs with their frost-like ashes and their throbbing cores of flame.

"I am waiting, Basil," said the young man, in a hard, clear voice.

He turned round. "What I have to say is this," he cried. "You must give me some answer to these horrible charges that are made against you. If you tell me that they are absolutely untrue from beginning to end, I will believe you. Deny them, Dorian, deny them! Can't you see what I am going through? My God! don't tell me that you are infamous!"

Dorian Gray smiled. There was a curl of contempt in his lips. "Come upstairs, Basil," he said, quietly. "I keep a diary of my life from day to day, and it never leaves the room in which it is written. I will show it to you if you come with me."[18]

"I will come with you, Dorian, if you wish it. I see I have missed my train. That makes no matter. I can go to-morrow. But don't ask me to read anything to-night. All I want is a plain answer to my question."

"That will be given to you upstairs. I could not give it here. You won't have to read long. Don't keep me waiting."

XI

He passed out of the room, and began the ascent, Basil Hallward following close behind. They walked softly, as men instinctively do at night. The lamp cast fantastic shadows on the wall and staircase. A rising wind made some of the windows rattle.

When they reached the top landing, Dorian set the lamp down on the floor, and, taking out the key, turned it in the lock. "You insist on knowing, Basil?" he asked, in a low voice.

"Yes."

"I am delighted," he murmured, smiling. Then he added, somewhat bitterly, "You are the one man in the world who is entitled to know everything about me. You have had more to do with my life than you think." And, taking up the lamp, he opened the door and went in. A cold current of air passed them, and the light shot up for a moment in a flame of murky orange. He shuddered. "Shut the door behind you," he said, as he placed the lamp on the table.

Hallward glanced round him, with a puzzled expression. The room looked as if it had not been lived in for years. A faded Flemish tapestry, a curtained picture, an old Italian *cassone,* and an almost empty bookcase—that was all that it seemed to contain, besides a chair and a table. As Dorian Gray was lighting a half-burned candle that was standing on the mantel-shelf, he saw that the whole place was covered with dust, and that the carpet was in holes. A mouse ran scuffling behind the wainscoting. There was a damp odour of mildew.

Contemporary engravings, published shortly before the opening of the Grosvenor Gallery in May 1877, showing the gallery's interior and exterior. "It is at the Grosvenor Gallery," wrote Wilde, "that we are enabled to see the highest development of the modern artistic spirit."

"So you think that it is only God who sees the soul, Basil? Draw that curtain back, and you will see mine."

The voice that spoke was cold and cruel. "You are mad, Dorian, or playing a part," muttered Hallward, frowning.

"You won't? Then I must do it myself," said the young man; and he tore the curtain from its rod, and flung it on the ground.

An exclamation of horror broke from Hallward's lips as he saw in the dim light the hideous thing on the canvas leering at him. There was something in its expression that filled him with disgust and loathing.[1] Good heavens! it was Dorian Gray's own face that he was looking at! The horror, whatever it was, had not yet entirely marred that marvellous beauty. There was still some gold in the thinning hair and some scarlet on the sensual lips. The sodden eyes had kept something of the loveliness of their blue, the noble curves had not yet passed entirely away from chiselled nostrils and from plastic throat. Yes, it was Dorian himself. But who had done it? He seemed to recognise his own brush-work, and the frame was his own design. The idea was monstrous, yet he felt afraid. He seized the lighted candle, and held it to the picture. In the left-hand corner was his own name, traced in long letters of bright vermilion.

It was some foul parody, some infamous, ignoble satire. He had never done that. Still, it was his own picture. He knew it, and he felt as if his blood had changed from fire to sluggish ice in a moment. His own picture! What did it mean? Why had it altered? He turned, and looked at Dorian Gray with the eyes of a sick man. His mouth twitched, and his parched tongue seemed unable to articulate. He passed his hand across his forehead. It was dank with clammy sweat.

The young man was leaning against the mantel-shelf, watching him with that strange expression that is on the faces of those who are absorbed in a play, when a great artist is acting. There was neither real sorrow in it nor real joy. There was simply the passion of the spectator, with perhaps a flicker of triumph in the eyes. He had taken the flower out of his coat, and was smelling it, or pretending to do so.

"What does this mean?" cried Hallward, at last. His own voice sounded shrill and curious in his ears.

1 Disgust and loathing in the face of evil are a staple ingredient of Gothic fiction. The terms in which Wilde describes Hallward's reaction recall those used by Wilde's great-uncle, Charles Maturin, in his novel *Melmoth the Wanderer* (1820) when the innocent Stanton re-encounters the satanic Melmoth: "The expression of [Melmoth's] eyes could never be mistaken or forgotten. The heart of Stanton palpitated with violence,—a mist spread over his eyes,—a nameless and deadly sickness, accompanied with a creeping sensation in every pore" (*Melmoth the Wanderer: A Tale,* ed. Alethea Hayter [Harmondsworth: Penguin, 1977], p. 85).

2 Dorian alludes here to Basil's confessions in Chapter VII: "I quite admit that I adored you madly, extravagantly, absurdly. I was jealous of every one to whom you spoke. I wanted to have you all to myself. . . . One day I determined to paint a wonderful portrait of you. It was to have been my masterpiece. It is my masterpiece. But, as I worked at it, every flake and film of colour seemed to me to reveal my secret. There was love in every line, and in every touch there was passion" (p. 172 above). But see also Basil's confession to Lord Henry, in Chapter I: "I have put into it all the extraordinary romance of which, of course, I have never dared to speak to him" (p. 85 above).

3 "The mind is its own place, and in itself / Can make a Heav'n of Hell, a Hell of Heav'n" (Milton, *Paradise Lost*, I:254–255). See also William Blake's *Marriage of Heaven and Hell,* in which Blake observes, "As a new heaven is begun . . . the Eternal Hell revives," and "Without contraries is no progression" (Plate 3).

"Years ago, when I was a boy," said Dorian Gray, "you met me, devoted yourself to me, flattered me, and taught me to be vain of my good looks. One day you introduced me to a friend of yours, who explained to me the wonder of youth, and you finished a portrait of me that revealed to me the wonder of beauty. In a mad moment, that I don't know, even now, whether I regret or not, I made a wish. Perhaps you would call it a prayer. . . ."

"I remember it! Oh, how well I remember it! No! the thing is impossible. The room is damp. The mildew has got into the canvas. The paints I used had some wretched mineral poison in them. I tell you the thing is impossible."

"Ah, what is impossible?" murmured the young man, going over to the window, and leaning his forehead against the cold, mist-stained glass.

"You told me you had destroyed it."

"I was wrong. It has destroyed me."

"I don't believe it is my picture."

"Can't you see your romance in it?" said Dorian, bitterly.

"My romance, as you call it . . ."

"As you called it."[2]

"There was nothing evil in it, nothing shameful. This is the face of a satyr."

"It is the face of my soul."

"Christ![a] what a thing I must have worshipped! This has the eyes of a devil."

"Each of us has Heaven and Hell in him, Basil,"[3] cried Dorian, with a wild gesture of despair.

Hallward turned again to the portrait, and gazed at it. "My God! if it is true," he exclaimed, "and this is what you have done with your life, why, you must be worse even than those who talk against you fancy you to be!" He held the light up again to the canvas, and examined it. The surface seemed to be quite undisturbed, and as he had left it. It was from within, apparently, that the foulness and horror had come. Through some strange quickening of inner life the leprosies of sin were slowly eating the thing away. The rotting of a corpse in a watery grave was not so fearful.

His hand shook, and the candle fell from its socket on the floor, and lay there sputtering. He placed his foot on it and put it out. Then he flung himself into the ricketty chair that was standing by the table and buried his face in his hands.

"Good God, Dorian, what a lesson! what an awful lesson!" There was no answer, but he could hear the young man sobbing at the window.

"Pray, Dorian, pray," he murmured. "What is it that one was taught to say in one's boyhood? 'Lead us not into temptation. Forgive us our sins. Wash away our iniquities.'[4] Let us say that together. The prayer of your pride has been answered. The prayer of your repentance will be answered also. I worshipped you too much. I am punished for it. You worshipped yourself too much. We are both punished."

Dorian Gray turned slowly around, and looked at him with tear-dimmed eyes. "It is too late, Basil," he murmured.

"It is never too late, Dorian. Let us kneel down and try if we can remember a prayer. Isn't there a verse somewhere, 'Though your sins be as scarlet, yet I will make them as white as snow'?"[5]

"Those words mean nothing to me now."

"Hush! don't say that. You have done enough evil in your life. My God! don't you see that accursed thing leering at us?"

Dorian Gray glanced at the picture, and suddenly an uncontrollable feeling of hatred for Basil Hallward came over him. The mad passions of a hunted animal stirred within him, and he loathed the man who was seated at the table, more than he had ever loathed anything in his whole life. He glanced wildly around. Something glimmered on the top of the painted chest that faced him. His eye fell on it. He knew what it was. It was a knife that he had brought up, some days before, to cut a piece of cord, and had forgotten to take away with him. He moved slowly towards it, passing Hallward as he did so. As soon as he got behind him, he seized it, and turned round. Hallward moved in his chair as if he was going to rise. He rushed at him, and dug the knife into the great vein that is behind the ear, crushing the man's head down on the table, and stabbing again and again.[6]

There was a stifled groan, and the horrible sound of someone choking with blood. The outstretched arms shot up convulsively

4 Basil conflates parts of the Lord's Prayer ("Forgive us our trespasses . . . And lead us not into temptation"), the best-known prayer in Christianity, with Psalm 51, the Lavabo prayer of the Roman Catholic Mass ("Wash me thoroughly from my iniquity, and cleanse me from my sin"). His confusion suggests the superficiality of his religious convictions and the purely ritualistic qualities of his religious upbringing. It is a moving, pathetic moment. Attempting (and failing) to recall accurately "what . . . one was taught to say in one's boyhood," Basil looks sentimentally to his own childhood as a source of spiritual strength.

5 Isaiah 1:18.

6 The brutality of the stabbing would undoubtedly have reminded Wilde's earliest readers of the gruesome Whitechapel, or "Jack-the-Ripper," killings of 1888.

7 The peacock was a favorite symbol of beauty for aesthetes of Wilde's generation. Here, however, the monstrosity of the peacock's tail, like that of the hidden portrait, reflects the corruption of Dorian's beauty and innocence. Like the sky itself, corruption and monstrosity spread themselves across the metropolis of London, implicating everything and everyone. The image conveys, too, the notion that secret vices cannot long remain hidden: the myriad stars in the night sky—the golden eyes—penetrate the darkness. The ocular-like designs in the peacock's tail are of course called "eyes." According to Ovid, it was Juno who placed the eyes in the peacock's tail, taking them from the head of her murdered watchman, Argus "with a hundred eyes," in order to better continue her jealous watch over her husband's extramarital affairs.

In the late 1870s and early 1880s, Wilde wrote a number of impressionistic poems, such as "Impression: Le Reveillon" and "Impressions 2: La Mer," that capture in words the dramatic effects of light and color in a darkened, wintry sky. In Wilde's later prose works, these skyscapes frequently operate as symbolic backdrops for decadent action. Wilde's story "Lord Arthur Savile's Crime," for instance, takes place against a backdrop in which "the gas-lamps round the square flared and flickered in the keen wind" and in which "the moon peered through a mane of tawny clouds, as if it were a lion's eye, and innumerable stars spangled the hollow vault." Similarly, near the beginning of *Salome*, the moon is likened to "the hand of a dead woman . . . seeking to cover herself with a shroud"; and before his decapitation, Iokanaan foresees a day when "the moon shall become like blood, and the stars of the heaven shall fall upon the earth like unripe figs."

8 The "prowling hansom" scurries away like a guilty thing, as if one of the very symbols of the modern metropolis were steeped in corruption. Indeed, the hansom is a "crimson spot."

three times, waving grotesque stiff-fingered hands in the air. He stabbed him once more, but the man didn't move. Something began to trickle on the floor. He waited for a moment, still pressing the head down. Then he threw the knife on the table, and listened.

He could hear nothing, but the drip, drip on the threadbare carpet. He opened the door, and went out on the landing. The house was quite quiet. No one was stirring. He took out the key, and returned to the room, locking himself in as he did so.

The thing was still seated in the chair, straining over the table with bowed head, and humped back, and long fantastic arms. Had it not been for the red jagged tear in the neck, and the clotted black pool that slowly widened on the table, one would have said that the man was simply asleep.

How quickly it had all been done! He felt strangely calm, and, walking over to the window, opened it, and stepped out on the balcony. The wind had blown the fog away, and the sky was like a monstrous peacock's-tail, starred with myriads of golden eyes.[7] He looked down, and saw the policeman going his rounds and flashing a bull's-eye lantern on the doors of the silent houses. The crimson spot of a prowling hansom gleamed at the corner, and then vanished.[8] A woman in a ragged shawl was creeping round by the railings, staggering as she went. Now and then she stopped, and peered back. Once, she began to sing in a hoarse voice. The policeman strolled over and said something to her. She stumbled away, laughing. A bitter blast swept across the Square. The gas-lamps flickered, and became blue, and the leafless trees shook their black iron branches as if in pain. He shivered, and went back, closing the window behind him.

He passed to the door, turned the key, and opened it. He did not even glance at the murdered man. He felt that the secret of the whole thing was not to realise the situation. The friend who had painted the fatal portrait, the portrait to which all his misery had been due, had gone out of his life. That was enough.

Then he remembered the lamp. It was a rather curious one of Moorish workmanship, made of dull silver inlaid with arabesques of burnished steel. Perhaps it might be missed by his servant, and questions would be asked. He turned back, and took it from the table.

"He rushed at him, and dug the knife into the great vein that is behind the ear," wood-engraved illustration by Eugène Dété, from a drawing by Paul Thiriat, published in *The Picture of Dorian Gray* (Paris: Charles Carrington, 1908 [1910]).

9 In Britain, death by hanging was the principal form
of capital punishment until its repeal in 1998, although
the last executions in Britain took place in 1964 and
the death penalty for murder was abolished in 1969. In
the nineteenth century, 4,182 men and 214 women were
"strangled"—an average of 3.6 hangings per month.
Hangings were carried out in public until 1868, after
which they took place in prisons out of public sight.
Wilde's poem "The Ballad of Reading Gaol" movingly
records one such execution, which was conducted at
Reading prison while Wilde was incarcerated there. At
the time of *Dorian Gray*'s composition, a parliamentary
commission under Lord Aberdare was examining hanging methods in Britain, following the unsuccessful attempt to hang the convicted murderer John Lee on
February 23, 1885 (the trap would not open, and he was
reprieved after three attempts to execute him). Part of
Aberdare's remit was to devise a table of drops, finally
issued in 1892, thereby making judicial hanging a more
exact science in the eyes of its proponents.

How still the man was! How horribly white the long hands looked!
He was like a dreadful wax image.

He locked the door behind him, and crept quietly downstairs. The
woodwork creaked, and seemed to cry out as if in pain. He stopped
several times, and waited. No: everything was still. It was merely the
sound of his own footsteps.

When he reached the library, he saw the bag and coat in the corner. They must be hidden away somewhere. He unlocked a secret
press that was in the wainscoting, and put them into it. He could easily burn them afterwards. Then he pulled out his watch. It was twenty
minutes to two.

He sat down, and began to think. Every year—every month, almost—men were strangled in England for what he had done.[9] There
had been a madness of murder in the air. Some red star had come too
close to the earth.

Evidence? What evidence was there against him? Basil Hallward
had left the house at eleven. No one had seen him come in again.
Most of the servants were at Selby Royal. His valet had gone to bed.

"The thing was still seated in the chair, straining over the table with bowed head,
and humped back, and long fantastic arms," from *The Picture of Dorian Gray,* illustr.
Madjeska (New York: Horace Liveright, 1930).

Paris! Yes. It was to Paris that Basil had gone, by the midnight train, as he had intended. With his curious reserved habits, it would be months before any suspicions would be aroused. Months? Everything could be destroyed long before then.

A sudden thought struck him. He put on his fur coat and hat, and went out into the hall. There he paused, hearing the slow heavy tread of the policeman outside on the pavement, and seeing the flash of the lantern reflected in the window. He waited, holding his breath.

After a few moments he opened the front door, and slipped out, shutting it very gently behind him. Then he began ringing the bell. In about ten minutes his valet appeared, half dressed, and looking very drowsy.

"I am sorry to have had to wake you up, Francis," he said, stepping in; "but I had forgotten my latch-key. What time is it?"

"Five minutes past two, Sir," answered the man, looking at the clock and yawning.

"Five minutes past two? How horribly late! You must wake me at nine to-morrow. I have some work to do."

"All right, sir."

"Did anyone call this evening?"

"Mr. Hallward, sir. He stayed here till eleven, and then he went away to catch his train."

"Oh! I am sorry I didn't see him. Did he leave any message?"

"No, sir, except that he would write to you."

"That will do, Francis. Don't forget to call me at nine tomorrow."

"No, sir."

The man shambled down the passage in his slippers.

Dorian Gray threw his hat and coat upon the yellow marble table, and passed into the library. He walked up and down the room for a quarter of an hour, biting his lip, and thinking. Then he took the Blue Book down from one of the shelves, and began to turn over the leaves.[10] "Alan Campbell, 152, Hertford Street, Mayfair." Yes; that was the man he wanted.

10 *The Royal Blue Book* was an annually published directory of London's most socially prominent individuals. Its complete subtitle reads: *Fashionable Directory and Parliamentary Guide; containing the town and country residences of the nobility and gentry, with a local arrangement, in conformity with the postal districts, of the squares streets, inns of court, &c., to assist in visiting and canvassing.* The April 1890 volume, published by B. W. Gardiner and Son, was the sixty-eighth in the series.

XII

1 Wilde's irony here is biting, since Dorian, corrupt and approaching middle age, can in no way be said to represent youth. While "images of pleasure or of pain" may not have disturbed Dorian's sleep, the night itself has been far from "untroubled."

2 Chocolate has been called "the Gods' breakfast." *Dorian Gray* was first published in the middle of "the great chocolate boom," when manufacturers in northern Europe and North America sought increasingly novel ways of bringing chocolate to the masses, and when consumption and imports of cocoa increased dramatically. But drinking chocolate had become an established part of the English aristocratic breakfast in the 1700s, and Wilde invokes it here for its long-standing associations with "a degenerate loose-living aristocracy, addicted to luxury and oblivious to . . . suffering" (S. Moss and A. Badenoch, *Chocolate: A Global History* [London: Reaktion, 2009], p. 45).

AT NINE O'CLOCK THE NEXT MORNING his servant came in with a cup of chocolate on a tray, and opened the shutters. Dorian was sleeping quite peacefully, lying on his right side, with one hand underneath his cheek. He looked like a boy who had been tired out with play, or study.

The man had to touch him twice on the shoulder before he woke, and as he opened his eyes a faint smile passed across his lips, as though he had been having some delightful dream. Yet he had not dreamed at all. His night had been untroubled by any images of pleasure or of pain. But youth smiles without any reason. It is one of its chiefest charms.[1]

He turned round, and, leaning on his elbow, began to drink his chocolate.[2] The mellow November sun was streaming into the room. The sky was bright blue, and there was a genial warmth in the air. It was almost like a morning in May.

Gradually the events of the preceding night crept with silent bloodstained feet into his brain, and reconstructed themselves there with terrible distinctness. He winced at the memory of all that he had suffered, and for a moment the same curious feeling of loathing for Basil Hallward, that had made him kill him as he sat in the chair, came back to him, and he grew cold with passion. The dead man was still sitting there, too, and in the sunlight now. How horrible that was! Such hideous things were for the darkness, not for the day.

He felt that if he brooded on what he had gone through, he would sicken or grow mad. There were sins whose fascination was more in the memory than in the doing of them, strange triumphs that gratified the pride more than the passions, and gave to the intellect a quickened sense of joy, greater than any joy they brought, or could ever bring, to the senses. But this was not one of them. It was a thing to be driven out of the mind, to be drugged with poppies, to be strangled lest it might strangle one itself.

He passed his hand across his forehead, and then got up hastily, and dressed himself with even more than his usual attention, giving a good deal of care to the selection of his necktie and scarf-pin, and changing his rings more than once.

He spent a long time over breakfast, tasting the various dishes, talking to his valet about some new liveries that he was thinking of getting made for the servants at Selby, and going through his correspondence. Over some of the letters he smiled. Three of them bored him. One he read several times over, and then tore up with a slight look of annoyance in his face. "That awful thing, a woman's memory!" as Lord Henry had once said.

When he had drunk his coffee, he sat down at the table, and wrote two letters. One he put in his pocket, the other he handed to the valet.

"Take this round to 152, Hertford Street, Francis, and if Mr. Campbell is out of town, get his address."

As soon as he was alone, he lit a cigarette, and began sketching upon a piece of paper, drawing flowers, and bits of architecture, first, and then faces. Suddenly he remarked that every face that he drew seemed to have an extraordinary likeness to Basil Hallward. He frowned, and, getting up, went over to the bookcase and took out a volume at hazard. He was determined that he would not think about what had happened, till it became absolutely necessary to do so.

When he had stretched himself on the sofa, he looked at the title-page of the book. It was Gautier's "Emaux et Camées," Charpentier's Japanese-paper edition, with the Jacquemart etching.[3] The binding

3 The "édition definitive" (definitive edition) of Gautier's *Emaux et Camées* [Enamels and Cameos] was issued in yellow paper wrappers by Charpentier et Cie. in Paris in 1872. It contained an etched portrait of Gautier, by Jules Ferdinand Jacquemart, and was printed on fine Japanese paper (an additional twenty-five copies were printed on laid paper, or *papier vergé*, of European origin; see Maurice Tourneux, *Théophile Gautier: Sa Bibliographie* [Paris: J. Bauer, 1876], p. 10). Japanese paper, made from the inner parts of tree bark, remains prized by artists and printmakers and is distinguished by its smoothness, luminosity, and thinness as well as by its handsome, mottled appearance. When shortly after the publication of *Dorian Gray* the *Daily Chronicle* disparaged Wilde's "obtrusively cheap scholarship," Wilde replied that *Emaux et Camées* was, along with Petronius's *Satyricon*, a work "that any fairly educated reader may be supposed to be acquainted with" (*CL*, p. 436). Wilde's own copy of *Emaux et Camées* was auctioned off in the bailiff's sale of his possessions, in April 1895. Near the end of his two-year jail sentence, Wilde wrote to Robert Ross asking for friends to supply him with a few books, since "I have a horror . . . of going out into a world without a single book of my own" (*CL*, p. 790). *Emaux et Camées* was one of the books Wilde requested (see *CL*, p. 792), and he possessed a copy at his death.

4 Like many nineteenth-century books, Dorian's copy of *Emaux et Camées* has been specially and privately rebound.

5 Gautier was not the only nineteenth-century writer fascinated by Pierre François Lacenaire (1800–1836), a poet and double-murderer. Lacenaire was the model for Dickens's Rigaud *(Little Dorrit),* Victor Hugo's Montparnasse *(Les Misérables),* and Dostoyevsky's Raskolnikov *(Crime and Punishment).* Following his execution by guillotine in 1836, Lacenaire's right hand was removed from his corpse and embalmed. The hand later came into the possession of the writer Maxime Du Camp, who displayed the gruesome curiosity in his salon (where Gautier observed it) (G. Wall, "Thinking with Demons: Flaubert and de Sade," *Cambridge Quarterly* [2007], 36:2, 101–128). According to Michel Foucault, Lacenaire "committed a whole heap of minor and shoddy crimes, mostly failures, hardly glorious at all, but . . . succeeded through his very intelligent discourse in making these crimes exist as real works of art, and in making the criminal, that is Lacenaire himself, the very artist of criminality" ("I, Pierre Rivière . . . An Interview with Michel Foucault," trans. John Johnson, in *Foucault Live: Collected Interviews, 1961–84,* ed. Silvère Lotringer [New York: Semiotext(e), 1996], p. 204). Elsewhere Foucault writes that Lacenaire's presence is "assured for ever in the paradise of the aesthetes of crime" *(Discipline and Punish,* trans. Alan Sheridan [New York: Vintage, 1979], p. 283).

6 These phrases—translated into English by Wilde's contemporary Agnes Lee as "not yet washed clean of deadly stain" and "faun-shaped fingers"—are from Gautier's poem "Lacenaire," the second of two "Etudes de Mains" [Studies of Hands] in *Emaux et Camées* (*Enamels and Cameos and Other Poems,* trans. Agnes Lee, vol. 24 of *Complete Works of Théophile Gautier* [Jenson Society, 1906], pp. 49–51). As Lawler observes, Dorian's fascination with this poem prefigures the description of his own murderous hand, in the next chapter, as "spotted with blood." See, too, Basil Hallward's remark, in the previous chapter, that "if a wretched man has a vice, it shows itself in . . . the moulding of his hands," and his subsequent confession that he re-

was of citron-green leather with a design of gilt trellis-work and dotted pomegranates.[4] It had been given to him by Adrian Singleton. As he turned over the pages his eye fell on the poem about the hand of Lacenaire,[5] the cold yellow hand *"du supplice encore mal lavée,"* with its downy red hairs and its *"doigts de faune."*[6] He glanced at his own white taper fingers, and passed on, till he came to those lovely verses upon Venice:

> Sur une gamme chromatique,
>   Le sein de perles ruisselant,
> La Vénus de l'Adriatique
>   Sort de l'eau son corps rose et blanc.
>
> Les dômes, sur l'azur des ondes
>   Suivant la phrase au pur contour,
> S'enflent comme des gorges rondes
>   Que soulève un soupir d'amour.
>
> L'esquif aborde et me dépose,
>   Jetant son amarre au pilier,
> Devant une façade rose,
>   Sur le marbre d'un escalier.[7]

How exquisite they were! As one read them, one seemed to be floating down the green water-ways of the pink and pearl city, lying in a black gondola with silver prow, and trailing curtains. The mere lines looked to him like those straight lines of turquoise-blue that follow one as one pushes out to the Lido. The sudden flashes of colour reminded him of the gleam of the opal-and-iris-throated birds that flutter round the tall honey-combed Campanile, or stalk,[8] with such stately grace, through the dim arcades. Leaning back with half-closed eyes, he kept saying over and over to himself,—

> Devant une façade rose,
>   Sur le marbre d'un escalier.

The whole of Venice was in those two lines. He remembered the autumn that he had passed there, and a wonderful love that had stirred him to delightful fantastic follies. There was romance in every place. But Venice, like Oxford, had kept the background for romance, and background was everything, or almost everything. Basil had been with him part of the time, and had gone wild over Tintoret.[9] Poor Basil! what a horrible way for a man to die!

He sighed, and took up the book again, and tried to forget. He read of the swallows that fly in and out of the little Café at Smyrna where the Hadjis sit counting their amber beads and the turbaned merchants smoke their long tasselled pipes and talk gravely to each other;[10] of the Obelisk in the Place de la Concorde that weeps tears of granite in its lonely sunless exile, and longs to be back by the hot lotus-covered Nile, where there are Sphynxes, and rose-red ibises, and white vultures with gilded claws, and crocodiles, with small beryl eyes, that crawl over the green steaming mud;[11] and of that curious statue that Gautier compares to a contralto voice, the *"monstre charmant"* that couches in the porphyry-room of the Louvre.[12] But after a time the book fell from his hand. He grew nervous, and a horrible fit of terror came over him. What if Alan Campbell should be out of England? Days would elapse before he could come back. Perhaps he might refuse to come. What could he do then? Every moment was of vital importance.

They had been great friends once, five years before, almost inseparable indeed. Then the intimacy had come suddenly to an end. When they met in society now, it was only Dorian Gray who smiled: Alan Campbell never did.

He was an extremely clever young man, though he had no real appreciation of the visible arts, and whatever little sense of the beauty of poetry he possessed he had gained entirely from Dorian. His dominant intellectual passion was for Science. At Cambridge he had spent a great deal of his time working in the Laboratory, and had taken a good class in the Natural Science Tripos of his year.[13] Indeed, he was still devoted to the study of chemistry, and had a laboratory of his own, in which he used to shut himself up all day long, greatly to the annoyance of his mother, who had set her heart on his standing

jected a portrait commission simply because "there was something in the shape of [the subject's] fingers that I hated."

7 From "Sur les Lagunes" [On the Lagoons], the second in a sequence of four poems in *Emaux et Camées* collectively entitled "Variations sur le Carnaval de Venise" [Variations on the Carnival in Venice]. These stanzas are from Agnes Lee's translation of the poem (*Enamels and Cameos and Other Poems*, pp. 54–55):

> Her bosom covered o'er
>   With pearls, her body suave,
> The Adriatic Venus soars
>   On sound's chromatic wave.
>
> The domes that on the water swell
>   Pursue the melody
> In clear-drawn cadences, and swell
>   Like breasts of love that sigh.
>
> My chains around a pillar cast,
>   I land before a fair
> And rosy-pale façade at last,
>   Upon a marble stair.

8 Wilde refers here to the world's most famous *campanile,* or bell tower, St. Mark's Campanile in Venice's Piazza San Marco. Wilde had visited Venice in 1875, eulogizing the city and its sights (including the Campanile) in two letters to his mother. In the first of these he remarks that "the scene was so romantic that it seemed to be an 'artistic' scene from an opera" (*CL,* p. 10); and in both letters Wilde dwells at length on the color effects to be witnessed throughout the city (*CL,* pp. 10–11).

9 Wilde had been less effusive in his own visit to "the picture gallery" when visiting Venice in 1875, remarking only, "Titian and Tintoretto in great force" (*CL,* p. 11).

10 Smyrna is the ancient name for the city of Izmir in modern Turkey; hadjis are Muslims who have successfully made the pilgrimage to Mecca. Wilde's story "The Happy Prince" features a busy swallow that delays jour-

neying to the East in order to carry out the prince's wishes. Dorian would have read about the swallows flying in and out of the café at Smyrna in "Ce Que Disent les Hirondelles: Chanson d'Automne" [What the Swallows Say: An Autumn Song] in *Emaux et Camées*. Agnes Lee's translation reads:

Rain stirs the pool with pelt and shock.
  The swallows to the roof repair,
Confabulating as they flock
  And feel the winter in the air.

By hundreds gather they to vow
  Their little yearnings and intents.
Saith one: "'Tis fair in Athens now,
  Upon the sun-worn battlements! . . ."

And one: "A ceiling meets my needs
  Within a Smyrna coffee-house,
Where Hadjis tell their amber beads
  Upon the threshold luminous.

"I go and come above the folk,
  While their chibouques their clouds upfling.
I skim along through silver smoke,
  And graze the turbans with my wing."

("What the Swallows Say: An Autumn Song," in *Enamels and Cameos and Other Poems*, pp. 140–141)

11 Distant from my native land,
  Ever dull with ennui's pain,
Lonely monolith I stand,
  In the snow and frost and rain.

And my shaft once burnt to red
  In a flaming heaven's glare,
Taketh on a pallor dead
  In this never azure air. . . .

Sparrows lean defile my head,
  Where the ibis used to light,
And the fierce gypaetus spread
  Talons gold and plumage white.

And the Seine, the drip of street,
  Unclean river, crime's abyss,
Now befouls mine ancient feet,
  Which the Nile was wont to kiss:

Hoary Nile that, crowned and stern,
  To its lotus-laden shores
From its ever bended urn
  Crocodiles for gudgeon pours.

From "The Obelisk in Paris," in *Enamels and Cameos and Other Poems,* pp. 80–82. "The Obelisk of Paris" and "The Obelisk of Luxor" are two related poems by Gautier collectively entitled "Nostalgia of the Obelisks." Wilde was fascinated by the vision of the Nile conjured up in the poems; many of the features Wilde cites here recur elsewhere in his works, notably in the swallow's description of the Nile region in "The Happy Prince" and in his poem "The Sphinx."

12 Wilde refers to Gautier's poem "Contralto," in which the poet eulogizes the Louvre's Roman replica of the Greek statue of Hermaphroditus, the twin-sexed offspring of Hermes and Aphrodite. *Monstre charmant* means "charming monster."

13 Cambridge University, which numbers Bacon, Newton, and Darwin among its alumni, has traditionally dominated scientific research in Britain. In 1851 it became one of the first universities in the world to institute a degree program, or "Tripos," in Natural Science; and in 1887 it established the renowned Cavendish Laboratory, placing it at the forefront of research in electrical physics and biochemistry.

14 Anton Rubinstein (1829–1894), the Russian composer, educator, and piano virtuoso. He performed in London in 1876, 1877, 1881, and again in 1886 as part of a Europe-wide series of recitals that he himself regarded as the culmination of his concert-playing career. Wilde heard Rubinstein play Beethoven's *Appassionata Sonata* in May 1877—he alludes to the event in his 1877 review of the Grosvenor Gallery—and, shortly afterward, he met the pianist at one of Rubinstein's soirées at the Hotel Dieudonné (Philip S. Taylor, *Anton Rubinstein: A Life in Music* [Bloomington: Indiana University Press, 2007], p. 166). In "The Critic as Artist" Wilde writes, "When Rubinstein plays to us the *Sonata*

for Parliament, and had a vague idea that a chemist was a person who made up prescriptions. He was an excellent musician, however, as well, and played both the violin and the piano better than most amateurs. In fact, it was music that had first brought him and Dorian Gray together, music and that indefinable attraction that Dorian seemed to be able to exercise whenever he wished, and indeed exercised often without being conscious of it. They had met at Lady Berkshire's the night that Rubinstein played there,[14] and after that used to be always seen together at the Opera, and wherever good music was going on. For eighteen months their intimacy lasted. Campbell was always either at Selby Royal or in Grosvenor Square. To him, as to many others, Dorian Gray was the type of everything that is wonderful and fascinating in life. Whether or not a quarrel had taken place between them, no one ever knew. But suddenly people remarked that they scarcely spoke when they met, and that Campbell seemed always to go away early from any party at which Dorian Gray was present. He had changed, too, was strangely melancholy at times, appeared almost to dislike hearing music of any passionate character, and would never himself play, giving as his excuse, when he was called upon, that he was so absorbed in science that he had no time left in which to practice.[15] And this was certainly true. Every day he seemed to become more interested in Biology, and his name appeared once or twice in some of the Scientific Reviews, in connection with certain curious experiments.[16]

This was the man that Dorian Gray was waiting for, pacing up and down the room, glancing every moment at the clock, and becoming horribly agitated as the minutes went by.[17] At last the door opened, and his servant entered.

"Mr. Alan Campbell, Sir."

A sigh of relief broke from his parched lips, and the colour came back to his cheeks.

"Ask him to come in at once, Francis."

The man bowed, and retired. In a few moments Alan Campbell walked in, looking very stern and rather pale, his pallor being intensified by his coal-black hair and dark eyebrows.

"Alan! this is kind of you. I thank you for coming."

Appassionata of Beethoven, he gives us not merely Beethoven, but also himself, and so gives us Beethoven absolutely—Beethoven reinterpreted through a rich artistic nature" (p. 165).

15 Campbell's sudden aversion to music is related to his rejection of Dorian and everything for which he stands. Both are attempts at repressing something essential in his character.

16 Critics have noted resemblances between Wilde's *Dorian Gray* and Stevenson's *Dr. Jekyll and Mr. Hyde,* "that other great fantastic tale of doubling and transformation" (Robert Mighall, Intro. to *The Picture of Dorian Gray* [London: Penguin, 2003], p. xiii). If Dorian's double life mirrors Jekyll's in suggesting the necessity for duplicity in a repressive late-Victorian era, then the chemist Alan Campbell's secret double life offers another, more particular reflection of Jekyll and Hyde. Dorian Gray is an aristocrat. But Campbell and Jekyll are both professionals and men of science. Their duplicity is precisely the large, unbridgeable gap that exists between their aspirations to professional middle-class respectability and their inability to live up to their own standards. As Jekyll confesses, it was "the high views . . . I had set before me" and the promise of a distinguished scientific career that "made me what I was" and "severed . . . those provinces of good and ill which divide and compound man's dual nature" (*The Strange Case of Dr. Jekyll and Mr. Hyde and Other Tales of Terror,* ed. Robert Mighall [London: Penguin, 2002], p. 55). Jekyll also says, "I was no more myself when I laid aside restraint and plunged in shame, than when I laboured, in the eye of day, at the furtherance of knowledge or the relief of sorrow and suffering" (p. 55).

17 Alan Campbell is to some extent based upon the British zoologist Sir Peter Chalmers Mitchell. In his memoir *My Fill of Days* [London: Faber & Faber, 1937], Chalmers Mitchell recalls a chance meeting with Wilde in Paris after Wilde's release from prison, when the two men discussed meeting during happier times: "We talked and talked and I asked you how to get rid of the body," Chalmers Mitchell recalls Wilde as saying: "I used you in *Dorian Gray,* but I don't think you would be easy to blackmail" (rpt. in *Oscar Wilde: Interviews and Recollections,* ed. Mikhail, 2:367).

18 Coat made from the pelts of very young Karakul lambs, the tight curly wool of which superficially resembles fur. "A man with an astrakhan coat is to me a suspicious character . . . one who is probably deep in treasons, stratagems, and spoils. . . . And if you ask me to give reasons . . . perhaps it is the dislike I have for artificial curls . . . it must be that sense of artificiality which is at the root of the dislike" ("Alpha of the Plough," "On Wearing a Fur-Lined Coat," in *Fact, Fancy, and Opinion,* ed. R. M. Gay [Boston: Atlantic Monthly Press, 1923], pp. 319–320).

Etched portrait of Théophile Gautier, by Jules Ferdinand Jacquemart, printed as a frontispiece to the "édition définitive" (definitive edition) of Gautier's *Emaux et Camées* (Paris: Charpentier, 1872). Both the etching and the 1872 Charpentier edition are mentioned in *Dorian Gray.*

"I had intended never to enter your house again, Gray. But you said it was a matter of life and death." His voice was hard and cold. He spoke with slow deliberation. There was a look of contempt in the steady searching gaze that he turned on Dorian. He kept his hands in the pockets of his Astrakhan coat,[18] and appeared not to have noticed the gesture with which he had been greeted.

"It is a matter of life and death, Alan, and to more than one person. Sit down."

Campbell took a chair by the table, and Dorian sat opposite to him. The two men's eyes met. In Dorian's there was infinite pity. He knew that what he was going to do was dreadful.

After a strained moment of silence, he leaned across and said, very quietly, but watching the effect of each word upon the face of the man he had sent for, "Alan, in a locked room at the top of this house, a room to which nobody but myself has access, a dead man is seated at a table. He has been dead ten hours now. Don't stir, and don't look at me like that. Who the man is, why he died, how he died, are matters that do not concern you. What you have to do is this—"

"Stop, Gray. I don't want to know anything further. Whether what you have told me is true or not true, doesn't concern me. I entirely decline to be mixed up in your life. Keep your horrible secrets to yourself. They don't interest me any more."

"Alan, they will have to interest you. This one will have to interest you. I am awfully sorry for you, Alan. But I can't help myself. You are the one man who is able to save me. I am forced to bring you into the matter. I have no option. Alan, you are a scientist. You know about chemistry, and things of that kind. You have made experiments. What you have got to do is to destroy the thing that is upstairs, to destroy it so that not a vestige will be left of it. Nobody saw this person come into the house. Indeed, at the present moment he is supposed to be in Paris. He will not be missed for months. When he is missed, there must be no trace of him found here. You, Alan, you must change him, and everything that belongs to him, into a handful of ashes that I may scatter in the air."

"You are mad, Dorian."

"Ah! I was waiting for you to call me Dorian."

"You are mad, I tell you, mad to imagine that I would raise a finger to help you, mad to make this monstrous confession. I will have nothing to do with this matter, whatever it is. Do you think I am going to peril my reputation for you? What is it to me what devil's work you are up to?"

"It was a suicide, Alan."

"I am glad of that. But who drove him to it? You, I should fancy."

"Do you still refuse to do this, for me?"

"Of course I refuse. I will have absolutely nothing to do with it. I don't care what shame comes on you. You deserve it all. I should not be sorry to see you disgraced, publicly disgraced. How dare you ask me, of all men in the world, to mix myself up in this horror? I should have thought you knew more about people's characters. Your friend Lord Henry Wotton can't have taught you much about psychology, whatever else he has taught you. Nothing will induce me to stir a step to help you. You have come to the wrong man. Go to some of your friends. Don't come to me."

"Alan, it was murder. I killed him. You don't know what he had made me suffer. Whatever my life is, he had more to do with the making or the marring of it than poor Harry has had. He may not have intended it, the result was the same."

"Murder! Good God! Dorian, is that what you have come to? I shall not inform upon you. It is not my business. Besides, you are certain to be arrested, without my stirring in the matter. Nobody ever commits a murder without doing something stupid. But I will have nothing to do with it."

"All I ask of you is to perform a certain scientific experiment. You go to Hospitals and Dead-Houses, and the horrors that you do there don't affect you. If in some hideous Dissecting-room or fetid laboratory you found this man lying on a leaden table, with red gutters scooped out in it, you would simply look upon him as an admirable subject.[19] You would not turn a hair. You would not believe that you were doing anything wrong. On the contrary, you would probably feel that you were benefiting the human race, or increasing the sum of knowledge in the world, or gratifying intellectual curiosity, or something of that kind. What I want you to do is simply what you

19 "To the man who has mastered *Grey's Anatomy,* life holds no further terrors" (Arthur Conan Doyle, "The Romance of Medicine" [1910], quoted in *Arthur Conan Doyle: A Life in Letters,* ed. J. Lellenberg et al. [New York: Penguin Press, 2007], p. 91). In Conan Doyle's "Study in Scarlet," Sherlock Holmes, who is "well up in anatomy, and . . . a first-class chemist," refines his forensic methods by "beating the subjects in the dissecting-rooms with a stick. . . . to verify how far bruises may be produced after death." Holmes "is a little too scientific," we are told; "it approaches to cold-bloodedness" (*Sherlock Holmes: The Major Stories, with Contemporary Critical Essays,* ed. John A. Hodgson [Boston: Bedford / St. Martin's, 1994], pp. 19–20).

20 "'Ask no questions . . . for conscience's sake,'" the teacher of anatomy, Mr. K—, tells students in Robert Louis Stevenson's story "The Body Snatcher": among the budding scientists, Stevenson goes on to say, "there was no understanding that the subjects were provided by the crime of murder" (*The Strange Case of Dr. Jekyll and Mr. Hyde and Other Tales of Terror,* ed. Mighall, p. 79).

21 Dorian is blackmailing Campbell. In the wake of Section 11 of the 1885 Criminal Law Amendment Act, which criminalized homosexual activity between men, practicing homosexuals were frequently blackmailed, and Section 11 became known as the "blackmailer's charter." The blackmailing of good men for youthful indiscretions is a motif in Wilde's writings: in *An Ideal Husband,* when informed of Mrs. Cheveley's attempts to blackmail her husband, Lady Chiltern states, "I know that there are men with horrible secrets in their lives—men who have done some shameful thing, and who in some critical moment have to pay for it, by doing some other act of shame."

22 According to *A Treatise on the Theory and Practice of Medicine,* by John S. Bristowe, 5th ed. (London: Smith Elder, 1884), ague is "a specific non-contagious fever, produced by malaria; characterised by enlargement of the spleen, and recurring attacks of fever, attended each with a cold, a hot, and a sweating stage; and having an indefinite duration" (p. 279). Wilde uses *ague* in a more obsolete and literary sense to denote acute or violent fever.

have often done before. Indeed, to destroy a body must be less horrible than what you are accustomed to work at. And, remember, it is the only piece of evidence against me. If it is discovered, I am lost; and it is sure to be discovered unless you help me."

"I have no desire to help you. You forget that. I am simply indifferent to the whole thing. It has nothing to do with me."

"Alan, I entreat you. Think of the position I am in. Just before you came I almost fainted with terror. No! don't think of that. Look at the matter purely from the scientific point of view. You don't inquire where the dead things on which you experiment come from.[20] Don't inquire now. I have told you too much as it is. But I beg of you to do this. We were friends once, Alan."

"Don't speak about those days, Dorian; they are dead."

"The dead linger sometimes. The man upstairs will not go away. He is sitting at the table with bowed head and outstretched arms. Alan! Alan! If you don't come to my assistance I am ruined. Why, they will hang me, Alan! Don't you understand? They will hang me for what I have done."

"There is no good in prolonging this scene. I refuse absolutely to do anything in the matter. It is insane of you to ask me."

"You refuse absolutely?"

"Yes."

The same look of pity came into Dorian's eyes, then he stretched out his hand, took a piece of paper, and wrote something on it. He read it over twice, folded it carefully, and pushed it across the table. Having done this, he got up, and went over to the window.

Campbell looked at him in surprise, and then took up the paper, and opened it. As he read it, his face became ghastly pale, and he fell back in his chair.[21] A horrible sense of sickness came over him. He felt as if his heart was beating itself to death in some empty hollow.

After two or three minutes of terrible silence, Dorian turned round, and came and stood behind him, putting his hand upon his shoulder.

"I am so sorry, Alan," he murmured, "but you leave me no alternative. I have a letter written already. Here it is. You see the address. If you don't help me, I must send it. You know what the result will be.

But you are going to help me. It is impossible for you to refuse now. I tried to spare you. You will do me the justice to admit that. You were stern, harsh, offensive. You treated me as no man has ever dared to treat me, no living man, at any rate. I bore it all. Now it is for me to dictate terms."

Campbell buried his face in his hands, and a shudder passed through him.

"Yes, it is my turn to dictate terms, Alan. You know what they are. The thing is quite simple. Come, don't work yourself into this fever. The thing has to be done. Face it, and do it."

A groan broke from Campbell's lips, and he shivered all over. The ticking of the clock on the mantelpiece seemed to him to be dividing time into separate atoms of agony, each of which was too terrible to be borne. He felt as if an iron ring was being slowly tightened round his forehead, and as if the disgrace with which he was threatened had already come upon him. The hand upon his shoulder weighed like a hand of lead. It was intolerable. It seemed to crush him.

"Come, Alan, you must decide at once."

He hesitated a moment. "Is there a fire in the room upstairs?" he murmured.

"Yes, there is a gas-fire with asbestos."

"I will have to go home and get some things from the laboratory."

"No, Alan, you need not leave the house. Write on a sheet of note-paper what you want, and my servant will take a cab, and bring the things back to you."

Campbell wrote a few lines, blotted them, and addressed an envelope to his assistant. Dorian took the note up and read it carefully. Then he rang the bell, and gave it to his valet, with orders to return as soon as possible, and to bring the things with him.

When the hall door shut, Campbell started, and, having got up from the chair, went over to the chimney-piece. He was shivering with a sort of ague.[22] For nearly twenty minutes, neither of the men spoke. A fly buzzed noisily about the room, and the ticking of the clock was like the beat of a hammer.

As the chime struck one, Campbell turned around, and, looking at Dorian Gray, saw that his eyes were filled with tears. There was

Photo-portrait of Anton Rubinstein, date unknown. Wilde heard Rubinstein play Beethoven's *Appassionata Sonata* in May 1877 and met the great pianist shortly afterward.

23 Alan Campbell's use of a small electric battery places him in the forefront of electrical research: the first dry-cell battery was invented in 1886, though it would not be used commercially for another ten years.

24 In the early 1890s "the golden age of orchid fever" was in full sway, transforming otherwise normal people into crazed collectors willing to spend exorbitant sums for rare species (Peter Bernhardt, "Orchidelirium," in his book *Wily Violets and Underground Orchids* [1989; University of Chicago Press, 2003], p. 189). The commonest species were yellow or purple, though the rarer "white-flowered forms . . . always commanded higher prices" (p. 190). Dorian rejects white orchids, however, not because of their expense but presumably because white is traditionally associated with purity and innocence. For many Victorians, there was something menacing and monstrous about orchids, some species of which were known in Britain as "dead man's fingers." In a passage added to the 1891 book version of *Dorian Gray,* Lord Henry Wotton cuts for his buttonhole an orchid "as effective as the seven deadly things" (*The Picture of Dorian Gray: The 1890 and 1891 Texts,* ed. Bristow, p. 334). Similarly Mrs. Allonby, in Wilde's play *A Woman of No Importance,* refers to "an orchid . . . as beautiful as the seven deadly sins." The protagonist of H. G. Wells's 1895 story "The Flowering of the Strange Orchid" is killed by a mysterious deadly orchid (a forerunner of John Wyndham's 1950s sci-fi novel *The Day of the Triffids*). See, too, Chapter VIII of the present edition of *Dorian Gray,* in which *Le Secret de Raoul* is described as containing "metaphors as monstrous as orchids, and as evil in colour."

something in the purity and refinement of that sad face that seemed to enrage him. "You are infamous, absolutely infamous!" he muttered.

"Hush, Alan; you have saved my life," said Dorian.

"*Your* life? Good Heavens! what a life that is! You have gone from corruption to corruption, and now you have culminated in crime. In doing what I am going to do, what you force me to do, it is not of *your* life that I am thinking."

"Ah, Alan," murmured Dorian, with a sigh, "I wish you had a thousandth part of the pity for me that I have for you." He turned away, as he spoke, and stood looking out at the garden. Campbell made no answer.

After about ten minutes a knock came to the door, and the servant entered, carrying a mahogany chest of chemicals, with a small electric battery set on top of it.[23] He placed it on the table, and went out again, returning with a long coil of steel and platinum wire and two rather curiously-shaped iron clamps.

"Shall I leave the things here, Sir?" he asked Campbell.

"Yes," said Dorian. "And I am afraid, Francis, that I have another errand for you. What is the name of the man at Richmond who supplies Selby with orchids?"

"Harden, Sir."

"Yes, Harden. You must go down to Richmond at once, see Harden personally, and tell him to send twice as many orchids as I ordered, and to have as few white ones as possible. In fact, I don't want any white ones.[24] It is a lovely day, Francis, and Richmond is a very pretty place, otherwise I wouldn't bother you about it."

"No trouble, Sir. At what time shall I be back?"

Dorian looked at Campbell. "How long will your experiment take, Alan?" he said, in a calm, indifferent voice. The presence of a third person in the room seemed to give him extraordinary courage.

Campbell frowned, and bit his lip. "It will take about five hours," he answered.

"It will be time enough, then, if you are back at half-past seven, Francis. Or stay: just leave my things out for dressing. You can have the evening to yourself. I am not dining at home, so I shall not want you."

"Thank you, Sir," said the man, leaving the room.

"Now, Alan, there is not a moment to be lost. How heavy this chest is! I'll take it for you. You bring the other things." He spoke rapidly, and in an authoritative manner. Campbell felt dominated by him. They left the room together.

When they reached the top landing, Dorian took out the key and turned it in the lock. Then he stopped, and a troubled look came into his eyes. He shuddered. "I don't think I can go in, Alan," he murmured.

"It is nothing to me. I don't require you," said Campbell, coldly.

Dorian half opened the door. As he did so, he saw the face of the portrait grinning in the sunlight. On the floor in front of it the torn curtain was lying. He remembered that, the night before, for the first time in his life, he had forgotten to hide it, when he crept out of the room.

But what was that loathsome red dew that gleamed, wet and glistening, on one of the hands, as though the canvas had sweated blood? How horrible it was!—more horrible, it seemed to him for the moment, than the silent thing that he knew was stretched across the table, the thing whose grotesque misshapen shadow on the spotted carpet showed him that it had not stirred, but was still there, as he had left it.

He opened the door a little wider, and walked quickly in, with half-closed eyes and averted head, determined that he would not look even once upon the dead man. Then, stooping down, and taking up the gold-and-purple hanging, he flung it over the picture.

He stopped, feeling afraid to turn round, and his eyes fixed themselves on the intricacies of the pattern before him. He heard Campbell bringing in the heavy chest, and the irons, and the other things that he had required for his dreadful work. He began to wonder if he and Basil Hallward had ever met, and, if so, what they had thought of each other.

"Leave me now," said Campbell.

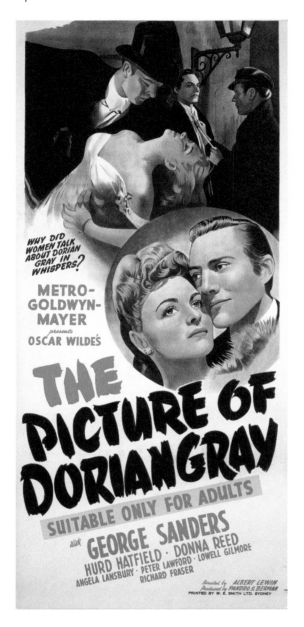

He turned and hurried out, just conscious that the dead man had been thrust back into the chair and was sitting up in it, with Campbell gazing into the glistening yellow face. As he was going downstairs he heard the key being turned in the lock.

It was long after seven o'clock when Campbell came back into the library. He was pale, but absolutely calm. "I have done what you asked me to do," he muttered. "And now, good-bye. Let us never see each other again."

"You have saved me from ruin, Alan. I cannot forget that," said Dorian, simply.

As soon as Campbell had left, he went upstairs. There was a horrible smell of chemicals in the room. But the thing that had been sitting at the table was gone.

Publicity poster for the 1945 MGM movie adaptation of *Dorian Gray,* directed by Albert Lewin. Billed as "suitable only for adults," with the accompanying caption, "Why did women talk about Dorian Gray in whispers?" Lewin's stylish, superbly acted film emphasized heterosexuality and expanded the role of the novel's female characters, partly to appease Hollywood's restrictive production code. Nonetheless, Hurd Hatfield and George Sanders give commanding performances as Dorian Gray and Lord Henry, respectively.

XIII

"THERE IS NO GOOD TELLING me you are going to be good, Dorian," cried Lord Henry, dipping his white fingers into a red copper bowl filled with rose-water. "You are quite perfect. Pray don't change."

Dorian shook his head. "No, Harry, I have done too many dreadful things in my life. I am not going to do any more. I began my good actions yesterday."

"Where were you yesterday?"

"In the country, Harry. I was staying at a little inn by myself."

"My dear boy," said Lord Henry smiling, "anybody can be good in the country. There are no temptations there. That is the reason why people who live out of town are so uncivilized.[1] There are only two ways, as you know, of becoming civilized. One is by being cultured, the other is by being corrupt. Country-people have no opportunity of being either, so they stagnate."

"Culture and corruption," murmured Dorian. "I have known something of both. It seems to me curious now that they should ever be found together. For I have a new ideal, Harry. I am going to alter. I think I have altered."

"You have not told me yet what your good action was. Or did you say you had done more than one?"

"I can tell you, Harry. It is not a story I could tell to any one else. I spared somebody. It sounds vain, but you understand what I mean. She was quite beautiful, and wonderfully like Sybil Vane. I think it

1 Here Lord Henry inverts the pastoral ideal that descends from late Greek and Latin literature, whereby the innocent simplicity of country life is invoked rhetorically in favor of the "teeming life, of flattery, of bribery, of organized seduction, of noise and traffic"—of "the city . . . itself, going its own way" (Raymond Williams, *The Country and the City* [Oxford University Press, 1973], p. 46).

2 *Dorian Gray* has seen numerous film, television, stage, opera, and dance adaptations. Between 1910 and 1918 alone it saw five film adaptations. More recently, it has been adapted for film eight times in the twenty-first century. The most famous and highly lauded film adaptation remains the one directed and written by Albert Lewin for MGM in 1945. That version considerably enlarges the role of Hetty Merton (Gladys Hallward), played by Donna Reed, in order to emphasize Dorian's heterosexual relationships. Hurd Hatfield's brilliant performance as Dorian would typecast him as a dandified beauty. George Sanders's performance as Lord Henry arguably matches John Gielgud's in the BBC's 1976 television production. In the MGM version, the Donna Reed character is engaged to Dorian when the story climaxes; the film closes with a teary-eyed Gladys/Hetty viewing Dorian's corpse and realizing how close she had come to marrying a monster. By contrast, the 1976 BBC production, directed by John Gorrie and scripted by John Osborne, eliminates the character of Hetty entirely and makes explicit the homoerotic dimensions of Wilde's plot.

3 For Victorians, apple blossoms in a woman's hair symbolized sexual fertility. See as an example Christina Rossetti's poem "An Apple Gathering":

> I plucked pink blossoms from mine apple tree
> And wore them all that evening in my hair:
> Then in due season when I went to see
> I found no apples there.
>
> With dangling basket all along the grass
> As I had come I went the selfsame track:
> My neighbours mocked me while they saw me pass
> So empty-handed back.

(*The Complete Poems,* ed. Crump, p. 37)

4 The heroine of Shakespeare's *Winter's Tale,* one of Wilde's favorite Shakespeare plays. Perdita is the daughter of Leontes and Hermione, the king and queen of Sicily. While still a baby, she is taken from her mother and abandoned upon the seacoast of Bohemia on the orders of her father, who wrongly suspects

was that which first attracted me to her. You remember Sybil, don't you? How long ago that seems! Well, Hetty was not one of our own class, of course. She was simply a girl in a village. But I really loved her. I am quite sure that I loved her.[2] All during this wonderful May that we have been having, I used to run down and see her two or three times a week. Finally she promised to come with me to town. I had taken a house for her, and arranged everything.[a] Yesterday she met me in a little orchard. The apple-blossoms kept tumbling down on her hair, and she was laughing.[3] We were to have gone away together this morning at dawn. Suddenly I said to myself 'I won't ruin this girl. I won't bring her to shame.' And I determined to leave her as flowerlike as I had found her."[b]

"I should think the novelty of the emotion must have given you a thrill of real pleasure, Dorian," interrupted Lord Henry. "But I can finish your idyll for you. You gave her good advice, and broke her heart. That was the beginning of your reformation."

"Harry, you are horrible! You mustn't say these dreadful things. Hetty's heart is not broken. Of course she cried, and all that. But her life is not spoiled. There is no disgrace on it.[c] She can live, like Perdita, in her garden."[4]

"And weep over a faithless Florizel," said Lord Henry, laughing. "My dear Dorian, you have the most curious boyish moods. Do you think this girl will ever be really contented now with any one of her own rank? I suppose she will be married someday to a rough carter or a grinning ploughman. Well, having met you, and loved you, will teach her to despise her husband, and she will be wretched. Upon the other hand, had she become your mistress, she would have lived in the society of charming and cultured men.[5] You would have educated her, taught her how to dress, how to talk, how to move. You would have made her perfect, and she would have been extremely happy. After a time, no doubt, you would have grown tired of her. She would have made a scene. You would have made a settlement. Then a new career would have begun for her.[d] From a moral point of view I really don't think much of your great renunciation. Even as a beginning, it is poor. Besides, how do you know that Hetty isn't

VAUDEVILLE THEATRE.

LOU-TELLEGEN'S SEASON

THE PICTURE OF DORIAN GRAY

BY

OSCAR WILDE

Dramatised by G. CONSTANT LOUNSBERY

MONSIEUR LOU-TELLEGEN

Theater program for the first theatrical adaptation of *The Picture of Dorian Gray* in 1913.

that Hermione has been unfaithful to him with his friend Polixenes, the king of Bohemia. Unaware of her royal parentage, Perdita grows into a beautiful young woman, raised by shepherds in a "rustic garden." When Florizel, the prince of Bohemia, falls in love with her, he initially incurs the wrath of his father, Polixenes; but when Perdita's true birth is revealed, Florizel unwittingly becomes the agent of reconciliation all around, and the parents of both children are happy to agree to their marriage. In September 1887, Wilde reviewed Mary Anderson's production of the play at the Lyceum Theatre, remarking, "Nothing has been seen in London for a long time more charming than the slight, graceful girl dancing with shepherds . . . or giving her flowers to the disguised King, or listening to the wooing of Florizel" (*"The Winter's Tale* at the Lyceum").

5 Stoddart or one of his associates deleted this sentence from Wilde's final typescript, along with the six that follow it, as well as Dorian's earlier comment, "[Hetty] promised to come with me to town. I had taken a house for her, and arranged everything." This was the most substantial of the Lippincott deletions as well as one of the most significant. Without these sentences, Hetty Merton is a somewhat unreal and idyllic figure. But here, in the restored text, we can see that Hetty was originally intended as one of Dorian's conquests. Is she a victim or a sexually adventurous woman of the world, not unlike Mrs. Erlynne and Mrs. Cheveley in Wilde's plays *Lady Windermere's Fan* and *An Ideal Husband*? At any rate, Lord Henry's characterization of the future life that awaits Dorian's would-be mistress still retains the power to shock.

6 Wilde alludes to Shakespeare's *Hamlet* and the drowning/possible suicide of Ophelia, who has been driven mad by her impossible love for Prince Hamlet. Ophelia's death is beautifully and hauntingly described by Queen Gertrude in her celebrated speech:

> There is a willow grows askaunt the brook,
> That shows his hoary leaves in the glassy stream,
> Therewith fantastic garlands she did make
> Of crow-flowers, nettles, daises, and long purples
> That liberal shepherds give a grosser name,
> But our cull-cold maids do dead men's fingers call them.
> There on the pendant boughs her crownet weeds
> Clamb'ring to hang, an envious sliver broke,
> When down her weedy trophies and herself
> Fell in the weeping brook. Her clothes spread wide,
> And mermaid-like awhile they bore her up,
> Which time she chaunted snatches of old lauds,
> As one incapable of her own distress,
> Or like a creature native and indued
> Unto that element. But long it could not be
> Till that her garments, heavy with their drink,
> Pull'd the poor wretch from her melodious lay
> To muddy death.

(*Hamlet*, IV:7, 173–176)

The scene of Ophelia's death was rendered in oil by John Everett Millais in *Ophelia* (1852), a painting that Wilde would have seen exhibited at the Grosvenor Gallery in 1886.

7 Jessamine, or *Jasminum officinale,* is a climbing shrub with white flowers, grown in England since the sixteenth century and notable for its beauty and fragrance. It is mentioned in the writings of Spenser, Milton, Johnson, Blake, Dickens, Gaskell, and Joyce, among others, where it often symbolizes rustic beauty and simplicity. The English heroine of Emma Brooke's 1894 novel *A Superfluous Woman,* swept up in a doomed sexual passion for a young peasant, is named Jessamine Halliday.

8 "Nowadays, with our modern mania for morality, everyone has to pose as a paragon of purity, incorruptibility, and all the other seven deadly virtues—and what is the result? You all go over like ninepins—one after the other. Not a year passes in England without somebody disappearing" (*An Ideal Husband*).

floating at the present moment in some mill-pond, with water-lilies round her, like Ophelia?"[6]

"I can't bear this, Harry! You mock at everything, and then suggest the most serious tragedies. I am sorry I told you now. I don't care what you say to me, I know I was right in acting as I did. Poor Hetty! As I rode past the farm this morning, I saw her white face at the window, like a spray of jessamine.[7] Don't let me talk about it any more, and don't try to persuade me that the first good action I have done for years, the first little bit of self-sacrifice I have ever known, is really a sort of sin. I want to be better. I am going to be better. Tell me something about yourself. What is going on in Town? I have not been to the Club for days."

"The people are still discussing poor Basil's disappearance."

"I should have thought they had got tired of that by this time," said Dorian, pouring himself out some wine, and frowning slightly.

"My dear boy, they have only been talking about it for six weeks, and the public are really not equal to the mental strain of having more than one topic every three months. They have been very fortunate lately, however. They have had my own divorce-case, and Alan Campbell's suicide. Now they have got the mysterious disappearance of an artist.[8] Scotland Yard still insists that the man in the grey ulster who left Victoria by the midnight train on the seventh of November was poor Basil, and the French police declare that Basil never arrived in Paris at all. I suppose in about a fortnight we will be told that he has been seen in San Francisco. It is an odd thing, but every one who disappears is said to be seen at San Francisco. It must be a delightful city, and possess all the attractions of the next world."

"What do you think has happened to Basil?" asked Dorian, holding up his Burgundy against the light, and wondering how it was that he could discuss the matter so calmly.

"I have not the slightest idea. If Basil chooses to hide himself, it is no business of mine. If he is dead, I don't want to think about him. Death is the only thing that ever terrifies me. I hate it. One can survive everything nowadays except that. Death and vulgarity are the only two facts in the nineteenth century that one cannot explain away. Let us have our coffee in the music-room, Dorian. You must play Chopin to me. The man with whom my wife ran away played Chopin exquisitely. Poor Victoria! She was desperately in love with you at one time, Dorian. It used to amuse me to watch her paying you compliments. You were so charmingly indifferent. Do you know, I really miss her? She never bored me. She was so delightfully improbable in everything that she did.ᵉ I was very fond of her. The house is rather lonely without her."

Dorian said nothing, but rose from the table, and, passing into the next room, sat down to the piano, and let his fingers stray across the notes. After the coffee had been brought in, he stopped, and, looking over at Lord Henry, said, "Harry, did it ever occur to you that Basil was murdered?"

Lord Henry yawned. "Basil had no enemies, and always wore a Waterbury watch.⁹ Why should he be murdered? He was not clever enough to have enemies. Of course he had a wonderful genius for painting. But a man can paint like Velasquez and yet be as dull as possible. Basil was really rather dull. He only interested me once, and that was when he told me, years ago, that he had a wild adoration for you."

"I was very fond of Basil," said Dorian, with a sad look in his eyes. "But don't people say that he was murdered?"

"Oh, some of the papers do. It does not seem to be probable. I know there are dreadful places in Paris, but Basil was not the sort of man to have gone to them. He had no curiosity. It was his chief defect. Play me a Nocturne, Dorian, and, as you play, tell me, in a low voice, how you have kept your youth.¹⁰ You must have some secret. I am only ten years older than you are, and I am wrinkled, and bald, and yellow. You are really wonderful, Dorian. You have never looked more charming than you do to-night. You remind me of the day I saw you first. You were rather cheeky, very shy, and absolutely extraordinary. You have changed, of course, but not in appearance. I wish you would tell me your secret. To get back my youth I would do anything in the world, except take exercise, get up early, or be respectable. Youth! There is nothing like it. It's absurd to talk of the ignorance of

9 Waterbury watches, made by the Waterbury Watch Co. in Waterbury, CT, were first sold in Britain in 1886; they were cheap, mass-made, and shoddy (in the United States they were sometimes given away free with clothing or merchandise), so they would hold little attraction for a thief. After his release from prison, Wilde wrote to Robert Ross requesting one (he had no other timepiece), adding, "A nickel watch is what I long for. . . . Silver is bimetallic" (*CL,* p. 918).

10 One of several references in this chapter to the Franco-Polish composer-pianist Frédéric Chopin (1810–1849), who lived briefly with his mistress George Sand on the Mediterranean island of Majorca and whose piano music Wilde greatly admired. In Wilde's "Critic as Artist," Gilbert remarks, "after playing Chopin, I feel as if I had been weeping over sins I never committed" (p. 127); and in *De Profundis* Wilde writes, "I hear . . . the cry of Marsyas. . . . in the deferred resolutions of Chopin's music" (*CL,* p. 756). In 1886 or 1887, Wilde invited A. G. Ross to a "smoking concert" featuring "Chopin and cigarettes" (*CL,* p. 291). Dorian was playing piano music when Lord Henry first met him, at the beginning of Chapter II, and in Chapter IX "Chopin's beautiful sorrows . . . fell unheeded on his ear" (p. 195 above).

11 In his memoirs, Edmund Yates writes that "dandies wore high stiff stocks [neckcloths or cravats], with an 'avalanche of satin' falling over the chest" as late as the mid-1840s (*Edmund Yates: His Recollections and Experiences* [London: Richard Bentley, 1884], p. 46).

12 According to classical myth, the faun Marsyas (often credited with inventing the flute) was so adept at flute playing that he challenged Apollo, god of music and master of the lyre, to a contest of skill. It was agreed that the Muses would judge who was the better musician, and also that the winner would be free to do with the loser whatever he liked. Marsyas lost the duel and was then cruelly flayed alive by Apollo. Wilde alludes to this myth elsewhere in his writings, notably in "The Decay of Lying," where he remarks that "the singer of life is not Apollo, but Marsyas" (p. 96), and in *De Profundis,* where he writes, "I hear in much modern Art the cry of Marsyas" (*CL,* p. 756). He connects Marsyas's cry to Baudelaire, Verlaine, and Chopin in particular.

13 Compare with Walter Pater's description of Leonardo's *Mona Lisa:* "It is a beauty wrought out from within upon the flesh, the deposit, little cell by cell, of strange thoughts and fantastic reveries and exquisite passions" (*The Renaissance,* ed. Hill, p. 98).

14 "How can we guard our unbelief?/. . . Just when we are safest, there's a sunset-touch,/A fancy from a flower-bell, some one's death,/A chorus-ending from Euripides,—/And that's enough for fifty hopes and fears" (Robert Browning, "Bishop Bloughram's Apology," ll. 180–185, in *Robert Browning: The Poems, Volume One,* ed. John Pettigrew, suppl. Thomas A. Collins [New Haven: Yale University Press, 1981], p. 622).

youth. The only people whose opinions I listen to now with any respect are people much younger than myself. They seem in front of me. Life has revealed to them her last wonder. As for the aged, I always contradict the aged. I do it on principle. If you ask them their opinion on something that happened yesterday, they solemnly give you the opinions current in 1820, when people wore high stocks and knew absolutely nothing.[11] How lovely that thing you are playing is! I wonder did Chopin write it at Majorca, with the sea weeping round the villa, and the salt spray dashing against the panes? It is marvelously romantic. What a blessing it is that there is one art left to us that is not imitative! Don't stop. I want music to-night. It seems to me that you are the young Apollo, and that I am Marsyas listening to you.[12] I have sorrows, Dorian, of my own, that even you know nothing of. The tragedy of old age is not that one is old, but that one is young. I am amazed sometimes at my own sincerity. Ah, Dorian, how happy you are! What an exquisite life you have had! You have drunk deeply of everything. You have crushed the grapes against your palate. Nothing has been hidden from you. But it has all been to you no more than the sound of music. It has not marred you. You are still the same.

"I wonder what the rest of your life will be. Don't spoil it by renunciations. At present you are a perfect type. Don't make yourself incomplete. You are quite flawless now. You need not shake your head: you know you are. Besides, Dorian, don't deceive yourself. Life is not governed by will or intention. Life is a question of nerves, and fibres, and slowly-built-up cells in which thought hides itself, and passion has its dreams.[13] You may fancy yourself safe, and think yourself strong. But a chance tone of colour in a room or a morning sky, a particular perfume that you had once loved and that brings strange memories with it, a line from a forgotten poem that you had come across again, a cadence from a piece of music that you had ceased to play—I tell you, Dorian, that it is on things like these that our lives depend. Browning writes about that somewhere;[14] but our own senses will imagine them for us. There are moments when the odour of heliotrope passes suddenly across me, and I have to live the strangest year of my life over again.

"I wish I could change places with you, Dorian. The world has cried out against us both, but it has always worshipped you. It always will worship you. You are the type of what the age is searching for, and what it is afraid it has found. I am so glad that you have never done anything, never carved a statue, or painted a picture, or produced anything outside of yourself! Life has been your art. You have set yourself to music. Your days have been your sonnets."

Dorian rose up from the piano, and passed his hand through his hair. "Yes, life has been exquisite," he murmured, "but I am not going to have the same life, Harry. And you must not say these extravagant things to me. You don't know everything about me. I think that if you did, even you would turn from me. You laugh. Don't laugh."

"Why have you stopped playing, Dorian? Go back and play the Nocturne over again. Look at that great honey-coloured moon that hangs in the dusky air. She is waiting for you to charm her, and if you play she will come closer to the earth. You won't? Let us go to the Club, then. It has been a charming evening, and we must end it charmingly. There is someone at the Club who wants immensely to know you. Young Lord Poole, Bournmouth's eldest son. He has already copied your neckties, and has begged me to introduce him to you. He is quite delightful, and rather reminds me of you."

"I hope not," said Dorian, with a touch of pathos in his voice. "But I am tired to-night, Harry. I won't go to the Club. It is nearly eleven, and I want to go to bed early."

"Do stay. You have never played so well as to-night. There was something in your touch that was wonderful. It had more expression than I had ever heard from it before."

"It is because I am going to be good," he answered, smiling. "I am a little changed already."

"Don't change, Dorian; at any rate, don't change to me. We must always be friends."

"Yet you poisoned me with a book once. I should not forgive that. Harry, promise me that you will never lend that book to anyone. It does harm."[15]

"My dear boy, you are really beginning to moralise. You will soon be going about warning people against all the sins of which you have

15 In what was doubtless a response to hostile critics who denounced *Dorian Gray* as "poisonous," Wilde added the following lines to Lord Henry's reply to Dorian for the expanded book version of 1891: "As for being poisoned by a book, there is no such thing as that. Art has no influence upon action. It annihilates the desire to act. It is superbly sterile. . . . But we won't discuss literature" (*The Picture of Dorian Gray: The 1890 and 1891 Texts,* ed. Bristow, p. 352).

16 The novel opens with the "heavy scent" of lilacs; Lord Henry may be remembering that Dorian had "buried" his face in lilac blossoms upon their first meeting, "drinking in their perfume as if it had been wine."

grown tired. You are much too delightful to do that. Besides, it is no use. You and I are what we are, and will be what we will be. Come round tomorrow. I am going to ride at eleven, and we might go together. The Park is quite lovely now. I don't think there have been such lilacs since the year I met you."[16]

"Very well. I will be here at eleven," said Dorian. "Good-night, Harry." As he reached the door, he hesitated for a moment, as if he had something more to say. Then he sighed and went out.

It was a lovely night, so warm that he threw his coat over his arm, and did not even put his silk scarf round his throat. As he strolled home, smoking his cigarette, two young men in evening dress passed him. He heard one of them whisper to the other, "That is Dorian Gray." He remembered how pleased he used to be when he was pointed out, or stared at, or talked about. He was tired of hearing his own name now. Half the charm of the little village where he had been so often lately was that no one knew who he was. He had told the girl whom he had made love him that he was poor, and she had believed him. He had told her once that he was wicked, and she had laughed at him, and told him that wicked people were always very old and very ugly. What a laugh she had! Just like a thrush singing. And how pretty she had been in her cotton dresses, and her large hats. She knew nothing, but she had everything that he had lost.

When he reached home, he found his servant waiting up for him. He sent him to bed, and threw himself down on the sofa in the library, and began to think over some of the things that Lord Henry had said to him.

Was it really true that one could never change? He felt a wild longing for the unstained purity of his boyhood, his rose-white boyhood, as Lord Henry had once called it. He knew that he had tarnished himself, filled his mind with corruption, and given horror to his fancy; that he had been an evil influence to others, and had experienced a terrible joy in being so; and that of the lives that had crossed his own it had been the fairest and the most full of promise that he had brought to shame. But was it all irretrievable? Was there no hope for him?

It was better not to think of the past. Nothing could alter that. It was of himself, and of his own future, that he had to think. Alan Campbell had shot himself one night in his laboratory, but had not revealed the secret that he had been forced to know. The excitement, such as it was, over Basil Hallward's disappearance would soon pass away. It was already waning. He was perfectly safe there. Nor, indeed, was it the death of Basil Hallward that weighed most upon his mind. It was the living death of his own soul that troubled him. Basil had painted the portrait that had marred his life. He could not forgive him that. It was the portrait that had done everything. Basil had said things to him that were unbearable, and that he had yet borne with patience. The murder had been simply the madness of a moment. As for Alan Campbell, his suicide had been his own act. He had chosen to do it. It was nothing to him.

A new life! That was what he wanted. That was what he was waiting for. Surely he had begun it already. He had spared one innocent thing, at any rate. He would never again tempt innocence. He would be good.

As he thought of Hetty Merton, he began to wonder if the portrait in the locked room had changed. Surely it was not still so horrible as it had been? Perhaps if his life became pure, he would be able to expel every sign of evil passion from the face. Perhaps the signs of evil had already gone away. He would go and look.

He took the lamp from the table and crept upstairs. As he unlocked the door, a smile of joy flitted across his young face and lingered for a moment about his lips. Yes, he would be good, and the hideous thing that he had hidden away would no longer be a terror to him. He felt as if the load had been lifted from him already.

He went in quietly, locking the door behind him, as was his custom, and dragged the purple hanging from the portrait. A cry of pain and indignation broke from him. He could see no change, unless that in the eyes there was a look of cunning, and in the mouth the curved wrinkle of the hypocrite. The thing was still loathsome, more loathsome if possible than before, and the scarlet dew that spotted the hand seemed brighter, and more like blood newly-spilt.[17]

17 Dorian's belated desire to overcome those elements in his own nature that are evil and corrupt—elements objectified in the portrait—recalls Dr. Jekyll's war against Hyde: "I was often plunged into a kind of wonder at my vicarious depravity. This familiar that I called out of my own soul, and sent forth alone to do his good pleasure, was a being inherently malign and villainous; his every act and thought centered on self; drinking pleasure with bestial avidity. . . . Henry Jekyll stood at times aghast before the acts of Edward Hyde; but the situation was apart from ordinary laws, and insidiously relaxed the grasp of conscience" (*The Strange Case of Dr. Jekyll and Mr. Hyde and Other Tales of Terror*, p. 60). Similarly, Dorian's horror at his own loathsomeness recalls Jekyll's disgust for "the full deformity of that creature that shared with him some of the phenomena of consciousness, and was co-heir with him to death" (p. 69).

18 "Of course the sinner must repent. But why? Simply because otherwise he would not be able to realize what he had done. The moment of repentance is the moment of initiation" (*CL,* p. 752). Although Wilde tells us in the next breath that "the death of Basil Hallward seemed very little to him," Dorian's acknowledgment that he ought to "tell his sin," to atone and suffer public shame, conveys a hint of remorse on his part. This hint is not sufficient to mitigate a more purely selfish impulse, apparent in the next few paragraphs, to free himself from the past and to destroy "the one bit of evidence left against him." But it is enough to make us question Dorian's motives in stabbing his own painted image. Does he strike it out of remorse or self-loathing? Is it another in a string of suicides in the novel, or is it a purely instinctive effort at self-preservation?

The novel's subtle hedging of the moral issue elicited fierce remonstrance when it was first published. The *Pall Mall Budget* complained that Wilde "does not take the trouble to make his moral logically cohere with his subject matter" (unsigned rev., "Mr. Oscar Wilde's 'Dorian Gray,'" *Pall Mall Budget,* July 3, 1890, p. 262). Wilde replied to such objections by insisting that his novel's ending was *too* moral—that "Dorian Gray, having led a life of mere sensation and pleasure, tries to kill conscience, and at that moment kills himself" (*CL,* p. 430) "The real trouble I experienced in writing the story," he notes, "was that of keeping the extremely obvious moral subordinate to the artistic and dramatic effect" (*CL,* p. 435). At any rate, when revising the novel for the expanded book edition, Wilde heightened Dorian's monstrosity to bring the novel to a less ambiguous, more easily understood, moral conclusion.

19 Dorian's preoccupation with the portrait as "evidence" echoes the obsessive efforts of Wilde's narrator in "The Portrait of Mr. W. H." to provide independent corroborating evidence of the existence of a boy actor with whom Shakespeare was allegedly in love. Without the physical proof of the portrait, the existence of the boy actor—and thus the true nature of Shakespeare's love—remains open to question since it can only be inferred from Shakespeare's sonnets themselves.

Had it been merely vanity that had made him do his one good deed? Or the desire of a new sensation, as Lord Henry had hinted, with his mocking laugh? Or that passion to act a part that sometimes makes us do things finer than we are ourselves? Or, perhaps, all these?

Why was the red stain larger than it had been? It seemed to have crept like a horrible disease over the wrinkled fingers. There was blood on the painted feet, as though the thing had dripped; blood even on the hand that had not held the knife.

Confess? Did it mean that he was to confess? To give himself up, and be put to death? He laughed. He felt that the idea was monstrous. Besides, who would believe him, even if he did confess? There was no trace of the murdered man anywhere. Everything belonging to him had been destroyed. He himself had burned what had been below-stairs. The world would simply say he was mad. They would shut him up if he persisted in his story.

Yet it was his duty to confess, to suffer public shame, and to make public atonement. There was a God who called upon men to tell their sins to earth as well as to Heaven. Nothing that he could do would cleanse him till he had told his own sin.[18] His sin? He shrugged his shoulders. The death of Basil Hallward seemed very little to him. He was thinking of Hetty Merton.

It was an unjust mirror, this mirror of his soul that he was looking at. Vanity? Curiosity? Hypocrisy? Had there been nothing more in his renunciation than that? There had been something more. At least he thought so. But who could tell?

And this murder—was it to dog him all his life? Was he never to get rid of the past? Was he really to confess? No. There was only one bit of evidence left against him. The picture itself. That was evidence.[19]

He would destroy it. Why had he kept it so long? It had given him pleasure once to watch it changing and growing old. Of late he had felt no such pleasure. It had kept him awake at night. When he had been away, he had been filled with terror lest other eyes should look upon it. It had brought melancholy across his passions. Its mere

"Lying on the floor was a dead man, in evening dress, with a knife in his heart," wood-engraved illustration by Eugène Dété, from a drawing by Paul Thiriat, published in *The Picture of Dorian Gray* (Paris: Charles Carrington, 1908 [1910]).

20 Elsewhere Wilde writes contemptuously of conscience: "The mere existence of conscience, that faculty of which people prate so much nowadays, and are so ignorantly proud, is a sign of our imperfect development. It must be merged in instinct before we become fine" ("The Critic as Artist," p. 148).

21 Wilde muted this sentence considerably in the 1891 book version, stating merely, "He seized the thing, and stabbed the picture with it." Wilde's description of stabbing as "ripping the thing from top to bottom" would once again have reminded his earliest readers of the gruesome Jack-the-Ripper killings of 1888, in which most of the victims were ritualistically disemboweled after their throats had been slashed with a knife.

22 "About the hearth the whole of the servants, men and women, stood huddled together like a flock of sheep. . . . A dismal screech, as of mere animal terror, rang from the cabinet" (*The Strange Case of Dr. Jekyll and Mr. Hyde and Other Tales of Terror*, pp. 38–44).

23 Sir Henry Ashton was one of the young men mentioned by Basil Hallward in Chapter X whom Dorian had previously "taken up" but who had ultimately "come to grief."

memory had marred many moments of joy. It had been like conscience to him. Yes, it had been conscience. He would destroy it.[20]

He looked round, and saw the knife that had stabbed Basil Hallward. He had cleaned it many times, till there was no stain left upon it. It was bright, and glistened. As it had killed the painter, so it would kill the painter's work, and all that that meant. It would kill the past, and when that was dead he would be free. He seized it, and stabbed the canvas with it, ripping the thing right up from top to bottom.[21]

There was a cry heard, and a crash. The cry was so horrible in its agony that the frightened servants woke, and crept out of their rooms.[22] Two gentlemen, who were passing in the square below, stopped, and looked up at the great house. They walked on till they met a policeman, and brought him back. The man rang the bell several times, but there was no answer. The house was all dark, except for a light in one of the top windows. After a time, he went away, and stood in the portico of the next house and watched.

"Whose house is that, constable?" asked the elder of the two gentlemen.

"Mr. Dorian Gray's, Sir," answered the policeman.

They looked at each other, as they walked away, and sneered. One of them was Sir Henry Ashton's uncle.[23]

Inside, in the servants' part of the house, the half-clad domestics were talking in low whispers to each other. Old Mrs. Leaf was crying, and wringing her hands. Francis was as pale as death.

After about a quarter of an hour, he got the coachman and one of the footmen and crept upstairs. They knocked, but there was no reply. They called out. Everything was still. Finally, after vainly trying to force the door, they got on the roof, and dropped down on to the balcony. The windows yielded easily: the bolts were old.

When they entered, they found hanging upon the wall a splendid portrait of their master as they had last seen him, in all the wonder of his exquisite youth and beauty. Lying on the floor was a dead man, in evening dress, with a knife in his heart. He was withered, wrinkled, and loathsome of visage. It was not till they had examined the rings that they recognised who it was.

Ivan Albright, *The Picture of Dorian Gray*, lifesize oil on canvas, 1943–1944. Albright was commissioned to create this painting for Albert Lewin's 1945 film adaptation of Wilde's novel. The painting was quite different when filming got under way: Albright gradually incorporated changes to reflect Dorian's growing corruption. Note "the scarlet dew that spotted the hand . . . like blood newly-spilt."

TEXTUAL NOTES

The following notes record all substantive changes made by J. M. Stoddart or his associates to the typescript (TS) of *The Picture of Dorian Gray* prior to its publication in *Lippincott's Monthly Magazine*. They also selectively record some of the deletions Wilde made in preparing the book edition of 1891, in order to indicate the depth of his self-censorship following the outcry of 1890. Wilde revised the *Lippincott's* text extensively for the book edition, adding to it substantially as well as deleting some of the most controversial passages. No attempt has been made here to document Wilde's additions to the 1891 text, and readers interested in studying his alterations for it are referred to *The Picture of Dorian Gray: The 1890 and 1891 Texts,* ed. Joseph Bristow, vol. 3 of *The Complete Works of Oscar Wilde* (Oxford University Press, 2005).

CHAPTER I

a. Wilde deleted the phrase "laying his hand upon his shoulder" from the 1891 book version.

b. In the TS, Stoddart or one of his associates altered "I sometimes wish she did" to "I sometimes wish she would."

c. Wilde deleted the phrase "shaking his hand off" from the 1891 book version.

d. Wilde deleted the sentence "I knew that if I spoke to Dorian I would become absolutely devoted to him, and that I ought not to speak to him" from the 1891 book version.

e. Stoddart or one of his associates altered "we are poaching" to "he is poaching."

f. In the TS, J. M. Stoddart altered "live with their own wives" to "live correctly."

g. In the 1891 book version, Wilde deleted the lines "Of course sometimes it is only for a few minutes. But a few minutes with somebody one worships mean a great deal," together with Lord Henry's following question, "But you don't really worship him?" and Basil Hallward's reply, "I do." He replaced these lines of dialogue in 1891 with the less-revealing sentence "He is absolutely necessary to me."

    h. Wilde made several alterations to this sentence for the 1891 book version, including the substitution of "curious artistic idolatry" for "extraordinary romance."

    i. Wilde deleted "I give myself away" from the 1891 book version.

    j. Wilde deleted the phrase "we walk home together from the club arm in arm, or" from the 1891 book version.

    k. Stoddart or one of his associates substituted "Gray" for Wilde's "him."

    l. Wilde added the mitigating phrase "of any kind" after "romance" when revising this sentence for the 1891 book version.

    m. Wilde deleted "that makes life absolutely lovely and" as well as "wonder or" from this sentence for the 1891 book version.

CHAPTER II

    a. Wilde deleted the sentence "He was made to be worshipped" from the 1891 book version.

CHAPTER III

    a. Stoddart or one of his associates altered ". . . to try and look young. . . . to try and talk brilliantly" to ". . . to try to look young. . . . to try to talk brilliantly."

    b. In the TS Stoddart or one of his associates changed "is Sybil Vane your mistress?" to "what are your relations with Sibyl Vane?"

    c. "How dare you suggest such a thing, Harry? It is horrible. Sybil Vane is sacred!" was changed in the TS by Stoddart or one of his associates to "Harry! Sibyl Vane is sacred."

    d. "Your mistress" was altered in the TS to "yours" by Stoddart or one of his associates.

    e. Wilde deleted the sentence "You don't mean to say that Basil has got any passion or any romance in him?" from the 1891 book version.

    f. Wilde deleted these two sentences from the 1891 book version.

    g. Wilde deleted "Never. . . . I am rather surprised to hear it" from the 1891 book version.

CHAPTER IV

    a. Wilde muted Hallward's reaction to the news of Dorian's impending marriage in the 1891 version, deleting this sentence and substituting in its place the line "Hallward started, and then frowned."

    b. Stoddart or one of his associates deleted "got" from "got some."

CHAPTER V

a. The following sentence was deleted by Stoddart or one of his associates: "A man with curious eyes had suddenly peered into his face, and then dogged him with stealthy footsteps, passing and repassing him many times." Previous editors have attributed this deletion to Wilde rather than to Stoddart. But the sentence is deleted, with an extended wavy pencil line through it, in a manner very similar to the way in which other sentences were censored by Stoddart or one of his associates.

b. *Lippincott's* and all succeeding editions have been printed without a paragraph break at this juncture; Wilde's paragraph break has been restored here.

CHAPTER VI

a. In *Lippincott's* text "a wonderful tragic figure to whom Love had been a great reality" was printed as "a wonderful tragic figure to show Love had been a great reality." The absence of editorial markings on the TS suggests that this change was the result of a typesetter's misreading. Without a text containing his original wording, Wilde used this change as the basis for a further alteration in the 1891 book version, where this phrase is rendered "a wonderful tragic figure sent on to the world's stage to show the supreme reality of Love."

CHAPTER VII

a. "I won't bear it" has been printed as "I won't hear it" in all previous editions. This is possibly the result of a typesetter's misreading, since Stoddart and his associates left "bear it" unaltered in the TS.

b. Wilde deleted "Rugged and straightforward as he was, there was something in his nature that was purely feminine in its tenderness" from the 1891 book version.

c. Stoddart or one of his associates changed "should ever give" to "usually gives."

d. Wilde deleted from the 1891 book version the four sentences from "It is quite true that I have worshipped you . . ." to "idle classes in a country," as well as the ensuing word "Well."

e. Wilde deleted "I quite admit that I adored you madly, extravagantly, absurdly" from the 1891 book version. He replaced it with "I was dominated, soul, brain and power by you. You became to me the visible incarnation of that unseen ideal whose memory haunts us artists like an exquisite dream. I worshipped you." He also made subtle refinements to the ensuing sentences.

f. Wilde deleted "It was all wrong and foolish. It is all wrong and foolish still" from the 1891 book version.

g. "There was love in every line, and in every touch there was passion" was deleted from the TS by Stoddart or one of his associates.

h. Stoddart or one of his associates deleted from the TS "something infinitely tragic in a romance that was at once so passionate and so sterile."

CHAPTER VIII

a. "*Le Secret de Raoul, par Catulle Sarrazin.*' What a curious title!" was deleted from the TS by Stoddart or one of his associates.

CHAPTER IX

a. "Raoul" was altered in the TS by Stoddart or one of his associates to "The hero."

b. "Catulle Sarrazin's fantastic hero" was altered in the TS by Stoddart or one of his associates to "the book's fantastic hero."

c. "Raoul" was altered in the TS by Stoddart or one of his associates to "the young Parisian."

d. In the TS, Stoddart or one of his associates altered "some ivory cell in the brain, or some scarlet nerve in the body" to the more anatomically correct description "some pearly cell in the brain, or some white nerve in the body"—a correction preserved in all subsequent editions. Wilde referred to the "ivory cell" of the brain again in his dialogue "The Critic as Artist" and his poem "Roses and Rue."

e. "Their child had been Brutus" and the sentence that follows, "The young priest of the Sun, who while yet a boy had been slain for his sins, used to walk in jewelled shoes on dust of gold and silver," were omitted from the text published in *Lippincott's* as well as from all succeeding published versions. Since these sentences were left intact by Stoddart and his associates in the typescript, we cannot ascertain whether they were omitted from the *Lippincott's* text simply as the result of a typesetting error or censored as the story was being prepared for the press.

f. Stoddart or one of his associates inserted a paragraph break into the printed text at this juncture, though none was marked on the typescript.

g. Stoddart or one of his associates changed "one night" in the TS to "some night."

h. In the TS Stoddart altered "till the people almost drove him out in horror, and had to be appeased by monstrous bribes" to "until he was driven away."

i. In the TS, Stoddart or one of his associates deleted the clause "who were jealous of the strange love that he inspired in women."

j. Wilde inserted the following into the TS in handwriting (having changed the preceding period to a comma): "and in the eyes of some it was a question whether that was an honour or a disgrace." This insertion, which directly quotes a passage Wilde had earlier deleted from the MS, was subsequently deleted from the TS and the comma preceding it reverted to a period. It is impossible to say who deleted this passage from the typescript, and previous editors disagree on this point (Bristow attributes it to Wilde, Lawler to Stoddart).

k. Stoddart or one of his associates deleted from the TS the sentence "It was said that even the sinful creatures who prowl the streets at night had cursed him as he passed by, seeing in him a corruption greater than their own, and knowing but too well the horror of his real life."

l. In the TS, Wilde substituted in handwriting "the death of those to whom she granted her favours" for "her lovers." Stoddart or one of his associates deleted the newly inserted phrase and reverted to "her lovers."

m. In the TS, Stoddart or one of his associates deleted "Raoul," capitalized "The," and deleted the comma after "life" so that this sentence read, when originally published, "The hero of the dangerous novel that had so influenced his life had himself . . ."

n. In the TS, Stoddart or one of his associates altered "the fourth" to "a" and deleted "us."

o. In the TS, Stoddart or one of his associates deleted "had drank the love-philter . . . by day a false gilded beard, and" and substituted "had."

p. In the TS, Stoddart made a number of significant deletions from this passage for the first published version: (1) he deleted "Lust," replacing it with "Vice"; (2) he initially deleted "courtezans," replacing it with "evil companions," before deciding to delete the entire clause "Here was Manfred . . . courtezans and buffoons," replacing the preceding period with a colon; (3) he deleted "that her guilty lover . . . that he fondled"; and (4) he deleted "Incest and." He also considered replacing "a harlot" with "one" before thinking better of it. Bristow attributes the deletion of "that her guilty lover . . . that he fondled" to Wilde, not Stoddart. But the pencil cancellation makes clear that (as Lawler contends) Stoddart or one of his associates deleted it.

CHAPTER X

a. Wilde deleted "things that I could hardly repeat to you" from the 1891 book edition.

b. In the TS, Stoddart or one of his associates deleted "Why is it that every young man that you take up seems to come to grief, to go to the bad at once?" and replaced it with "Why is your friendship so fateful to young men?"

c. In the TS, Stoddart or one of his associates deleted the sentence "It is quite sufficient to say of a young man that he goes to stay at Selby Royal, for people to sneer and titter."

d. In the TS, Stoddart or one of his associates deleted "He said that he suspected you" and in the previous sentence replaced "It was" with "Your name was implicated in."

e. Wilde altered "devoted" to "a staunch friend" for the 1891 book edition.

CHAPTER XI

a. "Christ!" was changed in the TS by Stoddart or one of his associates to "God!"

CHAPTER XIII

a. In the TS, Stoddart deleted this and the previous sentence. Initially he replaced them with "She would have come away with me," but then decided to delete his substitution as well.

b. In the TS, Stoddart or one of his associates deleted "said to myself 'I won't ruin this girl. I won't bring her to shame.' And."

c. In the TS, Stoddart or one of his associates deleted "her life is not spoiled" and changed "There is no disgrace on it" to "there is no disgrace upon her." Stoddart or one of his associates also crossed out Wilde's phrase "There is no" and the first syllable of "disgrace," suggesting that he initially intended to delete this sentence too but then thought better of it.

d. "Upon the other hand . . . would have begun for her" was deleted by Stoddart or one of his associates.

e. The sentences "She was desperately in love. . . . improbable in everything that she did" were deleted from the TS by Stoddart or one of his associates.

APPENDIX A

Accidental Changes Introduced into the Text
by J. M. Stoddart or His Associates

The following lists present only accidental changes to Wilde's typescript (made after Wilde had sent the novel to Philadelphia) that can be attributed with certainty to the editor of *Lippincott's,* J. M. Stoddart, or his associates. The term "accidental changes," as distinct from "substantive changes," is commonly used by textual scholars to distinguish seemingly small changes to a literary text, such as alterations of spelling, punctuation, and capitalization, from those that more clearly affect meaning and interpretation. As the Textual Introduction explains, Wilde's typescript was read—and possibly corrected—by at least six individuals upon its receipt in Philadelphia, and it contains numerous other accidental changes, including the insertion of commas, dashes, and exclamation marks, as well as the transposition of quotation marks (so that commas and periods fall within quotation marks rather than outside them), whose authorship is difficult to determine clearly. For a complete record of such accidentals, see *The Picture of Dorian Gray: The 1890 and 1891 Texts,* ed. Joseph Bristow, vol. 3 of *The Complete Works of Oscar Wilde* (Oxford University Press, 2005). Where accidental changes cannot clearly be attributed to Stoddart or his associates, they have been incorporated into the text of the novel as if they are Wilde's own and consequently do not appear here.

SPELLING CHANGES

annihlated   *annihilated*[1]   178
apologise   *apologize*   142

[1] Stoddart's correction of "annihlated" has been allowed to stand in the present edition.

ardour   *ardor*   194

armour   *armor*   84, 198, 204

candour   *candor*   90, 105

celestis   *caelestis*   194

characterises   *characterizes*   184

clenched   *clinched*   145, 170

colour   *color*   86, 104, 105, 140, 154, 159, 172, 173 (×2), 186, 194, 197 (×2), 230, 233, 246

coloured   *colored*   67, 78, 83, 89, 96, 98, 109 (×2), 114 (×2), 128, 130, 134 (×2), 148, 165, 175, 184, 196, 198, 199, 200 (×2), 201, 247

colourless   *colorless*   102, 132

colours   *colors*   85, 91, 160, 162, 187, 193 (×2), 206

coverlid   *coverlet*   177

curtsey   *courtesy*   176, 177

dishonour   *dishonor*   188

drunkeness   *drunkenness*[2]   83

favour   *favor*   179

favourites   *favorites*   89, 198

feign   *fain*   194

good-bye   *good-by*   92, 107 (×3), 113, 128

grey   *gray*   115, 146, 151, 162, 211, 244

honour   *honor*   170, 179, 208

idyll   *idyl*[3]   242

jessamine   *jasmine*   244

leant   *leaned*   141

leapt   *leaped*   104, 120, 139, 144, 156

Mahomet   *Mohammed*   200

moralise   *moralize*   247

neighbour   *neighbor*   133

odour   *odor*   67, 114, 186, 219, 246

over-emphasised   *over-emphasized*   140, 187

persperation   *perspiration*[4]   171

practice   *practise*   233

realisation   *realization*   190, 192

realise   *realize*   84, 94, 99, 152, 184, 204, 224

realised   *realized*   145, 154, 169

recognise   *recognize*   124, 211 (×2), 221

recognised   *recognized*   211, 252

2 Stoddart's correction of "drunkeness" has been allowed to stand in the present edition.

3 Wilde changed "idyl" back to "idyll" when preparing the 1891 book edition.

4 Stoddart's correction of "persperation" has been allowed to stand in the present edition.

reverie   *revery*   186, 193

rhumatism   *rheumatism*[5]   177

ribands   *ribbons*   80, 160

ricketty   *rickety*   223

rumoured   *rumored*   194, 218

rumours   *rumors*   188, 214

Sphynxes   *Sphinxes*   231

spiritualise   *spiritualize*   139

spiritualises   *spiritualizes*   139

splendour   *splendor*   202

spoilt   *spoiled*   133, 160

Sybil   *Sibyl*   114, 119, 120 (×3), 121 (×2), 122 (×5), 124, 130 (×2), 134 (×2), 136 (×4), 139 (×2), 140, 142, 146, 150, 151 (×2), 154, 155, 156 (×5), 157 (×3), 160 (×2), 162 (×2), 163 (×2), 167 (×2), 168, 178, 182, 184, 241, 242

symbolise   *symbolize*   194

sympathise   *sympathize*   83

syphons   *siphons*   213

tyrannised   *tyrannized*   130

waggons   *wagons*   146

CAPITALIZATION CHANGES

Agate   *agate*   197

Altar Frontals   *altar frontals*   201

Amethyst   *amethyst*   197

Angels   *angels*   194

Art   *art*[6]   128

Biology   *biology*   233

Bishop   *bishop*   72

Café   *café*   231

Chalice   *chalice*   194

Chalice-veils   *chalice-veils*   201

Charity Concerts   *charity concerts*   152

Chasubles   *chasubles*   201

Church   *church*   110

Club   *club*   142, 182, 186, 190, 202, 244, 247 (×3)

Clubs   *clubs*   188

5 Stoddart's correction of "rhumatism" has been allowed to stand in the present edition.

6 Wilde was inconsistent in his capitalization of "Art," using the lowercase numerous times elsewhere in the same paragraph.

Communion   *communion*   194
Cornelian   *cornelian*   197
Coronation   *coronation*[7]   200
Corporals   *corporals*   201
Costume Ball   *costume ball*   196
Dead-Houses   *dead-houses*   235
Democracy   *democracy*   83
Diamond   *diamond*   197
Dissecting-room   *dissecting-room*   235
Divine   *divine*   99
Doctor   *doctor*   208
Duchess   *duchess*   113
Duke's   *duke's*   76
Ecclesiastical   *ecclesiastical*   200
Frontier   *frontier*   80
Garnet   *garnet*   197
Giants   *giants*   199
Gods   *gods*   165, 199
Good Heavens   *Good heavens*   142, 238
Heaven   *heaven*   250
Hedonism   *hedonism*[8]   100, 192
Hood   *hood*   200
Hospitals   *hospitals*   235
Hyacinth   *hyacinth*   197
Hydropicus   *hydropicus*   197
King   *king*   119, 180
King's   *king's*   199
Life   *life*   129
Lordship   *lordship*   177
Man   *man*   192
Manager   *manager*   138, 142
Market   *market*   146
Meloceus   *meloceus*   197

7 "Coronation" was left uppercased in the typescript but printed lowercased in *Lippincott's;* it was presumably altered during typesetting or proofing.

8 Stoddart and his associates retained Wilde's capitalization of "Hedonism" when editing the TS, but "Hedonism" was changed to "hedonism" when the novel was set in type. Wilde restored "Hedonism" for the 1891 book version. Like his respelling of "idyll," this restoration constitutes evidence that Wilde was given no chance to correct proofs before the novel was published in *Lippincott's* in June 1890.

Moon   *moon*   197

Mother   *mother*   182

Nocturne   *nocturne*   245, 247

Oh, yes, plays the piano   *oh, yes, plays the piano*   80

Opera   *opera*[9]   110, 122, 157 (×2), 163, 165, 166 (×2), 167 (×2), 196, 233

Orchestra   *orchestra*   139

Palace   *palace*   197

Passion   *passion*[10]   194

Prince   *prince*   122

Professor of Elocution   *professor of elocution*   141

Queen   *queen*   180

Queen's   *queen's*   199

Restaurant   *restaurant*   133

Saints   *saints*   140

Science   *science*   231

Scientific Reviews   *scientific reviews*   233

Selenite   *selenite*   197

Sir   *sir*[11]   176 (×4), 179 (×2), 227, 233, 238 (×3), 239, 252

Studio   *studio*   134

Sudaria   *sudaria*   201

Theatre   *theatre*[12]   120, 121, 124, 134, 137, 138, 146, 156, 157

Thee   *thee*   141

Tomb   *tomb*   119, 120

Town   *town*   244

Tragedy   *tragedy*   196

West Gallery   *west gallery*   200

CHANGES TO COMPOUNDS

oneself   *one's self*   83, 94, 120, 139

9 Although Stoddart or one of his associates lowercased "Opera" in the typescript, the word was capitalized when the novel was set in type.

10 Although Stoddart or one of his associates lower-cased "Passion" in the typescript, the word was capitalized when the novel was set in type. Stoddart left the word capitalized in the typescript later in the same chapter.

11 Wilde was inconsistent in his capitalization of "Sir," on occasion using the lowercase elsewhere in the typescript.

12 Wilde was inconsistent in his uppercasing of "Theatre," occasionally using the lowercase elsewhere in the typescript.

CHANGES TO NUMBERS

30.000   *thirty thousand*   198
200,000   *two hundred thousand*   208
12.15   *twelve-fifteen*   212
seventh   *7th*   211, 244

PASSAGES IN WHICH DASHES OR PARENTHESES WERE INSERTED[13]

Your rank and wealth, Harry; my brains, such as they are, my fame, whatever it may
be worth, Dorian Gray's good looks; we will all suffer   75
Your rank and wealth, Harry; my brains, such as they are,—my fame, whatever it may be
worth, Dorian Gray's good looks,—we will all suffer

Sit down again, Harry. And now, Dorian, get up   92
Sit down again, Harry.—And now, Dorian, get up

And yet . . .   94
And yet—

I have caught the effect I wanted, the half-parted lips   97
I have caught the effect I wanted,—the half-parted lips

It is horridly hot in the studio. Basil, let us have something   97
It is horridly hot in the studio.—Basil, let us have something

Beauty is a form of Genius, is higher indeed than Genius,   99
Beauty is a form of Genius,—is higher, indeed, than Genius,

A new Hedonism! That is what our century wants.   100
A new hedonism,—that is what our century wants.

I congratulate you most warmly," he said. "Mr. Gray, come and look at
yourself."   101
I congratulate you most warmly," he said.—"Mr. Gray, come and look at yourself."

It will mock me some day, mock me horribly!   103
It will mock me some day,—mock me horribly!

13 None of the dashes documented here were incorporated directly onto Wilde's typescript.
They were inserted into the novel when it was being set in type.

It is the real Dorian Gray, that is all   103
It is the real Dorian Gray,—that is all

"I wish I could trust myself," said Lord Henry, laughing. "Come, Mr. Gray,   107
"I wish I could trust myself," said Lord Henry, laughing.—"Come, Mr. Gray,

I can drop you at your own place. Good-bye, Basil.   107
I can drop you at your own place.—Good-by, Basil.

I came in to look for you, to ask you something, I forget what it was. And I found
Mr. Gray here   113
*I came in to look for you, to ask you something,—I forget what it was—and I found
Mr. Gray here*

I have promised to drive with the Duchess. Good-bye, Mr. Gray. Good-bye,
Harry.   113
I have promised to drive with the duchess.—Good-by, Mr. Gray.—Good-by, Harry.

Faithlessness is to the emotional life what consistency is to the intellectual life,
simply a confession of failure.   116–117
*Faithlessness is to the emotional life what consistency is to the intellectual life—simply a
confession of failure.*

Oh, she is more than good, she is beautiful   132
Oh, she is more than good,—she is beautiful

I asked the question for the best reason possible, for the only reason, indeed, that
excuses one for asking any question, simple curiosity   135
*I asked the question for the best reason possible, for the only reason, indeed, that excuses one
for asking any question,—simple curiosity*

Will you have some coffee, you fellows? Waiter, bring coffee, and *fine-champagne,*
and some cigarettes. No: don't mind the cigarettes; I have got some. Basil, I can't
allow you to smoke cigars. You must have a cigarette. A cigarette is the perfect type
of a perfect pleasure. It is exquisite, and it leaves one unsatisfied. What more can
you want? Yes, Dorian, you will always be fond of me.   136
Will you have some coffee, you fellows?—Waiter, bring coffee, and fine-champagne, *and
some cigarettes. No: don't mind the cigarettes; I have some.—Basil, I can't allow you to smoke
cigars. You must have a cigarette. A cigarette is the perfect type of a perfect pleasure. It is exquisite, and it leaves one unsatisfied. What more can you want?—Yes, Dorian, you will always be fond of me.*

Dorian, you will come with me. I am so sorry, Basil   136
Dorian, you will come with me.—I am so sorry, Basil

lovely to look at, one of the loveliest creatures   139
lovely to look at,—one of the loveliest creatures

I really want to be alone. Basil, you don't mind my asking you to go?   143
I really want to be alone.—Basil, you don't mind my asking you to go?

"Horribly!" he answered, gazing at her in amazement, "horribly!   143
"Horribly!" he answered, gazing at her in amazement,—"horribly!

"Dorian," she answered, lingering over his name with long-drawn music in her
voice, as though it were sweeter than honey to the red petals of her lips, "Dorian,
you should have understood.   143
*"Dorian," she answered, lingering over his name with long-drawn music in her voice, as
though it were sweeter than honey to the red petals of her lips,—"Dorian, you should have
understood.*

Take me away, Dorian. Take me away with you   144
Take me away, Dorian,—take me away with you

I should never have known it if you had not kissed me, if we had not kissed each
other   145
I should never have known it if you had not kissed me,—if we had not kissed each other.

He would not see Lord Henry any more, would not, at any rate, listen to those subtle poisonous theories   151
*He would not see Lord Henry any more,—would not, at any rate, listen to those subtle poison-
ous theories*

Don't sneer at it, Harry, any more, at least not before me   156
Don't sneer at it, Harry, any more,—at least not before me.

But, my dear Dorian . . .   156
But, my dear Dorian—

Did Sybil . . . Oh, Harry, I can't bear it!   157
Did Sibyl—? Oh, Harry, I can't bear it!

I remember your saying once, that there is a fatality about good resolutions. That they are always made too late. Mine certainly were.   158
I remember your saying once, that there is a fatality about good resolutions,—that they are always made too late. Mine certainly were.

Well, would you believe it? A week ago   159
Well—would you believe it?—a week ago

You said to me that Sybil Vane represented to you all the heroines of romance. That she was Desdemona one night, and Ophelia the other. That if she died as Juliet, she came to life as Imogen   162
You said to me that Sibyl Vane represented to you all the heroines of romance,—that she was Desdemona one night, and Ophelia the other; that if she died as Juliet, she came to life as Imogen

"Ah, then," said Lord Henry rising to go; "Then, my dear Dorian,   162
"Ah, then," said Lord Henry rising to go,—"then, my dear Dorian,

when I heard that Sybil Vane had killed herself. . . .   167
when I heard that Sibyl Vane had killed herself—

You are not stronger. You are too much afraid of life. But you are better.   169
You are not stronger,—you are too much afraid of life,—but you are better.

He settles my flowers for me, that is all.   170
He settles my flowers for me,—that is all.

Form and colour tell us of form and colour, that is all   173
Form and colour tell us of form and colour,—that is all

it hasn't been opened for nearly five years. Not since his Lordship died.   177
it hasn't been opened for nearly five years,—not since his Lordship died.

I merely want to see the place, and perhaps store something in it. That is all.   177
I merely want to see the place, and perhaps store something in it,—that is all.

Now it was to hide something that had a corruption of its own, worse than the corruption of death itself, something that would breed horrors and yet would never die   177–178
Now it was to hide something that had a corruption of its own, worse than the corruption of death itself,—something that would breed horrors and yet would never die

I will certainly drop in and look at the frame, though I don't go in much for
religious art; but to-day I only want a picture carried to the top of the house
for me   179
*I will certainly drop in and look at the frame,—though I don't go in much for religious art,—
but to-day I only want a picture carried to the top of the house for me*

Some love might come across his life, and purify him, and shield him from those
sins that seemed to be already stirring in spirit and in flesh, those curious unpictured sins whose very mystery lent them their subtlety and their charm.   181
*Some love might come across his life, and purify him, and shield him from those sins that
seemed to be already stirring in spirit and in flesh,—those curious unpictured sins whose very
mystery lent them their subtlety and their charm.*

in the opinion of most people his frank debonair manner, his charming boyish
smile, and the infinite grace of that wonderful youth that seemed never to leave
him, were in themselves a sufficient answer to the calumnies, for so they called
them, that were circulated about him.   202–203
*in the opinion of most people his frank debonair manner, his charming boyish smile, and the
infinite grace of that wonderful youth that seemed never to leave him, were in themselves a
sufficient answer to the calumnies (for so they called them) that were circulated about him.*

The Renaissance knew of strange manners of poisoning, poisoning by a helmet and
a lighted torch, by an embroidered glove and a jewelled fan,   210
*The Renaissance knew of strange manners of poisoning,—poisoning by a helmet and a lighted
torch, by an embroidered glove and a jewelled fan,*

the most dreadful things are being said about you in London, things that I could
hardly repeat to you.   214
*the most dreadful things are being said about you in London,—things that I could hardly
repeat to you.*

Then there are other stories, stories that you have been seen creeping at dawn out
of dreadful houses   215
*Then there are other stories,—stories that you have been seen creeping at dawn out of
dreadful houses*

I told him that it was absurd, that I knew you thoroughly, and that you were incapable of anything of the kind   216
*I told him that it was absurd,—that I knew you thoroughly, and that you were incapable of
anything of the kind*

to destroy the thing that is upstairs, to destroy it so that not a vestige will be left
of it   234
to destroy the thing that is upstairs,—to destroy it so that not a vestige will be left of it

You are mad, I tell you, mad to imagine . . .   235
You are mad, I tell you—mad to imagine . . .

There is someone at the Club who wants immensely to know you. Young Lord
Poole   247
There is someone at the club who wants immensely to know you,—young Lord Poole

What a laugh she had! Just like a thrush singing.   248
What a laugh she had!—just like a thrush singing.

APPENDIX B

The 1891 Preface to *The Picture of Dorian Gray*

The Picture of Dorian Gray was vilified by British reviewers upon its appearance in *Lippincott's Monthly Magazine* in 1890. Feeling aggrieved and misunderstood, Wilde appended the following aphorisms to the novel, as a Preface, upon its publication in book form one year later. The novel has since rarely been printed without the Preface, though the Preface has often been printed or anthologized separately, as representing Wilde's artistic credo.

Many of the aphorisms are based on statements Wilde made in letters to the press defending his novel following publication in *Lippincott's*. Others are based on ideas contained in Gautier's Preface to *Mademoiselle du Maupin* (1835), a manifesto of "art for art's sake," also written in reply to critics who had attacked its author's moral character. Before attaching them to the novel, Wilde published twenty-three of the aphorisms in the *Fortnightly Review* in March 1891, where they appeared over his signature under the title "A Preface to *The Picture of Dorian Gray.*" The aphorism "No artist is ever morbid. The artist can express everything" was added, and one or two others were slightly altered, when the Preface appeared—again over Wilde's signature—in the book edition of *Dorian Gray* in April 1891.

Wilde's Preface is an example of what the critic Gérard Genette terms a "delayed preface" insofar as it serves a "compensatory" purpose and responds "to the first reactions of the first public and the critics" (*Paratexts: Thresholds of Interpretation*, trans. Jane E. Lewin [Cambridge University Press, 1997], p. 240). However, Genette himself treats Wilde's Preface as an example of the "preface-manifesto" (p. 228) whereby an author seeks to redefine or overthrow existing artistic conventions. In the breadth of its aims, says Genette, Wilde's Preface is comparable not merely to Gautier's Preface to *Mademoiselle du Maupin* but also to Conrad's Preface to *The Nigger of the Narcissus* and to Victor Hugo's never-completed "philosophical preface" to *Les Misérables*.

THE PREFACE

THE artist is the creator of beautiful things.

To reveal art and conceal the artist is art's aim.

The critic is he who can translate into another manner or a new material his impression of beautiful things.

The highest as the lowest form of criticism is a mode of autobiography.

Those who find ugly meaning in beautiful things are corrupt without being charming. This is a fault.

Those who find beautiful meanings in beautiful things are the cultivated. For these there is hope.

They are the elect to whom beautiful things mean only Beauty.

There is no such thing as a moral or an immoral book. Books are well written, or badly written. That is all.

The nineteenth century dislike of Realism is the rage of Caliban seeing his own face in a glass.

The nineteenth century dislike of Romanticism is the rage of Caliban not seeing his own face in a glass.

The moral life of man forms part of the subject-matter of the artist, but the morality of art consists in the perfect use of an imperfect medium.

No artist desires to prove anything. Even things that are true can be proved.

No artist has ethical sympathies. An ethical sympathy in an artist is an unpardonable mannerism of style.

No artist is ever morbid. The artist can express everything.

Thought and language are to the artist instruments of an art.

Vice and virtue are to the artist materials for an art.

From the point of view of form, the type of all the arts is the art of the musician. From the point of view of feeling, the actor's craft is the type.

All art is at once surface and symbol.

Those who go beneath the surface do so at their peril.

Those who read the symbol do so at their peril.

It is the spectator, and not life, that art really mirrors.

Diversity of opinion about a work of art shows that the work is new, complex, and vital.

When critics disagree the artist is in accord with himself.

We can forgive a man for making a useful thing as long as he does not admire it. The only excuse for making a useless thing is that one admires it intensely.

All art is quite useless.

OSCAR WILDE.

NOTE ON WILDE EDITIONS

For many years, the standard edition of Wilde's works was the fourteen-volume *Complete Works* edited by Robert Ross in 1908. The edition was published in Britain by Methuen and Co., except for *The Picture of Dorian Gray,* which was published uniform with the Methuen volumes by Charles Carrington in Paris. All fourteen volumes were published in the United States in 1910 by John Luce and Co. of Boston. Ross's edition restored Wilde's literary reputation at a single stroke, but it contains omissions and distortions and can no longer be relied upon as the standard edition.

In 2000 Oxford University Press issued the first volume in a multivolume *Complete Works,* under the general editorship of Ian Small, projected eventually to replace Ross's *Complete Works* and to become the standard edition. As of 2010, however, only four volumes have been published.

The current incompleteness of the Oxford edition has led me to adopt the following policy concerning bibliographic references for Wilde's works cited or quoted in the annotations to the present edition: with one exception, where the work in question has already appeared in the Oxford edition, readers are referred to the relevant Oxford volume. However, in the case of works by Wilde that have yet to appear in the Oxford edition, no bibliographic information has been given since no standard edition currently exists.

The exception concerns Wilde's long prison letter to Lord Alfred Douglas, first published in its entirety in 1962, though parts of it were first published under the title *De Profundis* in the decade following Wilde's death. Here I refer readers to the text edited by Merlin Holland and Rupert Hart-Davis in *The Complete Letters of Oscar Wilde* (Henry Holt, 2000), which is an exact transcription of Wilde's letter. Readers may also be interested in the facsimile edition of *De Profundis,* edited and introduced by Merlin Holland (British Library, 2000), which contains an exact photographic reproduction of Wilde's letter, warts and all.

FURTHER READING

EDITIONS OF WILDE'S WORK

The Complete Works of Oscar Wilde, gen. ed. Ian Small (Oxford: Oxford University Press, 2000–).
As of 2010, the following four volumes have appeared in the Oxford *Complete Works:*
Vol. 1: *Poems and Poems in Prose,* ed. Bobby Fong and Karl Beckson, 2000.
Vol. 2: *De Profundis; Epistola: in Carcere et Vinculis,* ed. Ian Small, 2005.
Vol. 3: *The Picture of Dorian Gray: The 1890 and 1891 Texts,* ed. Joseph Bristow, 2005.
Vol. 4: *Criticism: Historical Criticism, Intentions, and the Soul of Man,* ed. Josephine M. Guy, 2007.

The Complete Works of Oscar Wilde, ed. Robert Ross, 14 vols. London: Methuen, 1908. Except: Vol. 12, *The Picture of Dorian Gray.* Paris: Carrington, 1908.
The Complete Letters of Oscar Wilde, ed. Merlin Holland and Rupert Hart-Davis. New York: Henry Holt, 2000.
Oscar Wilde's Oxford Notebooks: A Portrait of Mind in the Making, ed. Phillip E. Smith II and Michael S. Helfand. Oxford: Oxford University Press, 1989.
The Picture of Dorian Gray, ed. Andrew Elfenbein. A Longman Cultural Edition. New York: Pearson Longman, 2007.
The Picture of Dorian Gray, ed. Donald F. Lawler. Norton Critical Editions. New York: Norton, 1988.
Table Talk: Oscar Wilde, ed. Thomas Wright, foreword by Peter Ackroyd. London: Cassell, 2000.

BIBLIOGRAPHICAL TOOLS

Beckson, Karl, ed. *Oscar Wilde: The Critical Heritage.* London: Routledge and Kegan Paul, 1970.

——. *The Oscar Wilde Encyclopedia.* New York: AMS Press, 1998.

Fletcher, Ian, and John Stokes. "Oscar Wilde." In *Anglo-Irish Literature: A Review of Research,* ed. Richard Finneran. New York: Modern Language Association, 1976.

——. "Oscar Wilde." In *Recent Research on Anglo-Irish Writers,* ed. Richard Finneran. New York: Modern Language Association, 1983.

Mason, Stuart [Christopher Millard]. *Bibliography of Oscar Wilde.* London: T. Werner Laurie, 1914.

——. *Oscar Wilde: Art and Morality: A Record of the Discussion Which Followed the Publication of Dorian Gray.* 1907; rpt. New York: Haskell House, 1971.

Mikhail, E. H. *Oscar Wilde: An Annotated Bibliography of Criticism.* London: Macmillan, 1978.

Mikolyzk, Thomas A. *Oscar Wilde: An Annotated Bibliography.* Westport, Conn.: Greenwood, 1993.

Small, Ian. *Oscar Wilde Revalued: An Essay on New Materials and Methods of Research.* Greensboro, N.C.: ELT Press, 1993.

——. *Oscar Wilde: Recent Research; A Supplement to "Oscar Wilde Revalued."* Greensboro, N.C.: ELT Press, 2000.

BIOGRAPHIES AND BIOGRAPHICAL TOOLS

Ackroyd, Peter. *The Last Testament of Oscar Wilde.* New York: Harper and Row, 1983.

Amor, Ann Clark. *Mrs. Oscar Wilde: A Woman of Some Importance.* London: Sidgwick and Jackson, 1983.

Bartlett, Neil. *Who Was That Man? A Present for Mr. Oscar Wilde.* London: Serpent's Tail, 1988.

Belford, Barbara. *Oscar Wilde: A Certain Genius.* New York: Random House, 2000.

Borland, Maureen. *Wilde's Devoted Friend: A Life of Robert Ross 1869-1918.* Oxford: Lennard, 1990.

Brasol, Boris. *Oscar Wilde: The Man, The Artist, The Martyr.* New York: Scribner's, 1938.

Brémont, Anna, Comtesse de. *Oscar Wilde and His Mother.* 1911; rpt. New York: Haskell House, 1972.

Coakley, Davis. *Oscar Wilde: The Importance of Being Irish.* Dublin: Town House, 1994.

Douglas, Lord Alfred. *Oscar Wilde and Myself.* London: J. Long, 1914.

——. *Without Apology.* London: Martin Secker, 1938.

——. *Oscar Wilde: A Summing-Up.* London: Duckworth, 1940.

Eagleton, Terry. *Saint Oscar.* Lawrence Hill, Derry: Field Day, 1989.

Ellmann, Richard. *Oscar Wilde.* New York: Knopf, 1988.

Fryer, Jonathan. *Robbie Ross: Oscar Wilde's Devoted Friend.* New York: Carroll and Graf, 2000.

Goodman, Jonathan, compiler. *The Oscar Wilde File*. London: Allison and Busby/ W. H. Allen, 1989.

Hare, David. *The Judas Kiss*. New York: Grove Press, 1998.

Hofer, Matthew, and Gary Scharnhorst, eds. *Oscar Wilde in America: The Interviews*. Urbana: University of Illinois Press, 2010.

Holland, Merlin. *The Wilde Album*. London: Fourth Estate, 1997.

———. *The Real Trial of Oscar Wilde: The First Uncensored Transcript of the Trial of Oscar Wilde*. New York: Perennial, 2003. Published in the U.K. as *Irish Peacock and Scarlet Marquess: The Real Trial of Oscar Wilde*. London: Fourth Estate, 2003.

Holland, Vyvian. *Son of Oscar Wilde*. 1954; rpt. Oxford: Oxford University Press, 1988.

Hyde, H. Montgomery. *Oscar Wilde: The Aftermath*. New York: Farrar Straus, 1963.

———. *The Trials of Oscar Wilde*. 1962; rpt. New York: Dover, 1973.

———. *Oscar Wilde: A Biography*. New York: Farrar, Straus, and Giroux, 1975.

Lewis, J. Lloyd, and Henry Justin Smith. *Oscar Wilde Discovers America, 1882*. 1936; rpt. New York: Benjamin Blom, 1967.

McCormack, Jerusha Hull. *John Gray: Poet, Dandy, and Priest*. Hanover, N.H.: Brandeis University Press, published by University Press of New England, 1991.

———. *The Man Who Was Dorian Gray*. New York: St. Martin's, 2000.

McKenna, Neil. *The Secret Life of Oscar Wilde*. London: Century, 2003.

Merle, Robert. *Oscar Wilde*. Paris: Hachette, 1948.

Mikhail, E. H. *Oscar Wilde: Interviews and Recollections* (2 vols.). London: Macmillan, 1979.

Moyle, Franny. *Constance: The Tragic and Scandalous Life of Mrs. Oscar Wilde,* forthcoming.

Murray, Douglas. *Bosie: A Biography of Lord Alfred Douglas*. New York: Hyperion, 2000.

O'Brien, Kevin. *Oscar Wilde in Canada: An Apostle for the Arts*. Toronto: Personal Library, 1982.

Page, Norman. *An Oscar Wilde Chronology*. Boston: G. K. Hall, 1991.

Pearson, Hesketh. *The Life of Oscar Wilde,* rev. ed. London: Methuen, 1954.

Pennington, Michael. *An Angel for a Martyr: Jacob Epstein's Tomb for Oscar Wilde*. Reading: Whiteknights, 1987.

Schmidgall, Gary. *The Stranger Wilde: Interpreting Oscar*. New York: Dutton, 1994.

Sherard, Robert Harborough. *The Life of Oscar Wilde*. London: T. W. Laurie, 1906.

———. *The Real Oscar Wilde*. London: T. W. Laurie, 1916.

Winwar, Francis. *Oscar Wilde and the Yellow Nineties*. New York: Harper, 1940.

Wright, Thomas. *Built of Books: How Reading Defined the Life of Oscar Wilde*. New York: Henry Holt, 2008. Published in the U.K. as *Oscar's Books*.

Wyndham, Horace. *Speranza: A Biography of Lady Wilde*. London: Boardman, 1951.

CRITICAL WORKS

Readers are referred also to the numerous essays and reviews to be found regularly in *The Wildean: A Journal of Oscar Wilde Studies,* published twice yearly by the Oscar Wilde Society; also *Oscholars* (www.oscholars.com), an electronic exchange and repository for research and news concerning Wilde and his works. Further critical tools may be found in the annotations and notes to the present edition.

Ablow, Rachel. "Oscar Wilde's Fictions of Belief." *Novel: A Forum on Fiction* 42, no. 2 (Summer 2009): 175–182.

Bashford, Bruce. *Oscar Wilde: The Critic as Humanist.* Madison, N.J.: Fairleigh Dickinson University Press, 1999.

Behrendt, Patricia F. *Oscar Wilde: Eros and Aesthetics.* New York: St. Martin's, 1992.

Bendz, Ernst. *The Influence of Pater and Matthew Arnold in the Prose Writings of Oscar Wilde.* 1914; rpt. Folcroft, Pa.: Folcroft Press, 1969.

Blanchard, Mary. *Oscar Wilde's America: Counterculture in the Gilded Age.* New Haven: Yale University Press, 1998.

Bloom, Harold, ed. *Oscar Wilde.* Bloom's Classic Critical Views. New York: Infobase, 2008.

Boker, Uwe, Richard Corballis, and Julie A. Hibbard, eds. *The Importance of Reinventing Oscar: Versions of Wilde during the Last 100 Years.* Amsterdam: Rodopi, 2002.

Bowlby, Rachel. "Promoting *Dorian Gray.*" In Bowlby, *Shopping with Freud.* New York: Routledge, 1993.

Bredbeck, G. W. "Narcissus in the Wilde." In *The Politics and Poetics of Camp,* ed. Moe Meyer, 51–74. New York: Routledge, 1994.

Bristow, Joseph. "Wilde, Dorian Gray, and Gross Indecency." In *Sexual Sameness: Textual Differences,* ed. Joseph Bristow. New York: Routledge, 1992.

——. "Wilde's Fatal Effeminacy." In Bristow, *Effeminate England: Homoerotic Writing after 1885,* 16–54. New York: Columbia University Press, 1995.

——, ed. *Wilde Writings: Contextual Conditions.* Toronto: University of Toronto Press, 2003.

——, ed. *Oscar Wilde and Modern Culture.* Athens: Ohio University Press, 2008.

Brown, Julia Prewitt. *Cosmopolitan Criticism: Oscar Wilde's Philosophy of Art.* Charlottesville: University of Virginia Press, 1997.

Buckton, Oliver S. "Defacing Oscar Wilde." In Buckton, *Secret Selves: Confession and Same-Sex Desire in Victorian Autobiography,* 107–160 (Chapel Hill, N.C.: University of North Carolina Press, 1998).

Chamberlin, J. E. *Ripe Was the Drowsy Hour: The Age of Oscar Wilde.* New York: Seabury, 1977.

Clayton, Loretta Ann. "Fashionably Wilde: Oscar Wilde and *The Woman's World.*" Ph.D. diss., University of Washington, 2005.

Clayworth, Anya. "*The Woman's World:* Oscar Wilde as Editor." *Victorian Periodicals Review* 30 (1997): 84–101.

Cohen, Ed. *Talk on the Wilde Side: Towards a Genealogy of a Discourse on Male Sexualities.* New York: Routledge, 1993.

———. "Writing Gone Wilde: Homoerotic Desire in the Closet of Representation." In *Critical Essays on Oscar Wilde,* ed. Gagnier, 1991.

Cohen, Philip K. *The Moral Vision of Oscar Wilde.* Rutherford, N.J.: Fairleigh Dickinson University Press, 1978.

Cohen, William A. "Indeterminate Wilde." In Cohen, *Sex Scandal: The Private Parts of Victorian Fiction,* 191–236. Durham, N.C.: Duke University Press, 1996.

Craft, Christopher. "Come See About Me: Enchantment of the Double in *The Picture of Dorian Gray.*" *Representations* 91 (2005): 109–136.

Danson, Lawrence. *Wilde's Intentions: The Artist in His Criticism.* Oxford: Clarendon Press, 1997.

Dawson, Terence. "'Man's Deeper Nature Is Soon Found Out': Psychological Typology, the *Puer Aeternus,* and Fear of the Feminine in *The Picture of Dorian Gray.*" In Dawson, *The Effective Protagonist in the Nineteenth-Century British Novel,* 67–127. Aldershot: Ashgate, 2004.

Eells, Emily, ed. *Two Tombeaux to Oscar Wilde: Jean Cocteau's* Le Portrait Surnaturel de Dorian Gray *and Raymond Laurent's Essay on Wildean Aesthetics.* High Wycombe: Rivendale Press, 2010.

Ellmann, Richard, ed. *Oscar Wilde: A Collection of Critical Essays.* Englewood Cliffs, N.J.: Prentice Hall, 1969.

Evangelista, Stefano, ed. *The Reception of Oscar Wilde in Europe.* London: Continuum, 2010.

Foldy, Michael. *The Trials of Oscar Wilde: Deviance, Morality, and Late-Victorian Society.* New Haven: Yale University Press, 1997.

Fortunato, Paul L. *Modernist Aesthetics and Consumer Culture in the Writings of Oscar Wilde.* New York: Routledge, 2007.

Frankel, Nicholas. *Oscar Wilde's Decorated Books.* Ann Arbor: University of Michigan Press, 2000.

———. "Vernon Lee and A. Mary F. Robinson—Two New Sources for *Dorian Gray.*" *Wildean: Journal of the Oscar Wilde Society* 36 (January 2010): 69–76.

Gagnier, Regenia. *Idylls of the Marketplace: Oscar Wilde and the Victorian Public.* Stanford: Stanford University Press, 1986.

———, ed. *Critical Essays on Oscar Wilde.* New York: G. K. Hall, 1991.

Gere, Charlotte, and Lesley Hoskins. *The House Beautiful: Oscar Wilde and the Aesthetic Interior.* Aldershot: Lund Humphries, 2000.

Gillespie, Michael Patrick. "Ethics and Aesthetics in *The Picture of Dorian Gray.*" In *Rediscovering Oscar Wilde,* ed. Sandulescu, 137–155.

———. *The Picture of Dorian Gray: "What the World Thinks Me."* New York: Twayne, 1995.

———. *Oscar Wilde and the Poetics of Ambiguity.* Gainesville: University Press of Florida, 1996.

Gomel, Elana. "Oscar Wilde, *The Picture of Dorian Gray,* and the (Un)Death of the Author." *Narrative* 12 (2004): 74–92.

Green, Stephanie. "Oscar Wilde's *The Woman's World.*" *Victorian Periodicals Review* 30 (1997): 102–120.

Guidicelli, Xavier. "Illustrer *The Picture of Dorian Gray:* les paradoxes de la representation." *Etudes Anglaises* 62, no. 1 (2009): 28–41.

Guy, Josephine, and Ian Small. *Oscar Wilde's Profession: Writing and the Culture Industry in the Late Nineteenth Century.* Oxford: Oxford University Press, 2000.

———. *Studying Oscar Wilde: History, Criticism, and Myth.* Greensboro, N.C.: ELT Press, 2006.

Han, Suh-Reen. "The Aesthete as the Modern Man: Discursive Formation in *The Picture of Dorian Gray.*" *Nineteenth Century Literature in English* 14, no. 1 (2010): 179–196.

Hanson, Ellis. "The Temptation of Saint Oscar." In Hanson, *Decadence and Catholicism,* 229–296. Cambridge, Mass.: Harvard University Press, 1997.

Horan, Patrick M. *The Importance of Being Paradoxical: Maternal Presence in the Works of Oscar Wilde.* Madison, N.J.: Fairleigh Dickinson University Press, 1997.

Ivory, Yvonne. "Poison, Passion, and Personality: Oscar Wilde's Renaissance Self-Fashioning." In Ivory, *The Homosexual Revival of Renaissance Style 1850-1930,* 83–108. New York: Palgrave Macmillan, 2009.

Joyce, Simon. "Sexual Politics and the Aesthetics of Crime: Oscar Wilde in the Nineties." *ELH* 69, no. 2 (Spring 2002): 501–523.

Kaplan, Morris B. *Sodom on the Thames: Sex, Love, and Scandal in Wilde Times.* Ithaca: Cornell University Press, 2005.

Keane, Robert F., ed. *Oscar Wilde: The Man, His Writings, and His World.* New York: AMS Press, 2003.

Kent, Julia. "Oscar Wilde's 'False Notes': *Dorian Gray* and English Realism." *Romanticism and Victorianism on the Net* 48 (November 2007). Available at www.erudit.org/revue/ravon/2007/v/n48/017437ar.html.

Killeen, Jarlath. *The Faiths of Oscar Wilde: Catholicism, Folklore and Ireland.* Basingstoke: Palgrave Macmillan, 2005.

Knox, Melissa. *Oscar Wilde: A Long and Lovely Suicide.* New Haven: Yale University Press, 1994.

Kofman, Sarah. "The Imposture of Beauty: The Uncanniness of Oscar Wilde's *The Picture of Dorian Gray.*" In *Enigmas: Essays on Sarah Kofman,* ed. P. Deutscher and K. Oliver. Ithaca: Cornell University Press, 1999.

Kohl, Norbert. *Oscar Wilde: The Works of a Conformist Rebel.* Cambridge: Cambridge University Press, 1989.

Kosofsky-Sedgwick, Eve. "Toward the Gothic: Terrorism and Homosexual Panic." In Kosofsky-Sedgwick, *Between Men: English Literature and Male Homosocial Desire,* 83–96. New York: Columbia University Press, 1985.

Latham, Sean. "The Importance of Being a Snob: Oscar Wilde's Modern Pretensions." In Latham, *"Am I a Snob?" Modernism and the Novel,* 31–56. Ithaca: Cornell University Press, 2003.

——. *The Art of Scandal: Modernism, Libel Law, and the Roman à Clef.* Oxford: Oxford University Press, 2009.

Lawler, Donald F. "Oscar Wilde's First Manuscript of *The Picture of Dorian Gray.*" *Studies in Bibliography* 25 (1972): 125–135.

——. "The Revisions of *Dorian Gray.*" *Victorians Institute Journal* 3 (1974): 21–36.

——. *An Inquiry into Oscar Wilde's Revisions of* The Picture of Dorian Gray. New York: Garland, 1988.

Lawler, Donald F., and Charles E. Knott. "The Context of Invention: Suggested Origins of *Dorian Gray.*" *Modern Philology* 73 (1976): 389–398.

Levine, Caroline. "Wilde's End of Realism." In Levine, *The Serious Pleasures of Suspense: Victorian Realism and Narrative Doubt,* 192–199. Charlottesville: University of Virginia Press, 2003.

Liebman, Sheldon W. "Character Design in *The Picture of Dorian Gray.*" *Studies in the Novel* 31, no. 3 (Fall 1999): 296–316.

Lloyd, Tom. "Oscar Wilde's *The Picture of Dorian Gray:* The Monstrous Portrait and Realism's Demise." In Lloyd, *Crises of Realism: Representing Experience in the British Novel, 1816-1910,* 156–171. Lewisburg, Pa.: Bucknell University Press, 1997.

Lorang, Elizabeth. "*The Picture of Dorian Gray* in Context: Intertextuality and *Lippincott's Monthly Magazine.*" *Victorian Periodicals Review* 43, no. 1 (Spring 2010): 19–41.

MacLeod, Kirsten. *Fictions of British Decadence: High Art, Popular Writing, and the Fin de Siècle.* Basingstoke: Palgrave Macmillan, 2006.

Mahaffey, Vicki. "Wilde's Desire: A Study in Green." In Mahaffey, *States of Desire: Wilde, Yeats, Joyce, and the Irish Experiment,* 37–86. Oxford: Oxford University Press, 1998.

McCormack, Jerusha H., ed. *Wilde the Irishman.* New Haven: Yale University Press, 1998.

McGinn, Colin. "The Picture: Dorian Gray." In McGinn, *Ethics, Evil, and Fiction,* 123–143. Oxford: Clarendon Press, 1997.

Mendelssohn, Michelle. *Henry James, Oscar Wilde, and Aesthetic Culture.* Edinburgh: University of Edinburgh Press, 2007.

Meyer, Moe. "Under the Sign of Wilde: An Archaeology of Posing." In *The Poetics and Politics of Camp,* ed. Moe Meyer. New York: Routledge, 1994.

Mighall, Robert. "Unspeakable Vices: Moral Monstrosity and Representation." In Mighall, *A Geography of Victorian Gothic Fiction: Mapping History's Nightmares,* 166–209. Oxford: Oxford University Press, 1999.

Milbank, Alison. "Sacrificial Exchange and the Gothic Double in *Melmoth the Wanderer* and *The Picture of Dorian Gray.*" In *Shaping Belief: Culture, Politics and Religion in Nineteenth-Century Writing,* ed. Victoria Morgan and Clare Williams, 113–128. Liverpool: Liverpool University Press, 2008.

Nassaar, Christopher. *Into the Demon Universe: A Literary Exploration of Oscar Wilde.* New Haven: Yale University Press, 1974.

Nunokawa, Jeff. *Tame Passions of Wilde: The Styles of Manageable Desire.* Princeton: Princeton University Press, 2003.

Oates, Joyce Carol. "*The Picture of Dorian Gray:* Wilde's parable of the Fall." In Oates, *Contraries: Essays.* New York: Oxford University Press, 1981.

O'Connor, Maureen. "*The Picture of Dorian Gray* as Irish National Tale." In *Writing Irishness in Nineteenth Century British Culture,* ed. Neil McCaw. Aldershot: Ashgate, 2004.

O'Malley, Patrick R. "'Monstrous and Terrible Delight': The Aesthetic Gothic of Pater and Wilde." In O'Malley, *Catholicism, Sexual Deviance, and Victorian Gothic Culture,* 165–192. Cambridge: Cambridge University Press, 2006.

Paglia, Camille. "The Beautiful Boy as Destroyer: Wilde's *The Picture of Dorian Gray.*" In Paglia, *Sexual Personae: Art and Decadence from Nefertiti to Emily Dickinson,* 512–530. New Haven: Yale University Press, 1990.

Pine, Richard. *The Thief of Reason: Oscar Wilde and Modern Ireland.* New York: St. Martin's, 1995.

Powell, Kerry. *Acting Wilde: Victorian Sexuality, Theatre and Oscar Wilde.* Cambridge: Cambridge University Press, 2009.

———. "Oscar Wilde 'Acting': The Medium as Message in *The Picture of Dorian Gray.*" *Dalhousie Review* 58 (1978): 104–115.

———. "Tom, Dick, and Dorian Gray: Magic-Picture Mania in Late Victorian Fiction." *Philological Quarterly* 62, no. 2 (Spring 1983): 147–170.

———. "Who Was Basil Hallward?" *English Language Notes* 24, no. 1 (September 1986): 84–91.

Raby, Peter, ed. *The Cambridge Companion to Oscar Wilde.* Cambridge: Cambridge University Press, 1997.

Ragland-Sutherland, Ellie. "The Phenomenon of Aging in *The Picture of Dorian Gray:* A Lacanian View." In *Memory and Desire: Aging—Literature—Psychoanalysis,* ed. K. M. Woodward and M. M. Schwartz. Bloomington: Indiana University Press, 1986.

Ransome, Arthur. *Oscar Wilde: A Critical Study.* 1912; rpt. New York: Haskell House, 1971.

Riquelme, John Paul. "Oscar Wilde's Aesthetic Gothic: Walter Pater, Dark Enlightenment, and *The Picture of Dorian Gray.*" *Modern Fiction Studies* 46, no. 3 (Fall 2000): 610–631.

Roden, Frederick S., ed. *Palgrave Advances in Oscar Wilde Studies.* Basingstoke: Palgrave Macmillan, 2004.

Roditi, Edouard. *Oscar Wilde.* 1947; rev. ed. New York: New Directions, 1986.

Ross, Iain Alexander. "The New Hellenism: Oscar Wilde and Ancient Greece." D. Phil. diss., University of Oxford, 2008.

Salamensky, S. I., ed. *Oscar Wilde, Jews and the Fin-de-Siècle.* Special issue of *Oscholars* (Summer 2010). Available at www.oscholars.com/TO/Specials/Wilde/ToC.htm.

Sammells, Neil. *Wilde Style: The Plays and Prose of Oscar Wilde.* New York: Longman, 2000.

Sandulescu, George, ed. *Rediscovering Oscar Wilde.* Gerard's Cross: Colin Smythe, 1994.

San Juan, Epifanio. *The Art of Oscar Wilde.* Princeton: Princeton University Press, 1967.

Sanyal, Arundhati. "Taboo in *The Picture of Dorian Gray.*" In *Bloom's Literary Themes: The Taboo,* ed. and intro. Harold Bloom, vol. ed. Blake Hobby, 147–156. New York: Infobase, 2010.

Sato, Tomoko, and Lionel Lambourne, eds. *The Wilde Years: Oscar Wilde and the Art of His Time.* London: Barbican Art Galleries, 2000.

Satzinger, Christa. *The French Influences on Oscar Wilde's* The Picture of Dorian Gray *and* Salome. Lewiston, N.Y.: Edwin Mellen, 1994.

Schaffer, Talia. "The Dandy in the House: Ouida and the Origin of the Aesthetic Novel." In Schaffer, *The Forgotten Female Aesthetes: Literary Culture in Late-Victorian England.* Charlottesville: University of Virginia Press, 2000.

———. "The Origins of the Aesthetic Novel: Ouida, Wilde, and the Popular Romance." In *Wilde Writings: Contextual Conditions,* ed. Bristow.

Seagroatt, Heather. "Hard Science, Soft Psychology and Amorphous Art in *The Picture of Dorian Gray.*" *Studies in English Literature 1500–1900* 38 (1998): 741–759.

Senelick, Lawrence. "Wilde and the Subculture of Homosexual Blackmail." In *Wilde Writing: Contextual Conditions,* ed. Bristow.

Shewan, Rodney. *Oscar Wilde: Art and Egotism.* London: Macmillan, 1977.

Siegel, Sandra F. "Wilde on Photographs." *Wildean: Journal of the Oscar Wilde Society* 17 (2000): 12–30.

Sinfield, Alan. *The Wilde Century: Effeminacy, Oscar Wilde, and the Queer Movement.* New York: Columbia University Press, 1994.

Sloan, John. *Oscar Wilde.* New York: Oxford University Press, 2003.

Smith, Philip E., II, ed. *Approaches to Teaching the Works of Oscar Wilde*. New York: Modern Languages Association, 2008.

Stokes, John. *Oscar Wilde: Myths, Miracles and Imitations*. Cambridge: Cambridge University Press, 1996.

Tanitch, Robert. *Oscar Wilde on Stage and Screen*. London: Methuen, 1999.

Thomas, Ronald R. "Poison Books and Moving Pictures: Vulgarity in *The Picture of Dorian Gray*." In *Victorian Vulgarity: Taste in Verbal and Visual Culture,* ed. Susan D. Bernstein and Elsie B. Michie. Aldershot: Ashgate, 2009.

Tufescu, Florina. *Oscar Wilde's Plagiarism: The Triumph of Art over Ego*. Dublin: Irish Academic Press, 2008.

Upchurch, David. *Wilde's Use of Celtic Elements in* The Picture of Dorian Gray. New York: Peter Lang, 1993.

Vaninskaya, Anna, ed. *The Soul of Man: Oscar Wilde and Socialism*. Special issue of *Oscholars* (Spring 2010). Available at www.oscholars.com/TO/Specials/Soul/ToC.htm.

Varty, Ann. *A Preface to Oscar Wilde*. New York: Longman, 1998.

Waldrep, Sheldon. *The Aesthetics of Self-Invention: Oscar Wilde to David Bowie*. Minneapolis: University of Minnesota Press, 2004.

Walker, Richard J. "The Psychopathology of Everyday Narcissism: Oscar Wilde's Picture." In Walker, *Labyrinths of Deceit: Culture, Modernity and Identity in the Nineteenth Century,* 91–115. Liverpool: Liverpool University Press, 2007.

Whyte, Peter. "Oscar Wilde et Théophile Gautier: le cas du *Portrait du Dorian Gray*." *Bulletin de la Société Théophile Gautier* 21 (1999): 279–294.

Willoughby, Guy. *Art and Christhood: The Aesthetics of Oscar Wilde*. Rutherford, N.J.: Fairleigh Dickinson University Press, 1993.

Womack, Kenneth. "'Withered, Wrinkled, and Loathsome of Visage': Reading the Ethics of the Soul and the Late-Victorian Gothic in *The Picture of Dorian Gray*." In *Victorian Gothic: Literary and Cultural Manifestations in the Nineteenth Century,* ed. Ruth Robbins and Julian Wolfreys, 168–181. Basingstoke: Palgrave, 2000.

Wood, Julia. *The Resurrection of Oscar Wilde: A Cultural Afterlife*. Cambridge: Lutterworth, 2007.

Woodcock, George. *The Paradox of Oscar Wilde*. London: Boardman, 1949. Rpt. as *Oscar Wilde: The Double Image*. Montreal: Black Rose Books, 1989.

CONTEXTUAL REFERENCES

While the range of contextual references is potentially limitless, readers may find the following short selection useful for understanding Wilde's novel in its broader contexts.

Adams, James Eli. *Dandies and Desert Saints: Styles of Victorian Masculinity.* Ithaca: Cornell University Press, 1995.

Beckson, Karl. *London in the 1890s: A Cultural History.* New York: Norton, 1993.

Caird, Mona. *The Morality of Marriage and Other Essays.* London: G. Redway, 1897.

Cannadine, David. *The Decline and Fall of the British Aristocracy.* New Haven: Yale University Press, 1990.

Charlesworth, Barbara. *Dark Passages: The Decadent Consciousness in Victorian Literature.* Madison: University of Wisconsin Press, 1965.

Cook, Matt. *London and the Culture of Homosexuality 1885–1914.* Cambridge: Cambridge University Press, 2003.

Corbett, David Peters. *The World in Paint: Modern Art and Visuality in England, 1848–1914.* Manchester: Manchester University Press, 2004.

Davidoff, Leonore. *The Best Circles: Society, Etiquette and the Season.* London: Croom Helm, 1973.

Dellamora, Richard. *Masculine Desire: The Sexual Politics of Victorian Aestheticism.* Chapel Hill: University of North Carolina Press, 1990.

——, ed. *Victorian Sexual Dissidence.* Chicago: University of Chicago Press, 1999.

Dollimore, Jonathan. *Sexual Dissidence: Augustine to Wilde, Freud to Foucault.* Oxford: Clarendon Press, 1991.

Dowling, Linda. *Language and Decadence in the Victorian Fin de Siècle.* Ithaca: Cornell University Press, 1986.

——. *Hellenism and Homosexuality in Victorian Oxford.* Ithaca: Cornell University Press, 1994.

Ellis, Havelock. *Studies in the Psychology of Sex,* 4 vols. New York: Random House, 1936.

Ellis, Havelock, and John Addington Symonds. *Sexual Inversion.* 1897; rpt. New York: Arno, 1975.

Feltes, N. N. *Modes of Production of Victorian Novels.* Chicago: University of Chicago Press, 1986.

——. *Literary Capital and the Late-Victorian Novel.* Madison: University of Wisconsin Press, 1993.

Foucault, Michel. *The History of Sexuality,* tr. Robert Hurley, 5 vols. New York: Vintage, 1986–1990.

Frankel, Nicholas. *Masking the Text: Essays on Literature and Mediation in the 1890s* High Wycombe, UK: Rivendale Press, 2009.

Freedman, Jonathan. *Professions of Taste: Henry James, British Aestheticism and Commodity Culture.* Stanford: Stanford University Press, 1990.

Gay, Peter. *The Bourgeois Experience: From Victoria to Freud,* 5 vols. New York: Oxford University Press, 1984–1998.

Gilman, Sander L., and J. E. Chamberlain, eds. *Degeneration: The Dark Side of Progress.* New York: Columbia University Press, 1985.

Gilmour, Robin. *The Idea of the Gentleman in the Victorian Novel.* London: Allen and Unwin, 1981.

Hamilton, Walter. *The Aesthetic Movement in England,* 3rd ed. London: Reeves and Turner, 1882.

Houghton, Walter. *The Victorian Frame of Mind.* New Haven: Yale University Press, 1957.

Hyde, H. Montgomery. *The Cleveland Street Scandal.* New York: Coward, McCann and Geoghegan, 1976.

Jackson, Holbrook. *The Eighteen Nineties: A Review of Art and Ideas at the Close of the Nineteenth Century.* 1913; rpt. Franklin, Tenn.: Tantallon Press, 2002.

Johnson, Robert V. *Aestheticism.* London: Methuen, 1969.

Koven, Seth. *Slumming: Sexual and Social Politics in Victorian London.* Princeton: Princeton University Press, 2004.

Lambourne, Lionel. *The Aesthetic Movement.* London: Phaidon, 1996.

Ledger, Sally, and Roger Luckhurst, eds. *The Fin de Siècle: A Reader in Cultural History, c. 1880–1900.* Oxford: Oxford University Press, 2000.

Ledger, Sally, and Scott McCracken, eds. *Cultural Politics at the Fin de Siècle.* Cambridge: Cambridge University Press, 1995.

Marshall, Gail, ed. *The Cambridge Companion to the Fin de Siècle.* Cambridge: Cambridge University Press, 2007.

Mason, Philip. *The English Gentleman: The Rise and Fall of an Ideal.* Cambridge: Cambridge University Press, 1997.

McDonald, Peter D. *British Literary Culture and Publishing Practice 1880–1914.* Cambridge: Cambridge University Press, 1997.

Moers, Ellen. *The Dandy: Brummell to Beerbohm.* New York: Viking, 1960.

Prettejohn, Elizabeth, ed. *After the Pre-Raphaelites: Art and Aestheticism in Victorian England.* Princeton: Princeton University Press, 2000.

Prettejohn, Elizabeth. *Art for Art's Sake: Aestheticism in Victorian Painting.* New Haven: Yale University Press, 2007.

Psomiades, Kathy Alexis. *Beauty's Body: Femininity and Representation in British Aestheticism.* Stanford: Stanford University Press, 1997.

Reade, Brian, compiler. *Sexual Heretics: Male Homosexuality in English Literature from 1850–1900.* New York: Coward McCann, 1971.

Reed, John R. *Decadent Style.* Athens: Ohio University Press, 1985.

Showalter, Elaine. *Sexual Anarchy: Gender and Culture at the Fin de Siècle.* New York: Viking, 1990.

Simpson, Colin, Lewis Chester, and David Leitch. *The Cleveland Street Affair.* Boston: Little Brown, 1976.

Stokes, John, ed. *Fin de Siècle, Fin du Globe: Fears and Fantasies of the Late Nineteenth Century.* New York: St. Martin's, 1992.

Thornton, R. K. R. *The Decadent Dilemma.* London: E. Arnold, 1983.

Veblen, Thorstein. *The Theory of the Leisure Class* (1899), ed. Martha Banta. Oxford: Oxford University Press, 1999.

Walkowitz, Judith R. *City of Dreadful Delight: Narratives of Sexual Danger in the Late-Victorian City.* Chicago: University of Chicago Press, 1992.

Warwick, Alexandra, and Martin Willis. *Jack the Ripper: Media, Culture, History.* Manchester: Manchester University Press, 2007.

Weeks, Jeffrey. *Coming Out: Homosexual Politics in Britain, from the Nineteenth Century to the Present.* London: Quartet, 1977.

West, Shearer. *Fin de Siècle: Art and Society in an Age of Uncertainty.* Woodstock, N.Y.: Overlook, 1994.

———. *Portraiture.* Oxford: Oxford University Press, 2004.

White, Chris, ed. *Nineteenth Century Writings on Homosexuality: A Sourcebook.* New York: Routledge, 1999.

PARODIES AND IMITATIONS

Hichens, Robert. *The Green Carnation,* ed. Stanley Weintraub. 1894; Lincoln: University of Nebraska Press, 1970.

[Leverson, Ada]. "An Afternoon Party." *Punch, or the London Charivari* 105 (15 July 1893), 13.

Reed, Jeremy. *Dorian: A Sequel to "The Picture of Dorian Gray."* London: Peter Owen, 1997.

Reed, Rick R. *A Face without a Heart.* Darien, Ill.: DesignImage, 2000.

Self, Will. *Dorian: An Imitation.* New York: Grove, 2002.

Street, G. S. *Autobiography of a Boy.* 1894; rpt. New York: Garland, 1977.

ILLUSTRATION CREDITS

Map of London in Wilde's day. Courtesy Harvard Map Collection.   *vi*

Oscar Wilde's tomb, designed by Jacob Epstein in 1909, Père Lachaise Cemetery, Paris, France. © David Jones/Alamy.   *3*

Front cover of British version of the July 1890 issue of *Lippincott's Monthly Magazine.* © The British Library Board Eccles 395.   *5*

Front cover of the 1891 book edition (large-paper issue) of *The Picture of Dorian Gray,* published by Ward, Lock, and Co. EC85.W6445.891pb, Houghton Library, Harvard University.   *8*

Calling card, left for Wilde at his club by the Marquess of Queensberry, Lord Alfred Douglas's father, on February 18, 1895. National Archives, UK.   *16*

Edward Carson Q. C., later 1st Baron Carson, caricatured by "Lib" [Libero Prosperi], from *Vanity Fair,* Nov. 1893. f *44WP-16, Houghton Library, Harvard University.   *17*

"It is your best work, Basil." Illustration from *The Picture of Dorian Gray* by Oscar Wilde (1854–1900), engraved by E. Dété (litho) by Paul Thiriat (19th–20th century). Private Collection/The Stapleton Collection/The Bridgeman Art Library.   *66*

Oil portrait of Lord Ronald Sutherland Gower, painted and gifted to Lord Gower by the artist John Everett Millais, R. A., in 1876. Royal Shakespeare Company.   *68*

Harry Furniss, pen and ink caricature of Wilde's mother, Jane Francesca Elgee, Lady Wilde. Harvard College Library, Widener Soc4895.26.   *68*

James McNeill Whistler, "Harmony in Blue and Gold: The Peacock Room," 1876–1877. Freer Gallery of Art, Smithsonian Institution, Washington, D.C.: Gift of Charles Lang Freer, F1904.61.   *71*

"Strictly Private View, Royal Academy," satirical engraving that appeared in *Punch* in 1890. Harvard College Library, Widener P 325.1 (1890).   *73*

Harry Furniss, "Our Academy Guide, No. 163—Private Frith's View," satirical engraving that appeared in *Punch* in 1883. Harvard College Library, Widener P 325.1.5 (1883). *73*

Charles Haslewood Shannon, lithographic portrait of John Gray, 1896. Courtesy of Charmian O'Neil and Leonie Sturge-More. *74*

"Dorian Gray? Is that his name?" frontispiece by S. A. Moss to *The Picture of Dorian Gray*, vol. 2 of *The Sunflower Edition of the Works of Oscar Wilde* (New York: Lang, 1909). Boston Athenaeum. *75*

Drypoint etching of Edward Carson Q. C., by John George Day, 1914. © National Portrait Gallery, London. *77*

Lord Alfred Douglas's father, the Marquess of Queensberry. Harvard College Library, Widener 23493.36.168. *82*

A "Vesta" case with a built-in match strike, by Archibald Knox (1864–1933), manufactured by William Hair Haseler of Birmingham in 1904. Courtesy Daniel Bexfield. *86*

A Private View at the Royal Academy, 1881 (oil on canvas) by William Powell Frith (1819–1909). Private Collection / Copyright Pope Family Trust / The Bridgeman Art Library. *88*

Lord Alfred Douglas at twenty-one. Harvard College Library, Widener 23493.36.168. *90*

"Dorian Gray," frontispiece to *The Picture of Dorian Gray*, intro. Osbert Burdett, illustr. Henry Keen (London and New York: John Lane / Dodd, Mead & Co., 1925). The William Andrews Clark Memorial Library, University of California, Los Angeles. *91*

Lifesize oil portrait of W. Graham Robertson, by John Singer Sargent, 1894. © Tate, London 2010. *92*

A house on Curzon Street, in the exclusive Mayfair district. © Illustrated London News Ltd / Mary Evans. *93*

Photo of Walter Pater, taken at Oxford around the time he published his controversial book *The Renaissance* (1873). Harvard College Library, Widener 20482.4.33.2 (v.1). *100*

Statue of Hermes and the Infant Dionysus, c. 330 BC (parian marble) by Praxiteles (c. 400–c. 330 BC). Archaeological Museum, Olympia, Archaia, Greece / The Bridgeman Art Library. *104*

A hansom cab, designed and patented in 1834 by Joseph Hansom. Harvard College Library, Widener Library Br 4719.02.20 (v.2). *106*

Aubrey Beardsley, "The Peacock Skirt," line-engraved illustration to Wilde's *Salome, A Tragedy in One Act,* trans. Lord Alfred Douglas (Elkin Mathews and John Lane, 1894). Harvard College Library, Widener 23498.55.605. *108*

Interior of the House Beautiful—An "Aesthetic" Drawing-Room, c. 1882. Harvard College Library, Fine Arts XFA56.3.7. *110*

Terracotta statuette, by "Clodion" [Claude Michel, 1738–1814], depicting two dancing bacchantes and a putto, 1800. Photograph © 2011 Museum of Fine Arts, Boston. *111*

Aubrey Beardsley, "The Wagnerites" (1894), line-engraving satirizing the blind devotion to Wagner among the British intelligentsia of the 1890s. Harvard College Library, Widener P 435.2 (v.3, 1894). *112*

Piccadilly, looking east, with Green Park on the right, early 1900s. Harvard College Library, Widener Br 4719.09 (v.2). *117*

Piccadilly in 1902. Harvard College Library, Widener Library Br4719.02.20 (v.1). *117*

Photo-portrait of Wilde, by Ward and Downey, c. 1892. Mark Samuels Lasner Collection, on loan to the University of Delaware Library. *118*

Photo-portrait of Constance Wilde, 1892. The William Andrews Clark Memorial Library, University of California, Los Angeles. *122*

Satirical engraving from *Punch,* June 25, 1881. Harvard College Library, Widener P 325.1. *123*

Sheet music cover for "The Oscar Wilde Galup," arranged by F. H. Snow (New York: R. A. Saalfield, n.d.). Mark Samuels Lasner Collection, on loan to the University of Delaware Library. *123*

Lifesize oil portrait of Oscar Wilde, by Harper Pennington, a student of Whistler's, commissioned by Wilde in or around 1884. The William Andrews Clark Memorial Library, University of California, Los Angeles. *125*

Aubrey Beardsley, "The Woman in the Moon," line-engraved illustration to Wilde's *Salome, A Tragedy in One Act,* trans. Lord Alfred Douglas (Elkin Mathews and John Lane, 1894). Harvard College Library, Widener 23498.55.605. *127*

Photo-portrait of Richard Le Gallienne, c. 1894. 1126. Harvard College Library, Widener 20467.25. *129*

"In her boy's dress," illustration to *The Picture of Dorian Gray,* intro. Osbert Burdett, illustr. Henry Keen (London and New York: John Lane/Dodd, Mead & Co., 1925). The William Andrews Clark Memorial Library, University of California, Los Angeles. *134*

"One afternoon, a month later, Dorian Gray was reclining in a luxurious armchair, in the little library of Lord Henry's house in Mayfair," from *The Picture of Dorian Gray,* illustr. Madjeska (New York: Horace Liveright, 1930). © The British Library Boardy Cup. 502.e.25. *135*

A brougham. Long Island Museum of American Art, History & Carriages, Gift of Ward Melville, 1971. *137*

Napoleon Sarony photo-portrait of Wilde, 1882. Mark Samuels Lasner Collection, on loan to the University of Delaware Library. *139*

The actress Ellen Terry (1847–1928), photographed at the age of sixteen, by Julia Margaret Cameron. f AP9 C1445, Houghton Library, Harvard University. *141*

"She crouched on the floor like a wounded thing, and Dorian Gray, with his beautiful eyes, looked down at her," from *The Picture of Dorian Gray*, illustr. Madjeska (New York: Horace Liveright, 1930). © The British Library Board Cup. 502.e.25. *146*

Wilde caricatured as an "Apostle of the Lily" in a satirical engraving from Harvard College Library, Widener Library 23493.36.53.5. *147*

Fruit auction at Covent Garden, London's main fruit, vegetable, and flower market. Harvard College Library, Widener Library Br4719.02.20 (v.1). *148*

Flower selling at Covent Garden. Harvard College Library, Widener Library Br4719.02.20 (v.1). *149*

"Dead! Sybil, dead! It is not true," illustration by S. A. Moss to *The Picture of Dorian Gray*, vol. 2 of *The Sunflower Edition of the Works of Oscar Wilde* (New York: Lang, 1909). Boston Athenaeum. *157*

The diva Adelina Patti, dressed for the lead role in Verdi's *Aida*, which she performed at the Royal Opera House, in London's Covent Garden, in June 1876. The Eda Kuhn Loeb Music Library. *159*

Front wrapper to *The Woman's World*, almost certainly designed at Wilde's instigation, by Lewis F. Day, 1888. The William Andrews Clark Memorial Library, University of California, Los Angeles. *161*

"Dorian Gray," by "Basil Hallward," published as the frontispiece to *The Picture of Dorian Gray* (New York: Charterhouse Press, 1904). Harvard College Library, Widener 23493.36.17.5. *163*

Engraved portrait of Théophile Gautier by L. Wolff, after a photo by Nadar, c. 1856. Harvard College Library, Widener 41542.7.5. *169*

Napoleon Sarony, photo-portrait of Wilde. The William Andrews Clark Memorial Library, University of California, Los Angeles. *173*

Pencil sketch of Vernon Lee, by John Singer Sargent, 1889. Art & Architecture Collection, Miriam and Ira D. Wallach Division of Art, Prints and Photographs, The New York Public Library, Astor, Lenox and Tilden Foundations. *175*

Joris-Karl Huysmans, *À Rebours* (Paris: Charpentier, 1884). FC8 H9876 884a, Houghton Library, Harvard University *182*

Napoleon Sarony, photo-portrait of Wilde seated with a book (1882). The William Andrews Clark Memorial Library, University of California, Los Angeles. *183*

William Rothenstein, lithographic portrait of Joris-Karl Huysmans, 1895. © The British Library Board Wq1/6110 DSC. *184*

Photo-portrait of Wilde by Hills and Saunders, taken in Oxford, 1876. General Research Division, The New York Public Library, Astor, Lenox and Tilden Foundations. *189*

Oil portrait of Robert Baldwin Ross, by William Rothenstein, © estate of Sir William Rothenstein / National Portrait Gallery, London. *191*

"As Anne De Joyeuse," illustration to *The Picture of Dorian Gray,* intro. Osbert Burdett, illustr. Henry Keen (London and New York: John Lane / Dodd, Mead & Co., 1925). The William Andrews Clark Memorial Library, University of California, Los Angeles.   *198*

Gustave Moreau, *Sappho,* watercolor, c. 1884. © V & A Images, Victoria and Albert Museum.   *207*

Photo-portrait of John Addington Symonds, 1886. Harvard College Library, Widener Harvard Depository 20485.50.15 (v.1).   *210*

Victoria Station, terminus of the London, Brighton, and South Coast Railway, early 1900s. Harvard College Library, Widener Econ3058.17 (v.1).   *212*

Grosvenor Square, in London's aristocratic Mayfair district, in the 1850s. Mary Evans Picture Library.   *213*

An ulster. Courtesy of the Library of Congress.   *213*

A "Gladstone bag," a small portmanteau bag, named after Britain's four-time prime minister, William Ewart Gladstone. Dorling Kindersley / Getty Images.   *214*

Carriages driving in Hyde Park, c. 1896. © The British Library Board Maps.20.c.31.   *217*

"'Come upstairs, Basil,' he said quietly," illustration by S. A. Moss to *The Picture of Dorian Gray,* vol. 2 of *The Sunflower Edition of the Works of Oscar Wilde* (New York: Lang, 1909). Boston Athenaeum.   *218*

Interior of the Grosvenor Gallery in May 1877. Harvard College Library, Widener Library P 229.10 F.   *220*

Exterior of the Grosvenor Gallery in May 1877. Courtesy of the Library of Congress.   *220*

"He rushed at him, and dug the knife into the great vein that is behind the ear." Illustration from *The Picture of Dorian Gray* by Oscar Wilde (1854–1900), engraved by E. Dété (litho) by Paul Thiriat (19th–20th century). Private Collection / The Stapleton Collection / The Bridgeman Art Library.   *225*

"The thing was still seated in the chair, straining over the table with bowed head, and humped back, and long fantastic arms," from *The Picture of Dorian Gray,* illustr. Madjeska (New York: Horace Liveright, 1930). © The British Library Board Cup. 502.e.25.   *226*

Etched portrait of Théophile Gautier, by Jules Ferdinand Jacquemart, printed as a frontispiece to the "edition définitive" (definitive edition) of Gautier's *Emaux et Camées* (Paris: Charpentier, 1872). Harvard College Library, Widener Harvard Depository 41542.8.   *234*

Photo-portrait of Anton Rubinstein, date unknown. Harvard College Library, Lamont Library Morse Music & Media ML410.R89 A32 1890.   *237*

Publicity poster for the 1945 MGM movie adaptation of *Dorian Gray,* directed by Albert Lewin. THE PICTURE OF DORIAN GRAY © Turner Entertainment Co. A Warner Bros. Entertainment Company. All Rights Reserved.   *240*

Theater program for a performance of *The Picture of Dorian Gray,* by Oscar Wilde (1854–1900), at the Vaudeville Theatre on August 20, 1913 (litho), by English School (20th century). Private Collection/The Stapleton Collection/The Bridgeman Art Library. *243*

"Lying on the floor was a dead man, in evening dress, with a knife in his heart," illustration from *The Picture of Dorian Gray* by Oscar Wilde (1854–1900), engraved by E. Dété (litho) by Paul Thiriat (19th–20th century). Private Collection/The Stapleton Collection/The Bridgeman Art Library. *251*

Ivan Albright, *The Picture of Dorian Gray,* 1943–1944, oil on canvas, 85 x 42 in. Gift of Ivan Albright, 1977.21, The Art Institute of Chicago. *253*

ACKNOWLEDGMENTS

I am immensely grateful to John Kulka, my editor at Harvard University Press, for the meticulousness, imagination, and generosity with which he has helped me edit and annotate *Dorian Gray*. Besides commissioning this book, John carefully nurtured it from very humble beginnings; any excellence it possesses owes much to him, while any errors or omissions are mine alone. Numerous colleagues at Virginia Commonwealth University supported this work. Fred Hawkridge, acting dean of the College of Humanities and Sciences, got the project off the ground by awarding me a Career Enhancement Grant in the summer of 2008; later he arranged a generous subvention to support the acquisition of illustrations. Terry Oggel, chair of the English Department, was a critical supporter at every stage, while Nick Sharp and David Latané, successive associate chairs, scheduled my teaching so that the book could progress rapidly while delivering maximum benefit to my students. Catherine Ingrassia, associate dean of the College, and Kathy Bassard moved mountains so that a great deal could be done in the summer of 2009 through an NEH grant. Eric Garberson, Laura Browder, Bryant Mangum, David Latané, Josh Eckhardt, Kate Nash, Susann Cokal, and Richard Priebe all provided important intellectual support, while work would have ground quickly to a halt without divine interventions from the angels in the office, especially Margret Schluer, Ginnie Schmitz, and the staffs of the VCU English and Interlibrary Loan offices. I am grateful to all of these individuals, departments, and administrators for making VCU a wonderful place to work.

A special debt is owed to Merlin Holland, Wilde's grandson, who generously granted me permission to publish material still in copyright, and whose own scholarship influenced the book profoundly. Michael Winship deftly and generously guided me through the labyrinthine archives of J. B. Lippincott and Co. Pamela Dalziel, Joseph Bristow, Josephine Guy, Peter Bernhardt, Jos ten Berge, George Bornstein, Linda Hughes, Margaret Stetz, Mark Samuels Lasner, Jerome McGann,

Bill Baker, Steve Arata, Phillip E. Smith, David Latané, Paul Van Capelleveen, and Chip Tucker all provided advice or help of various kinds. Mark Samuels Lasner and Daniel Bexfield kindly provided me with images from their personal collections, while Leonie Sturge-Moore and Charmian O'Neil generously granted me permission to publish Charles Shannon's lithograph of John Gray. Christine Thorsteinsson expertly guided the book through the press, and Matthew Hills oversaw practical matters. Graciela Galup, the book's designer, is responsible for its lovely form. Two anonymous readers for Harvard University Press provided useful criticisms and saved me from embarrassing mistakes, while my wife, Susan Barstow, commented incisively and frequently on the introductory essays during their composition. The book could not have been written without the support and partnership she offers on a daily basis. Together with my children, Max, Theo, and Oliver, she continues to be a source of inspiration.

Grants from the NEH and the Bibliographical Society of America enabled research and writing in summer 2009. I am indebted, too, to the staffs of the Pennsylvania Historical Society and the William Clark Andrews Jr. Memorial Library, especially Scott Jacobs, for many kindnesses; to Declan Kiely, curator of manuscripts at the Morgan Library, and to Rachel Foss, curator of modern literary manuscripts at the British Library. The work of previous editors of Wilde's novel—especially of Isobel Murray, Joseph Bristow, and Donald F. Lawler—constitutes the foundation on which I have built. My debts to these previous editors run deep and will be apparent throughout.

Finally, lest we think Wilde's story is passé, I would remember a number of teenage suicides in the fall of 2010, caused by bullying and the stigma still attached to homosexuality in many quarters. Publicity surrounding these untimely deaths overshadowed the latter stages of the production of this edition.